PLAYING
God
A NOVEL

michelle mckinney hammond

HARVEST HOUSE PUBLISHERS

EUGENE, OREGON

Published in association with the literary agency of Alive Communications, Inc., 7680 Goddard Street, Suite 200, Colorado Springs, CO 80920.

Cover design by Koechel Peterson & Associates, Inc., Minneapolis, Minnesota

PLAYING GOD
Copyright © 2008 by Michelle McKinney Hammond
Published by Harvest House Publishers
Eugene, Oregon 97402

ISBN-13: 978-1-60751-063-5

To all those who have waited patiently...or impatiently...for God to deliver their hearts' desires.
To those who are clinging to one last hope.
To those who have allowed themselves to become
consumed with disappointment, questioned God
and the hope of their faith.

I encourage you to hold on a little while longer. The promise
is on the way accompanied by a great "aha moment" that will
make the wait worthwhile!

> *Do not throw away this confident trust in the Lord,*
> *no matter what happens.*
> *Remember the great reward it brings you!*
> *Patient endurance is what you need now,*
> *so you will continue to do God's will.*
> *Then you will receive all that he has promised.*

HEBREWS 10:35-36

Lord, thank You for being patient toward us as we question
and wrestle with You over our hearts' desires. We're so glad
You love us enough to stay focused on the prize when we can't
see it. Truly You do know what is best for us and every good
and perfect gift comes from You. You are our hero. Amen.

Acknowledgments

Well Erin, my dear editor, you've done it again! Thanks for gently leading me across the finish line.

Barb Gordon, thanks for helping me break the ribbon, ha ha. Your patience is greatly appreciated.

To my entire Harvest House family for nurturing the novelist in me and allowing me to write about hard things. It's so needed.

To my dear friends, family, and office staff who have to put up with my descent into the black hole. Thank you for always being there when I come out. I love and appreciate you. Words cannot express... Imagine that! This writer has no words! So listen to my heart, it beats for you.

A [woman's] own folly ruins [her] life,
yet [her] heart rages against the LORD.

PROVERBS 19:3

one

"Tamara?" The voice halted her in her tracks, cutting through passing traffic and the hum of conversation on the busy sidewalk. Slowly she turned toward it.

"Charles?" A lifetime passed as she faced him. This was the man who had broken her heart. Shattered it into a million itty-bitty pieces she thought she would never find again. Forget Humpty Dumpty. That was just a nursery rhyme. Her heartbreak had been very real, and there had been no king's horses and no king's men to help her put her heart back together again. Yet, miraculously, time had done its work, and now she only felt the sting of love lost…if she stopped long enough to think of him—which she purposed not to do until not loving him anymore became a habit.

"How have you been? *Wow!*" He was grinning broadly. "It's been *years!*"

"Yes, it has." Tamara studied him while trying to get in touch with how she was feeling. It was a strange mixture of numbness and the familiar churning in the pit of her stomach that used to always happen when she anticipated being with him. The feeling was as fresh as it had been when they were together, much to her dismay.

"You look great!" he said.

"Thanks, so do you. How are you?" She sounded stiff, but she didn't quite know what else to say. Her question seemed to add wattage to his smile.

"Do you have time for a cup of coffee? I have so much to tell you."

"Um…" Before she could answer he guided her to a Starbucks that seemed too conveniently near. She sat numbly in the chair while he went to the counter to get her a coffee. She could hear him ordering her a vanilla latte, whole milk with an extra shot of almond. He hadn't forgotten. That had been one of the things she loved about him. He always seemed to know exactly what she liked and what she wanted. Now that it was safe to look at him without him being close enough to read her thoughts and feelings, she studied him. He'd never been what she considered a gorgeous man, but he was easy on the eyes. He would easily blend in with a crowd without inviting a second look. But there was something about him. The way he carried himself. The way he dressed. His sharp wit, charm, and fascinating mind that had taken her off guard and swept her off her feet. And then, as quickly as she had fallen in love, he was gone. His parting words were, "I don't know how I'm supposed to feel. I just can't reconcile being in love with someone I can't be sexually intimate with." And with that, the abyss that separated their love for one another from her faith and principles widened and swallowed him, leaving her with a gaping hole in her heart and a lot of questions for God.

"Here you go." He set the coffee in front of her, breaking into her thoughts. He sat and smiled at her.

"You know, I'm really glad I ran into you today."

"Really?" Tamara didn't quite know what to make of that statement. The intellectual side of her warned her heart not to make any assumptions. *Watch yourself, girl.*

"Yes. I've actually been meaning to call you…I owe you my life in a way."

Tamara felt her mind forming a question, but she couldn't vocalize it.

"What I'm trying to say is that I got saved, Tamara. And I owe it all to you! I know when we were together I didn't get where you were coming from. My pride was wounded because you wouldn't sleep with me, and I took it personally. I have to admit now that my breaking up with you was my way of punishing you for making me feel like I wasn't important enough to you...that I wasn't man enough to break you down."

Tamara could feel her mouth opening, but still no words came. Charles held up his hand to stop her. "The truth of the matter is, I didn't respect your faith and I am sorry. I just wanted to tell you that."

"I see." Tamara couldn't believe what she was hearing. Dare she hope that after all those tear-stained nights God had brought the man of her dreams back into her life? Could He have taken him away to clean him up and bring him back to her? A check in her spirit made her stop her train of thought.

Charles chuckled. "You know you were a woman a long time before I became a man. Talk about being unequally yoked, and I'm not just talking spiritually! I sulked for a long time after we broke up. I started reading everything I could about God, Jesus...I was going to come back and convince you that you were wrong, but in the midst of devising my argument I got slammed with the truth." He shook his head as if bemused at the irony. "Well, to make a long story short, I got saved, went off to seminary, got ordained, and I've just moved back to Chicago to take over a church on the south side."

"Charles, that's great! I can't believe you waited all this time to tell me! Why didn't you call me? I can't believe this." She realized she was repeating herself and stopped, not knowing what else to say.

"I can't explain it all now. A lot of things happened, but I know it was all for the best." He hit the table. "Wait until I tell my wife I saw you! We were just talking about you."

Tamara felt as if she'd been slapped. Her eyes dropped to mask her shock. For the first time she noticed the wedding band on his left ring finger. She was glad she was sitting, and yet suddenly her chair didn't feel so secure.

"Tamara…"

His voice snapped her out of her freefall back into pain. "You would love her. She reminds me so much of you. I met her at seminary. She knows all about you because you were an integral part of my conversion…"

His voice went on, but she no longer heard him. She was about to suffocate. She glanced at her watch and stood up suddenly. She was relieved that the action jolted her back to the present.

"I'm so sorry. I just realized what time it is. I'm supposed to be meeting Jamilah for dinner, and now I'm late. I'd better get going before she has a fit." She was lying about how her best friend would react to her tardiness, but she didn't care. All she knew was she had to get away. Away from him. Away from herself and how she was feeling. Away from the memories she'd managed to compartmentalize to a back file in her heart all this time.

Charles handed her a card. "It really was good to see you. Come visit one Sunday! I'd love for you to meet Valorie. You two would really hit it off."

You must be crazy, she thought.

"I will." She lied again.

"Oh and please give Jamilah my regards."

"I will. She won't believe I ran into you. I'm so happy for you!" She forced a smile that felt too wide. "Well, gotta run." She turned and headed toward the door, frantically in search of oxygen. Outside she stopped, took a deep breath, and exhaled. *Jamilah's never going to know it either.* A little voice had entered Tamara's head, making her resolve to blot this encounter from her mind for the sake of her sanity. Yet in spite of her resolve not to tell Jamilah what had just happened, as soon as she was clear of the door she yanked open her cell phone.

"Where are you, girl? It's eight o'clock! See? This is why I always tell you a half hour *before* we're supposed to be somewhere. You're always late!"

Tamara detected a smile in Jamilah's voice even though she was scolding her. "Look, I spend my life being on time for clients who drive me crazy, so I deserve to take my time getting everywhere else."

"I see!" Jamilah feigned shock. "Buuuuut...that's not really acceptable and obviously you're in a mood, so we'll talk about what's got you in such a snit when you get here."

"I can't..."

"You can't what?"

"I can't get there. I can't get anywhere...I've got to go home..."

"What?"

"I just ran into Charles on the street."

"What?"

"Stop sounding like a broken record. Charles. Remember him?"

"How could I forget?"

"I wish I could. Well he got saved. Got married. And he's pastoring a church on the south side."

"You're lying!"

"I wish I were. Actually I told several lies while I was with him. I told him I would visit his church, but I won't. I told him I was happy for him, but I'm not happy at all. How dare he get saved and get on with his life! I'm so upset, Jamilah." The tears began to flow. "And then he had the nerve to tell me he wanted me to meet his wife. What was he thinking? I'm so mad I can't see straight. I'm mad at him, and mad at myself for being stuck on a memory. I'm supposed to be able to get past this. I'm a therapist for Pete's sake! Oh, and speaking of God, I'm mad at Him too for letting the whole thing happen. Why couldn't Charles have gotten saved when he was with me? And don't give me a lecture about being out of the will of God because I don't want to hear it." The sobs were coming hard and fast now, and she didn't care who was looking. She threw up her arm to hail a cab.

"Oh Tamara..." Jamilah sounded satisfactorily sympathetic, but it wasn't enough to soothe Tamara.

She settled into the seat of a cab and slammed the door. "1563 North Dearborn," she barked at the driver. "I'm sorry, Jamilah, I've got to go." She closed the phone before her friend could say anything else.

They understood each other well. Jamilah knew she needed her space. Tamara was like a cat licking her wounds until they healed. Except this time she wondered if they ever would. She felt trapped, unable to divorce herself from what she believed, and yet constantly questioning it. And now she was mad at the One who had all the answers. She closed her eyes to help shut out her thoughts. What would she tell herself if she was one of her clients? She went down the list of tried and reportedly true answers. None seemed to fit, and that was when she knew she was in trouble. Deep trouble.

two

Corinne stepped out of the shower and reached for the bath sheet on the heated rack. Slowly and deliberately she dried herself off while pondering her fate. Most men would have found her flawless. Skin like glass, smooth and clear. An hourglass figure. Pert, beautiful breasts, a small, tight waist, perfectly flat abdomen, and taut backside…all perfectly sculpted by the finest plastic surgeon in Chicago. She could have been a poster child for the prominent doctor at Northwestern Reconstruction Center. Known for his handiwork, he was called Michelangelo—and that was the truth. She was a work of art—or so she'd been told…though how she felt didn't mirror that train of thought. She had subjected herself to surgery after surgery to be perfect for her husband, thinking if she could only be beautiful enough she could win his heart and attention. And still no response…at least not the warmth she was looking for. All this time she had believed her husband's disinterest in her was her fault. He was, after all, a man of God. One who counseled husbands and wives on how to have lasting marriages. But their own home didn't sound like the one he described when teaching about the family and what "kingdom living," as he liked to call it, looked like.

How ironic! She was the envy of many of the women in the congregation. Their church was a family church, approximately 10,000 members strong, in Barrington, one of the wealthiest suburbs of Chicago. Corinne was the beautiful young wife with the perfect husband overseeing one of the most prestigious churches in the country. How wonderful her life must be. Little did people know her husband was far more loving in public than he was behind closed doors. Oh he wasn't cruel or anything. Far from it. He was kind and indulgent—perhaps that was his way of assuaging the guilt of the secret he had kept all this time. No, the cruelty was not obvious abuse, it was his distance when she wanted to respond to his kindness. He made love to her on rare occasions, as if it was a duty, and left her feeling more alone than ever.

She smiled wryly, thinking of all the singles at church who were always bemoaning their fate. She wanted to scream at them so many times, "Little do you know it can be far more painful to feel lonely when you have someone than when you don't! Believe me it's far better to be lonely alone than lonely with someone." But these were things she kept to herself as she maintained the facade of the controlled, respectable first lady of her church. Elegant and gracious, but dying slowing inside with her congregation none the wiser.

She slipped on a silver-blue silk slip of a nightgown and crowned it with a beautiful matching robe, tying the knot on the belt to complete her ensemble. Reentering the bedroom she looked around the room, surveying the décor, all subtle shades of silver and mauve. It was a large room—large enough for a couple to coexist and still remain strangers. The king-size bed was crowned with a voluptuous draped canopy. The room was softly lit by a beautiful crystal chandelier. There was a sitting area, complete with a plush velvet love seat and settee. Heavy satin draping framed the room, creating a romantic picture that didn't really exist. And now the silence was deafening. She reached for the remote and flicked a button, flooding the room with music, instrumental easy listening that washed over her. A drink would be perfect. It was her way of numbing her pain. She could tell her troubles to the bottom of her glass, and it would be repeated to no one.

It was not only lonely being the wife of Randall Collins, it was also lonely being the wife of a preacher. It was a world of subterfuge where it was hard to know who could be trusted. She couldn't confide in parishioners from her church because her husband was their fearless and flawless leader and should remain that way in their eyes. She couldn't really confide in another preacher's wife either because in a sense her husband was the competition. Any sin revealed could be used to ruin her husband and steal his flock. Church life could be a complicated world of cardboard facades that fronted completely different lives behind the scenes.

She never knew when it was safe to be vulnerable. Even though all pastors' wives heard rumors of the husbands who played around, were involved with pornography, had gambling problems, and dealt with other issues on an unbelievable list that one would never associate with "men of the cloth," no one was brave enough to get involved or even make a phone call to get confirmation from the source. And so the wives sedated themselves with surface conversations at luncheons and shopping expeditions in the city without breathing a word of their troubles. It was called networking, but Corinne called it another occasion for catty comparisons that she could do without, and so she'd withdrawn to her own insulated world. And when her plastic surgeon refused to make one more adjustment, her bourbon tumbler had become her best friend. She never drank enough to get totally drunk because she didn't believe in excess, but she did appreciate the nice buzz that put everything in soft focus so the truth wasn't so jarring. That way she could be pleasant and present without hurting so much.

She took a deep breath, opened the bedroom door, and made her way down the hall toward the stairs. She stopped at Jada's door and was about to knock but then lowered her fist knowing she would be greeted by silence. Jada, her teenage daughter, was a whole separate issue. The once vivacious little girl had grown sullen and distant, practically a recluse in the last year. Hiding in her room and insisting her need for privacy be respected had led to many volatile showdowns but no solutions. Corinne was at her wit's end, but she could only juggle so many emotional balls at a time…and no one was cooperating with her. She had prayed about it to no avail. She finally "let go and let God," which felt precarious at best, so shaky was her faith of late. After all, she'd prayed for a godly man and gotten Randall. What other cruel jokes would God play on her before life was over?

She made her way down the staircase on a mission to claim a nightcap and something sweet before turning in for the night. A light coming through the partially opened door to the den caused her to pause. *Is Randall home?* She hadn't heard him come in. She walked toward the door, but another sound stopped her in her tracks. Low moans came from the room. She didn't know what made her tiptoe her way toward the door instead of walking normally, perhaps it was the Holy Spirit or mere human instinct. She felt a sharp intake of air, her hand going to her mouth to silence herself as she reeled backward in shock at the sight of her husband locked in the embrace of another man who was passionately kissing and fondling him.

Colliding with a pedestal next to the door, the sound of glass shattering snapped her out of her horror long enough to send the blood rushing out of her head, reverberating through her ears, causing her to feel faint for a moment as she teetered before she stabilized herself by catching the doorjamb.

She looked up and saw Randall staring at her. She couldn't tell if the look on his face was concern for her or guilt. Thoughts were traveling through her mind at the speed of light. Did she just see what she thought she saw? Surely there was some mistake, and she would sound foolish if she leveled an accusation that was wrong. No, she needed time to think. The room was spinning.

A strange man stood behind Randall, looking at her curiously. Randall was rooted to the spot and still hadn't said a word. She fought to recover.

"Oh, I'm so sorry…" though she wasn't clear on what she was apologizing for. She managed to squeeze out a hollow-sounding chuckle. "Oh my goodness! I'm so embarrassed." Then, realizing she was in her peignoir set, she didn't know if she should clutch her robe or begin picking up the broken vase. She decided to go for the glass. She stooped to the floor, trying to recover the shattered pieces, handling them as carefully as she would have liked her husband to handle her heart, grateful that she had an excuse not to look at him while she tried to collect her thoughts. What was she supposed to say or do now?

She wrestled inwardly, finding no answer, unable to hear God because she was screaming too loudly inside. She stood as Randall finally came to life.

"Here, let me help you before you cut yourself…"

"Thank you…but…please…don't let me interrupt your meeting. Mr.…." She looked toward his silent visitor, trying not to study him too closely lest her stare betray her revulsion.

"Leonard," he answered, looking awkward as he stepped toward her and extended his hand to shake hers before thinking better of it and dropping it to his side.

Corinne was relieved her hands were filled with large pieces of glass, though she couldn't decide if she wanted to discard them or take a swipe at the men. The slow realization of what had led to her husband's distance was washing over her like the shower she'd just left. The knowledge that she was not the reason for his coldness didn't make her feel any better. Why hadn't she discerned this from the beginning? And what should she do now? Should she confront him? Should she go to the church board and expose him? But would they believe her? And how would that affect the church? Her marriage? Her home? The consequences were too overwhelming to consider; the fallout would be devastating for everyone. The parishioners' faith would be shattered, and they would scatter. She and her daughter would have to endure unspeakable public shame. Her husband could be removed from the church, and they would lose everything they had.

Her thoughts careened over one another as if scrambling for an exit but, not finding one, they hit the wall of her mind and collected in an unsolvable heap. Where would they go from here? No one would want to do the damage control it would take to justify their association with him. He would be jobless, and so would she. She'd never officially worked a day in her life. It seemed like she'd always been his wife because they'd married fresh out of Bible school. She had no other identity. No other skills. No way to make a living that would afford her what she was used to. No, there was way too much at stake to just react. She would keep quiet to preserve what she did have. She may not be able to control what her husband did, but she would do her best to keep the rest of her world intact.

"It's been nice meeting you, Mr. Leonard, did you say? Although I wish I could have been a bit more graceful." She could hear her involuntary nervous laughter echoing in the foyer. "Tell him I'm not usually this clumsy, dear. There must have been something on the floor. I slipped."

Randall looked relieved, breathing out as if he'd been holding his breath in anticipation of what she would say. "It's all right, honey. Leonard was just leaving. Why don't you get rid of that before you cut yourself? I'll get the rest."

"Thank you." She was grateful to be dismissed and glad she'd managed to cover her shock. *Thank goodness Randall doesn't suspect I saw him and his lover. His lover.* She shuddered but managed to direct a weak smile at the men. Fighting the urge to run, she concentrated on taking measured steps down the hallway, toward a place where she could feel safe.

She made her way to the kitchen and dumped the glass in the trash. The sound of it landing closely imitated the noise inside her soul—the sound of her life falling apart around her. She felt strangely anesthetized, almost as if she were in a cocoon that sheltered her from the pain she knew she was really feeling somewhere deep inside. Almost robotic, she felt herself going through familiar motions that suddenly felt quite foreign. As a futile stab at normalcy, she cut a thin slice of her homemade apple pie she knew she wouldn't eat. Then she poured herself a shot of bourbon for good measure. She headed up the back stairs to avoid another awkward encounter. As she settled onto the love seat she heard the front door close. She listened to her husband's steps in the foyer, and then heard them retreating back down the hallway. She finished her drink, on the rocks of course, and left the pie untouched on the table beside her seat. The thought of eating made her sick to her stomach. Slipping off her robe, she shivered and climbed into bed...and waited, though she didn't know what she was waiting for. She tried to focus. To pray. To formulate a point of view, a plan, some type of clarity. She could do none of these. And so she lay there, staring at the ceiling waiting...holding her breath until it hurt. Slowly she released herself to breathe evenly and waited...and waited...until the haze and warmth of her drink folded her into its arms, cloaking her consciousness in the darkness, giving her a temporary respite from the painful knowing that tomorrow would come and she still would have no idea what to do.

three

Lydia made her way across the wide expanse of the lavish hotel lobby. So intent was she on reaching her destination she failed to see the swarm gathering around her until the first flash snapped her out of her thoughts.

"Mrs. Caldwell! Or should I say Miss? Any comments on your recent divorce?"

"What?" Lydia instinctively raised her hands to shield her face from the flashes that continued to flicker like lightning filling the sky.

"Would you care to comment on your recent divorce?"

"No, I would not!"

"Is it true your husband was having an affair?"

"What?" Her heels stopped beating a rhythm across the marble entryway. The paparazzi gathered even closer, hemming her in.

"Is it true your husband left you for another woman?"

"Where did you get such nonsense?" She knew she should keep walking, but she was rooted to the spot.

"Do you know your ex-husband is engaged to another woman?"

"Not to my knowledge!" she snapped. The shock of what had been said propelled her to press past the photographers blocking her departure. She quickened her pace toward the front door as their questions ricocheted off her back. She couldn't believe she was being subjected to this. It was one thing to be on the other side of the gossip rags watching her famous acquaintances being trashed, but to be on the receiving end gave her a new appreciation for what others had to endure. *I'm not going to take it. Mmm mm. I'm not going out like that,* she decided. Wheeling to face her pursuers, she planted herself for the face off.

"Just where do you people get off invading people's personal space? Notice I said *personal.* That's what you keep to yourself! If you want to ask me what my latest movie project is, I'll be happy to accommodate your questions. But my husband's or *ex-*husband's and my affairs are none of your business!"

"So he *did* have an affair! Or did *you* have an affair? I'm confused." The group began to laugh at the wit of the brave photographer.

"Yes, perhaps you are." With eyes of steel she bore a hole into the offender. "Perhaps if you had a life of your own, you wouldn't feel you had to dip in grown folks' business."

"Now wait a minute, lady! I'm just here doing my job."

"Then you need to get another one." She made her way out the door when one of the photographers jumped in front of her. Before she could think, she grabbed the camera. The photographer reached to get it back, and she turned to dodge his reach.

"*What* is going on here?"

Everyone swung in the direction of the questioner. Without missing a beat the cameras resumed flashing. This time their focus was a different subject. Richard Caldwell stood assessing the situation. But that was not Lydia's focus. Her eyes took in the woman standing next to her ex-husband.

This must be the woman they had alluded to. How long had everyone else known what she was the last to find out? Leave it to Richard to disgrace her publicly. But then again, they were newly divorced, and he could do what he liked whether it hurt her or not. She lifted her chin to reassert herself. She hated to admit that she was crumbling inside. No way was she going to let this group of vultures get a photo op of her crying like a pathetic castoff. "They were just asking me to comment on your affair." She looked at Richard levelly.

"I see. And what did you tell them?"

"I told them I had no knowledge of it."

"Good answer." He started toward the door, his arm on his companion's elbow, guiding her gently past Lydia.

The paparazzi followed, snapping pictures and barking questions behind the couple as they moved through the revolving door.

"Mr. Caldwell! Mr. Caldwell! Care to share with us who your friend is?"

Richard never looked back. Lydia looked after them, trying to collect her thoughts. A touch on her shoulder made her jump. She turned to the lone reporter left behind.

"*Now* do you care to comment on your husband's affair?"

"Didn't you hear anything I said? He is my *ex*-husband. And no, I have no comment." She pushed past him, afraid he'd see the tears forming in her eyes. She was thankful for the brisk Chicago wind and frigid blast that she could blame should they begin to fall while the doorman hailed her a cab. She had no comment because she hadn't had a clue...about the demise of her marriage, how she'd ended up in this situation, or how to handle the way she was feeling. She had acquired new wounds on top of old ones, and she didn't know which ones to address first.

Richard had a way of making her feel so small, vulnerable, and defenseless when he looked at her the way he had inside. It was the same withering look of disapproval her father used to give her that hurt more than any whipping or rejection. That attitude screamed, *You think you're something, don't you? Always have to be the center of attention!* And what was wrong with that? What was wrong with simply wanting someone to love you? Was that so terrible?

Well, she couldn't go back, but she could move forward. And she had no intention of letting anyone see her sweat. "To the Estate Room, please," she told the cabbie. Right now she had a very important business meeting, and she didn't intend to be late or let one monkey stop her show. Even though it felt like everything she'd managed to build for herself was falling down around her ears, life had to go on. If Richard wanted to embarrass himself by carrying on with women beneath his station, he could go right ahead. She didn't intend to make a fool of herself. He could try to intimidate her with his superior stares and posturing, but he should have known by now that she didn't go down without a fight. She'd felt helpless as a child when dealing with her father's distance and silent disapproval, but she was a woman now—and she was not having it.

The cabbie waited for traffic to clear and eyed her curiously through the rearview mirror, pulling her from her musings, making her conscious of how she must look.

She angrily wiped her tears away, adjusted herself in the backseat, and turned her face away from him and toward the window. Gazing outward she took in the scene. The paparazzi was still taking pictures and asking questions. Richard and whoever the woman was were slowly and deliberately making their way past them. A flash went off in her direction. She shuddered at the thought of what the headlines on the local gossip columns would say the next day. *Well, if you can't beat them, join them,* she thought. She lifted her chin in defiance. If they wanted something to talk about, she would give them something to talk about—but they wouldn't like the conversation.

four

Tamara's eyes slowly traveled around her office. Its cool colors were soothing to the eye. She took pride in creating an environment that those she counseled would find inviting. She'd established an oasis from their pain, a safe haven, all silver, taupe, and sea foam, with floor to ceiling windows. Her only regret was perhaps she left her clients too open to being emotionally manipulated by the external elements that seemed so close at 30 floors up. Their moods did seem to reflect whatever was going on outside. This led her to add whispers of organza drapes to soften the effects and shield them from the psychological ravages of the weather. But aesthetics could only serve as a temporary diversion at best, this she had found out soon enough. No matter how pretty the room was, it wasn't enough to protect them from the ugliness of their issues.

"Perhaps I would know what to do if it was another woman. But how do you compete for your husband's love and attention when the other woman is a man?"

They'd been around this mountain before. Tamara stifled the urge to yawn. That would not be good. Not when Corinne Collins was in mid cry. Instead Tamara shifted and twirled her pen before putting a mustache on the woman she drew on her notepad. There was no need for more notes. Every week was the same. She could practically recite her patient's dialogue with her in stereo. Corinne always started off the same. The brave smile that looked questionable around the edges. It quickly disintegrated after she proclaimed that she was feeling a little bit better this week. This self-deception would be betrayed by the wringing of her hands, narrowing down to twirling the three-carat diamond set in a cathedral mount that seemed to grow each week. It seemed so cruel in an ironic way. Why did unfaithful men always give such fabulous gifts? Did they think expensive baubles would make up for their direct or indirect battery of a woman's soul?

Tamara cocked her head to the side, studying her client once again. Corinne was slender and beautiful. Fine-boned and elegant. Naturally blonde with wide blue eyes that were now red-rimmed and framed with long, wet lashes that any woman would envy. Yes, she was beautiful. A vision in soft blue cashmere that seemed almost too pretty for the dreariness of the day. She was tragically beautiful, for in her mind she wasn't beautiful enough...even though she was supermodel perfect.

It was March, but it looked more like January. Spring was taunting Chicago again, making the inhabitants wait for the sun and some semblance of warmer days. Tamara shifted her gaze from her client to study the bleak sky that seemed to be brooding as it peered in on their session. She pulled her eyes back from the window, slowly exhaled, licked her lips, and said, "I'm sorry. That's all we have time for today."

Corinne opened her mouth as if she wanted to say something else, but then pressed her lips together. Almost in slow motion she uncrossed her legs and stood in one fluid motion. She walked slowly toward the door, and then turned back toward Tamara. "What will I tell my daughter?"

"We'll talk about that next week." Tamara let out the breath she'd been holding as the door closed behind her client. She looked at the door as if willing it to lock magically. The whisper of the water from the fountain in the corner of the room broke her concentration and brought her back to the immediate. Why didn't she feel more sorry for Corinne? Had she become that hard and jaded? Perhaps she'd been doing this too long. That was funny; she'd only been in practice for seven years. She recalled how zealous she was at the onset. She was going to revolutionize her field. Marrying the tools of psychology with spiritual knowledge and the power of prayer, she was going to be known for getting results. She and Dr. Jesus were in the house. And then the people had come. One by one with story after story of defeat, misery, and woe.

At first she internalized their troubles, finding them hard to shake at the end of the day. Late in the night hours she found herself tossing and turning, wrestling to find answers to their problems. Their sad faces invaded her personal prayer time, her thoughts when she was out with friends, her mind and body even in mid-sweat as she worked out, fighting to release the tension that was building within her. Their lives haunted her. Slowly the callus grew around her heart to shield her from the continuous angst she found herself feeling. It was a matter of survival. She couldn't continue to carry the load of her clients' wounded hearts. This she knew and so slowly she erected walls around her heart, hiding behind them where nothing could penetrate. It was the only way to keep her sanity. The mild irony of it made her giggle a closed mouth bubble of joyless mirth. When had the fire gone out? When had she lost her passion? She was tired of everyone's troubles. Even more tired of watching people's faith disintegrate. Tired of not having enough hope to offer them. Tired of not having any answers.

There was a time when she had all the answers—or thought she did. But then came the Corinne Collinses of the world. And more complex issues than Tamara ever anticipated facing. There seemed to be no clear-cut solution when she searched the Scriptures. Corinne's life was beautiful and perfect...a fairly tale...until you turned the page and read about her husband, a rather prominent Christian leader who was having an affair with another man. How do you deal with what should have been a perfect little Christian marriage? Why didn't God insulate Corinne from something that should have been foreign to her? Shouldn't her relationship with Jesus make her exempt from experiencing these kinds of traumas?

And on a personal level, how does a woman compete with the other woman who is actually a man? How could she help Corinne feel beautiful again? And what advice should she offer about talking to her daughter? Shoot, how does Corinne face her congregation? There would always be some who would accuse her of not being a good enough wife. How would she deal with that? So many questions that demanded answers Tamara honestly didn't know. Anything she said sounded "religious" or like a cliché, and she could no longer vouch for the effectiveness of the counsel she offered. And that was scary after thinking she was going to save the world. The more she discovered her lack of answers for others, the more the answers for her own life became elusive.

She sighed again. How could she tell Corinne she was probably wasting her money? That her counselor had nothing to give her... nothing that she believed anyway. She was fresh out of answers. And that was bad...very bad.

five

Jada leaned her elbow against the top of the piano, idly tinkling the keys with one hand while surveying the massive sanctuary. It felt different when it was empty. The notes rising from the keys she idly tapped echoed, creating an almost mournful call. She liked the sound. It echoed the cry of her soul, the cries she could no longer release unless she was singing. Worship was her solace. She smiled at the paradox. The same thing that gave her so much pleasure also brought her the most pain.

Many had commented on the purity of her praise as she led the worship team week after week, head thrown back, eyes shut, hands lifted to the heavens. But what they saw as surrender she knew was a desperate attempt to reach the heavens and pull God down. Pull Him down to her rescue. When she sang the words "Draw me close to You," she meant it from the core of her soul. She'd rewritten the rest of the words: "Hide me in the center of Your heart…Keep me hidden in the secret place…deep within the warmth of Your embrace…come, Lord Jesus, grant me gracious shelter…surround and keep me safe from every storm. Let me know You are here beside me…protecting me from every care and harm…" She would sing it a million times if she could—or at least until the words came true. She refused to believe God was not great. That He couldn't do something to save her from the hand of a man who made a mockery of his title and everything God stood for. To begin to doubt that God was not powerful, that He didn't love her, that He wouldn't do something to save her would be enough to push her over the edge. She didn't dare lose her faith. It was all she had. Where else could she turn? She couldn't go to her mother; she was an emotional invalid. She couldn't go to her father—that would uncover a Pandora's box she wasn't ready to deal with. She couldn't handle being responsible for completely ruining everyone's lives. So only God was left. Yet it seemed the more she called out to Him, the more silent He became.

And so she waited in the only place that felt safe to her. The empty sanctuary. It looked the way she felt. She'd finished rehearsing with the worship team. They had come, gone through the paces, laughed and talked in the easy, carefree manner of artists who truly enjoy using their gifts. They lingered just long enough for her to shoo them on so she could enjoy the temporary respite of being alone with her thoughts in a place that allowed her to breathe freely for a few stolen minutes. She used to hate this place. As a child she was under scrutiny from the moment she entered the building. As the pastor's daughter, the expectations for perfection and good behavior were at an all-time high. She hated the way everyone felt they could tell her what to do. She hated the label "PK" and what it implied. All "preacher's kids" were rebellious and got into trouble. The worst was expected of her when she hit her early teens, and now it seemed the worst was happening to her and no one knew.

Now in her mid-teens, no one scolded her any longer. She had grown up and blossomed beyond their critical expectations into someone seen as responsible and perfect. Gone was the magnifying glass she once was held under. She almost wished it would return. Perhaps then someone would at least suspect that something was very wrong and sound the alarm for her. Or perhaps they would blame her for what she suffered, just like the voices inside her head that said the situation was all her fault. She felt helpless to prove otherwise.

A loud rap interrupted her thoughts. Pastor Masters had dropped his Bible on the floor. Recovering from tripping over a loose corner of carpet, he looked annoyed. "I have to get that fixed. Ready to go, young lady?" He made his way down the center aisle toward her, a smile that his eyes betrayed as insincere. No, she wasn't ready to go. At least not where he wanted to take her. It was a ritual now. She waited in the sanctuary, clinging to God for as long as she could until the man appeared and ripped her from Jesus' arms again. Pastor Masters was a wolf circling her, licking his fat lips that always made noise when he talked.

"We'd best get going. Ruth hates it when I'm late for dinner."

Jada bit her tongue, killing the urge to say Ruth would hate discovering her wonderful, godly husband wasn't really who he pretended to be. He turned back toward the door leading out of the sanctuary. She gathered her things and slowly followed him to the foyer. The building was deserted, and she could hear her heels echoing his steps as he headed toward his office. She wondered where her father went every Thursday evening at this time, although she could guess what he was doing. He always gave some vague explanation for why Pastor Masters had to give her a ride home from church.

She knew her mother was in the city seeing her therapist, although she wondered why her mother even bothered. At this point it must simply be a social habit because Jada saw no improvement in her mother's disposition. She remained a hapless victim at home and at church as a "first lady." She was a disappointment to the congregation because she took no active part in anything, failing to live up to their expectation to be the fearless, anointed leader of the women's ministry. She seemed content to just be arm candy to her husband, who fawned over her in public but remained distant at home. Jada wondered if they ever stopped to think how she felt about living a life of appearances only. How long could they all live for the sake of other people? But, after all, isn't that why Christ died? She was beginning to wonder about the value of salvation. She failed to see the point.

"I forgot something in my office. Come along, and then we'll be on our way."

He always said that, looking about him to make sure the coast was clear. She shivered as she entered his office, more from the temperature of her heart than the room.

"Close the door. I want to show you something." His voice sounded distant to her as she retreated into herself, steeling herself against what was to come. She hadn't cried after the first time, lest he gain pleasure from thinking he had power over her. She wouldn't give him the satisfaction. It was the only thing she could control, and so she gritted her teeth and determined not to be a sniveling victim. He leaned into her, stroking her face with his pudgy, parched fingers. She squeezed her eyes shut, and turned her face away from him. He disgusted her. She resisted the urge to retch in his face.

"You are so beautiful…"

She pulled her face away from him, trying to escape his putrid breath.

"Just like your mother…so unspoiled." He seemed to be in a daze. She frowned. *Unspoiled? But you've spoiled me. And my father has spoiled my mother. We are both spoiled.* She pressed her lips together to keep from screaming as his hands raked down the front of her blouse. She found a spot on the opposite wall to concentrate on, as if waiting for someone to pull an arrow from her heart without the help of anesthesia. He had his way with her. It no longer hurt; she didn't feel him pressed against her. Didn't feel him touching what he shouldn't. Didn't feel him violating what was supposed to be holy and reserved for her wedding day.

She felt nothing. No anger. No hate. No despair. Gone were the initial responses of begging him to stop. Of asking why. Of wondering if he had no fear of God. Obviously he didn't. And perhaps he had no reason to. She now knew he was driven by his own perversion. And he'd seized his opportunity through brutal bribery because of her father's secret sin. She was fresh out of responses, reactions, or thoughts. She'd wondered until she could wonder no more, and all that was left was a vast yawning space of no conclusions.

Time was suspended in her world of nothingness, a place that offered safety, endurance, and survival, though she wasn't sure what she wanted to survive or live for anymore. She was never aware of how long his invasion of her lasted. His groping seemed endless. But suddenly it was over, and he was a heaving mass of vile humanity. He left her to rearrange her clothes and get presentable. Then she followed him wordlessly to his car. The fresh air slapped her back to consciousness. She blinked and swallowed the tears that threatened to come. No, she refused to give in to emotion. If she did, she might never recover. Sometimes she had visions of herself screaming endlessly; saw herself being carried away because she couldn't stop screaming, which further confirmed her worry that she might lose her sanity. Like Humpty Dumpty sitting on the wall. It only took one fall for him to be damaged beyond repair. She feared she would never be able to put the pieces of her soul back together again.

Subconsciously going through the motions of life, she opened the car door and got in, looking straight ahead. She refused to look at him. Perhaps it was guilt that made him attempt to have a normal conversation...as if nothing had happened. Good! Let him wallow in his guilt all by himself. She didn't answer. She was glad he felt something negative because she felt nothing...nothing at all.

six

Jamilah looked at her watch and then back at the lonely little girl before her. Her eyes were huge and forlorn. The look of rejection so acute it pierced the teacher's heart. "I'm sure she'll be here soon." She lowered herself down to sit on the school steps next to her seven-year-old student who looked smaller than ever in her oversized sweater and backpack. Arianna shrugged as if suggesting this was an old line. She seemed older than her years and weary from being forgotten by her mother time and time again. Her little wise face was studying Jamilah now.

"I'll be all right if you have somewhere to go, Miss Williams."

"Hmm…no, sweetheart, I don't have anything to do. And even if I did, I most certainly wouldn't leave you sitting here by yourself." Jamilah was embarrassed to be caught looking at her watch. The truth was she did have somewhere to go, and Tamara was going to kill her. It was six thirty. They were supposed to meet at six, and she was late again. But so was Arianna's mom. *What was the deal on this woman anyway?* Jamilah was getting angry. How many times was Arianna's mother going to forget to pick her child up? How could any man or drug distract a mother from caring for her precious child?

She took in Arianna's tiny oval-shaped face. She was smaller than most children her age. Her smooth, olive-colored skin framed large, luminous eyes, the cutest little button nose, and pink, pouty, heart-shaped lips. Her face was crowned with dense black ringlets. Jamilah guessed she was African-American mixed with Latina. She was going to be dangerously beautiful when she grew up. That is…if she survived her mother's neglect. The little girl was extremely bright and creative and had great promise. Jamilah hated to see her succumb to the elements and negative influences around her.

With many students in the same predicament, it broke her heart how callous they seemed to become at an early age. But there was something special about this child. Arianna had managed to claim Jamilah's heart, and she couldn't shake her concern for the girl. If only she could rescue this precious darling from her circumstances. As the evening grew darker and chillier, Jamilah felt more and more powerless. She put her arm around Ari, and wrapped her coat around her.

"Are you hungry? Perhaps we could go across the street and get a sandwich. We'll still be able to see your mother when she comes if we sit close to the window."

Ari brightened at this suggestion and nodded her head. Jamilah rose, took Ari's tiny hand, and led her across the street. Going inside, she lifted her up and placed her on a stool facing the street. She left Ari in charge of her briefcase and went off to order dinner. Once she was out of earshot she flipped open her phone and dialed Tamara's number.

"Where are you?" A slightly irritated voice crackled in and out on her cell phone.

"I'm sorry. I don't think I'm going to make it."

"Are you standing me up after I've been sitting here waiting for you?"

"I know you're not talking to me after standing me up for Charles the other night!" Jamilah countered, thinking, *Tamara sure has nerve.*

"Don't even go there with me." Tamara's tone was dark. "His name is to be forever stricken from the record."

"That's fine with me, but I still can't make it tonight. Ari's mother forgot to pick her up again."

"How does somebody forget to pick up her child?"

"I don't know. You're the therapist, you tell me."

"Chile, I'm off the clock and fresh out of answers. Somebody needs to call the Department of Children and Family Services on that woman. She is beyond triflin'."

"I don't know if that's the answer. If I call DCFS Ari could end up in a worse place than she is right now, per their record of late."

"This is true."

"Welcome to McDonald's. May I take your order?" The server was looking impatient.

"Hold on a minute, the natives are getting restless. Yes, I'll have a cheeseburger Happy Meal with a fruit punch."

"Ooh, now you're playing mommy! Girl, you have too many students like that to try to save them, you know."

"I'm not trying to save anybody, but what am I supposed to do? I can't leave her sitting on the school steps. There's no telling what time that woman will show up. What if something happens to Ari? And the office is closed, so I can't leave her there." Jamilah struggled to balance her phone on her shoulder while searching for money to pay for the food. One of these days she was going to invest in a headphone.

"That is not your problem, Jamilah. Ari is not your child. I've told you this before."

Jamilah rearranged the food on the tray. "I know that, Tamara! Have you ever heard of this little word called 'compassion,' oh great therapist? What's going on with you, anyway?" She moved away from the counter.

"I don't know..." Tamara sounded tired.

Jamilah was too wound up over Ari to pay attention to vocal cues. "Do you know what Ari said to me the other day? 'Miss Williams, do you think God loves me?' 'Of course he does,' I said. And then you know what she said? 'Well, if He loves me, why won't He make my mama love me?' How deep is that? So I said, 'Your mother does love you, honey. She's just sick and scared that's all.' 'Well, can't He make her better?' she asks. At that point I didn't know what to say. All I could tell her was people have to want to be better in order for God to help them."

"You did better than I would have done 'cause I'm beginning to wonder myself if the doctor is in the house."

Jamilah frowned as she neared the table. Ari was still looking out the window, swinging her legs beneath her. "What doctor? I'm confused."

"Dr. Jesus, stupid."

"Oh, you're going there. Well, this is way too deep a discussion for me to get into right now. I'll call you when I get home."

"All right. Just remember, don't go trying to save the world 'cause *you* might need to get saved by the time you're finished."

"Ooh, you're really in a mood. I'll call you back. Bye." Jamilah flicked the phone shut, and then shifted gears for Ari's sake. "Here you go, sweetie!"

As she tried to process Tamara's comments, she watched Ari scarf down her food and, with the other half of her brain, wondered vaguely if the child had eaten breakfast. She looked at her watch again. It was seven thirty. Time for plan B. They couldn't stay outside or shut the restaurant down as they had done before. She wasn't about to let Ari's mother make this a habit; she'd have to figure out a way around that later.

"Why don't we go to your house? Maybe your mother fell asleep."

"Okay." Ari wiped her lips with her napkin, looking like quite the little princess seated on a throne.

Jamilah smiled. Hoisting her down from her stool, they started the trek to Ari's house.

Jamilah shivered as they turned the corner and headed toward the project. The apartments loomed in the near distance, looking as cold and aloof as the young men standing on the corner. She nodded to them as they passed. They looked at her curiously, and then smiled at Ari. One of them reached out to rub her head.

"Hey, little bit. Where's yo' mama?"

Ari ducked under his hand, frowning at the young man. "She's at home. I told you not to mess up my hair."

The young man waved her off and feigned a mock apology. "Aw, I'm sorry, yo' highness. I'll remember dat next time. Tell yo' mama I'm lookin' for her."

"All right." Ari seemed fearless as she bounced back in step with Jamilah, who was nervous and doing her best to keep a calm facade in place.

Although she was black, Jamilah wasn't comfortable in this environment. Her neighborhood, only five blocks away, was markedly different. The lines of demarcation were drawn, and the unspoken code of who belonged where was solidly in place. The gentrified did not mix with the urbanized, and that was understood by all. There was always the suspicion that those who had "made it" felt they were better than those they'd left behind. And there was no convincing those who felt trapped where they were that this wasn't necessarily the case. They did nothing to mask their resentment and jealousy, which often made for volatile exchanges. Jamilah wasn't ready for an altercation like that.

Turning into the first building, Jamilah was saddened by the state of the hallway. It was littered with trash and dark. The lightbulb in the overhead fixture looked like it had been burned out for quite some time. By the time they climbed to the third floor, the young teacher was beside herself. As emotionally drained as she was winded, she couldn't understand how anyone could settle for living like this. Knocking tentatively on the door, she knew what the response would be before the silence came back to greet them. Now she was really mad. Where was Ari's mother?

Ari tugged her coat.

"I have a key." Tiny fingers produced a key tied to a string that was connected to her book bag. Jamilah stifled the urge to scream and took the key. Opening the door carefully, she peered in. She knew it. No one home. "Miss Jordan?" She would give her the benefit of the doubt. She walked through the living room that was in total disarray. The kitchen was even worse. Didn't the woman believe in washing dishes? She resisted the urge to look into the refrigerator, knowing what she saw would make her crazy. Her last stop was the only bedroom, just past the bathroom, with its door ajar. Nope. No one home. Now what? She couldn't leave Ari here by herself.

Pulling a sheet of paper out of her briefcase, she wrote a note and left it on the only bare spot on the coffee table, along with a twenty dollar bill. It wouldn't cost that much for Ari's mom to take a cab to get to Jamilah's house and back, but she didn't want to leave it to chance or give her an excuse.

> Dear Miss Jordan,
>
> Ari is with me. You can come to get her. I've left cab fare for you. I was nervous about leaving her home alone. If you get in late, you can wait until tomorrow to pick up Ari. I'll be happy to let her spend the night at my house and take her to school with me in the morning. Please call me.

She signed the note and included her address and phone number.

"Ari, I think you should go home with me. Your mother can pick you up if she comes in soon, okay?"

Ari looked uncertain.

"It'll be fun. I'll help you with your homework, and we'll watch a cartoon. See, I left your mother a note."

Ari was slowly warming to the idea.

"Why don't you get another sweater and some underwear just in case it gets too late for her to come tonight, okay?"

"Okay!"

Jamilah shook her head as Ari bounded off to the bedroom to retrieve her clothes. She quickly returned, and they left the apartment.

Back outside Jamilah heaved a sigh of relief while catching a breath of fresh air. Too tired to walk any further, she hailed a cab. Eight o'clock. It felt like eleven.

The doorman smiled at Ari as he swung open the door. "Good evening, Miss Williams."

"Hey, Emmett! How are you?"

"Just fine, Miss Williams, thank you. And who do we have here?"

"This is Miss Arianna Jordan."

"I see. How do you do, Miss Jordan?" He bowed low while reaching to shake her hand.

Ari extended her hand politely and giggled. "Hello."

"Her mother might be coming to pick her up soon. Please let me know when she arrives."

Emmett frowned. "Might?"

Jamilah raised an eyebrow to let him know now was not the time to discuss when or if Ari's mother would show up.

He straightened with comprehension. "I'll let you know when she gets here. My shift ends at eleven, so I'll let Ryan know if she hasn't come by then."

"Thanks, Emmett." Jamilah pushed the elevator button and escorted Ari inside when it arrived. As she watched the numbers lighting up as they passed each floor, Ari's eyes grew wider. The elevator stopped and the door opened. Jamilah smiled as she stepped out into the hallway and led her guest to her apartment. When she opened the door she heard the little girl gasp.

"Ooh, pretty!" Ari looked like Alice in Wonderland must have. She reverently turned slowly around in the middle of the living room. Jamilah was proud of her home, even though it was small. It was hers, and she'd found a way to fill it with light and make it inviting. Warm and eclectic, it was the type of home where you found treasures in every corner. Not that people noticed them all on a first visit, but on subsequent ones they would be delighted by the unusual treasures. They accumulated in view the way they had been collected—one by one with great care from Jamilah's travels. Each piece represented a place she'd visited and the heart of the people there—especially the women and children. Paintings and charcoals hung from the walls in old, rich-looking frames that made them appear as if they had been in place for a lifetime.

Ari's eyes grew larger as her eyes fell on one painting in particular. It was smaller than the others—a painting of a little girl looking out a rain-streaked window. Her expression matched the weather. The painting looked unfinished, a bit crude, almost elementary, but there was something haunting about it. "Miss Williams! That's my painting!" she exclaimed.

"Indeed it is." Jamilah grinned at Ari, taking delight in her surprise. "I told you that you were good." She could feel an awkward moment of emotion coming on, so not knowing what else to say, she reverted to teacher mode. "Now, young lady, you have a half hour to do your homework and then off to bed you go."

After setting Ari at the kitchen table, she sat across from her, watching intently as she bowed her head in deep concentration. *How could anyone not want to be home for such a beautiful child when she got out of school?* She sighed and rose to go in search of linens to transform her couch into a bed for her young charge.

A half hour later she sat on the edge of the couch, looking down on a very sleepy little girl. As she smoothed her hair back from her face she said, "Ari?"

"Yes, Miss Williams?"

"Do you pray before you go to bed?"

"No. Mama said God isn't interested in anything I have to say."

"That's not true! God is very partial to little girls. He loves you, and He loves it when you talk to Him."

"Really?"

"Really! Do you have something you want to say to Him?"

Ari hunched her little shoulders under the covers. "I don't know. Do you pray, Miss Williams?"

"All the time."

"What do you say to Him?"

"Whatever is on my heart at the time. You should try it. I know! Pretend that He's your father. What would you say to Him?"

Ari squeezed her eyes tightly until her whole face was scrunched up. Clasping her hands close to her chest, she said with all the intensity her little heart could muster, "Dear God, please make my mama be happy and love me. Amen." Then looking at Jamilah she said, "Do you think He heard me?"

The teacher swallowed hard, fighting to keep back the tears. "I'm sure He did, honey. Now get some sleep." She got up, turned off the light, and then hurried to her room before her student could see her fall apart.

Tamara was not as sympathetic as Jamilah wanted her to be.

"You can't save the world, Jamilah." She sounded world weary over the phone.

Jamilah sniffed into her tissue and snuggled even deeper into the bedding, while cradling the phone between her shoulder and her pillow. "I know that, Tamara. I'm not talking about the world. I'm talking about one little girl. There's just something about her…"

"Be careful, girl. I'm telling you now, if you get emotionally involved it will come back to bite you in the butt."

"How could caring be a bad thing, oh great and mighty counselor? I'm beginning to worry about your clients."

"Don't I do my job and keep them in the right perspective?"

"I don't know how you do it. I don't think I could sit and listen to people's problems all day without absorbing them and making myself crazy. Come to think of it, you do sound a little weird."

"Ha ha, very funny. But seriously, you have to learn to distance yourself."

"How can you distance yourself when a little girl wonders if God hears her prayers?"

"I'm with her on that one," Tamara muttered.

"What was that?" Jamilah wondered if she'd heard her correctly.

"Oh, nothing. I need to go. I've got an early morning."

"Don't you try to run from me, Miss Calm, Cool, and Collected. What is up with you? I don't like how you've been sounding lately. Maybe it's time for me to take your spiritual temperature, hmm?"

"You just said it…cool. But now is not the time for that discussion. I'll be all right. I just have some questions of my own for God right now. At any rate, none of the world's problems will be solved in one night so I suggest we get some sleep and revisit these issues and more when we are more awake, okay? I'll call you tomorrow to reschedule dinner, but only if you promise not to stand me up again."

"All right, girl. I'll talk to you tomorrow." Jamilah knew the conversation was over whether she wanted it to be or not.

As she settled into the warmth of her bed she pondered Tamara's state of cynicism. She understood her pain over Charles on some level but couldn't understand why disappointment over a man would corrupt someone's relationship with God. Where did trusting God to know what was best for her come in? After all, if Charles had been right for her, wouldn't God have put them together? Sleep overtook her thoughts that vacillated between Ari and Tamara. She found herself dreaming first of trying to hide Ari and then running after Tamara as she walked toward a sunset.

A sharp rap startled her out of the deep darkness that had finally enveloped her. At first what it was didn't register. At last it did. Someone was knocking impatiently at her door. Who could that be? The knocking didn't stop. Jamilah grabbed her robe and headed to the front door, intent on stopping the insistent rapping. Peeking through the peephole she saw Ari's mother, who looked extremely unhappy. Even through the tiny peephole she could see her black shiny eyes looking like hard marbles in a dark-chocolate face taut with rage. High cheekbones and patina smooth skin would have been beautiful if the ash of drug abuse didn't give away her secret. Hair pulled back so tight her hairline was in distress made her look even harder and meaner. Ryan, the night watchman, was behind her, looking deeply distressed.

Jamilah opened the door. "Miss Jordan?" *What time is it, anyway?* she wondered.

Before she could say anything else, the doorman said, "I'm sorry, Miss Williams, but she wouldn't wait for me to call you. She just..."

"Shut up!" Miss Jordan snapped. "Where is she?"

"Wh...?" Jamilah felt disoriented. She focused on the hallway clock. It was three thirty.

"Ari! Where is she?"

"Miss Jordan, she's here and she's fine. Look it's late and she's sleeping. Why don't you let her stay and I'll take her..."

"No, you will not! What's with you, anyway? Why don't you get your own kids? I could have you arrested, you know!"

"Mama?" Ari's voice came from behind Jamilah. She turned to see Ari looking even smaller than usual in the T-shirt she'd given her to sleep in. Miss Jordan stepped past her roughly, yanking Ari's arm while looking around.

"Git cho clothes and let's get outta here."

Ari obediently started gathering her things slowly, her face reflecting a sad mixture of sleepy and unhappy.

"Really, Miss Jordan, it's late and..."

"Back off, lady! I got this, all right?" She turned back to Ari. "Hurry up! And next time you keep your narrow little behind at home until I get there. What do you think you have a key for?"

Turning back to Jamilah she bared her teeth and squinted her eyes. "Next time stay out of my biz'ness or I'll report you. You got that?"

Jamilah opened her mouth and then closed it.

Miss Jordan pushed Ari toward the door. As she stumbled forward Ari turned back toward Jamilah, and her eyes said it all. Perhaps God really didn't hear her prayers after all.

It seemed like a long walk home for Ari. Her mother seemed oblivious of the night, spurning the cabbies that slowed down as they passed, hoping for early morning customers. She stomped in fury down the street, fussing all the way and yanking her daughter's arm every few minutes for emphasis.

"What chu mean by goin' home wit' dat woman?" she accused. "What chu tryin' to make me look like? An unfit mother or somethin'?"

She picked up her pace, and Ari could barely keep up with her.

"You keep foolin' 'round followin' her and see where you end up. If I get reported they'll take you away from me. And ain't no tellin' where you'd end up. And then sweet lil Miss Williams won't be 'round to help you."

"Mama, I'm sorry. I wasn't trying to make you look bad. It was just dark, and Miss Williams was worried about me staying home by myself. I wanted to wait for you, but I think Tyrone and them scared her."

"Tyrone!" At this her mother stopped on the sidewalk and looked at her intently. "Tyrone and who?" She licked her lips nervously.

"I don't know...Big Boy and Louis...I can't really remember." Had she said something wrong? "Tyrone tried to play with my hair, but I told him not to touch me."

"You stay away from them, you hear?"

"Yes, ma'am."

At that Ari's mama started her brisk pace again. They rounded the corner, heading toward home. The buildings looked ominous in the dark. Most of the lights were out, but a few young men lingered on the corner as usual, talking, laughing, and smoking as if it were Saturday afternoon. Ari's mother slowed her pace as they got closer to them, squeezing Ari's hand so tight she almost cried out.

"Hey there, Mama! You got somethin' for me?" one of the guys said.

"Man, you know I'm too young to be your momma! And naw, I don' have nothin' for you today. I didn't get my check. Tomorrow..."

Her mother's tone was light, but Ari could feel the tension in her grip.

"All right, but don' keep me waitin' 'cause I might have ta fin' another way for you ta pay!" His eyes took a long, leisurely tour of Ari from top to bottom.

Ari decided she didn't like him.

Again her mother squeezed her hand tightly...too tightly.

"Ouch!" Ari couldn't help it. Her fingers stung.

"Now, don' go there with me. I said I'd get it to you and I will. Anyway, I need to get my chile home. She has homework to do."

"At this time in the mornin'?"

"Yup. I'll hook up with you later."

"You better. I don' wanna hafta come lookin' for you."

"Come on, Ari." Her mother tugged at her again.

Ari looked back. The young men were still watching them. "Mama, who was that?"

"Nobody you need to know, chile. Nobody you need to know."

The moment they got in the door, Ari's mother made her way to the bathroom and closed the door.

Ari waited for her to come out, but she didn't. She finally yawned, took off her backpack, and went to the bedroom. Lying on top of the bed, still in her clothes, she drifted off to sleep, dreaming about young men laughing on street corners while her mother pulled her down the street and squeezed her hand and told her not to look back.

seven

"You did what?" Tamara hollered into the phone as she lurched forward in her chair, banging her knee and spilling her coffee at the same time. She couldn't decide which fire to put out first—the one in her lap or her knee. "Sh…" she caught herself. "I can't believe this…"

"What is going on over there?" Jamilah sounded irritated. "Did you just cuss, girl?"

"No! I mean…aw forget it. I just spilled coffee all over a cream-colored skirt. And I have to get ready for my next appointment, which isn't going to be pleasant. We need to finish talking about this later."

"You seem to be saying that a lot lately."

"I don't know what else to say right now, Jamilah. You can't go taking a little girl home and then being surprised when her mother doesn't like it—no matter how fit or unfit a mother you think she is."

"But…"

"Wait! I'm not finished! You have *got* to stay out of it. Hey, you're big on prayer. Pray about it, and stay out of it before you get into trouble. It's just not worth it." She took a deep breath. "I've really gotta go." She hated to cut off Jamilah in her time of distress, but she had to collect her thoughts before the larger-than-life presence of Lydia Caldwell entered her office.

Tamara always centered herself and secured her vantage point before Lydia entered her office. When Lydia wanted to, she could be very sweet, but Tamara could never relax. She never knew when Lydia would flip the switch and stab her with her acid tongue. Tamara could understand why Lydia's husband left her, and yet she also felt sorry for the woman at the same time. Lydia was a mixed bag. She reveled in being a Hollywood wife. Her husband was a high-profile producer. In time she took her place at his side, becoming just as respected in the business as he was, wheeling and dealing, brokering her own deals and making movie magic.

But now that was threatened by the fallout from the implosion of her marriage. She'd followed her husband to Chicago, hoping they would work things out while he was out of the limelight and in a new environment. Lydia and Richard landed in Tamara's office together. She spent hours listening to Lydia. Her husband, Richard, gave up trying to get a word in edgewise after two appointments. His parting words said it all, "Whatever she said, that's it—at least in her mind. There's no need for me to try to add anything." With that he strode through the door without looking back. The next time she faced a tear-streaked Lydia, Richard had left her. Tamara wasn't surprised.

But she was surprised by how much the victim Lydia became. Then the metamorphosis began. She watched her turn from a wounded little bird into a seething, vindictive shrew. Tamara didn't know how many more sessions she could tolerate with her. She hoped Lydia would return to Los Angeles now that her marriage was over. But her prayers seemed to be bouncing off the ceiling lately. Stifling the urge to sigh, she surrendered to the need to get ready to endure another session of listening to her hateful client rant and rave, just as she had every week. Lydia refused to listen to counsel and never came to any solid solutions. Perhaps she would finally grow weary of rehearsing the same speech over and over again and move on. But Tamara didn't see that happening anytime soon.

Right now she needed to take care of her coffee-soaked skirt. Scrubbing, Tamara frowned. The stain was not coming out. She would have to sit behind her desk for the entire session, which actually suited her just fine. The desk would be a welcome shield from her client, who felt more like an opponent at times. She gave her skirt one more pass with the hand towel and turned to enter her office from the washroom. She stopped short, catching her breath as she found herself withering under the disdainful gaze of Lydia Caldwell.

Tamara allowed her the luxury of perusing her soiled facade in silent repulsion before she positioned herself behind her desk and motioned to Lydia to sit in the chair across from her. Stella, her assistant, would be dealt with later for allowing a client into her office unannounced. She hated that. It put her on the defensive when she should be the one controlling the room.

Recovering quickly, she stifled the urge to giggle. She'd never noticed before that Lydia reminded her of Cruella De Vil from *101 Dalmatians*. Perhaps it was the way she held her hands that were thin and tapered. Her face was drawn. She could have been beautiful, but her unhappiness and anger made her cheekbones seem too pronounced, her face icy, leaving it hard to decide if she was attractive or not. Though she was black, she could have passed for white with her pale skin, sandy hair, and green eyes. Perhaps that was why she was so angry. Her "high yellow" looks were supposed to guarantee her the love of a black man, and yet he'd left her for what she considered a "lesser" woman.

"Hello, Lydia. How are you doing today?" Tamara asked.

"Have you seen this?" Lydia hissed. She threw a newspaper on the desk.

Startled, Tamara tipped back in the chair and banged the same knee again. She stifled the urge to cuss, making a mental note to replace her chair or get it fixed. Rubbing her knee with one hand and pulling the newspaper closer with the other, she perused the society column touting the happy countenance of Lydia's ex-husband Richard Caldwell, seeming quite self-assured and satisfied with his escort—who had to be the focus of Lydia's ire. She was small, petite in fact, and paper-bag brown. Her face was framed with short locks that had been deliberately coifed into a mini bob, giving her a look that Tamara termed "ethnic elegance." She had a beautiful, dimpled smile. Cute, yes. Not gorgeous...just cute. Her countenance revealed why Richard was smitten by her. She appeared to be a nice woman, sweet and simple. After Lydia, Tamara was sure Richard found in this woman a respite from the storm.

"He could at least have left me for someone attractive. How insulting!" Lydia burst out. "She's so..." She waved her hands as if to materialize the word to describe her nemesis and, finding none, settled for "ordinary." She sniffed. "No sense of style at all. Nothing going for herself. Honestly, what is he thinking?" she said for the umpteenth time.

"Perhaps he's thinking style and accomplishment aren't so important when it comes to love." Tamara tried to bring some reality to Lydia's over-inflated sense of self.

Lydia narrowed her eyes as she pressed her lips together and sent a silent threat to Tamara that her snide comments would not be tolerated. "Can you believe that hair?"

Lydia obviously wasn't listening. *Mmm mm.* Tamara wasn't about to get dragged into a hate session with Lydia. "Her hair is not the issue, Lydia. This session is about you, not her."

"But she's part of the reason I'm here!"

"No she isn't...unless you make her part of the reason. You are here to deal with what made your marriage fail and recover so you don't repeat the same mistakes again."

"Since when did everything become my fault?"

"I didn't say it was your fault, but since you are the only person you can control in the equation, dealing with you is a good place to start."

"I don't want to start with me. I want to start with *him*. I want his life to be ruined the way mine has been."

"And exactly how has your life been ruined?" Tamara was tired of listening to the same speech she'd listened to every week for quite some time. No matter what direction she tried to shift Lydia to, they always came to the same place.

"How dare he carry on like this! And our divorce isn't even final. I'm going to drag him through the muck and mire for this. He's stripped me of everything I hold dear. My personal and professional status, the admiration of our friends, my social standing, my home."

"What about your marriage?"

"What do you mean my marriage? Obviously I don't have one."

"But you didn't have that on the list of what you hold dear. You listed everything *except* your husband and your marriage."

"You cut me off!"

"Yes, I did. But you were on quite a roll. 'Out of the abundance of the heart the mouth speaks,' so are you telling me your husband was that far down on your priority list?"

"Don't you dare quote scripture to me!"

"Lydia, I'm a Christian therapist. That's one of the reasons you came to me." Tamara knew Lydia had chosen her more as a ploy to get back into Richard's good graces than because of any true interest in God at that time. The fact that she continued to come to counseling after Richard's departure had been surprising. Tamara believed God was working on her strong-willed client.

"Yes, you are, Tamara," Lydia breathed out the words slowly and deliberately. "However, I don't think you should be so self-righteous and judgmental about it."

"Lydia," Tamara was determined to stay focused. "I have not handed you a sentence or decided how you should be punished, which is what a judge does. But clarifying the difference between judging and discerning right from wrong is another discussion we can have, but not today. I want to get back to the point that your love for your husband was not on the list of things that were 'near and dear' to you. Is it possible that you are not as heartbroken as you purport to be? Is it possible that this is not about losing him but rather about losing what he represented for you?"

"What? What are you trying to say?"

Tamara thought Lydia's eyes were going to pop right out of her head. "We need to examine the root of your issues so we can get you on the road to healing."

Tamara had learned early in her career that no one responded well to being told what was wrong with them. Until they were ready to confess it themselves, there would be little moving forward. Until then she facilitated their musings and guided them toward realizing the truth for themselves. Eventually most clients admitted that changes needed to be made if they wanted something different to happen. The time for this process varied, depending on how in touch with themselves they were and how willing they were to "own their stuff," as she liked to put it.

Lydia didn't want to own her stuff. Her problems were always someone else's fault. At this point she was no longer a victim. Instead she was signing up for pain, embracing her woes and troubles with passionate abandon. She couldn't...or wouldn't...see that her refusal to forgive and release her ex-husband was like drinking poison and waiting for him to die. She was strangling on her own bile. In the end it would be her ruin if she didn't get a grip.

Tamara settled into her chair as the onslaught poured forth from Lydia's wounded pride and unacknowledged pain. At least she didn't have to say much. Lydia would do most of the talking. From time to time Tamara would see an opening and inject a question that Lydia didn't want to answer. The hour felt endless. On and on Lydia went until Tamara felt like screaming. She looked at her watch. *Ah, the torture will be over in five minutes.* When she looked up, Lydia was rising from her chair.

"I don't have to take this! I don't know why I even bother to come here. You never have anything good to say." She stopped as if a great epiphany had suddenly dawned on her.

"You don't like me do you? That's it. You don't like me! You're on *his* side, aren't you? Then why don't you collect your fee from *him?*" There were angry tears in her eyes now.

Tamara was calm as she rose to full stature in her chair while eyeing Lydia evenly. She realized she was throwing professional caution to the wind, but she was beyond caring. "I believe I already do. He *is* the one still paying all your bills, isn't he? It's not that I don't like you, Lydia." She cocked her head to the side, studying her subject as the realization took shape in her mind. "I don't like the fact that you refuse to own your part in the demise of your marriage. Your coldness and driven nature favored achieving over creating a home. This was your choice. You didn't make your husband a priority and nurture your marriage. Are you really surprised your husband would go for a woman who adores him and concentrates on pleasing him and looking after him?"

Suddenly Tamara was very tired, and she didn't want to say too much. "Lydia, I want you to consider this carefully. Look at yourself and your actions from Richard's point of view. If you can do that, this session will be on me. We'll discuss this next week." With that she rose from her chair and headed for the washroom, leaving Lydia standing speechless in the middle of her office.

eight

Felicia Sample strode across the empty loft space, seeing details that Tamara couldn't see. Through the eyes of an interior designer an empty wall became a whole new animal.

Tamara waited for Felicia to translate the transformation that would take place in the space before it would be ready for her to move in.

"It's all about tension and release," Felicia murmured. Her eyes were sparkling, making her pretty face glow.

Tamara was mesmerized. "Tension and release? I can relate to that."

"What was that?" Felicia looked confused, unaware she'd spoken aloud and jolted from her concentration.

"Never mind. Would you mind translating what you're envisioning on that wall?" Tamara asked. Her eyes grazed across the landscape of her future new home, a preconstruction loft that seemed to mirror how she was feeling—open and vacant. She was restless. What she wanted she didn't really know. She just longed for something different. Something that was a departure from the sameness of her life that seemed as sprawling and endless as the walls they were surveying. Apparently Felicia wasn't finding them as daunting as she was.

"The possibilities are endless! I think we should do a muted tone of white with a touch of taupe to cut the glare. It will be the perfect backdrop to make your African art pop. The walls are perfect for your paintings, but the arrangement will be everything. That's where tension and release come in. Groupings here...and knowing when and where to put nothing so the space can breathe and let the eye rest before moving to take in the next fabulous item on display. Got it? Tamara? Are you listening to me?" Felicia frowned.

Tamara wasn't listening; her mind was wandering. Whatever Felicia said would be fine, she was sure. Felicia was the best. She had recently been written up in *Elle Décor* as one of the up-and-coming interior designers in the country. But she was still sweet, demure, almost childlike in her wonder of everything. For her, life was obviously truly beautiful. Just as beautiful as she was. Some said she was a Vanessa Williams look-alike with her caramel skin, gray eyes, and wavy, textured sandy hair with a touch of gold.

Tamara had helped her resolve her shock and settle her identity issues after discovering the father she'd known all her life was not really her father. Her biological father was a wealthy white man who didn't want to know she existed. Or...rather...he didn't want anyone in his social circle to know she existed. After struggling through an unwanted pregnancy and facing the prospect of being a single mother, Felicia had weathered the storm and reconciled with her mother. Though it seemed that everything had worked out well in the aftermath of having the baby—becoming a born-again Christian and marrying the father of her child—severe postpartum depression had brought her to Tamara's office weeping bitter tears. Now she was one of the success stories Tamara could rejoice over, though in another respect her life placed Tamara in a personal quandary.

Felicia was a classic study of a woman doing all the wrong things but still ending up with a "made for television" wonderful life. She had chased her man, been insecure and desperate, gotten pregnant out of wedlock, not told the father, and, to top off all the drama, she'd finally made her way to church—only to have her water break at the altar in the middle of accepting Christ as her Savior. And now here she was, radiant and gorgeous, with a beautiful new baby, a wonderful, newly saved husband, a blossoming and incredible career—everything was great. In spite of her imperfections, she'd managed to attain the perfect life.

Tamara stepped closer to eye a beautiful diamond cross on Felicia's neck. "Ooh, that's pretty. Is it new?"

Felicia flushed. "Girl, Kenny is something else. He left it on my pillow this morning with a note saying, 'Just because.' Isn't that sweet?"

"Mmm, really sweet." The words tasted sour in Tamara's mouth as she realized that instead of celebrating Felicia's good fortune she was actually quite jealous. Moments like this magnified the fact that she had issues with God that needed to be resolved…hopefully before her emotions caused her to do something against her normally good judgment. She was single, celibate, trying her best to live holy, and she couldn't remember the last time she'd had a date.

Her days were spent listening to her clients struggling with the issues of life while sometimes clinging to a mere morsel of faith that God would come through for them in the end and flip the script on their circumstances. But Felicia's life defied the Christian reasoning that said only the right choices would lead to everything in life going right. *Why did life work out perfect for Felicia and not for me?* Tamara wondered.

How could she intellectualize this? There was no explaining the whims of a quirky God who allowed His faithful followers to struggle and writhe in their difficult circumstances while others who paid Him no mind skipped capriciously through the tulips of life and landed in a bed of roses without thorns at the end of the day. *Go figure!* Tamara felt tense. To avoid plummeting into despair she decided to switch to a more pleasant subject matter.

"How's your daughter?" Tamara loved children. Though she was ambivalent about having one of her own, she wasn't too happy that the opportunity might pass her by if she didn't nab a husband by the time the alarm on her biological clock went off.

Felicia brightened even more. "Simone is wonderful! Now I'm not saying this just because she's mine, but she has got to be the most perfect child on the planet! She is such an old soul. Before I came to know the Lord I would have said she must have been here before." Her eyes misted. "God is so good, Tamara. I just can't believe how much He has blessed me in spite of my past foolishness and mistakes. To think I almost blew it with Kenny! He's the greatest father and most wonderful husband." She grinned. "Hey! He signed up for the men's discipleship program at church last Sunday. Isn't that great?"

"Great!" Tamara didn't mirror her enthusiasm. Her smile twisted into a flinch as a twinge of pain ripped through her lower abdomen.

"Are you all right?" Felicia looked worried.

"Hmm? Oh, I'm fine. I keep getting this sharp little pain in my side. My doctor would probably say it's fibroids, but I say it's probably from eating food that's too spicy again."

"You should get that checked out. The last time I self-diagnosed it wasn't what I thought it was, if you know what I mean."

"Girl, I don't have that worry. I believe immaculate conception was slated for only once in history, and it already happened."

"Oh Tamara, you're probably too busy running everyone else's life to pay attention to all the men who have got to be tripping all over themselves to get to you."

"Really? Where are they? I was beginning to wonder if I had a giant wart on the end of my nose that I didn't know about."

"No, you do not!" Felicia giggled. "All I can tell you is to trust God. He has this amazing way of showing up when you least expect it. Just when I thought I'd never find true love, love found me. And my cousin...you remember I told you all about Tracy? She's seeing the most fabulous man! He's fine, he's saved, he's successful, and he loves her like nobody's business."

"Wait a minute! Didn't you say she wasn't jumping up and down about you getting saved? Where is she spiritually?"

"She's coming around. I think David is a big part of that. He refuses to compromise his faith even though he loves her."

"Whoa! Hold up! Didn't you say Tracy wasn't a Christian? How can David not be compromising his faith if he's dating a non-Christian? How do you tidy that one up? Felicia, I know you're a new Christian and everything, but 'missionary dating' is compromising."

"'Missionary dating'? What's that?"

"That's when you date someone thinking you're going to get him saved. It's a disaster waiting to happen." Even as the words left Tamara's lips she knew she was struggling to believe what she was saying. She felt like a parrot, mindlessly repeating words but having no real understanding of the meaning. Again she could hear that old green monster, Envy, whispering in her ear, "Just where do these people get off being happy when they're not paying God any attention? It just isn't fair." And then a more sinister suggestion was whispered into her mind, "So much for living holy."

"Hmm." Felicia looked as if the light was coming on.

"What?"

"Well, that might explain something. David won't kiss Tracy. He takes her out, and he does all kinds of nice things for her. I know he loves her; it's written all over his face. But he won't touch her. And he told Tracy that the woman he marries has to love the Lord more than him."

"Good for him, but he's still putting himself in a precarious position. What if Tracy never gets saved?"

"She will!" On this Felicia was resolute. "I've prayed and I know that God is going to bring her around. I think David knows that too, and he's willing to wait."

"I love the faith of new saints. I just hope for David's sake you're both right." *Then I'll have another thing to put on my list of things I'm upset with God about,* she decided.

"Oh! I've got to run. Kenny will be downstairs waiting for me. We're going to the greatest couples' Bible class."

"I'll go down with you. I'm meeting Jamilah for dinner."

"Which way are you going? Would you like us to give you a ride?"

"No, that's okay. I've got a stop to make along the way. On second thought, I want to stand here for a minute and see if I see some of that stuff you were talking about. Tension and release, right?" Tamara smiled. But inside she was thinking the last thing she wanted to do was sit in a backseat and observe anybody's oo-some twosome.

"You got it! I'll see you next week when I get the paint samples." Felicia hugged her in a warm, loving embrace. "Thanks, Tamara."

"For what?"

"For being here and walking me to the other side. Life is good."

"I didn't do anything but listen. You did the work. And yes, life is good." She said it as if talking to herself. She did basically have a good life. A prosperous business, a fabulous new home in the swanky part of town. No bubbles, no real troubles. Life *was* good...it just wasn't good enough. She hugged Felicia back and watched her skip out the door. She turned back to stare at the blank walls, seeing no more than she had originally.

After waiting about five minutes, long enough to make sure Felicia was safely on her way, she made her way down the hallway to the elevator. Jamilah would be waiting at their favorite restaurant. That is, if she hadn't stood her up for that child again.

nine

Jamilah looked into the eyes of Mr. Parker, who stared over the top of his glasses with a look of great consternation. Silently he motioned to the chair in front of his desk. She obediently followed his direction to sit and waited perched on the edge of her seat. She had no idea what she'd been summoned for, but then again, maybe she did. Mr. Parker continued to stare at her, saying nothing. This was the principal's ploy to put his "subjects" on the defense, and then he would home in for the kill. The silence went on longer than Jamilah's capacity to maintain her cool. She coughed nervously and shifted in her chair, averting her eyes from his discomfiting gaze.

"Miss Williams," he said, easing forward in his chair while fingering a worn pencil between his two forefingers and thumbs. "Do you know why you are here?"

"No I don't…" Her words trailed off in uncertainty, not knowing if she needed to be worried about something or not. Had something happened to Ari? She hadn't come to school today, but Jamilah assumed it was because of how late it had been when she left her house early this morning. She imagined Ari's mother had slept in late and allowed Ari to do so as well. Suddenly she panicked.

"Can you explain why you are taking students home with you? Especially without the consent of their parents?"

Jamilah let out a slow breath of relief. "I have *not* taken *students* home with me, Mr. Parker. I have only taken *one* student home, and it was under unique circumstances."

"And what might those circumstances be, Miss Williams?" He stressed the Miss purposely, reminding her of a bee buzzing. Jamilah was growing impatient with his attempts at intimidation.

"Her mother never showed up to get her from school. I waited with her on the school steps until six-thirty, and then I took her across the street to McDonald's for dinner. I then walked her home. When we got to her house, her mother wasn't around. I didn't feel comfortable leaving her in that environment alone."

"But doesn't she live in that environment? She's probably spent a lot of time alone there." His eyebrows arched.

Jamilah shook her head to clear it. "Not on my watch, she won't!"

"Not on your watch? Hmm…And why wasn't this reported to the office? You know the procedure for after-school care of students. Miss Williams, may I remind you your duties at this school consist of teaching the curriculum as mandated by those who issue the requirements of education according to government standards and reporting anything that you suspect might be an endangerment to your students. That does *not* include taking students home when their mommas decide not to show up." His voice was rising.

"No one was in the office; everyone had left by the time I discovered she was still here. I'm not trying to add to my job description. I *am*, however, concerned about one child. Ari is so bright. Her mother is a drug addict and a hazard to her safety. I can't stand by and watch someone with so much potential go down the drain."

"Well, that is downright admirable of you, Miss Williams. However, that line of thinking will only get you into a lot of trouble. Since I haven't been privy to the information you hold firsthand, and it would be hearsay coming from me, this is on you. If you suspect Arianna's mother is placing her daughter in any type of peril, you need to report it to the Department of Children and Family Services, not take matters into your own hands."

"I'm sorry, but…"

"Trust me. You will be sorry if you keep this up. Now I'm going to pretend we didn't have this conversation because if anything happens to Arianna and DCFS finds out you had prior knowledge of her being in a situation that compromised her safety, you could be fined, lose your job, and worse. You do understand you could lose your job? Is this child worth the trouble? In the end she'll end up just like her mother."

"Don't say that!" Jamilah couldn't decide if she was angry or horrified. "How can you say such a thing? It's not your job to sit here and predict the future of your students, Mr. Parker. We're supposed to be preparing them for the future and protecting them to the best of our ability."

"No. This is where you're a little misguided." He shook his head as if cajoling a confused child. "It is *not* your job or my job to protect anybody. Our job is to educate, plain and simple. And trust me, you'll be lucky if one of your students ends up using what you taught. Most of them end up on the street and die young." All of a sudden he looked old. "I used to be like you. I thought I was going to be the mighty savior of the urban school dilemma, going to the 'bad' side of town to make a difference in the lives of young people who needed me. But converting ruffian children into brilliant ones only happens in the movies. Real life versus Sidney Poitier in *To Sir, with Love.* No music, no magical transformations, just more of the same."

"I don't believe that, Mr. Parker." Jamilah felt sorry for him, but now she understood him. The hard crust she'd initially thought had always been there had grown over a soft heart filled with hopes that had been crushed by all he had seen and experienced during his years at this school. Though she could understand it, she refused to go there herself. She had come from a neighborhood like this and been surrounded by the same resignation about life. But she'd had a teacher who spoke life into her and blown on her dreams and led her to believe she could make a difference...and that was what she had come back to do.

Tamara had asked her why she wanted to buy a place so close to the projects instead of a luxury building on a safer side of town, especially since she was a single woman, but Jamilah wanted to keep her past in clear view so she would never lose the urgency to encourage others to dream beyond the edge of where they came from. It was so paradoxical. If her students couldn't see past where they were, they would be forced to see soon enough. The neighborhood around them was changing, and the last of the projects were being closed down and the tenants squeezed out. It was a matter of time before the school would be filled with children from more upwardly mobile families. But for now only the disenfranchised raced down the halls, trying to skip class and causing major chaos every time they were dismissed. Streetwise kids were already convinced they didn't need to be educated...just be slick.

Jamilah felt she was a good judge of character and pretty much knew which ones would sit in class for as long as they had to and slip between the cracks in the system later. She was determined not to allow that to happen as long as she stood at the front of her classroom. She had deliberately chosen to teach first and second grades because she knew she would have to plant big dreams in small hearts so they would take root. It was harder to plant seeds in soil that had been hardened from seeing and experiencing too much too soon. She prayed over her students, was firm but loving, and had won their adoration as well as their respect. Gradually she saw them responding, eager to learn the things she shared. She tried to instill in them that they could be anything they wanted to be. They were smart, and they could live a different life from what they were used to seeing. She even enlisted the help of her friend Dwayne, who ran a mentorship program. Together they took them on field trips to show them the world beyond the projects and their corner of the city. Not only was she determined to educate them, she was set on filling their hearts with hope. And now Mr. Parker sat there with a smug look on his face, trying to throw ice water on her heart. She refused to be bowed by his jaded outlook.

"I'm sorry you allowed your students to change you, rather than you changing them, Mr. Parker. Perhaps it's true that the teacher becomes the student. However, I don't agree with that. Ari is different, and I refuse to stand by and watch her life go down the drain. I don't see the harm…"

"The *harm*, Miss Williams, is when her mother calls here and makes your benevolence my problem! I don't need this! This school is coming up for review at the end of the semester, and a loud-mouthed trouble-maker might cause the school board to question how I'm running my school. I'm warning you now—if this comes up again, you will handle the heat alone. I don't want any part of it. I have enough problems getting funding for teachers and supplies. I'm not going to endanger that. I know you don't think I care about these kids, but I do. And I do my part by keeping the doors open. What they do when they leave here is their business, and you'd better adopt the same attitude. You want to help these kids? Then don't do anything that could endanger your being here. It's called survival. Have I made myself clear?"

"Perfectly clear." Jamilah's throat was tight, and she felt like bursting into tears. She wanted to flee before she fell apart. She had the feeling nothing would give him greater satisfaction. She took a deep breath and swallowed. "Are we finished?"

"Most definitely." The finality of his tone said it all. He was pleased at having the last word. It was potent with a silent threat to not even think about defying him. They sat for a minute, eyes locked on one another in silence. She had no interest in a contest of wills, and she was well aware that whether she agreed with him or not, he was her boss. There was nothing more to say, so Jamilah slowly rose from her chair and soundlessly left the room.

Tamara better have time to talk tonight, she thought.

ten

The sun rudely interrupted Ari's dreams. Stretching and relishing the last moments of sleep before reliving the events of the night before, she wondered why her mother hadn't awakened her. She thought she'd heard her angrily fussing about something earlier, but perhaps it had been a dream because the apartment was now completely silent. Maybe she was still angry at her. Gingerly Ari made her way to the kitchen, looking for signs of life…but there were none. The bathroom door was still closed.

"Mama?" No answer.

Slowly she opened the bathroom door. Her mother was still sitting on the toilet. Head nodding. Eyes glazed. Her face shiny with sweat. She looked at Ari as if struggling to recognize her. Her speech was slow and slurred.

"Hey, baby, help Mama to the couch, okay?"

Ari struggled to lift her, but she was too small to support her.

Her mom slumped back down on the toilet. Ari grabbed her hand but dropped it quickly. It felt as if it were on fire.

"Mama, you're hot!"

Her mother fought to focus on Ari but couldn't quite control her gaze. Her eyes wandered as if looking for an anchor; her voice was barely audible.

"I know…hot…bad stuff…I'll be all right…go on to school now."

"No, Mama! I can't leave you like this. You're sick. Should I call the doctor? I know! I could call Miss Williams. She would know what to do."

Her mother didn't even have the strength to react. "No…no…be all right. Go on now." She held a finger to her lips. "Don't tell nobody… go on now."

"No. Come on…you need to lie down. I'll be back in a minute." Ari ran out of the bathroom and out into the hallway and down five flights of stairs. Mr. Morrison would know what to do. She found the kindly old janitor mopping the entryway. She stopped to catch her breath.

Mr. Morrison frowned at her, squinting through his glasses that always looked as if they were fogged up. "What's up, little bit?"

By now Ari was so overwhelmed all she could do was stand there heaving and pointing in the direction of the stairs. She started to cry.

"Whoa! What's the matter? Calm down now. I can't do anything until you tell me something."

"Mama! She's sick. I can't get her out of the bathroom…too heavy… I can't…" on that note she collapsed into full-blown tears.

"Now, now, it's going to be all right. Come on! Let's go see what we can do." Mr. Morrison started toward the service elevator, rattling his keys, sounding as if he were talking to himself. "I ain't takin' nobody's stairs…"

Entering the apartment, they could see Ari's mother still nodding on the toilet. Mr. Morrison looked disgusted. "Sick, huh? Yeah, right." Then remembering that Ari was present, he changed his tone. "You go get a towel and wet it with some cold water for your mama's forehead. She'll be all right. It's just a matter of time."

Ari ran toward the kitchen while Mr. Morrison went into the bathroom. Picking up Ari's mother as if she were a paper doll, he carried her to the couch, still mumbling under his breath. "You used to be such a pretty thing...let that junk mess you up. Should be shamed of yo'self." Then turning back to Ari he said, "Don't worry. She'll be all right. Just need to watch her and towel her down. She'll sleep it off, but you call me if she gets worse. She might throw up, but that's good. Get it out of her system."

"She told me not to tell nobody." Ari was beginning to panic again, not quite sure of what Mr. Morrison would do or who he would tell.

"Don't worry. Your secret is safe with me. Besides ain't none of my business. My name is Wes, and I ain't in the mess...Honestly it's just a sad state of affairs..." He was talking to himself again as he made his way out of the apartment. Then looking back, he gave his final instructions, "Make sure you eat something, ya hear?"

And so for the next two days Ari sat and watched her mother sweat out her bad high. Falling off to sleep between her feeble ministrations, Ari dared to hope that God would hear one more prayer, even though the first one hadn't seemed to work. "God, I don't mind if Mama never says she loves me, just don't let her die..."

Her mother roused from her sleep. "Who you talkin' to?"

"Mama, you all right now?" Ari was relieved to see her mother looking at her in her right mind again. She was weak but seemingly none the worse for wear.

"Yeah, baby. Can you get Mama some water?"

"Yes, ma'am!" Ari jumped up and was back with the water in a flash. She sat watching her mother drink eagerly from the cup. When she was finished she looked back at Ari. "Was somebody here? Who were you talkin' to?"

Ari hung her head, and then looked up. "God. I was asking Him not to let you die."

Ari's mother reached out, cupping Ari's face in her hands, smiling faintly. "Thank you, baby. I guess God still answers prayer. I once had to pray that prayer for you. I almost lost you before you were born, and now here you are..." Her eyes fluttered. "Sleepy... You a good girl, Ari. You old enough to walk home by yourself now. No need...to tell..."

And she was asleep, but now it looked like a peaceful sleep, and Ari wasn't afraid anymore. She had her mother back, and that's all that mattered. Oh—and God had answered her prayer after all. One out of two wasn't bad. Ari was happy to take what she could get.

eleven

Tamara closed her eyes, chewing slowly, concentrating on the flavor of her food. Hot and spicy, just the way she liked it. "Mmm, my, my my," she said dabbing the corners of her mouth and looking a bit too satisfied. She reached for her water.

Jamilah laughed. "Girl, you need to stop that. People are looking at you. Or should I say staring…and one in particular." Jamilah's eyes did a slow sweep around the outer perimeter of the restaurant, taking in all its finery and trying not to look obvious before resting on who she was talking about.

Tamara followed the direction of Jamilah's eyes to land on one of the finest men she'd ever seen. The corner of his mouth lifted ever so slightly as he nodded in her direction. Suddenly she felt extremely self-conscious. Smiling demurely she lowered her eyes but couldn't resist the urge to look at him again. Without allowing her lips to move she breathed, "Now that is what you call a tall, smooth drink of chocolate. Chocolate uncut!"

Even Jamilah's carefully cultivated, proper facade had dropped. "Oo, sho' you right about that!"

The man was now in deep cahoots with a waiter and looking their way.

"Stop staring!" Tamara hissed at Jamilah, dabbing the corner of her mouth with her napkin again and regaining her composure. "Now, where were we? Ah yes, you were on the brink of being fired!"

"Don't say that! I cancel that in Jesus' name!"

"Oh puh-leeze!"

"Please nothing. You know the power of words. You can have what you say."

"I also know the power of having good sense and listening to your boss. Which I hope you will do before you get into trouble."

"I don't know, Tamara. I feel compelled to care for Ari's welfare, like she's an assignment from God for me. I can't just let her go like that."

"Excuse me…"

They both looked up and into the face of the waiter who had been in consultation with the handsome man across the room. They glanced over, and he was once again looking intently their way. His gaze was like a magnet, pulling Tamara's eyes toward him. She felt a little dizzy and warm when her eyes met his, so she shifted her attention back to the waiter.

"Yes?" She struggled to clear her throat.

"The gentleman over there has sent you a drink. He said that if you enjoyed it, he'd be delighted to treat you to a bottle for your table." With that the waiter set two wine glasses before them. Tamara looked toward the man, who lifted his glass in a toast to her. She followed suit, and took a sip after flashing a thank-you smile. "Oh my!" The rich, red liquid was the best wine she'd ever tasted.

"Would you like a bottle?"

"Ooh no. He would have to carry me out of here!"

"The way he's looking at you, I don't think he would mind that." Jamilah was laughing. "I'm a helpin' a sistah out." Looking at the waiter she said, "Please tell Mr…"

"Davis."

"Yes, Mr. Davis. We appreciate his kind gesture, but we will enjoy just a glass, although it is very good. Tamara?"

Tamara jumped as if someone had pinched her. "Hmm? Yes, very good." Her gaze went back to Mr. Davis, who was grinning broadly, revealing the most beautiful, even white teeth.

"Stop staring!" Jamilah hissed. "Plus, I need you to pay attention. This work issue is important to me!"

"All right, all right! But he sure is fine."

"Probably not saved, so forget about him."

"Now that is a shame."

"You know I'm telling the truth. When was the last time you saw a man that looked like that sitting in church?"

"I've seen a few, but they were all married."

"Exactly my point. Now, can we get back to Ari?"

"Jamilah, there is nothing to get back to. There is nothing you can do about Ari. You need to stay out of it. I deserve a break today after what I've been through, so why are you ruining my dinner? Aren't you the one who is always saying, 'Let go and let God'? Well how about letting go long enough to enjoy some dessert and this amazing wine sent over by the finest man I've been blessed to look at in a long time? You deserve a break today, and God knows I do! Just chill, girl. It will all work out, okay?"

"I can see I'm not getting anywhere with you this evening. I don't know what's up with you, but you'd better watch yourself!"

Tamara was beginning to get a little annoyed. "What makes you say that?"

"I'm sitting here looking at you. You better cool your jets and collect yourself. Remember, the devil knows what you like."

"So do I." Tamara smiled at the man across the room again as she took another sip of wine before turning her attention back to Jamilah reluctantly. "I think I'll have the watermelon soup. How about you?"

Jamilah did not look happy.

The waiter came, and they placed their dessert order.

"Oh, Jamilah, lighten up!" Tamara continued when the waiter left. "What's wrong with a little harmless flirtation? You know, I think you

take this 'being saved' business a little too seriously. I just don't think it's that deep."

"What are you talking about?"

"I'm talking about the fact that we are living our lives in a bubble, and life is passing us by. We are so busy being good little Christian do-bees, we're missing out on all the fun."

"Who says I'm not having any fun?" Jamilah arched her eyebrows.

"I am. Look at you. You're beautiful. Why are you sitting here having dinner with me?"

"Because you're my friend?" Jamilah hunched her shoulders and looked at Tamara as if she'd just grown horns.

"No. Because you don't have anybody else to have dinner with!"

"That is not true!"

"Yes, it is! I'm not trying to hurt your feelings, but that is the only reason I'm here. And you are not a fun date—at least not this evening."

"Tamara, you are tripping."

"Maybe I am. I just met with my interior designer, who was clueless about God until recently. She seems to be more blessed than both of us. She's got a great husband, beautiful baby, fabulous home and career, and a rock on her hand that gives bling a whole new meaning. Meanwhile, back at the ranch, we're sitting around dotting our spiritual i's and crossing our theological t's, bein' all righteous and holy and dating each other. What is wrong with this picture? Hmm? Think about it. Doesn't it seem as if we are the butt of a cruel joke?"

She took a taste of the watermelon dessert. "Mmm, this is so good!"

"What cruel joke might that be?" Jamilah said a little too quietly.

"The joke is that life is supposed to be wonderful when you know the Lord, and it is not. There are people just going about their business, living their lives, and things are turning out all right for them. The joke is we got sucked into believing there was some magic formula for living the good life, and it's just not working."

"Whew! I'm dizzy, and you are in deep trouble. First of all, let me set the record straight, if I may. God doesn't owe you anything. He already gave you everything when He sacrificed His only Son for your little hussified self! Second, the operative word is *seems.* You don't know what that girl went through to get what she got, and she got it by the grace of God! Third, you do have a good life. If something is missing from it, it's your fault, not God's." She lifted her arm and shouted across the room, "Waiter, can we have the check please?" Swinging back toward Tamara she said, "And another thing…" She narrowed her eyes at Tamara, whose eyes were beginning to wander. "If you look at that man one more time I will hurt you. And you're not such an exciting date yourself." She rummaged in her purse and threw her money on the table. "That should cover my dinner. I'm going to get the car and meet you outside." She started toward the door, and then turned to add a final caveat. "I know you told me never to mention 'you know who' again, but I think I need to break that rule for a moment to yank you back to reality. Don't set yourself up for another fall. The first time shame on them, the second time shame on you." She spun on her heel, heading toward the door, turning a few heads herself.

Tamara watched her wind her way through the restaurant and thought better of sneaking another peek at Mr. Davis. She sat back, waiting for the check, and pondered what Jamilah had just said. Perhaps she was right. The entire Charles debacle had been her fault. But would it really have been that deep if she'd slept with him long enough to get him in her grip? It seemed to have worked for everybody else. It was her fault she didn't have everything she wanted. Perhaps she expected too much of God, waiting for Him to drop a man out of the sky or at least pop him on the pew next to her. After all, she was a grown woman. She should be able to get a man without God's help, shouldn't she?

She reached absentmindedly for the check that had been placed before her. Flipping open the cover, she resisted the urge to giggle. Instead of the check there was a business card with writing on the back: "I enjoyed watching you enjoy your dinner. Next time I'd like to have a closer view." Mr. Kevin Davis had also written down his cell phone number. "I look forward to hearing from you." Tamara smiled. He sure was sure of himself. She slid his card into her purse, along with Jamilah's money. Smiling at Mr. Davis, she rose from her chair. *But then again, he should be, lookin' like that.* She shook herself, feeling a slight chill. He sure was fine, but for tonight she wouldn't let him know the effect he had on her. No, it was always good to leave men guessing and wanting more. She forced herself not to look back as she headed for the door. Pausing, she handed her business card to the waiter and said, "Would you please give this to Mr. Davis for me?" He would call. She was sure of it. And this time she wouldn't blow it. With that, she exited the restaurant to meet Jamilah. If Mr. Davis was truly interested he would call. She didn't call men, and she wasn't about to begin now.

twelve

Lydia Caldwell stretched in her chair like a cat just waking up. She pressed her lips together and adjusted her already low neckline, flicking her freshly blow-dried hair over her shoulder in anticipation of working her magic on her dinner guest. Her eyes sparkled in the dim lighting. *Perfect,* she noted. Yes, she looked perfect if she did say so herself. She scanned the restaurant. The perfect setting. The Peninsula was where all the stars stayed when they were filming in Chicago. There was sure to be some paparazzi hovering in the lobby waiting for a photo op. If Brandon Walker strode across the lobby, they would follow him to see who he was meeting…and he was meeting her. She smiled as she thought of the look on Richard's face when he saw the photo of her with Brandon, the leading man on the film he was shooting in Chicago, splattered on the front page of the *Sun Times.* Her ex would have a cow. She laughed out loud. *Good! Two can play this game.* If he wanted to disgrace her by moving on with someone less than her equal in full public view, she would move on with someone on his level and rub his face in it.

"Care to share your secret with me?" A rich, deep male voice interrupted her thoughts. She looked up into the handsome, chiseled face of

Brandon Walker, America's latest heartthrob, looking as fine as wine. He was delicious. Smooth, caramel skin, deep-brown eyes rimmed by lashes a woman would die for above an aquiline nose that flared just so over a lush mouth that parted in a smile to reveal the most beautiful teeth. She licked her lips and extended her cheek to him in expectancy of the usual Hollywood welcome kiss.

"Brandon! It's so good to see you…" she breathed.

Click.

Ah yes, she heard the clicks of cameras. *Don't anyone tell me I'm not a great producer!* She turned to let him kiss the other cheek. Um hmm, more clicks. She would give them plenty to record before the evening was over.

"Why don't you sit next to me?" She patted the chair beside her. "Across the table is too far away, and I want to gaze on your fineness up close."

Brandon lifted an eyebrow, and Lydia knew she'd hit his sweet spot. He had an ego the size of America, making him an easy pawn in her game. It amazed her time and time again how these actors, no matter how much adoration the public gave them, clamored for more and more. It was as if their hearts were bottomless pits, always thirsting for more praise. She would make a concerted effort to stroke Brandon's ego, which totally went against the grain of her nature. Proof of this was the major problem in her marriage. One of her husband's complaints was her blatant lack of affection and what he termed "disinterest." She had not been raised around what she termed "PDA." Public displays of affection made her uncomfortable. All that fawning seemed so contrived. It had been hard for her to understand why Richard needed so much affirmation from her. She'd never gotten it from her family, and she hadn't died. As a matter of fact, it had probably given her the edge required to become an overachiever. She didn't need all that stroking. She wanted to see the results of her labor from what she produced, not what others had to say about it. Praise she could do without; to her it was a sign of weakness to depend on others loving you. That just set you up to be hurt in her book.

But for now she would switch from producer to actor and become an adoring woman. Her attention shifted back to Brandon, who was lowering himself into the seat beside her. She lightly ran a finger along the top of his hand from his wrist to the tip of his first finger and then slowly circled to the tip of his thumb while smiling into his eyes. He definitely was eye candy. Though her heart wasn't really in it, he would make her mission easy. "There, I think I like the view from here a whole lot better." She leaned closer. "Mmm, you smell nice. Issey Miyake?"

Brandon smiled and raised an eyebrow. "I didn't know you were a connoisseur of men's cologne."

"That particular scent just happens to be my favorite. It always goes to my head. It's a bit intoxicating when someone with the right chemistry wears it." She looked at him purposely.

"Ooh, you're good! So tell me, how does one become so lucky as to win an audience with the amazing mega-visionary Lydia Caldwell?"

"I'm not so amazing or mega. I'm just a woman, flesh and bones, and now that I'm a free woman in a strange city who still has to eat, I decided you would be a 'less fattening but no less fabulous' dessert."

"Wow! I'm flattered." Brandon was beaming. Lydia knew she had reeled in her catch. She'd seen him looking at her before, and she knew he wanted her. And now he would have her—for as long as it suited her.

She had long ago decided to ignore the actors she was constantly surrounded by. They all flirted, but she knew not to believe the hype. Hollywood was the type of place where everyone did what they had to in order to get what they wanted. Sleeping one's way to the top was passé and the norm. She was as aware of her power to make and break careers of the players who surrounded her, and everyone played the game. She, however, was a traditionalist and had never been available to play before. Plus she had been married to a powerful producer. She didn't need them; they needed her. Her only consolation at this point was she'd managed to make a name for herself in her own right, which kept her power base even after the loss of Richard.

She had watched all of the behind-the-scenes repartee between actors, producers, and directors. Seen the fallout from the empty flirtations and fly-by-night affairs. Watched the devastation after a movie wrapped, signaling not just the end of a project but in most cases romantic relationships as well. She had comforted many a wife whose husband had fallen prey to his character's lust for his leading woman. It never failed to fascinate her how these men seemed to lack the ability to separate fact from fiction until they were no longer in the close proximity of flying adrenaline from the short-lived fantasy of the films they created. But in the aftermath, a husband faced the reality of a wife who could not reconcile either his brief flight of whimsy or their marriage. Thus the constant turnover of front-page tabloid news.

The series of events was predictable. The more action-packed and tension-filled the script was, the more the exchange of flying pheromones heightened. Hours of rehearsing and filming, spending long days together, the rush of emotions and heightened chemistry from the excitement of the scenes. It didn't take a brain surgeon to figure out that if life was normal to boring at home, it was easy for the deception to take root that a scene partner was more exciting and would provide a fascinating escape. And new passion was always more combustible than old love. Proximity feeds passion, which makes someone forget what he has at home, no matter how good or solid it is.

But this was no movie, and her marriage was over, and that was painfully real to her. And now she was breaking her own personal rules about mixing and mingling with those who stood to gain everything from her with little to give in return. Except in this case she was the producer, and she was not invested emotionally. This was her scene to direct as she wished, and what she wanted more than anything was to inflict as much pain on Richard as he had inflicted on her. She couldn't decide which was worse, the pain or the shame. It was time for Richard to feel what he'd subjected her to. She could sport arm candy too, and what a morsel Brandon was.

Interrupting her thoughts, Brandon, looking slightly concerned, said, "Isn't my being here with you a little bit awkward? I am in the film your husband is producing right now. I wouldn't want to do anything to..."

"You mean *ex*-husband. It's a matter of the ink drying love. He is well occupied and couldn't possibly care what I'm doing. We're all adults, aren't we? I like you and you like me, right?" She took his hand in hers, turning it over, allowing her fingers to linger and trace light teasing lines in the center of his palm. She felt his hand relax. "Trust me. I doubt Richard would put his film in jeopardy by messing with his biggest box office draw." *Brandon's ego would be such a terrible thing to waste,* she decided. Especially if it worked to her benefit.

Brandon drew close. "Well, in that case, I'm glad you called." He kissed her lips lightly.

Click. Click.

Lydia lingered, touching his jaw to give the cameras more fodder. Breathing in his cologne and letting it go to her head, she decided this wouldn't be a difficult acting job after all.

thirteen

Corinne made her way down the hallway in search of her customary bedtime libation, otherwise known as a nightcap. She stopped short at the sight before her. Jada was abstractly drifting up the stairs, looking nowhere in particular. Mother and daughter stood staring at one another for a moment before Corinne broke the silence.

"What have you done to your hair?" Corinne was practically whispering. The horror of the sight before her had taken her voice. Jada's previously beautiful blonde hair that Corinne had to get a colorist to copy on her own hair was dyed the darkest shade of black with maroon glints. The effect robbed Jada's face of the soft innocence it once possessed. Now her blue eyes seemed more pronounced and startling against the sharp contrast of her hair. Pale matte lipstick drained the rest of the color from her face, reminding Corinne of the rebellious youth who prided themselves in being part of the grunge movement.

Jada lifted her chin defiantly. "I dyed it, mother. Do you like it?"

"No, I do not, young lady! What has gotten into you? Honestly, I don't understand you these days, Jada. If this is a cry for attention…"

"Actually, I've grown quite used to not having attention."

"Don't get smart with me. If you would come out of that room sometimes and act like a member of this family, that would not be a problem."

"Oh really? And just where would you suggest I find my family in this house? Dad is never here, and when he is he's polite at best. As for you, well…"

"You'd better watch your mouth when you're talking to me. And don't you dare try to divert the issue." Corinne knew Jada was telling the truth, but she didn't want to acknowledge it. Besides, she reasoned, in her own defense she was the mother, Jada was the child, and she had no right to talk to her that way. "What were you thinking? Why would you do something like this?"

"Why do you do what *you* do, Mother?" Jada stared intently at Corinne, and then cocked her head to the side as if having a revelation. "Were you on your way somewhere? To get a drink maybe?" Her voice barely veiled her disgust. "Perhaps if you could answer your own questions, you'd have the answers to mine." She pressed past her mother, went into her bedroom, and closed the door.

Corinne looked at the closed door, not quite knowing what to do or say. She knew she'd lost the right to speak into her daughter's life because she'd abdicated her position as a mother in the midst of wallowing in her own sorrows. Listening to the silence on the other side of the door, desperation rose in her chest. She could feel Jada slipping from her grasp. She was losing her, and she didn't want that. Jada was all she had. She needed to shake herself out of her malaise and find a way to reconnect with her daughter before it was too late.

Male laughter wafted up to the landing from the study below, distracting her from dwelling on the situation she knew couldn't be immediately solved. Randall's meeting must be ending, and that was a relief. Based on past experience, she was hesitant to enter open doors uninvited. Moving down the stairs, she walked to the study and stuck her head in the doorway. "Hey, you two, break it up in here!"

"Corinne, you're still up!" Roger Masters, their church's kindly old associate pastor, looked pleased to see her.

"Yes, I'm in search of a missing husband and a piece of apple pie. I baked it today. Care for a piece?"

"Well, if it wasn't after ten, I'd say yes, but Ruth would kill me. We're on a campaign—no eating after seven. She's determined to get rid of my spare tire. I tell you, that woman runs a tight ship even when I'm not in it. I believe if I snuck a bite she would smell it on my breath when I got home."

"Ooh that's good. You better be glad I don't have that great a nose, honey," she said, smiling at Randall, who grinned back.

"I like your nose just the way it is."

"Thanks, dear." Blowing him a kiss she reverted her attention to Pastor Masters. "You give Ruth my love, and I'll see you two on Sunday. You *are* still coming for dinner, aren't you?"

"Wouldn't miss it. Make sure you save some of that apple pie until then!"

"I'll have a fresh one waiting." She turned back toward Randall. "Do you want anything before I go back up?"

"No, I'm fine, thanks." His voice was filled with warmth.

"Then I'll see you upstairs."

"I'm right behind you."

"Take your time." She made her way down the hallway to the kitchen. She shook herself slightly. She didn't know what it was, but she really didn't like Pastor Masters. He seemed slimy. Perhaps it was because he smiled too quickly and broadly. People like that always seemed to have something to hide. Randall had pooh-poohed her observance on more than one occasion, so she'd settled into being the cooperative wife who had nothing more to say on the subject. After all, they were stuck with Masters. The man was practically an institution at the church. No one would dare say anything against him, and if she did she'd be viewed as a villain. She wondered if actresses felt as drained as she did from pretending to be something she was not.

She poured amber liquid into a glass. The smell of it held the promise of a peaceful night's sleep. Cutting a sliver of apple pie, she balanced her acquisitions in one hand and made her way up the back stairs to her room. She didn't feel like faking her way through another cheerful encounter. She knew Randall would stay downstairs as long as he could to avoid her, so she settled into slowly eating her pie and sipping her bourbon. She sucked the last of its flavor from the ice cubes and crawled into the bed.

The bed was lush but without warmth. Lying there, she wondered how much longer she would tolerate her husband's charades and her daughter's decline into who knew what. She berated herself for not being more proactive in the recovery of her family. Although she felt as if she were straight-jacketed, she was becoming impatient with not being able to undo the buckles that held her captive. Part of her wanted to stand and fight, but she felt powerless. Jada was right. She had to pull herself together for her daughter's sake, if not for her own. She could understand Jada's anger at her. It was the same anger she felt when she'd watched her own mother take abuse from her father. She was angry at Randall for putting her in this position, and at herself for being so pathetic.

She tossed and turned angrily, pulling the covers up around her shoulders to fend off the draft that made her shiver. *Snap out of it, Corinne!* She had to. Life could not continue as it was. *If you're not going to do anything about your situation, why not end it?* The thought was a jolt to her system. What was she thinking? She couldn't do that...but she must do something.

Her husband's negligence was no longer his fault alone. She was allowing it to continue, and that was her fault. Jada had made that very clear. Corinne had waited for God to wave His magic wand long enough. *Enough is enough. Yes, that's right. What are you going to do about it? I don't know, but something.* Thoughts were blurring together in her head as the bourbon started to pull down the curtains of consciousness. Memories of when Randall loved her blended with visions of Jada looking at her accusingly with black-rimmed eyes. Randall was coming toward her and then backing away, moving toward a man who was beckoning him from a distance. But Randall was saying something. Something she had to strain to hear. "I'm right behind you." His voice echoed on the edge of her mind. "Yeah, right." She sighed before slipping into a dreamless sleep.

fourteen

Jada heard her mother hovering outside her door and prayed she wouldn't knock. She didn't move, didn't breathe. She couldn't bear to look at the pain in her mother's eyes anymore. She hated the pathetic victim role she played. And she was tired of casting wary glances at the elephant in the room that everyone in the house did a polite dance around. Her father was gay. Why wouldn't they just say it? Why would her mother allow him to continue his charade? A charade that was costing them all. It was costing her mother her beauty. She kept trying to salvage her looks by constant visits to her plastic surgeon to smooth away the lines of grief and loneliness that slowly crept around the corners of her eyes, her forehead, and her mouth that were slowly and mercilessly betraying her hidden emotions. But there was no surgery for the red-rimmed eyes from too many nights spent crying when her sedatives or midnight cocktail didn't work fast enough.

Jada had tried to erase any resemblance to her mother since so many commented that she was a miniature version of her. The same delicate features, the same clear blue eyes. From the exterior she'd looked like other beautiful sixteen-year-old girls. But now that she'd dyed her hair midnight black, her eyes were more prominent, revealing a complete lack of emotion. She had the empty stare of a doll purchased at the store, pretty but cold and lifeless. The air about her seemed old, as if she'd seen too much too soon...and indeed she had.

She shuddered at the sound of the men laughing downstairs. No way was she going out of her room. She wished she could stay in her room for the rest of her life. Since that wasn't possible, she would at least stay until Pastor Masters left. The thought of him made her squeeze her eyes tightly shut to blot out the vision that came to mind. She shook her head as if to shake his hands off her body. She hated his hands even more than his breath, which smelled hot and putrid, repulsing her to the point of vomiting by the time he left her. Those horrible hands...rough, dry, and cracked...that scraped against her skin leaving telling marks of what she could not vocalize. Or didn't dare to. She was the silent guardian of her family's welfare. Her father's secret had not only cost her mother her beauty, but it also had cost his daughter her innocence. Her purity and the security of believing her father could keep her safe was gone. And how about God?

Why won't God keep me safe? she wondered. Pain tilted the corners of her lips ever so slightly. She was a prisoner of her father's secret, and no one could save her—not her mother, not her father, not God, though she kept hoping that if she kept praising Him and worshiping Him He would finally hear her cries, honor her worship, and deliver her. It seemed a mockery that the same place that gave her solitude was also the place of her greatest torment. Though she clung to leading the worship team and releasing her pain through singing, there was that flip side of what happened when the music stopped. She dreaded worship rehearsal because she knew he would be waiting. Waiting to give her a ride home. The irony that he violated her at church didn't escape her. His threat to expose her father if she breathed a word to anyone was his power. And to add insult to injury, he had the audacity to visit her father in her home even before the smell of his sweat could leave her nostrils. This was as abhorrent and shocking to her as his disgusting fumbling of her body.

Who could she tell? No one. She was filled with quiet rage so intense she was numb. If she closed her eyes now she could usually will herself not to remember his hands or the pressure of his body on hers. She no longer flinched at his threats. She just gave him an empty stare, straightened her dress, and walked away. Her lack of response seemed to throw him, but not enough. He kept coming back.

She took a deep breath and pondered her fate. The horror was that she lifted her hands and sang praises to God and then was subjected to such violation in a place where she should feel the safest. An open, mirthless laugh choked her.

Her mother's laughter filtering up the landing cut her off. Why didn't her mother save them both? What kept her silent? Did she fear the congregation that much? Who cared what they had to say? How much shame was too much in comparison to the silent torture they were both experiencing? What did they stand to lose? They had both lost everything already.

But the teen dared not say anything to her mom because she seemed so fragile. At least Jada's anger kept her strong. For this reason she clung to it, refusing to feel sorry for herself...choosing to not feel anything at all. Let her mother play the victim; she would not. Though she understood that bad things happened to good people because God gave everyone free will that He would not circumvent, she wished in the case of the innocent He would. Would she ever be saved from falling deeper and deeper into the deep abyss of nothing? If she closed her eyes and held out her arm she could imagine her mother standing before her, ready to comfort her. But open eyes revealed that her mother had nothing to offer. She too was trapped inside her own loneliness and rejection, a pitiful guardian with nowhere to turn and no recourse of her own.

Did her mother really think she didn't know what was going on? How long would her mom pretend things were normal? Things had been wrong for a long time. Home had never felt warm, just accommodating. Her father was always benevolent but not demonstrative or sincere. She would never have known life at home should be different if she didn't observe him interacting with his parishioners. At church he was overt, warm, and attentive. At home he was introverted, distracted, and distantly kind. She longed for the kinds of hugs she saw him give to others after the church services. But the only embrace she got came from the lecherous associate pastor. She comforted herself with visions of him burning in hell. But if God wouldn't save her, did hell really exist? If it didn't, it should. And Pastor Masters should be the first one in. But until that time she remained locked inside herself, searching for a way out.

She made her way across her bedroom, grabbed her purse, and plopped onto her bed. Her mother should be nursing her pain with bourbon by now so she wouldn't be interrupted. Digging in her bag she found what she was looking for. Fresh razor blades. Unwrapping them, she reverently selected one and placed the rest back in their container. Pulling back her sleeves she surveyed her arms. Her scars were healing, leaving little trace of the wounds that had been inflicted before. Too bad her heart couldn't mend as well. She thought of what would happen if she accidentally cut too deep, but that was never a solid enough thought to stop her from doing it again. She tried to resist the urge, but it grew stronger and stronger. Just as the scars closed, she would cut again. As the razor raked along her flesh and the sting grew stronger, she felt an odd sense of release. Yes, she was all right. She could still feel something. And at least in this instance she was in control of her pain. She was not the one being subjected to it; she was the inflictor. It gave her great satisfaction. It was hypnotic, as if she stepped outside of herself and stood as a silent observer. She rotated her hand ever so slowly, controlling where the blood flowed until it formed a deep-red liquid bracelet around her fragile wrist.

Again she wondered what would happen if she cut too deep, but even this was a distant thought as she concentrated on the pain. She heaved a sigh of relief as the throbbing became more insistent. At least she knew she wasn't dead.

fifteen

Jamilah wrung her hands as she related the story of her run-in with Ari's mother. Half looking at Dwayne, she could almost anticipate what he was going to say by the look on his face. However, he patiently chomped on his popcorn, studying her as she went on and on about how she hadn't wanted Ari to feel like a pawn being pulled between her teacher and her mother, but she was sure that's how she felt.

"It's just too much for a little heart to bear." Jamilah was talking to herself out loud, trying to sift through her thoughts and emotions and make sense of them. "Her mother is still her mother, no matter how crazy she is. I can understand that Ari's first loyalty would naturally go to her. But if you could have seen the look of peace she had when she was at my apartment, Dwayne, it would have broken your heart. I want her to feel that way all the time! It's a shame that at such an early age she should be this stressed out and unhappy. She's got a lifetime ahead of her, and there'll be enough stress when she grows up."

"That's for sure!" Dwayne threw another kernel of popcorn in his mouth.

Jamilah was getting annoyed at his lack of participation in the conversation. "Don't you think it's unfair of Miss Jordan to burden that child with her issues?"

"Yes, I do." Dwayne looked straight into Jamilah's eyes. "However, there is absolutely nothing you can do about it. You are the teacher; Ari is your student. And there is an invisible line you can't cross."

"I worried all weekend long when she didn't show up for school the rest of the week. I didn't know what to do. Do you think I made things worse?" She looked at Dwayne but didn't wait for an answer. She put her hand on her hip in disgust. "You know, I bet she kept Ari home for the rest of the week just to show me who's really in control."

"Sounds like you've instigated a power struggle that nobody can win…but someone can definitely be injured—that someone being Ari." Dwayne's look was gentle but serious.

"Now you sound like Tamara." Jamilah was disappointed by his response.

"Know and understand I feel for you, and I can relate to why you did what you did. But you can't be taking folks' kids home like that, baby. You could end up losing your job over that one."

"Don't you ever feel this way about the kids you work with? Even though you go from school to school, it has to be disheartening when you see the plight and hopelessness some of these children are forced to live in because their parents aren't there for them."

"Mentoring kids gives me the opportunity to give them glimpses of hope, a chance to see the world beyond where they live, and plant seeds that hopefully will take root and grow long after I'm gone. I do feel what you feel, and yet I don't act on it. I'm not going to endanger my access to them for a momentary fix."

"What do you mean?"

"I mean I keep the big picture in mind. So regardless of my compulsion to rescue one of the kids I'm mentoring, I know that kind of move can cost them and me in the long run. In short," he said taking her hands in his, "if you lose your job you can't be there for Ari at all."

Jamilah reached behind her and pulled a piece of paper from the table behind her. "Look at the painting she created. She looked so pleased with herself when she gave it to me." Jamilah felt tears spring into the corner of her eyes. She swallowed to press them back down. It was a painting of a little girl hugging a woman...a woman who looked like Jamilah.

"She told me the woman was me and the little girl was her."

Dwayne studied the painting. "She's good."

"Yes, she is. I told her I was going to frame it and keep it with the other one she gave me." Jamilah chuckled. "She giggled when I told her one day she was going to be a famous artist, and I would be a wealthy woman because I would have two of her originals."

"See, that's what I mean. You have to be smart so you can be around to show her how to dream." With this he lifted an eyebrow and kissed her on the top of her head before settling back down on the couch. She joined him, and they both sat noshing and watching TV.

Moments like these always confused Jamilah. She and Dwayne had been friends for a long time, but sometimes he felt more like a boyfriend, and she wasn't trying to go there. She knew she was vulnerable to Dwayne—but who wouldn't be. He was fine, had his act together, was an official BMW (Black Man Working), was financially sound, loved the Lord, and knew how to treat a woman. What was there not to like? Even Tamara had suggested they would make an ideal couple since their interest in children was mutual. And yet Dwayne had never approached her in any way other than that of a protective big brother, though his overt displays of affection sometimes left her wanting more...until he brought up his latest potential romance. The women never seemed to be quite right, and it was always a matter of time before he realized what she already knew. Then he would end up right back on her couch until there was another date to be had. The man was confused—there was no doubt about it. He couldn't see it, but she could. However, she wasn't about to fall into the trap of waiting for him to wake up and realize she was the one for him. The pragmatist in her often scolded her not to set herself up for disappointment. She had learned to keep her heart in check.

Though she sometimes wondered if she should resent playing second string to his series of girlfriends, she was too happy for his company to dwell on the matter for long. Besides, it didn't really matter. They were, after all, just friends. And guys were known for disappearing when in hot pursuit of romance. She chuckled. She always knew Dwayne would be back.

"What?" Dwayne was looking curious.

"Oh nothing. I'm just glad you're between marriage candidates so I can have your ear, that's all."

"Thanks a lot. You only want me for my mind?"

"I thought that was all I could have. You mean I could ask for more?" Jamilah sat up on the couch, a huge smile brightening her face and adding light to the mischief in her eyes.

Dwayne looked a little uncomfortable.

"Hold up, sistah!" Then he switched to his favorite defense. "You know you couldn't handle all of this man right here."

Jamilah threw back her head and laughed. She knew she was letting him off the hook, but she didn't care. "Aw, you know I would hurt you. You mean *you* can't handle all of this woman, 'cause you keep playing with all those girls!" Her laughter was cut short by the serious look on Dwayne's face.

"Is that really what you think? That I date girls?"

"Well, they're not really on your intellectual, spiritual, or emotional level, if the truth be told." She was still trying to keep it light. "Sometimes I wonder what you're really afraid of." She jabbed him in the side.

"Hmm...interesting." He cocked his head to the side, and then, with a glint of mischief coming into his eyes, he grabbed her, pinning her to the couch. "Maybe I'm afraid of you!"

This time Jamilah decided not to let him off the hook. "Maybe you are," she said, looking straight into his eyes and refusing to divert her stare. She could feel his hands loosening their hold. He flopped back on the couch.

"Aw, I ain't afraid of you, woman!" He waved her off and reached for a handful of popcorn.

"Well, thanks for recognizing..." She hesitated and then decided again to let him off the hook for now.

"Recognizing what?"

"That I'm a woman."

He looked her up and down appreciatively. "That would be kind of hard to ignore."

"Sho you right!" She sat up straight to emphasize her womanly attributes. "Now, back to a serious conversation..."

"You mean we weren't having one?"

"Obviously not 'cause you are scared."

"I am not!"

She knew that would get him, and she decided to leave his ego writhing for a while. "Moving on, let's get back to Ari. You mean to tell me there is nothing I can do?"

"Not much except be there for her when she needs you. You could report her mother to DCFS—the Department of Children and Family Services."

"But what if they take her away and I never get to see her again?" She shook her head and her stomach felt funny. "I don't know, Dwayne. I don't feel led in my spirit to do that. Even though I don't want her around her mother, I could be putting her in a worse situation."

"Well then, you better listen to God and lay low." He took a deep breath, as if struggling to be patient. "I know it's hard for a control freak like you, Jamilah, but you've got to let go of this one. Hey, you're the big prayer warrior! Have you prayed about it? Or have you been too busy getting in God's way?"

Jamilah threw her hands up in the air. "Why does everybody keep saying that to me?"

"If everybody is saying it, maybe it's true. Did it occur to you that God has a plan for that little girl's life in the midst of all this? Even if you don't like or understand what's going on right now, it's going to work out if you can stay in the right place."

"But..."

"Hey! Everybody has their own custom-made journey that makes

them who they are. You have a heart for that girl because of what you've been through. You know what it's like to grow up in that type of environment. However, you don't know what God is going to do with her. But if she has your attention, perhaps your job for now is to pray and watch the story unfold. Trust me, baby, God's plan will definitely unfold without any help from you."

He stood and stretched. "Well, I gotta go."

"You always do when it's time to get deep."

"Oh stop it! You better watch out before I kiss you again—and then you'll really want me."

"Puh-leeze, don't nobody want you!" She stood and copped a sister-girl pose.

"Ooh, such good grammar for a teacher." Then, looking forlorn, he added, "You really don't want me? I was counting on you in case the others don't work out. I'm feeling hurt."

"You are going to be physically hurt if you don't get out of my house." Jamilah hoisted a pillow from the sofa. Feigning fright, Dwayne made it to the door. He stopped and looked back.

"Jamilah?"

"Yes, D?"

"I really do love you for that."

"For what?"

"For caring about Ari the way you do. And trust me, God is going to do something. Remember, He cares about her more than you do. All you have to do is pray, wait, and stay out of His way."

"Even if He isn't moving fast enough?"

"Especially then because you don't know what He's doing."

"All right, all right, all right. I give."

"Whew, it's about time. It's hard work keeping you under control! Gotta go."

"Yeah, you said that already."

"Bye, silly girl."

"I'm a woman, remember?"

Dwayne rolled his eyes in mock resignation. "How could I forget?

Bye!" He closed the door just in time to avoid being hit by the pillow Jamilah hurled in his direction.

Falling back on the couch, Jamilah let out a sigh. "Don't get in God's way, huh? That is easier said than done."

sixteen

Tamara waited for her last appointment of the day. Corinne Collins was late. The counselor leaned back in her chair, tapping the top of her pen impatiently. *Where is she?* A card on the corner of her desk caught her eye. Retrieving it from its resting place, she asked the question she really wanted to know: *Where is he?* He being the mysterious Mr. Davis who had captivated her last week. Several times she'd taken out his card and gazed at it, as if staring would will him to call. She'd almost broken her own rules and called him, but she chose to pace the floor instead.

Perhaps Jamilah was right. Maybe God's prevention really was His protection. She pressed her lips together and narrowed her eyes. *Hmm, does God really have anything to do with it? Or is Mr. Kevin Davis just another trifling brother?* She looked at her watch again. *Where is Corinne?*

Her intercom buzzer sounded, and Stella's weary voice came through. "Corinne is running a few more minutes late, and you have a call holding on line one."

Before Tamara could ask who it was, Stella was gone. She gritted her teeth. She didn't know what Stella's deal was lately, but she was going to have to have a "come to Jesus meeting" with her secretary soon. Her sullen attitude and disrespectful, almost-off-the-cuff way of doing things was getting on her nerves. She pushed a button, putting her caller on speakerphone.

"This is Tamara Watson, how may I help you?"

"We could begin by you sounding happier to receive my call."

A melodious male voice filled her office, sending a thrill down her spine. Tamara took a deep swallow and eased forward in her chair, leaning toward the sound of the voice. This must be Kevin Davis. She decided to play it cool. "Perhaps I would be happier if I knew to whom I was speaking?"

A husky chuckle surrounded her and then turned to a sigh.

He sounded as good as he looked.

"I'm disappointed, Miss Watson. Do that many men call that you can't tell them apart?"

"I am a therapist. Many troubled men call me. Are you troubled?"

"No, but I will be if you can't meet me for dinner tonight."

"Aw…" Tamara pouted at the phone. "I can't make that decision until I know to whom I'm speaking, Mr…?"

"Davis. Kevin Davis. I believe we met across a crowded restaurant last week."

"Ah, yes! Which would explain why I might not recognize your voice, since I've never heard it before." She picked up the phone, taking him off the speaker.

"What's a little mystery between friends destined to be much closer, I hope."

"Ooh, you don't mess around do you?"

"I believe adults should get to the point, don't you? Now how about that dinner? I know just the place…" His words hung in the air, a potent invitation behind the up-front invitation.

For a moment Tamara was speechless. An internal war raged. Somewhere deep in the recesses of her spirit a "not a good idea" flag was waving. But a loud voice inside her head was screaming, "You owe it to yourself, girl!" She hesitated a moment longer and then broke her first rule: Never let a man disrespect you by assuming you are available on the day he calls.

"Dinner sounds good." She ignored the butterflies in her stomach, which were usually the Holy Spirit's last stand to warn her not to do something.

"Great! Shall we meet at Tru at seven? I'll take you home from there."

Tamara's eyebrow shot up. Tru was very expensive and very exclusive. She'd wanted to go there for a long time, but it was definitely on her list of restaurants where someone else would have to foot the bill. Even though she did well and was financially sound, she couldn't reconcile spending the same amount of money on a meal that would only be enjoyed for a few hours and gone the next in lieu of something more lasting—like designer shoes.

She broke her next rule: Never meet a strange man in a secluded spot alone.

"Sounds good. I'm already close to Tru, so that's perfect."

"Me too! So I'll see you at seven. I can't wait."

"Ah, but unfortunately you'll have to." Tamara couldn't resist giggling mischievously, though it was more out of nerves than relishing her mastery of a coy line.

"Alas, I must. See you then."

"Bye." She could hardly get it out. "Yes!" she breathed as she hung up the phone. Looking up from her desk, her eyes met the gaze of her assistant, Stella, who was looking at her quite quizzically.

"Who was that?"

She has her nerve! "That is what you were supposed to ask *before* you let the call through."

"Well, obviously you didn't mind, whoever it was!"

"Stella, we're going to have to talk." Tamara was more than a little irritated.

Stella seemed unmoved and clueless. "About what?"

"It's too long a conversation to get started now. *Where* is Corinne?"

"She's here. That's what I was coming to tell you."

Oh, now you decide to be the dutiful assistant, nosy wench! Tamara pressed her lips together and looked at Stella for a moment before opening her mouth that was filled with way too many wrong things to say right now. Regaining her composure she smiled, feeling very happy about not satisfying Stella's curiosity. "Good. Give me five minutes and then send her in."

Stella turned to leave.

"Oh, and please let her know we will still finish at her scheduled time. I have a commitment after that."

Stella opened her mouth, but then closed it, narrowing her eyes at Tamara. She knew Corinne was her last appointment of the day, but she left without another word.

Tamara figured it was none of Stella's business what she planned to do. Her mind was already racing. She needed to buy a new outfit for dinner tonight. She knew just the thing. On her way to work she'd spotted it in the window at Saks. A beautiful chocolate turtleneck sheath of a dress that stopped right at the knee. The material was a whisper of soft cashmere knit. Not too heavy; just right for the transitioning time between seasons. It was rich in color with just the right mahogany undertone to enhance her skin, and the sleeves were slightly sheer. A beautiful bronze belt gently hugged the hips of the mannequin, accentuating its waist. It was perfect. Not revealing but sexy just the same.

Tamara was convinced that mystery was ten times more provocative than overt displays of body parts that were supposed to be your best kept secret. She was not into advertising her wares. If a man couldn't recognize her worth by the wrapper, he would never be able to appreciate the contents, as far as she was concerned. Less was always more. She would trip right down to Saks, come back to the office, change, and be camera-ready for a romantic dinner in no time flat without looking like she tried. After all she wasn't desperate.

She powdered her nose, refreshed her lipstick, and spun around in her chair, catching herself before the chair lurched back again. She felt like a little girl who'd just opened a present and found something she'd always wanted. Her eyes were shining in a way they hadn't for a long time. Her diamond studs twinkled in harmony with her smile. She took a deep breath and reached for the intercom button. Now that she had taken the time to revel in a few pleasurable moments, she was ready to descend into the bleak chasm of Corinne Collins' life.

The door opened and the sleek form of her client entered, one fluid movement in soft silver gray. Tamara thoughtfully watched as Corinne settled into her chair. From the top of her head to the tips of her toes—perfect. If only she could see how flawless she really was. Tamara was aware Corinne had had some help—help she probably never needed. But if it made Corinne feel better about herself, she wouldn't have much to say about it. Unless it became an obsession, which might be the case.

"Well, don't you look great today? Nice outfit." Tamara attempted to inject some cheer into the atmosphere.

"Thank you. It's nice to have someone notice."

"Corinne, how do *you* feel about you? Is it really that necessary to have someone tell you that you're beautiful for you to feel beautiful?"

"I guess it isn't, but when you're used to having a man in your life who should notice and respond to how you look, perhaps it heightens your need to be validated or affirmed if you don't get it. I don't know…" Her eyes wandered off toward the window to gaze at the gray sky that matched her outfit. After a moment she started a sad and rambling commentary of her week. The chasm between her and her daughter, Jada, and the shock of her physical transformation.

Although she interrupted and added her observations, Tamara found it difficult to listen. Her mind kept straying to the evening ahead of her as she imagined different scenarios. She pulled her attention back to Corinne as she ended her lengthy soliloquy by blaming herself for not being enough for her husband…again.

"How can he continue to pretend he loves me so much in public and then make me feel like less than two cents in private? Perhaps he's right. Am I only getting what I deserve? Maybe it's my fault he's turned to men. What do I really have to offer? It's apparent I'm a disappointment to him…as well as to my daughter, who won't even look at me."

"Corinne, what does God say about you? Do you know that no matter what anybody thinks, it doesn't take away from who you really are or diminish your true value?"

"Tamara, I don't care what God says about me! Obviously my husband doesn't agree, and God can't hold me in the middle of the night. I'm so sick of all the religious clichés. I've gone over them in my head a thousand times, and I don't feel any better for knowing God loves me or thinks I'm fearfully and wonderfully made." Her tone grew sarcastic. "I just want my husband to love me." She was crumbling. "To act just as happy to see me as when he's pretending to love me in front of his congregation. I want my daughter to come out of her room and talk to me. I want people at church to stop treating me as if I'm invisible. I want my plastic surgeon to stop refusing to see me again. I want to stop feeling like an unwelcome guest in my own home. I want a lot of things, Tamara. And don't tell me to pray because I haven't got one prayer left. And I think the last ones I sent up must have disintigrated before they reached the throne room." She stopped and pressed her hand against her lips, shocked at her outburst.

Tamara looked at her in fascination. She sifted through her thoughts, deciding which ones were permissible to share with her patient, who had never shown this much life in a session. *Oo, there's fire in them there hills!* No, she couldn't say that. *You need to go off on your husband like that just once and stop beating around the bush.* She couldn't say that either because that needed to come from Corinne. She settled for a standard therapist line. "You sound angry."

"And shouldn't I be?"

"Should you?"

"Yes, I think I should! Who does Randall think he is? How long does he think he can get away with this? How long does he think I will live like this?"

"Now there's the question you need to ask yourself."

"What is that?"

"Aren't you listening? You said, 'How long does he think I will live like this?'" Tamara mimicked her perfectly. "That's a good question, and one I think you should mull over until we meet next week. I'm sorry, but our time is up."

"That's about all I can bear for today anyway. Sorry I was late. I...I just couldn't get myself together today, and then I got caught in traffic. I thought it was supposed to be stacked up going *out* of the city not into it."

Wearily Corinne rose from her chair.

She reminded Tamara of cotton candy. All soft and fluffy and air-spun.

Corinne was staring at her, studying her in analytical kind of way. "You look different," she finally said.

"I do? In what way?" Tamara was stymied by her observance.

"It's the kind of look a woman has when she just met someone, and she's excited and full of hope for the future." She smiled a wry smile. "If that's the case—and not to dash cold water on your little parade—remember that things aren't always what they seem. But then again, maybe that's only in my case. I hope he ends up being all he promises."

With that she was gone, leaving Tamara to ponder her words and wonder what was coming over the sweet, demure Corinne. Glancing at her watch, she switched her focus. She had a date, and she didn't intend to be late. *True dat.* She laughed to shake off her apprehension. She wasn't about to allow anyone to ruin her evening. She was sure Mr. Davis was all he promised to be...even though he hadn't promised anything yet beyond a very expensive dinner. She thought about calling to share her excitement with Jamilah, but she knew what she'd say. And Tamara was in no mood for warnings or caution signs. Perhaps, at least for now, she would keep her business to herself. And who knows, maybe there'd be nothing further to tell...but then again, there just might be. She glanced at his card still sitting on the corner of her desk before placing it in a safe corner of her top drawer, out of Stella's sight.

Mr. Davis was the president of his own business—Davis & Associates Financial Management. She laughed again. She had always told Jamilah, "No finance, no romance," and obviously Mr. Kevin Davis had plenty of both.

seventeen

Corinne strolled along the avenue, putting off the inevitable for as long as she could before retrieving her car from the parking garage to go home. Eventually she must head home. The excuse of out-waiting the rush hour traffic had played out a long time ago, and now it was only partially true. Her love of shopping had waned some time ago; it had given her more pleasure when it was forbidden. Now she shopped on automatic because she could and out of boredom…and perhaps even a bit on purpose to extract something out of her husband. Since she couldn't get what she wanted from him, shopping had become her drug of choice as a comforting companion to alcohol.

She thought back. Once upon a time, when Randall seemed to care about her, he teased her about her love of shoes when she arrived home from a day in the city. "What is it about you women and shoes? We'd better have a boy! I refuse to be outnumbered." Corinne giggled and rubbed her bulging stomach as he bent over to peer curiously into her bags and grasp his chest as if she'd spent his last dollar. Now he no longer asked.

Had it been an illusion that he really loved her? He used to tell her she was beautiful. And when she was assaulted with self-doubt, reeling from criticism by his new congregation, he tenderly reminded her that all he'd ever wanted from her was for her to be his wife. She remembered those nights of lying in his arms, feeling safe by his reassurances.

"I asked you to be my wife, not my co-pastor. You are my first and last lady, and that's all that matters. Do you know how many marriages in ministry fall apart because the wife forgets her first call to minister to her husband?"

Corinne opened her mouth to say she would never be guilty of that, but before she could say a word, he pressed his finger against her lips to silence her.

"Your ministry is to *me,* that's all I ask of you. The church is the Lord's bride, and you are mine. I'm clear on that. So don't let a bunch of women who are jealous of your beauty make you doubt your position and value, okay?"

"I love you! Ooh!" She grabbed her side.

"What is it?" He looked panicked.

"Oh, she just kicked again." She rubbed her tummy and smiled.

"You mean *he,* don't you? This house can only hold so many shoes!" She laughed and settled again into his arms feeling loved and protected.

His voice was husky as he drew her to him, "Now, let's have church…"

But that was then, when they were a young couple with lots of dreams and great plans. He was the up-and-coming, charismatic, promising pastor who was going to set the world on fire, and she was the loving wife. She felt blessed and beautiful then, but now she was none of those things. She was alone and isolated, lost and hopeless, existing for what she knew not.

She had no specific place or space of time she could pinpoint when things changed. It was almost as if he loved her and then suddenly he did not. She hadn't initially personalized his distance and lack of attention. She assumed he was consumed by the matters of the church, which had grown quickly, along with his popularity. The expectations of his congregation and those beyond the walls of their church had become overwhelming, sometimes taking him away from home to be a guest speaker, placing an even greater strain on him as he struggled to master the accelerated pace of his ministry.

She was consumed with the newness of motherhood. Jada had been an especially sensitive child requiring a lot of attention, and draining her energy in the early months after her birth. Corinne had been relieved when Randall didn't ask for her attention at night. She would fall into a thankful sleep, praying that Jada would allow her to sleep through 'til morning.

When Corinne once again turned to Randall, he would mutter that he was tired. He would hold her, but not with the same passion as before. At church he would be attentive and affectionate, inspiring the envy of those who were struggling in their marriages. But at home the strain set in. Corinne at first assumed it was because her body had changed after giving birth, so she went in search of cosmetic help. Still no response. Thus began the cycle of nipping and tucking anything that she studied long enough to find something wrong. Her breasts. Her nose. Her butt. Botox. Lipo. Collagen. She became a master of them all.

Her obsession with adjusting imagined imperfections only invited her husband's growing disdain.

Unhappy, she searched for other ways to numb her pain. She lost herself in her daughter, and after she'd put her to bed, a nightcap became her companion, kissing her goodnight through a soft haze.

The more her husband was gone, the more Corinne submerged herself in Jada. Her daughter became her everything. But when she reached her teen years, Jada developed her own interests. Corinne's active social calendar and involvement in church activities kept her busy but she had no close friends. She became more isolated. Suddenly she realized that all the things that had made up her world and given her identity had escaped her grasp. Her husband, her daughter, her friends.

Jada. Corinne frowned as she eased her car onto the expressway leading to the suburbs. She had changed. She used to be so happy and vivacious, talented and bright—a quadruple threat. Singer, dancer, pianist, and artist. She was so much like her father. She had a way with people, being a sanguine. Everyone said she was going to follow in her father's footsteps. Corinne knew she had a calling on her life, but lately Jada had become moody and introverted. The sparkle had gone out of her eyes. The laughter that had made their home bearable was gone, leaving a coldness in the air that magnified her husband's distance and made Corinne afraid.

She had tried reaching out to Jada, but the wall her daughter had erected around herself was impenetrable. Corinne didn't know what to pray about first. So she often found herself just sitting with no words to say, staring into space, and wondering what was becoming of her world and those she loved. She felt powerless, not knowing where, when, or how to find the end of the thread that had unraveled in her home and left her emotions a tangled mess.

She eased onto her street. It was such a beautiful neighborhood. Pristine, with large beautiful homes set back off the street proudly displaying perfectly manicured lawns complete with flowers and hedges that were a gardener's dream. She wondered how many other shipwrecked lives were hiding behind such fabulous facades. They'd had many of their neighbors over for dinner and backyard barbecues, more out of religious duty than a real desire to know them. The people were nice enough but kept their distance, which was fine with Corinne. She had no intention of trying to convert them or drag them to church. Surviving their visits was enough work.

She leaned forward as she recognized the car just pulling next to the curb in front of her house. Jada was getting home awfully late from worship rehearsal. She should have been home an hour ago.

Before Pastor Masters had completely stopped the car Jada was out of it without a backward glance. Pastor Masters lowered his window and called to her, but she kept walking without answering him.

Corinne's stomach twisted as she sensed something was wrong.

She shrugged it off and concentrated on her daughter's behavior. She would have to talk to Jada about being so rude. Pastor Masters didn't have to bring her home. He was doing them a favor. He must not have seen her pulling up because he slowly drove away just before she turned into the driveway.

Gathering her packages, she headed toward the house. Honestly, didn't that girl know how to turn on a light? One day she was going to trip on the stairs and get hurt. She'd told her daughter that a thousand times. Flipping on the lights she called, "Jada!" There was no reply. She started up the stairs, getting more irritated with every step. "Jada!" Still no answer. She leaned into Jada's bedroom door, knocking with an impatient rap. "Jada, answer me!" She opened the door, bent on telling her daughter she was no longer going to tolerate her insolent behavior, but the only thing that greeted her angry glare was an empty room and the sound of running water muffled by the bathroom door. That was fast.

Still trying to process Jada's need to take a shower so quickly, she retreated from the bedroom and made her way down the hallway to her own haven. Perhaps she would get a dog so that somebody would be happy to see her when she came home. The thought made her giggle. She must be more desperate for attention than she thought. She wouldn't forget to have a talk with Jada about her rudeness. And Randall too, for that matter. *Where does he go every single Thursday night?* She had to find a way to make him come clean with her. Whether she liked it or not, perhaps it was time to confront the silent demons that had taken up residence in her house. Her house. She looked back down the hallway. She had managed to make her house beautiful so she should be able to make her life just as beautiful...and yet clearly she'd failed. She had to find a way to get her family back, but for now she was tired. Very tired. Tired of trying to figure out her daughter. Tired of being alone in a marriage. Tired of praying prayers that seemed to go nowhere. Tired of no one responding when she reached out. Tired of the nothingness of her existence. What had she done to deserve this? She had the feeling her question would not be answered.

She entered her room and closed the door. She was too exhausted to even get the drink she craved. Slowly putting her new purchases away, she finished her night-time ritual. Sitting on the edge of the bed she idly perused the mail she'd picked up on her way into the house. She frowned. One packet was thick and had no return address. It was addressed to Randall. Something or someone compelled her to open it. It felt like photographs. Why would someone be sending photos anonymously?

Carefully she peeled back the sticky lip of the envelope and extracted the stack of photos inside. She heard the air leave her body. Her hand flew to her face as the pictures spilled onto the floor before her. If she'd wanted to avoid the truth, surely she no longer could. There it was at her feet. The naked truth…in more ways than one. The photos were of Randall and a man, both seemingly naked and unashamed. A note settled on top of one: "Wouldn't your congregation love to get a load of these?" She heard the front door close. Heard Randall's steps walking reluctantly toward their room. Hurriedly she gathered the pictures, stuffing them back into the envelope. She shoved them into the side compartment of her purse and dove into bed. She turned over, nestling deeper into the folds of the comforter, and closed her eyes. She heard him open the door and stop. She could feel his eyes on her, yet she didn't open hers. She dared not look at him lest she start screaming. She fought the urge to confront him; she knew she should have a plan before doing that. Her mind was racing as she willed herself to slow her breathing.

Everything done in the dark eventually comes to light, this she knew. But for the sake of Jada, she was going to figure out what to do with the light she'd been given.

eighteen

Tamara stopped long enough to smooth her hair and blow into her hand to check her breath before entering the restaurant.

The maitre d' was waiting. "Miss Watson?"

"Yes…" She was a little taken aback that he knew her.

"Mr. Davis is waiting for you. Right this way." With that he turned to lead her to a table.

Turning the corner, Tamara could see Kevin Davis over her guide's shoulder. He smiled as she came into view. Little butterflies rose from the pit of her stomach. She waved them away and ignored caution in lieu of a smile and the intent to enjoy her evening. Kevin rose to meet her as she approached the table. Taking both of her hands in his, he kissed her lightly on both cheeks and then lingered in front of her lips before planting a wisp of a kiss there also, sending a full-blown shiver straight down Tamara's spine.

"You look beautiful," he breathed.

Tamara was tempted to say, "You too." Instead she stuck to the appropriate, "Thank you."

The maitre d' pulled out her chair, and she sat down to face her date, who was looking much finer than she remembered. It was then she became aware of the presence of two waiters on either side of the table. One placed a glass stair-step topped with various flavors of caviar in the center of the table, while the other lowered flutes of champagne in front of them both. Kevin raised his glass to toast her, and she mirrored him, waiting for him to clink her glass.

"I took the liberty of ordering the chef's picks for us this evening. I hope you don't mind. Here's to beautiful beginnings."

Tamara raised an eyebrow. "I like that. And just what are we beginning?"

"Why, a beautiful relationship, of course." He gave a breathtaking smile that silenced her. "Whether it be friendship or something deeper...but I vote for something deeper."

"And how can you know that so soon?" The words of one of her favorite authors came to mind: "Dating is not for mating. It is for collecting data." A flare of resentment rose in her. She wasn't sure she was interested in listening to reason right now, and yet a silent war had begun inside. One part of her voted for caution, while the other relished throwing caution to the wind just once. Although she was really attracted to Kevin, her gut instinct cautioned her to maintain her sensibility and get a lot more information before deciding if this was going to be a love connection.

As their glasses touched, he laughed a low, sensuous laugh. "But why wouldn't I? My career is all about making quick, qualitative decisions and being willing to take a gamble to make great gains. I'm good at it; that's why I'm successful. So let's see, in front of me sits a beautiful, intelligent, confident, self-made, successful woman with a zest for life. What is there not to like or want?" He looked at her, awaiting an answer.

Tamara felt slightly off kilter. She voted for buying more time to collect her thoughts. She smiled. "Impressive. And how could you possibly know so much about me already?"

"I observe people. I figured you do too. That is what you do for a living, isn't it?" He placed some caviar on a sliver of toast and held it to her lips. "Taste this. It's infused with miso. If I were a betting man, and I am, I'd wager this is your flavor."

Tamara opened her mouth obediently and tasted his offering. She closed her eyes as the flavor exploded in her mouth. It was hot and spicy, a mixture of sensation and taste that she couldn't describe. "Mmm..." She couldn't hold in the response, the flavor was so intense.

"I'm glad you like it. Now, where were we? Oh, you were asking me how I can know so soon in the game that I want you. Every real man knows what he wants when he sees it." A light of challenge entered his eyes. "I thought real women operated the same way."

Tamara refused to be bested by him. "Indeed they do. So tell me why a real man like you hasn't found a real woman before now?" She decided it was best to see if the coast was clear before going any further.

"Perhaps I've been waiting."

"Waiting for what?"

"Waiting for the right woman. A person does have to be discriminating when one has a lot to bring to the table, and I don't believe in wasting time. Counterfeits are a waste of time, and I definitely know the real thing when I see it."

"I see," was all Tamara could muster. Her eyes took him in and decided after checking out the cashmere suit and Rolex watch that he definitely was into "the real thing" as he had put it.

She settled into her chair as the waiter brought the next course and then the next. She allowed herself the pleasure of savoring every delicious bite, along with conversation that proved to be just as delightful. *A real man. Now this is what I've always talked about. A man who knows what he wants and isn't afraid to go after it. These men are few and far between.* She couldn't believe her good fortune at finally meeting one. She shook off the thought that he was too good to be true and chose to enjoy the evening instead. Kevin was interesting, funny, world savvy, and he had wonderful taste. What was there not to like? Jamilah's words came unbidden to her mind, "But is he saved?" Right now Tamara didn't care. She felt she owed it to herself to just have a good time. Who said it would go any further, and a girl shouldn't turn down an expensive, wonderful meal now, should she? "Heck no!" That's what she would have said in jest to Jamilah had she proven to be in better humor, but these days her best friend wasn't much fun at all.

Kevin was a breath of fresh air, and she was going to breathe it in and savor it for a while. She saw no need to ask him about his spiritual state. To be perfectly honest, she really wasn't interested. She was more focused on having a good time with a man who was totally into her. She felt like a woman for the first time in a long time, and she loved every minute of it. Besides, he hadn't asked her to marry him or anything, so it wasn't a present concern anyway. *Carpe diem!* Seize the day and enjoy it—that was her motto tonight. With that she took another sip of champagne, allowed him to stroke her hand, laughed at all his jokes, and thoroughly relished dinner.

Deep in mid savor of the most wonderful crème brûlée she'd ever had, a voice interrupted her enjoyment.

"Tamara?"

She glanced up. "Lydia?" Her eyes went to the man standing behind her with movie star good looks. Younger, much younger than Lydia. Tamara had seen him somewhere before, though she couldn't remember where just now.

Lydia looked very pleased to see her. Her eyes were alight. Tamara studied her face as Lydia checked out Kevin and gave a smile of approval. Lydia looked different. She couldn't put her finger on exactly what was different about her as she watched her stroking her date's arm.

"Oh, forgive me for being rude. Tamara this is Brandon, Brandon Walker." She emphasized his name the second time as if to signal that she should know him. The light came on. Ah yes! *Oo...bad Lydia, bad, bad Lydia...not a good move, girl.* But now wasn't the time to get into that. She was careful not to let what she was thinking show on her face.

"Nice to meet you, Brandon." She was still watching Lydia's face, which was practically glowing. That was it! Lydia looked happy. And that was so foreign it had taken Tamara a moment to figure it out. Gesturing to her own date, she introduced him. "This is Kevin, Kevin Davis."

Lydia was leaning forward to shake Kevin's hand, still stroking

Brandon's arm with her left hand. "So nice to meet you, Kevin." She glanced back, smiling conspiratorially at Tamara. "Fancy meeting you here."

"Yes. I'm sorry I didn't see you earlier. I missed you."

"We'll have to get together soon. I'll give you a call." Lydia backed away from the table, and Tamara took the hint.

"Do that. And do enjoy your dinner. I highly recommend the lamb."

"Mmm, sounds good. I'll see you later." Looking at Brandon, Lydia asked, "Brandon, honey, are you ready?"

He nodded and obediently followed her to their table, but not before taking another look at Tamara.

"Someone you've known for a long time?" Kevin was looking after them in amusement.

"Yes." She finished her crème brûlée. "And she isn't being very smart at the moment."

"Cougars seldom are."

"Cougars?"

"You know. Older women who fool themselves into thinking the boy toys they acquire are actually serious about them. I foresee much trouble in that woman's life."

"Oh, I don't know. Lydia is on a different type of mission, and believe me, the woman doesn't have a soft spot in her body."

"Well, she does now, and judging from the way the young man was scoping you out, now is not a good time for her to get vulnerable. I fear she is hooked and he is not."

"Wow! You read all that in a three-minute encounter?"

"It was blatantly obvious. Where were you? I'm beginning to worry about your qualifications, Miss Therapist."

"Oh, don't even go there! I am off the clock and enjoying my dinner with a very handsome, charming man. I'm totally not interested in analyzing intruders who encroach on my personal time and space. I'm sure I'll have plenty of opportunities to watch Lydia's drama unfold, but not tonight. Okay?"

"That's fine with me...and on that note, back to us. Are you ready?" He hailed the waiter for the check.

Tamara felt a small thrill go through her. "Ready for what?"

"For us. To leave. Or both."

"I most certainly am."

"For which one?"

"For now, to leave. The jury is still out on us." She suddenly decided to play the game smart.

"Ah, well, I suppose I'll wait if I must." He signed the check with a flourish and rose. Leaning over her chair as she pushed it back to stand, he squeezed her shoulders, his lips grazing her ear, "And what must I do to move the jury along?"

Tamara waited a beat to allow her head to clear. "Just keep doing what you're doing. Consistency is the key."

"Ooh, are you a burned woman?"

"No, just a careful one."

"I see." He studied her face and then steered her toward the door. "No need to worry. Your knight is here and your chariot awaits."

"I like the sound of that." Giggling shyly, she allowed him to lead her to the door and out to his car. Settling into his Bentley, she stifled the urge to laugh out loud. Either this was a wonderful dream or a very cruel joke. But for now she was content to go with the flow and see where it led. As he pulled in front of her apartment building, she debated whether she should invite him up or not. It had been so long since she'd had a date, and she didn't know what the protocol was anymore. And she wasn't sure how far she wanted this to go yet. Now that the possibility to have what she'd always wanted was right here next to her, she wasn't sure exactly what to do. She felt a battle begin within. Her spirit was saying one thing; her flesh was saying another.

Kevin got out of the car, walked around, and opened her car door.

Taking his hand, she exited. They walked silently to the door. *You don't have to decide anything right now, girl. Enjoy it for what it is...in the moment. Slow down, girl.*

And then they were standing at the door…and he was looking into her eyes.

"I had a good time, Miss Watson."

"Me too, Mr. Davis."

"Let's do it again."

"I think that would be nice."

He kissed her. A light brush across her lips. A teaser.

He knows what he's doing, she decided.

"I'll call you." And then he was gone.

Famous last words, but she hoped not in this case. Time would tell…it always did.

nineteen

Lydia rolled over and reached for Brandon, finding only a lush pillow where his body once had been. She stretched and smiled like a satisfied cat. A lot had happened in a week's time. More than she'd ever expected. After her strategically designed photo op dinner, Brandon had swept her off her feet. With photographers in hot pursuit, he'd wined and dined her all over the city whenever he had a moment away from the movie set. She couldn't remember the last time she'd felt so alive, so beautiful…so…happy. She hadn't known it was possible.

She tried to figure out what was so different about this relationship. *"Relationship?" Hah!* She couldn't believe she actually thought of that word. A relationship had not been her plan. She'd wanted to use Brandon to raise the ire of her ex-husband and force a dialog so Richard would reconsider their divorce. But she hadn't heard from him, and suddenly she realized she didn't care.

The press had been abuzz about Brandon and her liaisons. Lydia read that one reporter asked Richard outright how he felt about his ex-wife running around town with his leading man. Richard had responded that everyone deserved to be happy and wished her well. He then diverted the interview back to the movie he was shooting. He sang Brandon's praises and rolled out enough rhetoric to make people wait with bated breath for the film's release.

Lydia was ecstatic. She'd never felt this way before. Brandon was attentive, supportive, and oh so romantic. He told her she was beautiful and made her believe it. Richard had never taken the time to do that...at least not in years. It seemed now as if their entire relationship had been a business partnership. To hear him tell it she was cold, aloof, and uncaring. But she remembered when they first met and how much she adored him and hung on his every word. When he walked into a room her heart pounded. She couldn't get enough of his presence. She loved working with him, being his muse and co-conspirator. They were quite the power team. But work became his other woman. Though she enjoyed the fruit of their work and the trappings it provided, she longed for him even more. The deeper into his work he burrowed, the more she erected walls around her heart. She learned to acquire other lovers, such as the prestige of success, the accolades of her peers, the material trappings and perks, the social outings. She let them consume her and replace him.

Though they continued to work together, they grew apart. For a long time she wondered if he even noticed. If he did, it wasn't apparent. She refused to dwell on the sadness she felt because it made her feel powerless; instead, she allowed her anger to become her best friend and motivator. She became fierce in business, a force to be reckoned with, her tongue becoming a weapon that chiseled everyone down to size. No one dared cross her. Even her husband learned not to question or oppose her when she was on a roll.

Then abruptly Richard "got religion," as she had laughingly called it. All of a sudden he wanted to be the loving husband she'd dreamed of for years. But it was too late; her wounds had healed and formed a hard ball of bitterness. She wanted him to suffer like she suffered. Wanted him to feel what it was like to have affections unreturned. She resented the fact that it took "the Lord" to make him want to love her the way she wanted to be loved. Shouldn't he have loved her all along? Why did God have to tell him how to treat her, how to love her? She wanted no part of Richard or God at this point. Religion seemed so contrived. How could someone change so drastically overnight? Surely this was a temporary thing, and she was not going to put herself in the position to be drop-kicked after he grew weary of doing things "God's way." Why get used to something if it wasn't going to last?

Her fear of being hurt again was greater than her past pain or her desire for his love, which added fuel to the fire of her offended heart. The more he tried to cross the great divide between them, the colder she grew toward him. She enjoyed watching him writhe in the agony of trying to do the right thing in spite of her hatefulness. *Good,* she thought. *Now you know how I feel.*

But too late she learned that listening to her wounded spirit had cost her more than she wanted. She'd overplayed her hand. Though Richard continued to be kind, he pulled back. Considerate to the point of sickening politeness, he remained physically with her, but she could feel his spirit leaving the building. She watched the light go out of his eyes. Watched him lose interest, his heart fading into the distance like a ship over the horizon line of a vast ocean. Being so rooted in her bitterness, she couldn't climb out of the deep well she'd allowed herself to sink into. She couldn't do what it would take to get him back.

When he announced he was leaving because he could no longer live in this state, she challenged his faith. "Is this God's way?"

That was the last nail in the coffin.

At first he didn't even answer. He packed his bags in silence and finally said, "Even Jesus knew when to shake the dust off his shoes. I've tried." And he left.

That's when the tables turned. She tried reaching out to him, but her heart was buried under so many years of pain she couldn't find the soft side of herself. She became a poor imitation of the woman he once knew. The fact that she was not interested in sharing his faith or controlling her mouth long enough to stop her bitter accusations delivered the death blow in the midst of their last disastrous counseling session. It was over. Though she should have anticipated this, she had to admit she hadn't. The reality of it sent her reeling in a way she hadn't expected. She landed in a bitter heap that had seemingly affected no one but herself. Broken, she called out to God, turning to him for comfort. It wasn't long before she was lured back into bitterness because God didn't do what she wanted, which was to bring Richard back to her.

And now here she was, lying in the bed of another man. A man much younger than she and who managed to make her feel brand-new in the course of one week. Wow! So caught up was she in creating misery for her ex-husband that she'd overlooked the possibility of finding happiness for herself. Perhaps it was too late to get Richard back, but it wasn't too late to learn a lesson and find new happiness! She wouldn't let this relationship slip away. How crazy that she would find happiness in the midst of a scheme to cause the unhappiness of someone else. Fancy that.

Even her therapist had a life. A rather good-looking one, for that matter, as she recalled the handsome visage of Kevin Davis. She'd been pleasantly surprised to see another side of her counselor's calm, cool, and collected demeanor. She gave her credit where credit was due. She didn't know why she'd imagined Tamara had no life outside of her office. Well, she'd been proven wrong, and it wasn't the first time. Tamara had looked downright stunning and seemed to be in rare form with her date. Brandon had asked who she was, to which Lydia had replied vaguely "an old friend." He didn't need to know what their association was. Besides, she wouldn't be seeing Tamara anymore. Lydia had found the fix she was looking for.

Lydia frowned. *Where is Brandon?* She'd slept so deeply she never heard or felt him arise. Looking at the clock, she gasped. It was ten o'clock! She never slept this late. He was probably up studying his lines. Slipping into the shirt he'd left at the foot of the bed, she slowly opened the bedroom door, padding barefoot into the living room of his suite. "Braaaandon? Didn't you forget some…thing…"

She stopped in her tracks as two pairs of eyes stared at her. She instinctively pulled Brandon's shirt tighter around her as Richard took in her rumpled appearance from the tip of her toes to the top of her head. He seemed very interested in perusing her fully, a look of mild fascination on his face. Brandon looked slightly uncomfortable but amused at the same time. Her heart was pounding in her ears so loudly she almost couldn't hear herself.

"Oh, I didn't know anyone else was here…"

"That's all right. I was just leaving." Richard rose. Turning toward Brandon, he said, "Let me know what you think of the changes. I think it's going to be great." He headed toward the door without a backward glance at Lydia. "Sorry to interrupt your morning, but I wanted you to be ready for the scene."

"No problem, man. I like the new direction. I'll be ready."

"I know you will. See you later." Then Richard was gone.

Lydia studied the door, trying to decipher what she was feeling before the reality that she was being watched shifted her gaze back to Brandon. She fought to rearrange her trembling lips into a smile, shifting uncomfortably from foot to foot while he studied her, a slight smile playing around the sides of his mouth.

"You all right?" he asked.

"Why wouldn't I be?"

"Well, he is your…"

"Ex-husband." She put her best brave face forward. If Richard didn't care, then neither did she. "Life goes on," she added, talking more to herself than to him. She moved closer and snuggled into his arms, pulling him close. "Right?"

"Right!" he said, pulling her even closer. "Just checking."

"Just checking what?"

"To see if there were any regrets."

"No regrets."

He kissed her. "Are you sure?"

"Positive!" And in that moment she was. She had to be. There was no turning back now. If Richard didn't care what she did, she would go to where she was celebrated and not merely tolerated. She took another look at Brandon before returning to the bedroom to dress. He sure was fine. This may not have been her first choice but she would enjoy the view.

twenty

Corinne sat on the chaise in her bedroom, the comforter enveloping her as she lounged with her morning cocktail. Her Bible lay at her feet abandoned. She had gotten up early, well aware of the swirling chaos in her soul. Going over the information she'd discovered the night before, she gathered her artillery. And now she had to do something…but what? Watching the sunrise she sat in silence, knees drawn to her chest, crying out to God inaudibly lest she wake Randall. She sat waiting for God to say something…anything…but she heard nothing. He hadn't spoken to her for a long time. Or perhaps she was unable to hear Him through the haze of the drinks that had replaced Him as her comforter. If He wouldn't talk to her, she had to numb the pain somehow.

Sighing, she turned her attention to Randall, who was sleeping far too peacefully for her taste. She resented his ability to be so self-possessed that he was totally unaware of the turmoil raging beneath their roof. What would he do if he knew about the photographs? Would the fact that someone was poised to blackmail him jolt him into reality? He seemed to be in his own cocoon of denial about the dire straits his household was in and how his reckless behavior was ultimately going to affect his family. Had he stopped to reflect on the deterioration that had already taken place? Was he aware of how much Jada had changed?

Jada. He was so proud that she was so much like him, but lately that wasn't the case. Corinne frowned. Reflecting on last night, she wondered too late after the fact if she had heard crying amid the din of the running shower. Waving it off as her imagination, she'd been too weary to retrace her steps to find out. But the sound haunted her in her sleep, causing her to rise early. Something was wrong. She could feel it. But she didn't have enough information. Furthermore, she didn't know if she could handle it if she did. And now there were those disgusting pictures on top of whatever was wrong with Jada. How high would the mountain grow before they all were crushed beneath its weight?

The rhythm of Randall's breathing became the beat of her thoughts. Her morning cocktail wasn't taking effect, and her frustration mounted as her musings tumbled over one another. She looked at Randall again. How could a man of God allow himself and his family to sink to such a low? How could he be so sensitive in the spirit when it came to his congregation and yet so clueless when it came to those he was supposed to love and treasure most? How could he continue his deception with no trace of remorse or display of conscience? Didn't he fear God at all? How long did he think God would let him get away with living a lie?

Her thoughts shifted back to God. *Yes, Lord, how long will You let this go on?* She took another sip. Somehow she knew He would let it go on as long as she let it. But what was she supposed to do? What would happen if she confronted her husband about what she knew? What would be the fallout? She didn't know if she had the strength to cope, and yet she knew she was going to have to suck up courage and deal with it. She was quickly coming to the end of herself. Her faith was at an all-time low. If God would allow her life to unravel like this, would He really take care of her in the aftermath of what would undoubtedly be a major storm? She wasn't sure.

But what did she really have to lose at this point? She'd had enough time for nursing and rehearsing her woes. Now it was time for action. She knew it was a waste of time to keep repeating herself over and over to Tamara each week. She wasn't getting any answers there either, and Tamara looked bored. To tell the truth, so was she. She gave a deep, throaty chuckle. She could have had a nice nest egg to fall back on if she'd saved the money she spent on Tamara and cosmetic forays. She could have been more prepared to handle the eventual disintegration of her marriage. One thing she did know was that every trial had an expiration date. She had allowed the dysfunction to go on long enough to earn the title of being certifiably insane—hoping for different results when she'd done nothing to promote a change.

She was done with the isolation of her secret misery. But who could she tell? Her friends? To tell the truth, she didn't really have any. It was hard to know who could be trusted with confidences when you're a pastor's wife. She'd learned to have surface friendships without sharing anything that could be used to hurt her or her family. She had no siblings. Oh how she wished for a sister at a time like this! Her mother? That would go over well. Her mom had never liked Randall, and she was too ill to deal with this anyway. Perhaps she should have listened to her, but she'd been too caught up in the handsome, debonair man with his promises to have and to hold forever and ever, amen. Promises, promises…

Randall opened his eyes and stared at her without moving. She stared back, slowing taking another sip of her drink.

"Isn't it a little too early for that?" He looked irritated.

She cocked her head, eyeing him evenly over the rim of her glass. "What time would you suggest? Ten? Eleven?"

"Oh for crying out loud!" He angrily threw back the covers and stomped into the bathroom.

"Maybe I should."

"Maybe you should what?" He looked at her, appearing completely baffled.

"Cry out loud." She could feel her insides crumbling but no tears came. She continued staring at him. She took another sip for good measure.

"Corinne, what do you have to cry about?" He slowly walked toward her. "You have quite the life, you know that? Beautiful home, a life of leisure, money to do as you please. I subsidize your shopping, your little trips to the plastic surgeon, and that…therapist…or whatever she is that you sit with and talk about God only knows what."

She sat up and pointed at him. "Now that is the truth…only God knows. Wouldn't you like to know what's going on with your wife? Your daughter? Yourself, for that matter?" She stopped and studied him as he stared back at her in silence. She took a deep breath. "Randall, do you pray?"

He arched his head back and looked at her as if she was crazy. "What?"

"Do you pray?"

"What do you mean, do I pray? Of course I pray. That is part of my profession. I'm a pastor for God's sake!"

"Now there's a novel concept. For God's sake. And for your family's sake. I haven't seen you pray for a long time. I was trying to find a reason for why you could be so out of touch with me and Jada. We're your family, and we used to pray together every morning before you left for work. What happened to that?"

A faint glimmer lit his eyes for a moment and then retreated. "Life happens, schedules happen. You got busy with Jada; I got busy with church."

"I haven't been busy with Jada for years, Randall. And if you were honest, you were busy first. What is happening…no…what has happened to us? You don't pray with me, and I don't see you praying at all. But who am I to tell you what you're not doing? I'm trying to understand where you are. So do you just pray up a sermon for every Sunday? Do you ever ask God anything about me or your daughter? I've been asking Him why you treat strangers and people at church like family and your family like strangers, but He's not answering." Now she felt the tears coming. She took another sip. For the first time, as she slowly came to grips with who Randall was and wasn't, she wondered if needing him was habit, true love, or a selfish need to be validated as a woman. The truth of her own neediness disgusted her.

"Maybe if you put that glass down long enough, you would be able to hear Him. As for me, I don't have anything to say to you. You're rambling, and I don't have time for this."

"When will you have time, Randall?" She could hear her voice rising. "When time runs out on our marriage?"

He took a step toward her. "What are you suggesting? Do you want to leave me? On what grounds? You have no biblical grounds." His tone had changed to his official pastor voice.

She wanted to scream, "Yes, I do! On the grounds of adultery!" She was tempted to pull out the pictures and throw them in his face, daring him to deny his indecencies. But she knew better than to reveal her cards before she had a plan. And the truth was, she still had none. So she whimpered instead. "How about abandonment? Because you aren't here, Randall. Where is my husband?" Even in her pain and new awareness she hoped for a caring response. That her appeal to him would make him want to be the man he was supposed to be.

He looked at her coldly as a fleeting glimmer of pity passed like a shadow over his face and disappeared just as quickly. "He's standing right here, Corinne. Looking at you. Sick and tired of seeing you in this state. Wondering when you'll pull yourself together. That is not a matter of prayer. That is a matter of decision. And that decision is up to you. Now I have to get ready for a meeting. I don't have any more time for this."

He headed toward the bathroom but turned to look back at her. "Perhaps you have too much time on your hands. You know what they say, 'An idle mind is the devil's workshop.' Maybe you need to find something to do with yourself. Charity or something." He closed the door.

Corinne stared at the door in disbelief. No, he hadn't said that. If 'an idle mind was the devil's workshop,' then what was his excuse? How dare he lecture her on biblical standards! He thought he had the upper hand because she had nowhere else to go. How would he feel if he knew she knew? How cocky would he be then?

In that moment she hated him. And she hated herself for vacillating between fear and doing what she needed to do. He'd turned her into her mother, and that was not a good thing. All her life she had thought her mother most pathetic as she tolerated her husband's emotional abuse. Now she understood why her mother had suffered silently until he'd finally passed away. Her mother's only skill had been being a wife. And Corinne had followed in her mother's footsteps. Here she sat in the same position—a loveless, pain-filled marriage with nowhere to go. Her mother had been fortunate enough to receive a nice chunk of life insurance money after her father's death. She doubted Randall would die anytime soon. Perhaps her mother had seen the warning signs, seen what was coming. Corinne hated it when her mother was right.

If God wouldn't answer her prayers, she would take life into her own hands…but she didn't know how yet. A wave of desperation swept over her. She would not die quietly! She would not let Jada watch her be as helpless as her mother had once been.

Corinne's arm rose. She felt the weight of the glass in her hand and heard it shatter against the bathroom door. She watched the pieces fall to the floor, and then she dissolved into a river of tears that she feared would drown her. Randall was right. She did need to get herself together. Though she knew anger could be destructive, she chose to cling to it as a motivator. In an odd way, she felt stronger. "You'd better watch your step, mister," she growled at the closed door, feeling far more dangerous than she was. It was time to rise to the occasion, if for no other purpose than to save Jada. In her moment of resolve, she was certain this whole situation would get worse before getting better. Although, on second thought, what could be worse than this?

twenty-one

Lydia breezed out of the elevator and across the lobby. Invigorated by her romantic tryst with Brandon, she felt vital and alive. Now all that would make her life complete was a tall caramel macchiato from Starbucks. She chuckled. *What did people do before Starbucks?* She shrugged and wrapped her shawl tighter around her to insulate her from the nip in the morning air. Usually this type of weather would have her complaining, but today she found it pleasant and refreshing. Chicago was growing on her, she admitted. It was a beautiful city. A chic, European-style flavor gave it a certain class that was surprising. The city was a little jewel no one really knew about that kept serving up pleasant sparkles with every turn as another great restaurant or unique boutique was discovered. She found the people real and earthy. There was no need to guess what they thought or if they liked you. They shot straight from the hip. They were entrepreneurial and very social. It made for an interesting life without the angst of false pretense. The city and the people had settled in to an even pace that she liked. No facades, no rush, no posturing. It was all new to her, and she liked it.

She had begun to look for an apartment to purchase, trying to decide between the conventional condo or one of the new artsy lofts that were going up everywhere. In the meantime she chose a small month-to-month suite just off Michigan Avenue, within minutes of the best shopping. It was interesting how each city had its own flavor. She was enjoying the sophistication of those who moved through Chicago's choice social circles. These people liked to dress up, and so did she. In short, she considered Chicago a quieter, cleaner, nicer New York. A happy medium between two worlds—a big city with a small town feel and sensibilities. She loved it, and she was loving it more every day she spent here with Brandon.

He was an explorer at heart with inexhaustible energy. Each day he came up with something for them to discover—the Botanical Gardens, the zoo that bordered the exclusive neighborhoods of Lincoln Park, and Navy Pier. Her favorites were the Museum of Natural History and the Frank Lloyd Wright homes. She relished every moment she spent with Brandon, knowing that his time would be limited when they began shooting. She smiled, remembering how he leaned in to her when giving her his key. She had pouted, saying that soon he wouldn't have time for her.

"I always have time for pleasure. So if you promise to be waiting for me when I get home, I promise to have time for you. Deal?"

"Deal!" she announced and giggled. She giggled again as the thought of their exchange sent a thrill through her. Turning out of the wind, she ran straight into the chest of a man. His hands caught her, breaking the force of their collision.

"I am so sorry…"

"It's quite all right, but we must stop meeting this way."

Her head snapped up to face Richard, who was still holding her arms and smiling.

"Although you do have more clothes on now. The other look was kinda cute. Not you at all."

"I didn't think you noticed." Her face felt hot, though she didn't know why.

"Oh, I noticed all right. But then again, isn't that what you wanted?"

"What do you mean by that?" She was annoyed that he might be on to her game.

"Come on, Lydia. Brandon Walker? You can't be serious. He's half your age."

"What does age have to do with it? He's brilliant and smart and has a lot going for him—much more than that chile you're dating. What's her name? Minnie…"

Richard threw back his head and laughed. "Ooh, down, girl! I believe her name is Winnie."

Lydia snorted. "Just as bad. Who ever heard of anybody worth anything being called Winnie?"

"Mmm…perhaps Nelson Mandela would beg to differ with you."

"No, he wouldn't. They're divorced too, remember?"

He pointed at her and smiled. "You have a point there." Then growing more serious, he said, "You know, maybe Brandon is good for you after all. He's gotten you to loosen up, let down your coif, take off your clothes. Whew! I might have stayed if all that was going on in our marriage!" He laughed and slapped his thigh as if he were truly enjoying a funny joke.

Lydia's eyes narrowed. "Perhaps if you'd stayed home long enough and paid attention you would have seen me that way in your house… *our* house."

Richard sobered. "Look, this is not the time or the place to get into all of that."

"Oh, I think this is as good a time as any to set the record straight. We certainly paid enough money to avoid the subject several times, so why not settle it once and for all for free?"

Click. She heard the camera, but she didn't care. A deep well had sprung up inside her, and she couldn't stop the water's flow. All the pain and loneliness of years past flooded out…her need for his attention and the lack of love she felt. Her fears that their marriage was one of convenience, for business only. Her fear that she was being used by him. The abandonment she felt when he got "saved." She'd felt she was on the outside looking in on something that gave him more joy than she could and that hurt. She'd been left out of some elite club because she didn't have the right qualifications.

She paused, mortified that her feelings were still so close to the surface in spite of her newfound happiness.

Oblivious to the curious onlookers studying the intensity of their exchange, she spewed even more of the hurt, anger, bitterness, and angst she'd felt over many years. The chasm they created in her couldn't be filled by accomplishments and accolades. Nothing had been able to put a dent in the emptiness she felt. To round it all off, she accused him of being jealous of what she'd been able to do without him.

But Richard had his own laundry list. His words slapped her as he accused her of causing the rift between them. He cited her voracious appetite for more of everything—more power, more possessions, more attention, more, more, more! His face was clouded with anger and taut with disgust as he spat, "I am so sick of women throwing out that stupid line about strong, accomplished women intimidating men. That's not it. I never had a problem with you being accomplished. What I did have a problem with was how impressed you became with yourself. Being self-serving has never been an attractive feature, in case you didn't know. Did it ever occur to you that I wasn't interested in curling up with a list of your accomplishments? After a while I couldn't find you anymore. You were too busy loving yourself to leave room for anyone else to love you. Lydia, did you consider that?"

She reeled back in shock. "What are you saying? I loved you, Richard! But all you could think about was your work." She lifted her chin, daring him to deny that fact. "Was I supposed to pine for you forever? How dare you blame me for the demise of our marriage just because I chose to get on with my life and go where I could receive what I wasn't getting at home."

"Perhaps you loved me, but you loved things more. I find it fascinating that women always run around looking for a rich man, and then they accuse the man of being bad because the poor guy has to spend most of his time working for the riches the woman wants. Make up your mind! Do you want a man with money or a man who has time for you? What was I supposed to do? You wanted this, you wanted that. You had to have the house. You had to style and profile. Just how did you think we were going to pay for all the things you wanted?" He was inching closer to her. His eyes clouded for a moment. "So sue me for trying to give you all the things you wanted. I loved you, and I wanted you to have them. So I worked and I worked to get them for you. And all the thanks I got was your cold attitude. Well, you're welcome—even though you never said thank you."

He stopped as his voice caught. "You can accuse me of a lot of things, Lydia, but don't ever accuse me of not loving you. I did the best I could, but my best wasn't good enough for you."

Lydia opened her mouth to say something, what she didn't know. But Richard put up his hand to cut her off.

"Let me finish. I think we're even here. You ran to your work, and I ran to God. Unlike you, I can admit when I've come to the end of myself. I couldn't make you love me, so I found Someone who did. For you to laugh at my faith was the ultimate insult. No one shut you out; you shut yourself out. But then again, it's easier to always play the victim, isn't it? Then you never have to deal with yourself. Well, you need to take a cold, hard look in the mirror while you're painting your face and trying to be twenty years younger than you are…"

Lydia didn't feel her arm raise. She heard the sound of her hand crashing across the side of his face. The impact rang in harmony with clicks of cameras. The paparazzi were like bees drawn to honey. Where they came from, she didn't know.

Richard stepped back as if stung. He eased away. She moved toward him, tears gathering in her eyes. No words came.

Click. Click. The sound finally jolted her back to reality as Richard spun on his heel and walked away, leaving her to face the cameras and onlookers alone. She stopped and viewed her audience, thinking better of going after him. Slowly wiping the tears that streamed down her face, she backed away from the curious throng, feeling her feet turning automatically, steering her in the opposite direction. Some things were beyond control and couldn't be produced to your liking. From these things you walk away. She didn't feel the pavement beneath her as she made her way down the crowded avenue.

Her mind was racing, still reeling from all Richard said. She was shocked by his pain and his anger. Horrified as the realization of her part in the disintegration of what she had held most precious began to settle and seep into her consciousness like a blanket sodden with oil. His words clung to her, weighing down her spirit. There was no getting away from the truth she had never considered 'til now. She wanted to cry out, but she'd created enough of a scene already. There was so much to absorb and make sense of.

Her mind went to Brandon. Perhaps he was her chance to start over again. This time she would do things the right way. What will he say when he sees Richard and my exchange splashed across the front page of the paper or in one of those gossip rags? For the first time she prayed that something of more import would upstage her story. Brandon didn't need to be privy to this exchange.

She couldn't get around the corner fast enough as she sought to leave the eyes she could still feel piercing her back. For once in her life she wished she could disappear, but that too was beyond her control. And so she didn't look back. Didn't see Brandon standing on the sidewalk watching, the reporters closing in around him, seeking a reaction to what had just taken place.

Sometimes looking back costs you more than you care to pay, she noted. Little did she know how true that was.

twenty-two

Jamilah sat back on the couch, watching Dwayne busy himself behind the bar in the kitchen. She liked his apartment. Spacious and open, with furniture that was contemporary with clean lines and Afrocentric touches and art. It was warm and comfortable without being overdone or prissy. The consummate bachelor pad. He had taken great pride in decorating it himself, allowing her access to give her opinion only after he'd moved in. When he spread paint palettes in front of her, she'd never seen him look so serious. This was his first home, and he was determined to have it reflect not only good taste but the level of accomplishment he'd finally achieved.

"What do you think?" he'd said in deep concentration. Jamilah had fought to stifle a hoot. All the palettes looked the same to her. Obviously taupe was going to be the color whether she liked it or not.

"Umm, I think this one looks good."

He brightened. "Really? That's the one I picked!" On that note he swung around, scooping up a painting. "Which wall do you think this should go on?" And with that they were off and running, settling every decision that had hung in the balance. Careful to make sure the final decision was really his, Jamilah had been mildly amused at his intense attention to every detail of setting up his home.

Ending her reverie, she glanced at Dwayne. He looked rather

happy doing whatever he was doing across the room. She could see him across the length of the large living room as he hummed under his breath along with Al Jarreau, whose voice flowed out of the suspended speakers surrounding her, inviting her to "Take Five."

Dwayne was truly in his glory. The king of his domain. For a moment she allowed herself to imagine what it would be like to live with him, wake up with him, be a part of his world for more than the times they shared whenever he went on a girlfriend sabbatical. She hovered there, but then chose not to remain, knowing that was a dangerous place. *Nope, nope, nope. Not smart, girl. The more you dwell on it, the deeper you'll sink,* she warned herself. So she took a moment to enjoy the daydream and then tucked it carefully back inside her fantasy file. Unless Dwayne declared his feelings toward her romantically, she would assume there was no chance for a deeper relationship. She had no intention of having a relationship with him all by herself, unlike many other women she'd observed who fancied themselves practically on their way to the altar with him, only to be rudely awakened when he turned left, leaving them standing alone.

"Hey, what are you so deep in thought about over there?"

His question snapped her back to the present. She didn't dare tell him what she'd been thinking.

"I was just thinking how great it looks in here. You've added a few pieces since the last time I was over."

"Thanks for noticing. You like?" He was coming toward her with a tray.

"Mm hmm. Although I don't know if I like the fact that you can have good taste without me."

He laughed. "To tell you the truth I did have a 'what would Jamilah do' moment before I bought it, so you did have some influence even though you weren't there." He frowned. "Hmm…I don't know if that's good."

She leaned forward and bit the shrimp off the tip of the fork that Dwayne extended to her. "That is good!"

"Your influence or my shrimp?"

"Both! But especially the shrimp." She decided to keep the evening light and avoid the former.

"Thank you. I made them myself." Dwayne looked very pleased.

"Come on, tell the truth and shame the devil. Your mama cooked this, and you're just perpetratin'." She watched his face for a reaction, but it was the picture of perfect innocence.

"Now do you really believe I would lie to you? I am wounded to the core." With that he slapped his hand over his chest, gripped it, and fell off the couch in a dramatic display of heart failure.

Jamilah laughed, "Boy, you crazy!"

"Now is that any way for a teacher to talk? Didn't you forget a verb in there somewhere?"

Jamilah leaned forward to swat him. He ducked and grinned.

"I may be crazy, but that's why you like me!" he asserted.

Trying to maintain a stern look she replied, "You are also incorrigible. And who told you I liked you?"

Dwayne did his best imitation of a sister-girl, swiveling his neck and pursing his lips, "Yo mama…"

"Aw, you know, you better leave my mama outta this!"

"Why? You brought my mama into it. One good turn deserves another."

"You know you're going to make me hurt you!"

"Ooh, promises, promises."

Jamilah threw a pillow at him. "You need to repent."

He ducked and laughed. "I refuse to!" Then straightening he said, "Hey, you know you've had a tendency toward violence these days? What's up with that? You keep throwing things at me. You don't have a crush on me, do you, girl?"

"Boy, you wish! Now get serious. I need your help."

"Aw, I knew it." He hung his head. "I feel so used. What is it this time?"

"You are so dramatic." She rolled her eyes and then sobered. "I need you to introduce me to your friend Stacy at DCFS. I think I need to begin the paperwork for becoming a foster parent."

Dwayne leaned back in his chair. "Whoa! Hold up! What brought this on?"

"I have this feeling deep in my spirit that I need to be ready for whatever. I can't explain it any other way. You told me to pray and stay out of God's way, and that's what I'm doing. But I keep getting this nudge to do whatever I need to do to be in position for what God does next."

"Let me guess. This wouldn't have anything to do with Ari, would it?"

"You know it does. But to be perfectly honest, I don't have the whole picture on what it's about. All I know is that from the time Ari told me her mother said it was all right for her to walk herself home from school, I felt like something bad was going to happen." Jamilah's eyes filled with tears.

Dwayne put his arms around her. "All right, little savior. What makes you think that girl's mama is going to let you have her child? Hmmm?"

"I don't." Jamilah shrugged in his embrace and then settled back into it. It felt good. "I don't know anything; I just know what I feel led to do. The rest is up to God to work out."

"I'm glad you know that much! But do you know what's involved in the process? They don't make it easy." With that, he dove into a full-blown tour through the world of fostering. Jamilah's head began to swim at the laundry list of things that needed to be done before she could even be cleared to be considered for foster care or adoption. By the time Dwayne ended his soliloquy on being approved by the state—the home studies, psychiatric examinations, interviews, FBI background checks, and full financial disclosure—she was exhausted and feeling overwhelmed. It sounded like a mountain she wouldn't have the strength to climb. But most of all, it sounded like a very lengthy process. She wasn't sure she had that kind of time. And yet she knew God had told her to get the process started, though she really couldn't figure out how He was going to use it.

Dwayne was right. Ari's mother would never allow her to leave.

Getting approved for foster care seemed like a futile exercise, and yet she couldn't shake the urgency to follow through, no matter how difficult it might be. All she knew was that she needed to be ready for whatever God intended. She just wished He would let her in on the plan so she'd know what to expect. She voiced this to Dwayne.

"But then you wouldn't be walking by faith, would you?" he replied.

"Well, who said I had to like it?"

"You don't. You just keep walking and not giving up. What's that scripture? 'In due season we shall reap if we do not lose heart'? Don't give up, my child." He tried his best to look pastorly.

"Hey, how come you know so much about this process anyway?"

"I've looked into it before." His eyes gave away buried hurt.

Of course he knew so much. Lost in her own focus on Ari, Jamilah had forgotten, but it came back to her now. A couple of years ago Dwayne had become attached to a little boy he was mentoring who was in a similar position as Ari. Dwayne talked the mother into letting him take her son until she could get herself together. Just as he was about to claim his little charge, the mother changed her mind. Afraid Dwayne would pursue adopting her son against her wishes, she took him and moved to Atlanta. Dwayne was devastated, fearing the boy would fall into a worse state with no respite or mentor. He never spoke about it anymore, and Jamilah never brought it up.

Now it made sense why he would discourage her from going through the same thing. She reached out and squeezed his hand.

"I'm sorry. I…"

He waved her away.

He doesn't want me to be hurt. How sweet is that?

He was looking at her strangely.

"What?"

"So you think you can be a single mother? It's a lot of work…"

"You don't think they would deny me because I'm single, do you?"

"They're not supposed to, but it depends on who you're dealing with. They always prefer two parents." He was studying her seriously.

"Well, I don't have a husband, so what am I supposed to do?"

There was a pregnant pause.

Jamilah stared at Dwayne; he stared back. He suddenly jumped up from the couch and began clearing away the dishes…without looking at her.

"Guess you'll have to find someone to marry."

"Any suggestions? Got a friend you want to hook a sistah up with?"

"Girl, do you want me to get run out of town after you drive one of my friends crazy?"

Another pillow went sailing across the room in the direction of the kitchen bar. Dwayne ducked in time to miss being hit and pointed at her. "You really need to get that condition checked out."

Jamilah laughed. She was glad Dwayne had such a great sense of humor and even more grateful that he knew when to get off a subject. Who she would marry and when was not a topic she cared to delve into at that moment. She wasn't ready to face her feelings about Dwayne yet. She knew she couldn't handle it if he didn't feel the same way…to hear him say he didn't like her "that way." If he said they should be "just friends," it would push her over the edge, especially while she was stressing over Ari. If he said that, it would be official. If he didn't say it, the possibility existed. For now ignorance was bliss. She could only take one "maybe" at a time, and for now settling the matter of Ari's life was more important.

"What does Tamara have to say about this?"

Jamilah frowned. *Tamara.* She hadn't spoken to Tamara in a couple of weeks. Or…at least they hadn't had a real conversation. When she'd called, Tamara was distant, citing weariness as an excuse. After a while Jamilah had voted to let her go until she was ready to share where she was and exactly what was going on.

"I suspect that Tamara is up to something she shouldn't be; therefore, I don't think she has too much to say."

"I think I'll stay out of that one. The two of you are weird."

Dwayne always said that. He always said he didn't understand how someone as earthy and sweet as Jamilah had ended up with someone as sa-diddy as Tamara for a friend. Surprisingly, he had been right on target when he diagnosed Tamara as being what he called a "convenient Christian." Tamara tried to do all the right things, but she seemed happy to do things God's way only as long as He was cooperating with her plans. Maybe this explained her present disenchantment with God. If her heart were really sold out to Him, she wouldn't vacillate the way she did when He didn't live up to or deliver on her expectations.

Jamilah remembered accusing Tamara of using living holy as a bargaining chip to get what she wanted. There were definitely terms to her devotion, even in their friendship. It was her way or the highway. Dwayne's prediction was that it would take a faith crisis to truly break her and bring her to a true decision about her faith once and for all. Jamilah had tried to defend Tamara, but as of late she was beginning to think he was right.

She wished Tamara was here to support her through this foster parenting decision, but she was prepared to forge on. She just hoped her dear friend hadn't gotten herself into something she couldn't handle.

A pillow slammed against the side of her head.

"Hey! Snap out of it! You can't save Tamara from her bad decisions. Besides, you've got a lot of work to do yourself. Stay focused!"

"I can always trust you to put things back in perspective."

Dwayne grinned. "You got that right."

Settling back on the pillow Dwayne had thrown at her, she smiled, full and content with an air of expectancy as she watched him cleaning up the kitchen. It felt so right being here with him...playing house. For a moment she let herself savor the feeling, and then she returned to reality, considering the gravity of what she was about to undertake. She was going to be a mother. A single mother. She didn't know when or how—all she knew was God was up to something.

twenty-three

Felicia smiled sheepishly as she maneuvered Simone's stroller into Tamara's office while balancing a book of fabric swatches and a brief-case. Stella hovered in the background, cooing and ready to pounce on the beautiful little girl in the stroller. Amber curls framed the little caramel face that displayed beautiful almond-shaped eyes and perfect pink cupid-bow lips. The toddler was a beauty, a miniature version of her mother. Tamara was mesmerized. For a moment she forgot that children had never been high on her list of priorities. Perhaps she was feeling a little more maternal because of Kevin. Whatever it was, Simone captured her heart hook, line, and sinker with one baby smile. Stella moved in to scoop her out of her stroller.

"Isn't she the most beautiful thing you've ever seen? Hi, baby!" Her attention was centered on the petite bundle she held.

"I'm so sorry, Tamara. I had to bring her with me. Kenny was sup-posed to keep her, but he had to go to the doctor. He's been having these really horrible headaches. I think it's stress but...well...here we are. I hope you don't mind."

"Not at all!" Tamara gently took Simone out of Stella's arms and gave her assistant a get-back-to work look. Stella glared at her before retreating to her desk. Tamara turned her attention back to Simone and squeezed her, planting a kiss on her cheek. The child looked up at her, reaching for her nose and giggling. Tamara was totally mush now. Simone smelled so good and felt even better. Tamara squeezed her again, feeling tears gathering in her eyes. She blinked them back and continued rocking Simone, who seemed to sense the tenderness of the moment. She melted into Tamara's arms even more, allowing herself to be held and loved without a struggle. Tamara didn't know how long she stood there cradling the little girl, but when she looked up Felicia was watching them with a strange smile.

"Well, I'm seeing a whole new side of Miss Tamara today, Simone. I think you bring out the mother in her."

"You think so?" Tamara felt a little embarrassed about being so emotional.

"Oh, I know so! I never imagined I would say these words, but I think you would be a good mother. As a matter of fact, a child would probably be good for you."

"You really think so?" Tamara's thoughts went to Kevin. "I guess I'd better get more serious about finding a husband then."

Felicia laughed. "That goes without saying. Please don't make the same mistake I made."

"But things worked out perfectly for you. You've got a handsome husband, a beautiful daughter, an awesome career. Is my envy showing?"

"Everything has a price, Tamara. You know that. There are consequences for every bad decision and choice we make."

"Okay, give me one 'for instance' in your case."

"I always wonder if Kenny would have married me if I hadn't gotten pregnant."

"Of course he would have. He loves your toe jam!"

"But I don't *know* that, Tamara. I would only be sure if he'd asked me *before* I got pregnant. How do I know he doesn't feel trapped sometimes or regret marrying me just because he wanted to be with his daughter? No matter how many times Kenny reassures me that he loves me, I always have that little question mark in the back of my mind. And it makes me do and say crazy things sometimes. I push his buttons, and then when I see the look on his face I want to shoot myself. And he just takes it, which makes me feel worse. And even though I know it's wrong, I can't seem to stop. My insecurity constantly makes me ask, 'Do you love me now? Do you love me now?' And my greatest fear is one day he'll say no." Her face crumpled.

Simone began to whimper, and Tamara rocked her back and forth, giving Felicia time to recover.

"Felicia, I know your fear is very real to you, but I have to tell you, it is totally unfounded. Every time that man looks at you his eyes are filled with love. He could just as well wave a humongous banner with 'I love you!' in huge, bright letters."

Felicia laughed. "I know. I feel schizophrenic. One moment I'm totally sure he loves me, and the next I'm freaking out. Maybe I need to come back to therapy. I think I have 'fear of abandonment' issues."

"I think you just need to relax and save your money."

Simone gurgled.

"And enjoy this beautiful baby, 'cause I sure would." She kissed Simone again and handed her to Felicia, feeling the need to change the subject. She felt bad about envying Felicia, concluding that everything is never what it seems to be. Perhaps her need to believe in happy endings had made her suspend reality long enough to overlook one of life's rules: "When you don't do things God's way, though forgiven, the natural consequences of wrong actions and choices can't be circumvented." Tamara focused her attention on the fabric samples.

"Now, what have we here?"

Felicia brightened. She placed Simone back in her stroller, giving her a biscuit to pacify herself, and turned to the swatches she'd brought. "These are the fabrics I was telling you about. They're from Italy. I just got them in yesterday. Aren't they beautiful? I thought any of them would work well in your space. It's just a matter of what you personally prefer."

"Ahem!" Stella was standing in the door, a bouquet of flowers in her hands. "Where would you like me to place this? Does this man have you set up on a weekly plan or something?"

Felicia's eyebrows shot up, and she looked at Stella. "What man?"

"You know just as much as I do. He's a mystery. He sends flowers every week and has a really sexy voice."

"Stella!" Tamara hated it when her employee crossed the line to familiarity.

"Perhaps you can solve the mystery," Stella whispered to Felicia as she scooted out the door.

Felicia folded her arms and turned to face Tamara. "Well, well, well! Have you been holding out on me? A man, huh? Sending flowers and all...sounds serious. Could that explain your new softness? Hmmm?"

Tamara felt the rush of blood to her cheeks. "I can't say it's serious yet, but it looks promising. And that's all I'm going to say!" She leaned back over the samples, picking one. "How about this one?"

Felicia took the swatch from her. "Not so fast! Who is this person, where did you meet him, how long have you been seeing him? Come on! Give up the information."

"I met him a little over three weeks ago at a restaurant. He's handsome, accomplished, smart, funny, romantic, and has been inundating me with flowers and dinners. It's been wonderful. The end. Now, back to my decorating choices."

"Is he saved?"

Tamara put up her hand. "I'm done with this subject."

Felicia looked deflated. "Oh, Tamara, he isn't saved, is he? What are you doing? You can't go out like that."

Tamara frowned. "Can't go out like what?"

"You've been holding out all this time. What about that lecture you gave me about 'missionary dating'? Don't give in now. It's not worth it. What's that scripture? 'Let us not grow weary while doing good, for in due season we shall reap...'"

"Yeah, yeah. 'If we don't lose heart.'" Tamara was getting irritated. This was why she hadn't discussed Kevin with anyone. For the first time in a long time she was enjoying life, loving the attention, feeling like a beautiful, normal woman. She didn't want to hear anything that would spoil it. And she didn't want to get into a spiritual debate about dating an unsaved man—"missionary dating," as Jamilah sarcastically called it.

Tamara didn't know whether she thought her dating Kevin really mattered to God. Look at Corinne with her highfalutin' on the "down low" pastor of a husband. And then look at Felicia, who had married an unsaved man who was now a model Christian. Where had following "the rules" gotten Jamilah who was in love with Dwayne and wouldn't admit it? For all their holy posturing, where had it gotten them? Tamara was tired of adhering to a bunch of rules that didn't seem to make much sense, especially based on the lack of romantic activity she'd been experiencing for quite some time.

"Well, I've lost heart, okay? I'm tired of sitting home alone. And I'm going to tell you how I *can't* go out. I can't go out alone, that's how I can't go out. And besides, it can't be all that deep. Look at you. For starting off all wrong, you certainly ended up all right."

Felicia reacted as if someone had slapped her.

Tamara noticed. "I'm sorry. I didn't mean it like that."

"Yes, you did. I'm just sorry you don't realize that what starts wrong gets right only by the grace of God. And that's only if regrets are acknowledged and dealt with...if it ever gets right. And there are no guarantees. It takes hard work. And you wouldn't have to do that if you do things the right way—God's way—in the first place. I'd give anything to be able to go back and do things the right way, Tamara. It would silence a lot of voices in my head."

Tamara opened her mouth, but Felicia silenced her with a raised palm.

"No, let me finish. I know my life must look perfect to you, but things are not always what they seem. I'm not going to go down the long laundry list of my struggles, but life isn't easy for anybody. So don't make it harder than it has to be, okay? Because there's a price to be paid for everything."

"I will take that under advisement. Now, can we get back to the fabric?"

Felicia stared at her for a long time.

Tamara felt uncomfortable. She cleared her throat and shifted her attention to the swatches before her. Pointing to one she said, "I really like this one. What do you think?"

Felicia was still studying her. "I think they are all beautiful, but what is the best choice for your space is the question."

"Are we talking about the fabric or Kevin?"

"Kevin! We're making progress! At least I have a name now. I guess the comment could cover both. I think I'll let you live with the swatches for a while...as well as your personal decisions. Sometimes it takes time for the best choice to become apparent." She turned her attention back to Simone. "Come on, baby. Your Auntie Tamara needs to counsel with herself for a while."

"Now see, that is not even right..."

"It may not be right, but it's true. I'm going to leave you with your thoughts 'cause I see you need to play this whole thing out."

"Fine!"

"By the way, my girlfriend Adrian is having an art exhibit, and you're officially invited. We're going to have dinner afterward, and you can finally meet my other good friends. I had her send you an invitation, so put the date on your calendar. It's next week on Wednesday." Felicia broke into a big smile. "That concludes my business for today. Gotta go!"

It was Tamara's turn to stare at Felicia. "Umm...you know..."

She was interrupted by the intercom buzzing. Stella's voice announced, "It's that man for you on line one."

Tamara pushed the button on the phone. "I believe that is Mr. Davis to you," she told Stella.

Felicia's eyebrows shot up, and she gathered the rest of her belongings. "Ooh, a first and last name. I'm really making progress."

Her back was already to Tamara as she headed out the door, so the glare leveled at her was wasted.

Felicia stopped and turned, her eyes intense and serious. "Be careful." With that she was gone.

Tamara reached for the phone and pressed another button. The warm, mellow voice on the other end quickly made her forget Felicia's warning. She'd been careful all her life. Now it was time to live a little. She liked how it felt to be a desired woman.

"Hey there! I'm on my way." And indeed she was.

twenty-four

Jamilah settled down onto the worn couch her mother refused to part with. Looking around the room she heaved a sigh. She didn't know why her mother insisted on staying in the same apartment she'd lived in all these years. She had long since earned enough money to move to a nicer neighborhood and safer environment, and yet she chose to remain in the place that held less-than-pleasant memories for Jamilah. The stigma connected to the projects and her address had followed her all the way through school. But her mother had never been moved by what other folks thought.

Her mother's simplistic reasoning was that this was where all her friends were, and she was reluctant to build a new life at this "late hour in the day," as she always put it. She clearly had her routine. For as long as Jamilah could remember, her mother would rise before the sun came up. Sitting in her prayer corner in the living room, she would open her Bible and the prayer journal where she recorded every request she'd ever made to God and the people she cared about. Pouring over the list of names, she would intercede for others.

The whole neighborhood knew about that list, and there were frequent knocks on her door with requests to be added to it. After she exhausted the list, she'd hum a song to God and then sit in silence, as if waiting for His reply. After a time of silence she would open her Bible and intently study a passage. Slowly she would shut the worn book and reverently fold her hands on top of it, closing her eyes as if to seal into her memory what she'd read. Again she would wait, and then she'd make final notes in her journal…as if she'd received closing comments from on high.

After that she would set the table, make breakfast, wake Jamilah to eat and check what she was going to wear to school, and then leave her to finish getting dressed. Her mother's clients awaited her. She treated her cleaning jobs as if she were off to work at a bank or law firm. "You should always be on time no matter what. It's a sign that you are serious about what you're doing," she always said. "'Cause if you aren't there, someone is always ready and willing to take your place." While Jamilah couldn't see having pride in cleaning other people's homes, her mother was quick to point out the value of serving others and waxing eloquent on the honor of lowliness. She also reminded her little daughter that Jesus came to earth to serve and not to be served. Besides, somebody had to clean rich folks' houses. They were too busy doing whatever made them rich, and it would be a pity for those pretty homes to go to pot.

Obviously her mom was good at what she did. Her clients loved her and showed it by paying her well and loading her down with things they were done with. Her mother viewed it as God's provision. Beautiful clothing, china, even some pieces of jewelry found their way into their humble little apartment, causing Jamilah to believe they were far richer than they really were…except for the looks she got when she told people her address. Having all these fine things was all the more reason for them to move out of the projects, in her opinion. But her mother didn't believe in "cutting her garment bigger than the cloth they had."

"That's why folks are so much in debt and in trouble. Living beyond their means. You can't place a price on peace of mind. Owe no man nothing, that's what the Word says, and I agree. We are doing just fine, Jamilah. We've got a roof over our heads, food on the table, fine china, and good friends. That's plenty to be thankful for."

That was all well and fine for her mother, but the moment Jamilah graduated from school she put as much distance as she could between the Southside Project and her. She moved to the prestigious north side of town. Not able to completely shake her mother's sensibilities, she'd moved into a small studio. When she'd saved enough to get a bigger place, she'd found a loft in her price range in an up-and-coming neighborhood…but within blocks of the Northside Project.

Jamilah chuckled and shook her head. Her mother's housecleaning had blossomed into a business. Over the years, as more and more of her clients' friends sought her services, she'd enlisted the help of friends to keep up with demand. Soon other women who needed work flocked to her door. Taking a small commission from the women she referred to others, her mother had made a comfortable living. She felt it was her ministry to help others. And so it was. Now she only worked for one family. They had paid Jamilah's college costs out of gratitude and appreciation for her mother's years of dedicated service. Jamilah's mother was still a beautiful woman with not a line on her face. She was petite and shapely enough to draw many a man's attention, which she chose to ignore. She kept her hair pulled back in a neat bun at the nape of her neck. Everything about her radiated peace from the simplicity of her life.

Jamilah looked around the room, taking it in. Small, comfortable, and clean, it looked the same as when she was growing up except for a new coat of paint on the walls. Her mother set the last dish on the table and looked at her, placing her hands on her hips.

"Did you hear anything I just said? Where is your mind, girl?"

"My mind is on the rolls and sweet potatoes you just put on that table! And I did hear what you said. You said, 'These young girls just don't clean like we did back in the day. They want a job, but they don't want to do the work.'" Jamilah mimicked her mother perfectly and broke into a grin. "Did I get it right?"

"You are impossible! Yes, you did, and never mind. Obviously you don't feel the depth of my concern. This generation has a lot to learn about service. Fooling around with them, my reputation is liable to be ruined and I'll have to go back to work myself." She wagged a serving spoon at Jamilah. "I know what I'm going to do. I'm going to stop hiring them and just find older women who understand the value of doing things right."

"You have a point there, Mama. But you have to understand that parents have a lot to do with the attitude of young people these days. Young adults have no work ethic because, for the most part, parents aren't instilling those values in their kids anymore. As a matter of fact, it seems they leave raising their kids to teachers these days."

"You have a point. I hear younger mothers talking, saying, 'I don't want my kids to go through what I went through,' and I think, 'But isn't that what made you the person you are today?' All this saving kids from hard times by giving them everything is making a bunch of spoiled brats with no character or work ethic. And I can't find a scripture to support 'time out' in my Bible anywhere. Whatever happened to a good, old-fashioned spanking? I tell you, I endured plenty of them and lived to tell about it. Well, don't get me started. Come and eat before the food gets cold."

Jamilah chuckled. This was her mother's favorite bone of contention—old folks versus young folks. The great generational divide. She headed to the kitchen to wash her hands. Grabbing one of the rolls from a baking sheet on the counter, she bit into it and sighed. Her mother baked some serious rolls. And every weekend she put some out for the kids in the neighborhood who came by to eat all the delights she created and then stayed for a Bible story. That was the agreement: free treats in exchange for hearing something from the Word of God. *Perhaps that's where my love of teaching came from.* Jamilah remembered the pride she felt as the young people paid rapt attention to her mother. They respected her and loved her, even when they grew older. While many folks in the neighborhood suffered from the rampant crime in the projects, their home remained untouched. The unspoken code was "You don't mess with Mrs. Williams. She good people." Her mother

was an anchor for many in the midst of mayhem and peace in the
middle of countless storms.

And she was still that for Jamilah. Sitting down to dinner and
bowing her head in prayer, she took a deep breath, releasing all the
worries and stresses that had been accumulating over the last few
months. "Amen."

Her mother lifted her head from prayer, took a bite, and then
looked straight at Jamilah. "So, what's on your mind?"

"Nothing…" Jamilah didn't know how to broach the subject on
her heart. She couldn't bear to have her mother disagree with what
she wanted to do.

"Don't give me that. You're talking to your mother. I know you.
Your mind has been churning ever since you came in the door. So you
want to tell me or do I have to ask Jesus?"

"No, you don't have to ask Jesus. I'm thinking about fostering or
adopting a child." Jamilah held her breath, waiting for her mother's
response.

Her mother studied her quietly. "That's a big deal, don't you think?"
Then she smiled. "I'm proud of you, Jamilah."

Relief flooded over her. "Really? You're not going to tell me it's too
hard? Or I need a husband first?"

"Well, you know I'm not from the school of sitting around waiting
for a man to show up before getting on with your life. As for it being too
hard, well, that's relative, isn't it? After all, I raised you by myself, and
you turned out all right, didn't you? I rest my case. There's a difference
between birthin' babies and being a mother. I raised you to serve others
whatever way God puts on your heart. And even though in a perfect
world I would have you married to Dwayne and having babies…"

"Mother!"

"Don't mother me! And don't tell me that wouldn't put you over
the moon. But I'm glad to see you're not waiting for life to happen.
Should God say so, Dwayne will have to take whatever comes with
the package. So I say go for it!"

"Mama, thank you! I pray I can be half as good a mother as you've been to me." Jamilah's eyes misted.

"Oh, I'm sure you'll be better than that." Her mother looked at her intently...and then past her, as if seeing something behind her. She looked back at Jamilah. "Baby, sometimes the path to your dreams can be difficult, but God always comes through. Remember that. I'm just going to believe God that somehow, someway He'll work things out for you to get that little girl that's on your heart. Ari, that's her name, right?"

Jamilah's mouth flew open. "How do you know? I..."

"You should know by now never to underestimate a praying woman or your mother...especially when they're one and the same. God tells me things. I can't say I know the end of the matter. All I can tell you is to stand in faith and leave the rest to God."

"That seems to be the message of the hour," Jamilah said, thinking back to her conversation with Dwayne.

"That should be the message always. Remember, He is God; you are not. And that is a good thing, baby girl. Now shut up and eat your food before it gets cold."

Jamilah knew that was the end of the discussion for now, and that was fine with her. She was perfectly in line with focusing on what she could control, which was the moment at hand and some mighty fine dining. For a brief moment she considered asking her mother exactly what she was praying about when it came to her and Dwayne but then thought better of it. No sense dwelling on that either. That too was beyond her control.

twenty-five

Tamara lingered in the doorway and smoothed her dress before entering the restaurant.

"You look absolutely beautiful." The voice coming from her side made her almost jump out of her skin.

"Oh! Kevin, you scared me!"

"Did I?…Or *do* I?" He was studying her while pressing in close for a kiss. She loved that about him. She'd always envied couples that she saw in the midst of PDA and had wondered what it felt like to let the whole world know you are in love.

In love. She couldn't believe the thought even entered her mind. And yet she had to admit that she was really falling for Kevin. He'd been totally intentional from the first time they met, pursuing her passionately. He'd wined and dined her, taken her to art exhibits, the theatre, and more. She was seeing a new side of Chicago. She discovered there was a whole level of society interaction and cultural affairs she'd missed that was exciting and vibrant. People were moving and shaking and going places. They had and exuded an energy that made her come alive. She even managed to pick up a few new clients.

Kevin proudly introduced her to his colleagues. They'd been admiring and even a bit flirtatious at times. When she mentioned this to him, he laughed it off, saying they had good taste but she should remember she belonged to him—no matter what they might offer. "She belonged to him." She liked that. It felt good to belong to someone. Kevin was thoughtful, romantic, and debonair. She thought about the scripture that said "he who finds a wife finds a good thing." She'd always told other women they didn't need to pursue a man. That if he was interested, he would do the pursuing. And that is exactly what Kevin did, proving her point. Morning, noon, and night he called, saying he wanted to be the first and last voice she heard every day. She could count the times she had called him on one hand because he always beat her to the punch. Yes, it had been a whirlwind romance, and she was loving every moment of it.

She was grateful that Jamilah had been too busy to be around to barrage her with questions or voice her disapproval of her "missionary dating." So far religion hadn't been a problem. Kevin honored the fact that she wouldn't sleep with him and stuck to choosing activities that kept them out and about where temptation couldn't close in on them. That didn't mean she didn't have to beat her own flesh down at times. The first time he really kissed her, it was like he invented the art of it. She had to keep herself from sliding to the floor. Rendered breathless and speechless, she opened the door and backed into her apartment, closing the door on his smiling face. She heard him laugh as he left, not pressing the issue, and she thanked God for deliverance.

So far she managed to dance around the issue of their intimacy quite effectively, but the elephant in the room was growing larger as the weeks went by and their feelings for one another grew.

"For you my love," Kevin said, interrupting her thoughts. He was leaning forward, smiling conspiratorially, and handing her a gift-wrapped envelope.

"What is it?" She felt like a little girl in a candy store.

"Open it and see."

She opened the envelope and smiled as the light of comprehension came and she focused on a vacation brochure for a tropical paradise.

"Oh my!"

"I take it that means yes?"

"Yes what?"

"Yes, you'll go, silly. I have a business conference in Grand Cayman right before Memorial Day. I thought we'd make it a getaway for the holiday weekend. I promise to behave if you will."

Tamara didn't know if she could say the same, but she wasn't about to turn down a free island vacation.

"I will go on one condition."

"You name it."

"That we have separate rooms." She watched his face for a reaction. It remained passive. "You may behave, but I may not." She decided to tease him to soften her stance. She didn't want to come off too religious, but that was also the truth. She was self-aware enough to admit that at this stage of the game she didn't trust herself.

With a slow, seductive smile, he said, "Well, I can't have you seducing me now, can I? I think I can arrange an extra room—if you insist."

"I do." She heaved a sigh of relief. He was so sweet. She reached out to touch his hand. "Thank you for understanding."

"No problem. It's all about being with you. Now, let's have dinner."

He then launched into an account of his day, painting a colorful tale of crazy clients and financial high jinks that had her laughing all the way through the meal. This was the life she'd always dreamed of. Being romanced by a handsome, successful man who was confident and in control. It was so refreshing to have a man who knew what he was doing—from ordering the right wine to selecting just the right weekend getaway. And he gave fabulous gifts, such as the beautiful bracelet he'd placed on her wrist.

"For dessert everyone should have a little ice," he said, looking at how the tennis bracelet lay just so on her wrist.

"Kevin! This is too expensive. I can't accept this."

"Why? Aren't you worth it?"

"Of course I am. It's just that…"

"That what? That you've never had a man who knew how to treat you before? Or should I say one who treated you the way you *should* be treated?"

She hated to admit that what he said was true. So she tipped up her chin and smiled instead, watching the light dance off the diamonds. It was absolutely beautiful. Wait until Jamilah sees this. *Jamilah!* She would never approve. She would think Kevin was way too slick and had unsavory intentions. Yes, Jamilah would hit the ceiling if she knew about this.

As she settled into Kevin's car for the ride home a tug-of-war began within her. Everything that she knew spiritually and everything she wanted in the flesh collided. She could hear her mother's voice saying, "Baby, if you've got to keep secrets, that's enough to let you know that what you're doing is not right." And Tamara knew that, but she didn't want to hear it right now. She was frustrated. How could something that felt so right be so wrong? All she wanted was a man to make her feel like a woman. To make her feel valued and loved…and she finally had that. Despite any warnings that Jamilah or her mother gave her, she felt she had to take this chance. Couldn't God redeem it the way He redeemed Felicia's life? It wasn't as if she hadn't tried to wait for a "saved" man. She had waited…and waited…and waited. And no one had come. Those that had straggled onto her path were weak and indecisive at best. They seemed to have lost their masculinity when they found salvation. The only great men she'd met who loved and served God were already married. So what did God want from her? Could He really blame her for grasping at happiness when she got the opportunity?

Besides, she wasn't doing anything wrong. She'd told Kevin she was a Christian and didn't believe in sex outside marriage. He'd said he would respect her wishes, and that it wasn't about sex, it was about being with her. This was refreshing and quite different from what she'd experienced in the past. She had encountered more trouble trying to maintain her sanctification with the men in the church than with

Kevin, who didn't profess to be Christian. He'd been raised in the church but strayed away after witnessing what he viewed as hypocritical behavior. He said he was fine with God all by himself. "At least I don't play games with Him."

In light of what she'd witnessed with Corinne's ruse of a marriage, Tamara was prone to agree with his viewpoint. She decided to ride it out and hope for the best. Kevin might come around, and that would solve all her problems. Except the real problem was her generally bad attitude toward God, which was also a difficult thing for her to reconcile. She loved Him. She just didn't like the life she felt He wanted her to live.

Though she intellectually understood that in God's mind life was all about the long-term journey and the process of becoming what He wanted her to be, she felt He had taken all the pruning, purging, and refining to the extreme. Why did some people get to get married first and then learn all their lessons while others had to struggle alone year after year? And to what end? This had been her one-sided discussion with God for months now. She heard no reply when she asked Him this question. Jamilah had told her once that she'd learned when God didn't answer your question, you needed to pick another question because you were asking the wrong one. Well, she didn't want to change her question. She wanted an answer to this one.

What was the point of the exercise she was tortured to endure? How could she come out better if all the waiting led to her having a bad attitude with God? She didn't want to, but she felt herself spinning deeper and deeper into cynicism, second-guessing God and His Word at every turn. She didn't know if the things she'd previously believed and insisted on were really necessary, and yet she was afraid to completely cross the line in the opposite direction because she wasn't quite sure. So she clung to the basics. But even some of those were slipping from her grasp. She had a vision of packing her bags and walking away from Him. It made her sad, but she wanted what she wanted, and she wouldn't deny herself any longer.

As she withdrew from God she felt a void she couldn't explain. Her prayer life dried up from true intimacy with God to almost a courtesy call. The lens of her spirit changed, shifting her outlook on life to one of negativity except in those moments when she was distracted by Kevin's charm and attention.

"Hey, are you with me?" Kevin's voice broke into her thoughts.

"Very much so!" She noticed they were pulling up in front of her building.

"So where were you? Were you on the beach already...without me?"

"No way! I wouldn't go without you. It just wouldn't be the same."

"Good! I'm glad to know that. Which reminds me...I have something else for you."

"You do?"

"You sit right there and let me get it." With that he was out of the car. After opening the trunk he reappeared and opened her door. Extending his hand to help her out, he presented her with a Louis Vuitton suitcase.

"Since it was such short notice on our holiday weekend, I packed for you."

"What?"

"Complete with swimsuit, evening gown, golf outfit. You can exchange what you don't like. I'm pretty sure I got your size right." He was grinning like a Cheshire cat.

"But how did you know I would say yes?"

"Let's just say I'm an optimist." He leaned forward, kissing her lightly on the tip of her nose, each cheek, and finally landing a soft whisper of a kiss on her lips. "Let me help you to the door, and then I must be off. Late client meeting. I'll call you when I get home, okay?"

"Okay." Shaking her head in disbelief, she followed him into her apartment building.

Depositing her at the front door, he turned to the doorman. "Take care of this for her, will you?" Giving him a twenty dollar bill and the suitcase, Kevin shook his hand. "Thanks, man." And he was gone.

Tamara sifted through her feelings that were tumbling over one another like a tidal wave. Avoiding the eyes of Cedric, the doorman who was looking at her quite curiously, she headed toward the elevator, finding great relief when the door opened immediately, as if anticipating her. She entered and as the doors closed the thought slowly dawned on her that she was in way over her head.

twenty-six

Tamara frowned as she entered her apartment. Had she left the light on? She jumped as her mother rose from the couch. That was the problem with giving people keys to your place, even though her mother usually called before she came.

"Mom! You scared me." She couldn't take many more surprises in one night. She jumped again as someone knocked on the door. She opened it. It was Cedric delivering the suitcase.

"I was trying to tell you your mother was here before you got on the elevator."

Tamara's mother eyed the suitcase, eyebrows up, before returning her gaze to Tamara's face. "Hmm, fancy. Going somewhere?"

"As a matter of fact I am." Then remembering that Cedric was still standing there, she turned and said, "Thanks, Cedric." As he turned away she closed the door. "I'm going to Grand Cayman with Kevin."

"With Kevin?" Her mother paused a beat. "The mysterious Kevin I haven't met yet? The one that's had my baby running all over the city for the past two-and-a-half months so I can't catch up with my own daughter?"

"Oh Mother…"

"Don't oh mother me! What's in the suitcase?"

"Kevin bought me clothes for the trip."

"Really? This Kevin is something else! Let's see…island getaway, expensive luggage, clothes. And I take it he bought you the bling on your wrist too?"

Tamara could feel it coming. "What are you implying?"

"Kevin sounds too good to be true, and usually when something is too good to be true, there's a lie in the middle of it. Something in my spirit is waving a caution sign."

Tamara didn't like what she was hearing. Her mother had the uncanny ability to predict the future. Usually when she didn't feel good about something, there was good reason to be wary. Every time she said something it seemed to come to pass. But what did she know about Kevin? Tamara countered. She hasn't even met him. Perhaps she resents the fact that she hasn't been invited to scope him out yet. Tamara had been waiting until she knew where the relationship was going before she introduced Kevin around. She'd long grown weary of taking men home and then being asked what happened to them when the relationships faded to black. She waved away the butterflies of worry that fluttered in her stomach from her mother's cautionary advice.

"Why does something have to be wrong just because he buys me presents and showers me with attention? Would you prefer he be like the other deadbeats I've dated?"

"Don't get defensive with me, young lady. 'What will it profit a man if he gains the whole world, and loses his soul?' Presents don't mean a thing. I'm more concerned about you. You're different."

"Different how?"

"Well, first off you're a little too swayed by all the surface stuff. You've become an enigma. I can't reach you by phone. You don't return calls. You don't remember appointments. Did you forget you were supposed to meet me for dinner this evening? You don't think I came all the way in from the suburbs just to check on you, did you?"

Tamara's hand flew to her mouth. "Oh no! Mom, I am soooo sorry! I completely forgot."

"Well, you'd better not forget how I raised you! I don't care how fine or generous Mr. Mystery Kevin is. Watson women don't lose their minds the minute some man comes along. And we certainly don't fall over just because they present us with a bauble!"

Tamara knew her mother was right. After her father died Tamara had watched her mom navigate the waters of reentering the dating scene. Shapely and attractive, she hadn't been at a loss for suitors. And she had fielded them with such wisdom and class that Tamara and Jamilah said she should write a book on how to capture a man's heart. Her only reply was "Watch and learn."

A devout Christian, she didn't compromise her standards. As a matter of fact, that was part of her process of elimination. If the man in question couldn't deal with or adhere to her convictions, he was history. "I only need one man...the right man," she often said. She told Tamara and Jamilah that if a man didn't want to break God's heart he wouldn't break theirs either. She never wavered in her standard, and her resolve paid off. Finally God gave her the man of her dreams. Tamara had asked God for a clone of her mother's husband several times. Not only was he handsome and successful, he was also grounded in the things of God. When he came into her mother's life he was the one who raised the bar by insisting they pray together and discuss God's Word daily.

Before she met her stepdad Tamara often commented to Jamilah, "Now that's what I'm saying. How come the woman always has to prop the man up spiritually? Where are all the real men?" But then she thought it was so cute and wonderful to see her mother on the phone discussing the agreed-upon passage every evening. And when her stepdad had come to ask if it was all right to propose to her mother, wanting to do everything decently and in order, Tamara gave her blessing enthusiastically. They had a dream wedding and honeymoon, and her mother hadn't stopped smiling since, remarking that he was worth the wait. He was the essence of a true godly man, wonderful husband, and fine representation of what a man should be. He'd been the guideline for Tamara and Jamilah...until now. Until Kevin.

Her mother was still standing there, looking at her. "Well? What do you have to say for yourself? What do you really know about this man?"

"I know how he makes me feel. He's funny, sweet, generous, and attentive…"

"But what do you really know about him, Tamara? All I've heard about in passing is you were on your way to dinner or the theatre or somewhere else. What about his friends and family? Have you been to his church? To his house? After all this time you should know more than how he makes you feel. How much solid and pertinent information do you plan on collecting about him while you're in Grand Cayman? Make sure he's not collecting anything from you that he shouldn't be…and vice versa. I don't think it's appropriate for you to be going. You're setting yourself up for a fall. How are you going to maintain holiness off in seclusion with no accountability?"

"Mom, I…"

"Oh what am I saying? Obviously you've made up your mind to go. Does Kevin have a relationship with Jesus?"

"Here we go! I'm not going to get into the whole saved issue."

"What? Tamara, what has gotten into you? All right, Satan, where have you hidden my daughter!" She looked around the room.

"Mother, stop it! I've met a lot of his friends."

"But you haven't met his family. I'm assuming that because he hasn't met yours. And yet you're going off to a remote island with him. This is not good."

"Mother, I am a grown woman. What if you lived in another city? You probably wouldn't meet him until we were close to being engaged or already engaged, so what difference does it make?"

"The difference is that I don't live in another city. I am right here. And you have ceased being the transparent and accountable daughter I once knew, which tells me you are in trouble—whether you choose to acknowledge it or not. I suggest you get on your knees and in God's face to get some discernment, before you find yourself in a major mess that even your psychology can't solve for you. You can't think your way out of a broken heart. And you've got enough clients to prove that, I'm sure."

Tamara could feel her mouth tremble. "Mother, I have not slept with Kevin and won't until...or if...we get married! I told him I wasn't going to compromise my faith or my standards. Yes, I had a lot of questions for God even before he came along. I didn't want to introduce you to Kevin because I didn't want to waste your time if he wasn't going to remain in my life. I'm tired of answering questions about what happened to this one or that one. And maybe I don't expect Kevin and me to get serious at this point. Maybe I'll just enjoy myself when I can, free of expectations, if that's all right with you."

"No, Tamara, that is not all right with me. Where is your faith? If 'faith is the substance of things hoped for, the evidence of things not seen,' that means we stand with God even when we can't see anything. That's what faith is all about. Just because God didn't give you what you wanted today doesn't mean He won't tomorrow. Not now doesn't mean never. It means He's waiting for the right person and the right time because His blessings are always perfect. You can't give him a deadline."

She folded her arms and cocked her head sideways, eyes still pinned penetratingly on Tamara. "So what happens when God doesn't do things the way you want and when you want? Do you stop loving Him and serving Him? Then I have to ask, Did you really love God in the first place? Because true love doesn't have conditions. It doesn't bail on the relationship just because the beloved doesn't do things according to a person's plan. If that was the case, God would dump all of us!"

"I can't handle this tonight, okay? I'm tired." She dissolved into tears.

Her mother moved to hold her. "Aw, baby, I totally get that piece. But you have my life as an example of what waiting can produce. Don't you know how lonely I was after your father died? Sometimes it's even worse when you know what it's like to be loved and cared for by a good man. To suddenly find yourself on your own, having to learn how to survive and care for a young daughter alone was more than a notion. I cried myself to sleep many a night. But I had no choice. I had to trust God. I could have fallen for the first man who came along, but that would have been a disservice to you and a lack of honor for your father. I couldn't accept less than the best. So I waited. Twelve years I waited. I often wondered what was taking God so long and why He allowed life to pan out the way it did. But He didn't owe me an explanation. He is God, and He knows what's best. When I made peace with Him and accepted His will for my life, I told Him if I never married again I would be fine with just Him. Then He brought Roland into my life."

She took Tamara's face in her hands and looked into her eyes. "It's got to be God first or nothing will work long term, whether you like it or not. He will not be ruled by you or moved by your pouting, whining, or acting out. You will only get yourself into trouble, you hear me? And I've got the scars to prove it."

Tamara frowned. "What are you talking about? You always do the right thing."

Her mother sighed. "I haven't always. We've all been young and foolish, trust me." She studied her. "Baby, I love you very much. I'm not trying to rain on your parade, but I'm telling you don't do it. Run—do not just walk—away from this man. He will hurt you. I feel it to the bottom of my soul. Take your heart back while you can. It's a hard climb back from falling when you've thrown grace out the window." She kissed her. "That's all I'm going to say. You're a grown woman. I'm just the mail carrier. I've delivered the message and now I'm leaving." She headed toward the door, but then looked back. "Even as I tell you this, I know you have to finish your journey 'cause everybody's got to walk in their own shoes. I've certainly run down a few pairs myself. I'll see you, baby girl." She let herself out, quietly closing the door.

Tamara stewed in the swirl of her emotions. What her mother said made perfect sense. But it rolled around in her head with her personal theology and stopped short of her heart. She didn't want her mother to be right, and she hoped she wouldn't be. Perhaps just once her mother would be the one who was surprised.

Dragging the suitcase to her room, anxious to open it and see the goodies inside, her excitement was dampened by the anxiety that was building inside of her. She reviewed the questions her mother had asked. Some of them hadn't occurred to her. She hadn't been to Kevin's house. She hadn't met his family. And she would have told any client of hers that this was cause to be wary.

The phone rang.

"Hello?" She anticipated a last warning from her mother, but it was Kevin.

"The thought occurred to me that it might be too late by the time I was finished with my meeting, and I didn't want to wake you, so I'm calling to tuck you into bed now. Did you like your new things?"

Warmth flooded her being. Truly her mother was worried about nothing.

"Actually I had unexpected company, and I'm just opening the suitcase so your timing is perfect!"

"Oh? Anybody I know?"

"Just my mother, and you'll meet her soon enough."

"I'm looking forward to it. Is she as beautiful as you?"

"Well, if there's any truth to the rumor that if you want to know what the woman you are seeing will look like in twenty years look at her mother, I think you'll be pleased."

Kevin laughed. "I suspected that. Well, beautiful, go and enjoy your findings. I'm headed into my meeting."

"All right. Hey, thanks in advance."

"No need to thank me; it's an even exchange. Pleasure for pleasure. I'll call you in the morning."

"Okay. Good night." Hanging up the phone she turned her attention to the suitcase. Unzipping it she was greeted by a wisp of cream-colored gauze, beautiful and very expensive. As a matter of fact all the outfits were. And they were all the right size. In the midst of her mini Christmas experience, her mother's words came back to haunt her, "If something's too good to be true there's a lie in the middle of it." She certainly hoped that wasn't true.

twenty-seven

Jamilah crossed the street, balancing the dry cleaning she'd collected on her way to work and the papers she'd corrected the night before. Just as she made it to the first step a wind gusted, flipping the cleaning wrappers upward and causing her to drop the homework as she frantically tried pull the plastic from her face.

"I got it, Miss Williams!" Ari's little voice piped through the mayhem as she and several other students scattered to retrieve the flying papers.

"Thanks, kids!" Jamilah looked down at the faces looking up at her. Extending her arm she gathered them like a mother hen, shooing her brood inside and out of the sudden burst of rain. Though it was May, that was no guarantee of good weather. Just when people thought it was going to be warm, the weather would play tricks as a last-minute reminder of who was really in control—Mother Nature. And she would let the sun stay only when she said so. Chicago's forecast was dependably unpredictable until mid July. Then the sun displayed consistent glory.

As they herded into the classroom, Jamilah took note of Ari's appearance. She could always tell when Ari had been left to her own devices because her hair would be in disarray. Her naturally curly hair was hard for a little girl to manage on her own. Today she'd attempted to make two ponytails, but they were hopelessly lopsided and one was in danger of escaping its holder any moment. Jamilah gave the class an assignment and when they'd settled into deep concentration, she took a tour around the room, looking over each student's shoulder to check their progress before finally reaching Ari's desk. She tapped her gently on the shoulder, and when the girl looked up Jamilah motioned for her to follow. Ari hesitated but she gave her an encouraging nod to follow her out of the classroom. Gently she took her by the hand and led her to the girls' bathroom.

"How are you, Ari? I see you did your hair today." Jamilah smiled.

Ari brightened. "How did you know?"

"Oh, I could tell. It's very nice, but do you mind if I help you out a bit?"

"No, Miss Williams, that's fine. I couldn't get it to do exactly what I wanted it to. Mama was asleep so I did it myself."

"You are such a good girl. I think you did a great job. I'm just going to adjust this one right here so it matches the other one, okay?"

"Okay." Ari stood perfectly still while Jamilah took the ponytail down, redid it, and gently brushed it into place.

The door swung open, causing them both to start. Miss Chavez, the assistant principal, stopped when she saw their looks of alarm.

"Is there a problem?"

"No, you just startled us. Ari was having a problem with one of her ponytails, so we were just adjusting it. Come on, Ari, let's get back to class." Jamilah guided Ari gently past Miss Chavez, who was looking at her suspiciously.

"And who is watching your classroom while you're out taking a beauty break, Miss Williams?"

"My classroom is fine, Miss Chavez. They are in the midst of an assignment, and we've been gone less than five minutes."

"I don't think it's appropriate to leave your classroom unattended."

"Neither is it appropriate to have this discussion at this time." Jamilah purposefully looked at Ari and then back at Miss Chavez.

Miss Chavez looked at her and opened her mouth to continue, but Jamilah decided not to give her that option.

"Now, if you will excuse me..." And with that she let the door close behind her and she and Ari walked back down the hallway.

"We're not going to get in trouble are we, Miss Williams?"

"No. We didn't do anything wrong. Miss Chavez just has control issues..."

"Control issues?"

"Never mind. You're too young to understand—and hopefully you'll never have to."

"Oh." Ari walked on in silence. Just before entering the classroom she turned suddenly and gave Jamilah a big hug around her waist, which was as high as she could reach. "Thank you, Miss Williams. You're the greatest."

Jamilah hugged her back and then straightened, sensing someone staring at her. She turned just in time to see Miss Chavez disappearing around the corner. She was sure this wouldn't be the last she heard about this, but she decided not to worry about it right now. "So are you! Now, get back to work," she said, shooing Ari into the classroom.

She smiled as Ari happily skipped back to her desk. She took her own seat, studying Ari as she bent her head to concentrate on her assignment. The teacher sighed. Summer was coming. She didn't know what she was going to do when she couldn't see Ari. When she would have no way of knowing how she was doing. She'd filled out all the paperwork required for foster care and was currently going through the interview process. Next would come a psychological evaluation. She'd been playing phone tag with Tamara in an effort to find out what she should expect, but the best she'd been able to do was leave a message and then listen to hers. Tamara certainly seemed busy these days. Jamilah knew her friend was seeing the man they'd seen at the restaurant. Tamara made a passing remark in one of her messages about being on her way out to dinner with him but had remained vague on the details.

Jamilah wondered about this mystery man. He was certainly good looking, but that didn't mean he was any good. She tried not to jump to conclusions. Just because Tamara didn't say much about him didn't necessarily mean they were doing something wrong. Plus, she couldn't address something she hadn't been given entrée to discuss. Still, she couldn't shake her feeling that if all was well, Tamara would be calling to share her excitement.

It wasn't like Tamara to drop off the face of the planet like this. She'd been getting stranger and stranger in the past months, and Jamilah was at a loss about what to do. She honestly didn't know what else to say to her friend that she hadn't said already. *Is she still smarting because I warned her about the man?* she wondered. She knew Tamara well enough to know that no news usually meant she had news she wasn't willing to report because she didn't want feedback.

Jamilah hadn't seen her friend at church for several Sundays, and she hadn't been able to pin her down for a get-together. This had been fine with her as she tried to balance her own schedule of teaching, doing volunteer work at The Kid's Club at the mission downtown, and taking the classes necessary to qualify for foster care.

Jamilah toyed with whether she should call her again or not and decided against it. It was a no-win situation. She knew they would end up arguing, and she had too much on her plate to get bogged down with going around and around about what God owed Tamara. Besides, God didn't need Jamilah's help to protect His reputation. Perhaps it was best to get out of the way and let the two of them duke it out, although Jamilah already knew who would win. When all was said and done, she was convinced Tamara had already decided God wasn't good, though she refused to admit it. Her actions clearly revealed what she felt in her heart. Jamilah had seen a plaque somewhere that said, "Never explain yourself to anyone. Because the person who likes you doesn't need it, and the person who dislikes you won't believe it." God surely knew that. Perhaps that's why He didn't bother to explain Himself or just give Tamara what she wanted in an effort to win her undivided affection. He knew that giving Tamara her heart's desire would divide her heart even further. Jamilah hoped that eventually Tamara would end her war with God and trust Him. She resolved to pray about it and avoid heated arguments.

Jamilah also had her own selfish reasons for not pursuing her overly frank and pragmatic friend. She was relieved not to be in a situation where Tamara might try to talk her out of becoming a foster parent. She couldn't bear to be ridiculed or told she was setting herself up for disappointment. Out of the corner of her eye she could see Mr. Parker observing her from the hallway. When her eyes met his, he resumed walking. She was sure Miss Chavez had practically broken her neck getting back to report their little exchange in the girls' restroom. Oh well, let her if she had nothing better to do with herself. Unhappy people were always trying to make others as unhappy as they were. Jamilah refused to enter into the assistant principal's petty little fray. If that's what she needed to do to make herself feel necessary, so be it. She, on the other hand, would not allow herself to be distracted. Right now her main care was what was going to happen to Ari. God had to do something...and soon.

twenty-eight

Corinne idly played with her pearls as she listened to the chatter around her. The usual drivel, in her opinion. They sat in the Zodiac Room at Neiman Marcus, having their usual First Ladies' Luncheon. The title "First Ladies" always made her laugh. *First for what?* she'd wondered the first time she'd been addressed as such. Less and less she considered her role as the wife of a pastor a special privilege. It was a difficult life at best. Every woman at the table was married to a pastor and had her struggles with how their church consumed their husbands and left very little for them to enjoy. This was the time they generally commiserated among themselves. Between accepting the fact that the church and its congregation would always be the other woman in the middle of their marriages and dealing with the interesting quirks that every "manna God" they knew seemed to have, they were all in the same boat. And though they'd also heard of some pastors who didn't fit the stereotype, that was a way of life not familiar to them. Gone were the fairy tale dreams of knights in shining armor carrying them away to a land of love and romance.

Complaining was their main conversation because it was their common bond of pain. They all knew what it was like to feel second or last on their husbands' lists of things to do. This was what they'd come to accept, and they compensated by talking and throwing themselves into their own children, ministries, charity work, shopping. Some anesthetized themselves in secret with alcohol or simply became numb and oblivious. Collectively they painted on empty smiles and moved through life by putting one foot in front of the other. They had all become masters of masking their pain and looking serene enough to cause other women to envy their positions.

Corinne wondered what would happen if they held a forum and told the whole truth and nothing but the truth. The church world would probably be set on its ear, and some folks' hair would be on fire! It seemed that God knew believers could only handle a maximum of two church scandals a year, so that was all He allowed. Corinne could tell that though the wives seemed to be forthcoming on general issues that bore no direct reflection on them, there was more going on than what they were sharing. Whenever a new drama unfolded and a high profile minister got outed on the news, the comments would be reserved, sympathetic, and muted...always ending with "but for the grace of God go I." The relief that it wasn't their story being magnified for all to see was obvious.

As she sat gazing at them, she knew they all had stories. She'd heard rumors of womanizing, squandering church funds, and general wheeling and dealing that had transpired with many of their husbands. There was only one woman at the table, Barbara Mathis, who seemed to have risen above it. She was older and had such a grace about her that it was obvious she'd suffered to acquire it. She was the only one who never postured and acted as if everything was hunky-dory. She had a wonderful marriage, though she admitted it hadn't always been that way. Today her husband was balanced and supportive. Her main problem was her child, who was autistic. But she remained upbeat, displaying the patience of Job. Corinne didn't know how she managed. Whenever she shared her latest trial and triumph, the women looked at her with awe. She always ended with "God is so good!" which made everyone at the table ashamed and repentant over their own

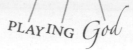

complaints on things that seemed surface in comparison. *Oh well,* Corinne decided, *we each have our cross to bear.* But she wondered if life would be easier if they put down their facades, got real, and actually supported one another.

Her inner musings were interrupted by a story unfolding at the table. A young woman at Sharon Crawford's church had been abused by her uncle for the last three years, and it had finally come out to the church leadership. And the family wanted to keep it quiet. The problem was that the uncle was a deacon at the church, and the church board was scrambling to do damage control.

"I should have known! The girl displayed all the classic signs of abuse. She was such a bright child. Very outgoing and artistic. Top of her class at school. Almost overnight she withdrew into a shell. Her mother brought her up for prayer several times. She said her grades had plummeted, and her teacher said that she was unresponsive and surly. No one could figure out what was wrong with her. We prayed for her, and she would just look at the floor. She wouldn't even look us in the eye. I mean, the girl went from Miss Effervescent to Miss Doom and Gloom. Couldn't get a smile out of her. I don't know why she didn't tell someone."

"Do you know the level of shame she endured? He probably had her thinking it was all her fault. They always say the victim blames themselves in these circumstances, you know, like abused wives do," Yvonne Dannings chimed in. Spoken like someone who should know, Corinne thought as she remembered the rumors she'd heard about Yvonnes' charismatic husband who had heavy hands.

"That's what the mother said!" Sharon Crawford was truly up in arms. "To think this could happen in church is frightening. I mean, where do you go to feel safe? The congregation is upset although they don't know who was abusing her. My husband is livid but trying to be tactful at the same time. I told him he needs to tell the man he has to step down. And then my husband needs to be real with the church about it and report him to the police. I don't think he has any other option. I don't know why we always tiptoe around these issues at church. To cover these things over is just celebrating people's bad behavior, and for what? That's what I want to know. To protect the church from scandal? But what about the girl?"

Sharon went on and on, but suddenly her words were coming from a distant place as Corinne's thoughts clamored louder than the conversation. Her stomach twisted. This girl sounded like Jada, who hadn't been herself for quite some time. Gone was the friendly, outgoing, creative daughter she once knew. Her way of dressing had even changed. She'd concluded it was just a stage her daughter was going through. And Jada had even dyed her hair dark. The soft, feminine things she used to wear had been replaced by all black or drab-colored clothing that was Goth in nature and covered her from head to toe. The girly girl was replaced by a rebellious, hard-looking tough who mimicked what "hip" teens were wearing. *Is she hiding beneath a mask to cover her beauty?* As for withdrawn…if she withdrew any further into her room they would never find her again. Her teacher had called yesterday voicing concern about her grades. She too had noted that Jada had become unresponsive and seemingly resigned to everything around her. The teacher had asked if there was trouble at home that could be contributing to the change.

"Jada used to be my best student. I hate to see this happening. I've tried talking to her, but I get nothing. I thought perhaps you would know what was going on with her."

Corinne had thanked Miss Hawkins and then made her way home. She went to the study to discuss this with Randall. As she approached she heard him shouting.

"You have to have a better reason than 'you don't want to do it anymore' to get off the worship team, Jada! You're the leader. What type of example do you think you're setting? Hmm?"

"I just need a break, that's all." Jada's voice sounded small against his booming one.

"I need a break too, but I don't get to have one! I wish it were that simple." Randall sounded exasperated. "I don't know what has gotten into you lately, but you need to get your act together! And I'm telling you right now, whatever this getup is that you have on, it's unacceptable for the stage. You can rebel on your own time, but not at church. You understand?"

"Obviously you don't!" Jada burst out of the room, practically knocking Corinne over in the hallway as she ran toward the stairs to go to her room.

Corinne was shocked. She couldn't believe Jada wanted to quit the worship team. She loved to worship; it had always been her favorite thing to do. And she was so gifted at it. Something was very wrong, but she just couldn't figure out what. She eased into the study to find Randall pacing back and forth and looking none too pleased. Now was not the time to bring up the call from Jada's teacher. That would add fuel to the fire.

Perhaps she should do a little investigating on her own. But where would she begin? Jada wasn't going to talk to her. As a matter of fact, she was sure Jada resented her. For what, she didn't know.

"Corinne, are you all right?"

Breaking out of her thoughts, she looked around.

Barbara was staring at her in concern.

She suddenly realized she was twisting her pearls to such a state that her knuckles were white. She felt the tenseness in her body.

Everyone's eyes were on her. All of a sudden she didn't care anymore. She could hardly breathe because her heart was pounding so hard.

"I'm sorry but that girl…the way you described her. She sounds just like my Jada. I've been so worried. I don't know what's wrong. I'm sorry…I…to think someone might be…oh…" She could feel the tears coming. It wasn't as if she knew anything definite, but something deep inside her spirit exploded, and she knew that Jada was in trouble. She just didn't know who the abuser was.

"You think someone is taking advantage of her?" Sharon was looking worried now. So were the others.

"Yes."

"But who?" Yvonne asked.

"I don't know...I don't know...I have to go..." Her voice was rising as panic rose in waves. She tried to stand up, but she suddenly couldn't breathe.

Barbara leaned forward to take hold of her hands.

Corinne slumped back into her chair. "Oh how could I not have known something was so very, very wrong? I've been so selfish, so consumed with my own problems."

"Take a deep breath. Tell us what's happening. Are you sure about this? It could be something else, so let's not panic," Yvonne said, taking a deep breath herself. "We all do it, Corinne." She was getting teary eyed too.

"Do what?"

"Let stuff fall between the cracks. Stuff it and just keep going. You're just one person. You can't do and know everything."

Corinne was about to ask her who she was really trying to convince when Barbara interrupted.

"I think we should calm down. Look at us! Here we all sit as if we don't know what to do. I know one thing that is always effective in situations like this...when you know nothing for sure and feel as if you can do nothing."

"What's that?" Sharon asked over the top of her wine glass.

"Pray! You do still believe in the power of prayer, don't you?" Barbara was looking at Sharon with a worried expression on her face.

Corinne let out a slightly hysterical giggle. "Oh, that's comforting. My prayers seem to be worth two cents these days...and for some time now."

"You're not alone on that one," Sharon mumbled.

Noting that maybe Sharon's "glass" was in the way, Corinne started to comment but then felt stabbed by conviction herself.

Barbara was kinder. "When you can't get a prayer through, that's what friends are for. We're in this together, Corinne, so pull yourself together and decide that you are not going to let the devil win. It's time to stop rolling over and pretending. Either you believe God will do something about your situation or you don't. And if you don't, then what's the point of us getting together? So are we in this together or not?" She looked around the table. All the women were looking at her.

"And let's get real here. Corinne is not the only woman having problems at this table. I don't know about you, but I'm tired of lunch as usual. Styling and profiling for what? To prove what? Nothing at the end of the day if our lives are falling apart around our ears. I have better things to do with my time. I say we decide to take back our families and everything else we've allowed to fall by the wayside. Let's be honest with one another and honor the rule that what gets said at this table stays at this table. Just like Vegas. Got that?"

A new side of Barbara was revealed. Corinne felt braver than she had in a long time. Besides she was desperate. She had rolled over, she could admit that. She'd been so busy feeling sorry for herself that she barely noticed her child was drowning. And now she was going to find out why. She'd had enough. She rose up in her chair. "Well I'm in. I've got nothing to lose at this point."

She was feeling like Esther, her favorite Bible heroine. "If I perish, I perish," she quoted.

Sharon lifted her glass again. "I'll drink to that!"

Corinne felt as if she was standing outside of her body listening to herself. "Sharon, put the glass down and let's pray!"

twenty-nine

Tamara was impressed. Adrian's work was amazing. As she meandered through the gallery, she was struck by how the paintings Adrian had created made her feel. There was so much emotion in her work. It pulled you in and surrounded you. This was her second collection, and the gallery was filled with people. Many had been at the unveiling of her first works and were back to purchase another painting for their collection. They oohed and aahed their way through the gallery, taking in the passionate renderings of love and romance. Felicia giggled beside her.

"Ever since Adrian got back with her husband, her style has truly gone up a notch."

"No doubt he is her inspiration. I can feel the heat coming off this one." Muriel said as she gaped at the couple on the canvas before her. They were locked in an embrace, their passion palpable. "It's almost embarrassing."

Muriel's husband, Brad, leaned forward. "Wow! And I thought we were hot, babe!"

"Brad!" Muriel yanked his arm, pulling him away from the painting. She put a finger to her lips. "Shhhh! Don't be tellin' all our biz'ness!" With that they both laughed as if they were the only ones in on the joke.

Tamara was mystified until Felicia explained, "Can you tell they waited until they got married to do 'the do'? Makes me wish I'd waited. I always wonder how much more special it would have been on our wedding night. Kind of like Christmas…" She looked a little wistful.

Tamara looked back at the couple. She was about to rationalize that she'd been just as excited about opening her presents before Christmas as waiting until the day of, but she got what Felicia was saying. There was something different about their interaction. They were tender and thoughtful, almost reverent, as if what they had was a priceless treasure. They were totally into one another, there was no doubt about that.

Felicia's inner circle was truly interesting and unique. Refreshing actually. Because she'd heard so much about them, Tamara tried to guess who was who before they were introduced. She laughed. They were so true to Felicia's descriptions that figuring out who they were wasn't difficult at all. She was surprised to discover that she was just as easy to recognize.

Adrian came toward her with her husband, Ron, in tow, looking every bit the proud supportive spouse. "You must be Tamara! Felicia has told us so much about you. I'm glad you were able to make it. You'll be joining us for dinner, won't you? Ron, stop that!" She pulled back from him as he nuzzled her neck and then turned to kiss him on the lips quickly. "Hold your fire, boy!" She laughed.

Tamara smiled. She saw Kenny come in the door. He came over and embraced Felicia while she looked up at him, paying rapt attention to what he was saying.

"How can I resist with so much energy in the room? You all are making me believe in the power of love," Tamara responded to Adrian.

"More like the power of God, honey!" A little blonde arrived, practically vibrating, while her husband looked as if he were trying to contain her energy.

"You must be Carla." Tamara laughed.

"That's me! And who might you be?"

"I'm Tamara."

A look of knowing crossed Carla's face. "Ooh! Al, this is Tamara."
Al looked puzzled, trying to decide why he should know her.

"You know...*Felicia's* Tamara." Carla spoke slowly hoping that
would clarify Tamara's identity to Al, who still looked confused. "Oh
forget it. I'll tell you later." Then turning back to Tamara she said,
"Don't worry. It's all good."

Tamara laughed again. Carla was everything Felicia had described.
Her enthusiasm was infectious. She kept them laughing all the way to
the restaurant by doing a very bad imitation of Adrian singing as they
rounded the corner by the gallery and spilled into Adrian's favorite
Armenian restaurant.

As Tamara sat and looked at all their happy faces, she reviewed
their stories. Until now they had been characters in a novel, with
Felicia sharing their adventures. There was Carla, who had introduced
Brad to Muriel, who had run for her life from his advances because
of her past. Well, her present was looking pretty wonderful as Brad
leaned forward to feed her some pita bread topped with hummus.
Carla had issues of her own, but she and Al had recently adopted
a baby girl from Ethiopia. And then there was Adrian. You would
never tell from looking at how happy she and Ron looked together
that he had left her for another woman. He was truly the proud husband tonight, beaming and hovering over his wife, fielding inquiries
about her art. And, of course, there was Tracy. She seemed like someone fun to know. After listening to her, Tamara wanted to meet her
friend...boyfriend...whatever he was. Unfortunately he didn't make
it because of a meeting at church.

"David really wanted to be here and sent his blessing, but you know
how he is. Nothing comes before his 'duties.'" Tracy made quote signs
with her fingers as she relayed his message to Adrian.

"Tell him I totally understand and appreciate the fact that he is a
man of integrity who honors his commitments." She glanced at Ron.
"Isn't that right, babe?"

"Yup, he's a keeper. I like him. Solid guy."

"Why? Because he couldn't skip one meeting at church to be here with me?" Tracy looked slightly annoyed.

"And that's a good thing, girl." It was Muriel's turn to chime in. "If he is that serious about what he's doing for God, he'll be just as serious about the promises he makes to you. Remember that."

"I never thought about it that way." Tracy brightened. "Okay, I guess I'll forgive him then."

"You should! You know what your problem is, girl? You are too used to 'no good' men to appreciate a good one. You need to get saved and go to church with him."

Brad punched Muriel to get her to stop.

She looked at him. "What?"

Adrian interrupted in an effort to change the subject. "Ahem! So, Tamara, did you enjoy the exhibit?"

Tamara swallowed the chuckle that was threatening to escape. "Yes, I did. Very much. It was so passionate, so bold, so…emotional. It was quite refreshing. I have to admit it wasn't what I was expecting."

"Really? What were you expecting?"

"Well I…how do I say this without insulting you? Because that's really not my intention. But I knew you were a Christian, and, well, your work was very hot!"

Adrian smiled at her, looking highly amused.

"Ah, I see. So Christians shouldn't be hot? Or romantic?"

"No, no, that's not what I'm saying at all."

"I mean, you do agree that God created romance?"

"Most definitely."

"And in the right context, He wants a couple to be uninhibited and…how did you put it? Hot!"

"Amen for being hot in the right context!"

It was Muriel's turn to punch Brad for this outburst.

Everyone at the table laughed.

"You all are funny and fun! Perhaps I've been hanging out with the wrong group of Christians. You seem so comfortable in the skin you're in. It's nice to see."

"They're all right as long as they leave me alone about getting saved." Tracy shot Muriel a look before turning to Tamara. "I'm the only sinner in the group."

"Now, that's not true. We're all sinners saved by grace, and we want what's best for you," Carla piped up.

"I get that piece, but it's still my journey. I have to find my way in my own time."

"I just hope you hurry up before you lose David."

"Carla!" Al looked apologetically toward Tracy and then back at Carla. "Honey, now lighten up. You know that whatever God has for Tracy will still be there at the right time. She can't choose the Lord because of David. She has to choose Him because that's what she really wants. And none of us can make her want Him. Think back…" He motioned as if trying to make her look into a crystal ball that would show her a vision of her past before she came to the Lord.

"Yeah, you're right. Forgive me for wanting to hurry up and get everybody married off. It's just such a marvelous invention of God, and I want everyone to experience it." She squeezed Al, who beamed in return.

Tamara touched Tracy's hand, feeling very protective of her. "If I may add my two cents as the only other single person at the table? You're right. You do need to decide about God for yourself. It's not an easy thing to handle sometimes, so you need to make sure your motive is all about having a relationship with Him. It can't be about anything else. That way no matter what happens—disappointments, whatever—your love for Him won't waver."

"Very well said. And now I think it's time to toast Adrian for her amazing exhibit, which I'm sure is one of many to come." Kenny lifted his glass while everyone agreed loudly.

Again Tamara was touched by their sense of togetherness and tenderness. She reflected on what she'd just said to Tracy, feeling a pinprick of conviction. She knew what she said sounded good, but she also knew it wasn't where she really lived, though somewhere in her heart she wanted to. For the first time, sitting among such a refreshing group of people who were just being Christians with nothing to prove, she considered the fact that perhaps she was unknowingly "religious," and it had robbed her joy without her noticing. She shifted in her chair. She wasn't ready to go there yet...not ready to give up what might be required if she surrendered totally to what she knew. She sighed. It was certainly far easier to tell others what their attitudes should be than it was to live it out yourself. Much easier said than done.

thirty

The plane touched down smoothly and made its way to one of the gates at Los Angeles' LAX. Lydia checked her text messages on her Blackberry as they pulled to a stop. "Happy landing. Hurry back. I'm waiting!" She smiled at the note from Brandon. She was going to miss him. She had tried to wrap up her project from Chicago, not relishing the idea of leaving him behind, but Hollywood had beckoned. And now that she was divorced, she discovered not only was she free to do as she pleased, she was also free to find a way to make a living for herself. It had never been a necessity before. She'd had the option of picking and choosing projects and working at her leisure. She couldn't afford to languish any longer. Though she would receive a nice settlement from Richard, if she wanted to maintain the standard of living she was used to, she had to get back to work.

Sylvia, her best friend, was waiting for her when she pulled her bag outside to the curb. She bounced out of the car to hug Lydia and grab her suitcase. Slamming the trunk, she grinned. "Girl, I thought you weren't ever coming back. I missed you!" She stopped, taking time to really look at her long-time friend.

"Look at you! I like the hair! It's very flattering, and it makes you look so much younger!"

Lydia smiled and bounced her new bob. "Really?"

"Really! Now get into this car and tell me everything about this man you've been running all over Chicago with. I was standing in the grocery store minding my own business and who do I see in a lip-lock but you and the finest man I've laid eyes on in a while. How old is he anyway, girl? I need to pray for you, I know!"

Lydia laughed. Sylvia was her oldest friend, and the one she felt safest with. Though they had their differences when it came to faith, Lydia had always admired Sylvia's beliefs and secretly coveted her relationship with God. When Lydia was at her lowest point, Sylvia had prayed for and with her. She truly led by example rather than making Lydia feel like a heathen, the way Richard had. They'd been friends since school. She was not in show business at all and was, for the most part, pretty oblivious to all its drama—except what she read on the front pages of the rags at the grocery store. She admitted this was her guilty pleasure. But being her pastor's executive assistant, she felt she shouldn't buy the magazines. So if it wasn't on the front cover, she didn't know anything about it.

"That man is one of the hottest new stars in the business, Sylvia. And I'm not going to tell you how old or young he is. I'll just say that he is all that and a bag of chips."

"Well, he must be something 'cause I haven't seen you looking this perky in quite a while. What does Richard have to say about all this?"

"Richard! I guess the big fight we had didn't make it to the front page here, huh?"

"Nope. You must have gotten bumped by Brad and Angelina."

They both laughed. Lydia decided it felt good to be home. Since she'd stopped seeing Tamara, she didn't really have a sounding board to air her concerns. She didn't dare share her struggles with her new friends in Chicago. It was far too early to know who could be trusted... who wouldn't repeat what would be considered juicy pieces of gossip for entertainment hounds. But now that she was back, she could talk to Sylvia about everything without fearing that what she said would find its way to the *Enquirer* or on an *Extra* report.

As they wove their way through the city, heading toward Beverly Hills, Lydia told Sylvia about how she'd planned to go to Chicago to get Richard back, only to discover the damage that had been done to their marriage was irreparable. She'd been angry and embarrassed when he got involved with someone else, so she sought to turn the tables and devastate his pride by showing him he could be replaced. But not by just any man, by his leading star.

Sylvia's eyes grew large. "Now, Lydia, you know God can't bless no mess. Getting bitter and seeking revenge is the quickest way to get yourself into more trouble than you bargained for. You're setting yourself up for a hurting, girl. Pride comes before a fall. Ah, I now see. I knew I wasn't praying over you for nothing. I tell you, I can't trust you to go anywhere unsupervised."

"Sylvia, please, let me finish. I did start off being an evil shrew trying to hurt Richard, but all of that changed." She chuckled. "It's wonderfully ironic. The 'gamer' has been captured by the game. I'm happy. I'm in love. Brandon is wonderful. I've moved on."

"Really? You've moved on? With a man half your age? What's going to happen when he moves on? And with someone younger? How are you going to deal with that?"

"I don't think I'll have to. Brandon loves me." In the face of Sylvia's unclouded candor, what Lydia was saying felt flimsy, and she was blindsided by her own insecurity.

"How can you be sure of that? How do you know he's not using you to heighten his own profile?"

"It's something I can feel. I just know. I know how I feel when I'm with him…" Lydia's words trailed off as she searched for solid footing on what she was saying.

"Girl, you couldn't *feel* your way out of a paper bag right now. You're too wounded. Anytime you make a decision out of hurt, anger, or fear, you make the wrong one. Your discernment is off right now, along with your prayer life, and you know it. You're using that man as a Band-Aid, and he is using you. I can feel it in my bones. And you know I have no interest in any of this except for your well-being." Sylvia shook her head. "I knew something wasn't right. But it's your journey, and some folks have to find out fat meat is greasy on their own. You can't tell them anything. So enjoy yourself while you can. Just remember, Band-Aids fall off."

"Thank you for the vote of confidence!" Lydia hated it when Sylvia talked like this because she was always right.

"You know me. I'm going to keep it real."

"Well, thanks for the unwanted reality check!" Lydia could feel herself growing defensive to ward off fear.

"Don't look so glum about it. I'm not trying to be a killjoy. It's just that…oh never mind. Forget about it." Sylvia heaved a long sigh and pulled into the driveway.

Lydia looked at her house. The beautiful, classic Beverly Hills home had always given her a great sense of pride. The lawn was beautifully manicured, and the house rose pristine in all its glory. But now it seemed too large. She could feel the loneliness emanating from it. She sat there staring at the front door, reluctant to leave the warmth of the car even though she didn't like the conversation.

Sylvia turned off the car and looked at Lydia soberly. "Well, here we are. Look, I know you've been busy running around Chicago, caught up in the euphoria of a new romance and all. But now that you're back, I suggest you stop running from yourself and your pain and reconnect with God. He's really the only one who can heal you. I can't do it. What's that boy's…I mean man's name? Ah yes, Brandon! He can't do it either. Even if Richard came back right now it wouldn't deal with the roots of your issues."

"Wow! When did you get a psychology degree?"

"I'm no psychologist, Lydia. I'm just a praying friend who loves you. And I'm telling you, until you're ready to deal with the heart of your love issues and face what's really wrong, you'll always be frustrated and looking for replacements that will be temporary fillers at best.

Nobody likes pain, but it's a necessary part of healing you can't escape. Treat it like a friend and let it talk to you. Shoot, chile, you're not the first person to suffer trauma and have a wounded spirit, so deal with it. You're a big girl now."

"I haven't been feeling so big lately. I've been feeling very small and lost. Brandon has been my only respite in the storm. If he…" She bit her lip to stop from saying the thing she feared the most. "I don't know what I'd do…" Tears were welling inside Lydia, and she was afraid the dam would break. "Oh Sylvia, what is going to become of me? I'm so scared! I've got to make this work. I couldn't bear to look like an idiot in front of Richard. You should have seen how he looked at me the other day…so disdainful…so…he reminded me of…" She threw up her hands and looked at Sylvia. "How do you get to be this old and still feel as if you can't do anything right?" The tears were freely flowing now, and she felt they would never subside.

Sylvia looked shocked by Lydia's sudden vulnerability but recovered quickly and gazed at her with compassion. She got out and made her way around the side of the car, opening the door and pulling Lydia out. "Here. Let's get you into the house. You'll feel better after you've had some tea."

Sitting in the living room, her hands wrapped around a steaming cup of tea, Lydia struggled to collect her thoughts as Sylvia sat across from her in silence. *It's such a lovely room,* she noted. She'd taken great pride in decorating it. Richard hadn't wanted to buy this house because of the awful condition it had been in. It had belonged to an old star who had allowed its glory to fade along with his fame. But she'd seen the possibilities and delivered her vision in style. She had done such a good job of making everything look beautiful…up to this last year. Now it all meant nothing. She thought of how Job must have felt sitting amid the ashes in sackcloth as he pondered his losses. Though she hadn't lost everything, she had lost enough. And she'd lost what mattered most. There was no way around the awful facts any longer. You just can't dress up a torn-down life. No matter how you look at it, the pain of all that transpired bled through and marred the perfect finish. She suddenly felt depleted. Lydia was completely out of energy to pretend. Totally drained from being angry. At the end of herself. What that meant she didn't know, and for once it was okay to admit it.

thirty-one

Jada had had enough of everyone around her doing as they pleased. Sick of her father's selfishness that had put her in this position. Fed up with her mother being clueless. Or was her mother really that out of touch? She pondered this thought as she unlocked the front door carefully, although she knew there was no reason to. Her mother was at her usual appointment in the city. Was this what had caused her to spend half her life in the city? Running away from the truth at home? Had she confronted her father, or did she suffer silently too?

A flush of anger washed over her and then dispersed just as quickly. To whom could she direct a tirade if she chose to do so? No one. There was no safe place. Not church. Not her mother. The vote was still out on God. Part of her felt completely abandoned by Him, but a small part of her held out hope. Why didn't He do something? She could understand her earthly father being flawed, but where was God when she needed Him? Why was He leaving her and everyone else to their own devices? Why wasn't He protecting her? Wasn't He supposed to be the perfect Father? If God disappointed her, she had nowhere else to go.

The door closed behind her with a thud. The sound was predictably hollow as it announced that, as usual, no one else was home. That much was a relief. She didn't want to argue about quitting the worship team again. Her father's angry message on her cell phone voicemail today demanding to know why she'd skipped rehearsal yesterday made something inside her snap. His voice had crackled on the line as if his anger was creating the static. "I will see you when I get home, young lady. And you'd better have a good reason for your insubordination."

Insubordination. Is that what it is? Was life about doing what *he* said no matter how she felt? He sounded like he was speaking to a stranger. Well, she wasn't going to be subjected to his railings again. She didn't care what he said, she wasn't going back. He hadn't heard her the first time, and he wouldn't hear her now. She didn't want to rehash old dialog. She didn't want to be questioned about why she wasn't there. She didn't want to be accused of attitudes she didn't harbor. She was trapped inside herself, afraid and hurting, her emotions a prison she couldn't escape. And there was no one on the outside to mediate for her.

She wondered what her mother would do if she told her everything. Would she believe her or go into denial, shut down, and continue the charade? What if her mother already knew? Will she ever do anything about it? But to conclude that her mother knew about what her father was doing and did nothing was more than Jada could bear. Just the thought made her scream silently until she thought her heart would explode.

Obviously her mother wasn't happy; it was clear she was merely existing. But why? Pastor Masters said that if the truth came out about her father, they would be ruined. Her father would lose the church and everything that came with it. Her mother had never worked. So what would happen to them? They wouldn't stay together as a family if she faced such devastating news and suffered such disgrace. Surely she would leave him. But leave him and go where? And Jada would stay with her mother. But how would they support themselves? They wouldn't be able to count on her dad's support if he didn't have a job. She'd rehearsed these same thoughts over and over, finding no solutions.

As she climbed up the stairs to her room, Jada's thoughts were like an avalanche, starting as a small snowball of fear, tumbling over itself again and again as it gained momentum and size and eventually overwhelmed her with despair. The thought of facing her father again tightened her chest, crushing her lungs and cutting off her breath. Her chest was heaving by the time she got to the top, leaving her light-headed with anxiety. She moved into her room and sat on the edge of the bed, trying to calm down and weigh her options.

Different scenarios played out in her head. If she went to her father and told him she knew he was gay, he would only deny it and fly into a rage. If she told him she was being abused by his beloved associate pastor…well, she didn't know what he would do. The thought of what he wouldn't do troubled her more. If she went to anyone at church, it would cause a mess she couldn't even begin to picture. Same thing if she went to a teacher at school. She'd already withdrawn from her friends, fearing they could clearly see her shame. Besides, what could they do except pity and commiserate with her?

She got up and paced back and forth, her thoughts rambling. She hated herself. Perhaps this situation was all her fault. No matter how much she tried to hide behind a mask or make herself undesirable, Pastor Masters' advances grew more insistent. She jumped as her cell phone rang. She retrieved it from her coat and frowned. She didn't recognize the number.

"Hello?"

"Jada?" It was Pastor Masters.

"Yes?" Chills ran down her legs, rooting her to the spot.

"Why weren't you at worship rehearsal yesterday?"

"I wasn't feeling well. I told Simone to let the rest of the team know I wouldn't be there and to give them the music."

"Really?"

She held her breath.

"When I spoke to your father earlier today and mentioned your absence, he said you were considering quitting the worship team. He asked me to speak with you about it. Is that true?"

She still said nothing.

"That would be such a shame." There was a hint of menace in his voice. "It would just be such a sin to allow such a gift to go to waste. Do you think it's really fair to withhold what you have to offer when it blesses so many people? You need to be very sure that your decision is being led by God and not your own impulses." He waited.

Jada cleared her throat. "I haven't made any decision. I just didn't feel well yesterday." She couldn't think of anything else to say.

"Well, I hope you're feeling better. And do pray about this. It might affect countless *others* besides yourself." Again the menacing undertone brought his threat to life.

"I have to go." Jada felt tension rising, cutting off her breath, choking her.

"All right then. See you next we…"

She flipped the phone shut, cutting him off. Again a scream rose in her throat but never made it to the surface.

The vise around her throat grew tighter and tighter. She hated him. She hated herself. She hated her mother…her father…God. She was groping through pitch darkness, unable to find her way out of a tunnel. She was so tired. She was caught in a long nightmare that would never end. She needed a release. The more she focused on Pastor Masters, the dirtier she felt…an internal filth that no amount of water could wash away. But she had to try. She'd take a bath. Perhaps she could soak him and the stain of his violation off her spirit.

She went into the bathroom and turned the water on in the tub. The sound soothed her, but the tightness in her throat threatened to choke her. She returned to her room and fumbled in the bottom of her nightstand drawer until she found them. Her new best friends. Her collection of loose razor blades. Selecting a brand-new one and pressing it against the soft flesh on the inside of her wrist, she watched as a faint line of red followed the trail she drew with the blade. Relief flooded over her as the pool deepened and the pain diverted her attention from her internal suffering. In time a strange sense of calm overtook her.

She cut again, watching the patterns the blood made on her arm until the tightness subsided from her throat. A stab of shock jolted her as more blood than usual spurted from a fresh incision. She pressed tissues against the wound, but they disintegrated as the blood kept flowing. Rushing to the bathroom, she grabbed a towel and wrapped it around her wrist...only to watch it turn a brilliant red. Amid the panic, she suddenly felt very lightheaded. She gazed at the red wrapping in fascination. The sound of running water in the background lulled her. She barely felt herself sliding to the floor. Her hold loosened on the towel. It felt so good to relax. She felt nothing, but it was a different kind of nothing, a good nothing. As the water flooded over the side of the bathtub and onto the floor, touching her, she semi-giggled as she remembered her mother talking about a bubble bath commercial that voiced her sentiments: "Calgon, take me away."

Nothing mattered anymore. She felt good. Warm. Light. Free. She closed her eyes floating...floating...a million miles away from home, basking in the warmth of the sun. So good...so good...so good...not to be tired anymore...

thirty-two

Ari skipped around the corner and into the sudden darkness of the hallway. After coming out of the light, her eyes had to adjust as she made her way down the corridor toward home. She wished she could live in a pretty place like Miss Williams. She loved her hallways with the pretty lights lining either side. And the floors. Marble, Miss Williams said. The prettiest Ari had ever seen. She tried to duplicate the design in one of her paintings because it was almost as if someone had drawn on the stone. And the doorman was so nice that night she'd gone over there. It would be nice to have a doorman welcome her home, especially when her mother wasn't here. She would feel safe knowing someone was looking out for her.

Sometimes if he was still there cleaning the hallways, the janitor would stop and talk to her. He always looked out for her, bringing her little sandwiches. Sometimes he would save a piece of the cake his wife packed for his lunch. He told her she could call him Uncle Jay, but she still called him Mr. Morrison. When Mr. Morrison was there she felt safe. But today he was nowhere to be seen. She wondered what had happened to the light in the hallway. Perhaps she should pray and ask God to let them move into a building like Miss Williams'. The hallway was filled with shadows, and she shivered in apprehension. She breathed a sigh of relief when she finally reached her door. As she bent to pull out her key, the door eased open of its own accord.

Stepping into the room, her eyes adjusting to the gloom, she called out tentatively, "Mama?"

A shadow moved, catching her attention out of the corner of her eye. She jumped when Tyrone stepped out of the corner of the living room and into the light. Big Boy rose from the couch. Instinctively she backed toward the door.

"Tyrone? What are you doing here? Where is my mama?"

"That's what we were wonderin'."

"H—how did you get in? What do you want?"

"We want our money, that's what we want!" Big Boy walked toward her threateningly. Tyrone put out his arm to stop him.

"Hold up, Big Boy. The chile ain't got no money. Our beef ain't with her, man. Now sid down somewhere. We just gon' sit here an' wait 'til this heifer comes home. She been givin' us the run around long enough." His lips strained across his teeth, highlighting his agitation. His tone softened as he stepped toward Ari. "Don' worry, little bit. We jus' need ta have a conversation with your mama. You know when shes comin' home?"

"No. I thought she'd be here. I don't know where she is." Ari clutched her book bag tighter, taking another step backward toward the door.

Tyrone stepped toward her, taking her by the arm and leading her into the room. "No need to be scared. Let's just all sit an' wait for your mama together, okay? Now jus' come on over here and sit." With that he firmly pushed her down on the couch.

Ari sat on the edge, hugging the arm of the couch for dear life.

Big Boy glared at her. "What's wrong wit' chu? You ack like we gon' eat you a'somethin'."

"How many times I got ta tell you ta leave dat girl alone, man? Now just chill. I gotta take a leak." Turning to Ari he asked, "Where's the bathroom, little bit?"

Ari pointed toward the bathroom door.

He headed toward it but then turned back to her. "Hey, why don't you do some homework or somethin' 'til your mama get home?"

He shut the door. Ari reached into her book bag and retrieved her reading book. Still perched on the edge of the couch, she spread the book over her knees and bent over it, trying to concentrate. The words blurred before her eyes. She could feel Big Boy sliding closer to her.

His breath on the back of her neck, he peered over her shoulder, looking into her book.

"What chu readin'?"

"A story. You want to read it with me?" She smiled at him, forgetting her fear until he grabbed her arm, pressing his face menacingly close to hers.

"What chu mean? You makin' fun o' me or somethin' 'cause I can't read?"

Ari felt faint, but the pain shooting through her arm where he grabbed it kept her conscious. "I...I...didn't know you couldn't read. I'm sorry. I..."

"You think you betta dan me wit' cho propa talkin' self?"

"No!" Ari didn't mean to scream, but fear pushed the answer out of her throat.

Big Boy grabbed her throat and slammed his hand over her mouth. "Shut up!"

Ari thought she was suffocating, which heightened her panic as she struggled to break free. Her second scream for help resulted in a muffled but shrill sound.

The bathroom door flew open.

"What's going on in here! Man! What chu doin'?"

"I think we should teach Little Miss Uppity a lesson. Besides, her mama ain't gon' pay us no way."

"Big Boy, have you lost your mind? I just want my money. I ain't goin' down for no mess like this!"

But Big Boy seemed to be in a daze. He took his hand off her mouth and stroked the side of Ari's face. "She's a pretty little thing, ain't she?" He glanced at Tyrone. "You sho you don't want a piece a' this?"

Ari screamed again and tried to wrench free, but Big Boy's grip was like iron. She scratched his hand. He released her arm and attempted to put his hand back over her mouth. She clamped on to the soft part of his hand with her teeth until he pulled back, waving his hand as if it were on fire. He slapped her hard across the face. Ari fell off the couch, but jumped to her feet as Tyrone tackled Big Boy.

She thought she heard someone screaming, and suddenly realized it was her.

"Man, get off me!" Big Boy struggled to get free of Tyrone.

"I tol' you ta leave her alone!" Tyrone yelled.

"What's going on here?" The door swung open with a bang, and Mr. Morrison filled the doorway. Any other time he would have been a welcome sight, but in the haze of her terror it was the impetus Ari needed to shoot through the door. She headed toward the stairwell, not chancing being stopped and caught at the elevator. Taking the steps two at a time she didn't even feel them beneath her feet. She didn't know where she was going; all she knew was she was running...running for her life. She prayed to God that Tyrone and Big Boy wouldn't catch her. Her breath was coming hard and fast, and her lungs were burning, but still she ran on. Just in case God didn't answer her this time, she was going to put as much distance between her and Big Boy as she could. The world around her was a blur. She was falling...falling...falling...and she had no strength to get up. And then she felt arms lift her. She cried out silently to God, *Help me!* And then there was nothing.

thirty-three

Tamara let the beautiful cream-colored gauze fall around her ankles and softly caress her like the breeze that gently blew through the window. She went to the balcony to take in the scenery. It was absolutely beautiful. The sun was just setting, and the sky was smiling a welcome to her. The perfect period to the sentence of her journey. She couldn't believe she was here with Kevin and getting ready to have a romantic dinner in the lap of luxury. The Ritz Carlton resort gave plush a whole new meaning. After landing this afternoon, Kevin had left her at the door of the spa, handing her a schedule of appointments to keep her occupied while he was at meetings.

"I want you to feel as beautiful as you look by the time I get back." With that he'd given her a loaded kiss, leaving her breathless as he departed.

The attendant raised her eyebrows before beckoning Tamara to follow her to a private dressing area to disrobe and prepare for a series of beauty treatments. As she submitted to being pampered from head to toe—facial, hot stone massage, reflexology, manicure, pedicure, hair—she chuckled. If you could name it, Kevin had thought of it.

He made sure she had plenty to occupy her so she wouldn't have time to pout over his absence. He was good. Very good. She thought about pinching herself, but she didn't want to wake up…didn't want to interrupt the dream. This was what she'd always wanted! A man who was romantic and thoughtful. A man who had the means to give her nice things and take her to beautiful places. Kevin was all that and more. And he was so fine! She saw the way the flight attendants looked from him to her and back to him as they sat in first class. She could see their envy as he focused his attention on her. She felt so proud. She had to stifle the urge to shout, "This is my man!" Instead she met their gazes, knowing her look said it all: "Look…but don't even think about touching."

Up until now Kevin had honored her no sex policy, but tonight she was more worried about herself than she was about him. He'd been the total gentleman, conceding to her two bedroom rule, but he'd gotten around it a bit by getting a suite with two rooms that shared a fabulous living room and dining room. It was perfect with its ocean view and sprawling balcony that ran the length of the entire apartment. She wished they could stay here forever. Away from the city. Away from everyone who would hold her accountable. Away from Jamilah, her mother, even Stella.

Stella had sniffed when told to cancel Tamara's appointments for Thursday, Friday, and Monday. Her disapproval hung in the air, but she didn't utter a word of what she was thinking, even though it showed clearly on her face. She finally quipped, "You sure you don't need a chaperone? My weekend is free, thanks to you!"

"No, that won't be necessary," Tamara answered. Nothing Stella could say could affect her mood today. She was in love and on her way to a romantic island getaway with her man. Her assistant was just evil 'cause she didn't have anybody. "Don't be a hater, Stella. It's not Christian."

"Let's not get started on what's Christian and what ain't…"

Tamara arched her brow signaling that Stella should take no further liberties.

Stella cleared her throat and went back toward her computer. "Have a nice time," she shot over her shoulder.

"I will!" Tamara shot back before breezing out of the office and closing the door. Shaking off any reservations as well as those voices playing in her head, she focused on the excitement she'd felt before Stella tried to rain on her parade. She went outside.

As she settled into the car Kevin sent, the driver headed to the airport. Kevin had an early morning meeting and would meet her there. Tamara couldn't help but think of the good times she'd missed while she waited for a "super Christian man" to show up and carry her away. If she was still in that mind-set, she'd still be waiting! She'd be heading to the office for yet another day of listening to woes and complaints that no one seemed able to pray away. Perhaps she'd gotten it wrong thinking she had to wait around for God to fulfill the desires of her heart. Maybe the popular saying was true, "God helps those who help themselves." Since she'd taken her life back into her own hands, everything was looking up.

Why didn't I do this sooner? she questioned as she spotted Kevin waiting for her curbside. Besides, it's just a matter of time before Kevin would see her point of view when it came to her faith and join in. Then everything would be perfect. They could get married before her biological clock sounded its last alarm. Surely God wouldn't let her miss this opportunity at happiness! That would be too heartless and cruel. She felt a twinge in her lower side again. She would have it checked when she got back home. Perhaps Felicia was right. But for now she was going to focus on the pleasures at hand.

"Hey, baby!"

She loved it when Kevin called her that. Yes, it was a perfect day for flying and a perfect day for love.

A knock at the door broke her out of her reverie. It must be Kevin. She took one last twirl in her dress, savoring the flowing fabric caressing her skin in a loving whisper. She was still amazed at how every garment he'd chosen for her was a perfect fit, flawless in taste, and totally her. She looked fabulous, if she did say so herself.

"Hey, you didn't let anyone steal you while I was away, did you?"

She giggled as she opened the door. "Now why would I let anyone do that when I have such a phenomenal man?"

He looked her up and down approvingly. "Mmm, and it seems a phenomenal man has a phenomenal woman." He nuzzled close to her. "You look incredible," he whispered in her ear before kissing her neck. His lips branded her skin and set off a fire inside her. She fought to compose herself before asking, "So, what's the plan for the evening? How did your meetings go?"

"Meetings were great, but the evening is going to be better. I've made reservations at one of my favorite restaurants, and then I have a little surprise for you."

"Another one? I don't think I can take any more."

"A woman like you should know what she deserves and always expect more."

"All righty then," she breathed, accepting his arm.

She was in a daze when the waiter pulled out her chair as they literally sat on the edge of a cliff in one of the most exclusive restaurants she'd ever been to. She could tell the clientele was a different breed than she was used to. They were bedecked and bejeweled in muted sophistication. There were no prices on the menu, and the chef specially selected each course according to the individuals he was serving. Every bite melted in her mouth, and every sip of wine was an elixir that went straight to her head. By the time they made it back to their suite, all she felt was delicious pleasure. As Kevin opened the door she was greeted by soft music floating from the balcony. The curtains had been drawn back to reveal a trio softly playing next to a table set with fruit, pastries, and champagne.

"Shall we dance?" Kevin swept her into his arms and danced her onto the veranda.

She didn't know if it was the wine they'd consumed, the perfume of the night wind, or the overall euphoria she felt, but she was suddenly lightheaded and overwhelmed. The beating of her heart and myriad emotions signaled she was losing the fight to contain herself. Jamilah's voice cut into her thoughts. "You know, it's just as easy to fall in love with an unsaved man as it is to fall in love with a saved one, so why even put yourself in that position?" Well she was in that position, and it was too late to back out now.

"Are you okay?"

Kevin's face clouded with concern as she almost swooned. "Hmm? Oh, yes, I'm fine. But I think you've gone to my head. I need to lie down for a minute."

"Let me help you." Kevin was at her side, gently leading her toward her room. He sat her on the edge of the bed and lifted her legs onto the soft duvet. Leaning over her, he smoothed her hair back from her face, gently kissing her forehead, her eyes, her lips, until she yielded beneath him.

As he began undressing her, the music drifting in from the balcony dissolved the last strains of her resistance. She melted beneath his touch, giving way to the intoxication of the night, his arms, his lips, his love. Nothing else mattered...nothing at all...

thirty-four

Jamilah hovered over Ari as she slept. She looked so small nestled in the layers of bedding. She frowned as she perused the rising welt on the side of the child's face and wondered how a mother could do such a thing to her child. She'd been shocked when she opened the door of her apartment to find Emmett standing there holding Ari in his arms.

"Poor thing. I don't know where she was coming from, but she shot through the door as if the hounds of hell were on her heels. She passed out in front of the counter."

Jamilah had anxiously watched over her as the paramedics who responded to her 911 call checked her over. Citing she had probably passed out from stress and exhaustion, they gave her some oxygen and waited until Ari revived. From what they were able to get out of Ari, she'd almost been attacked by two boys and her mother wasn't at home. She didn't know where she was, and she was too afraid to say who had attacked her.

After making sure the girl was all right, the paramedics left. Jamilah hovered over her little student.

"Miss Williams, please don't make me go home. I'm scared. Please…"

Jamilah's heart broke. If Ari only knew how much she longed to make that request a reality. But the sad fact was that the girl would have to go back home…but not tonight. No way was Jamilah going to send her back home in the state she was in. And it was highly likely her mother was still not home. Jamilah would not chance putting Ari in danger. So she tenderly put her to bed, reassuring her as best she could not to worry about anything. Keeping vigil over Ari as she drifted into a fitful sleep, the young teacher went over her options.

Moving to the living room, she called Ari's house. There was no answer, which made her angry. Where could Ari's mother be? And would she be angry if she got home and Ari wasn't there? *Well, just let her worry about where her daughter is. Perhaps it will teach her a lesson,* Jamilah decided.

She considered calling DCFS, but once again this alternative made her shudder. She couldn't bear to think where Ari could end up in the system. And she wasn't in the position to step forward to foster her because the process wasn't completed yet. Nothing would make her crazier than Ari disappearing within the system and going to some family she didn't know and where she might never see her again. No, that wouldn't work. She tried calling Dwayne but then remembered he was taking some of his young mentees on a field trip for the long Memorial Day weekend. She thought about calling her mother, but thought better of it. She didn't want to worry her. But as time ticked away, she dialed her number, only to get her mom's answering machine.

"Where did she have the nerve to go without telling me?" Jamilah wondered. Any other time she would have been happy to know her mother had taken a long weekend off. Somewhere in the back of her mind she had a faint recollection of her mentioning going to Galena with a friend of hers to go antiquing. "Perfect timing" was all she could think right now. She finally went away for a weekend when her daughter needed her most.

Tamara came to mind, but that didn't seem like a good choice. Besides, she hadn't heard from her for a couple weeks now, and Tamara would only repeat what she'd been saying all along. She didn't need to hear that she couldn't save the world right now. She just needed to know how to do it.

"Lord, you've got to help me. I'm trying so hard not to take matters into my own hands, but I truly don't know what You want me to do right now. I can't send her back home. You know what's happening there. Please do something…anything. I need to know You're here. I love this little girl so much it makes my heart ache, and yet I feel so helpless. I can't stand by and watch her life go down the drain. You've got to do something!" The tears fell as she silently prayed her heart. Then she returned to the bedroom.

Ari nestled deeper into the covers and then opened her eyes.

"Why are you crying, Miss Williams? Did I do something bad?"

"No, you didn't do anything wrong. I'm just…praying and asking God to give me wisdom, that's all. Sometimes even I don't know what to do."

"Do you think God hears us more when we cry?"

Jamilah laughed and blew her nose. "I don't think tears are really necessary to get God's attention, Ari. He hears us anyway, and He cares about the things we worry about. The problem is sometimes we just don't know what He'll do or when He'll do it. And in our limited faith sometimes we make bad decisions that kind of mess up what He had in mind and complicate things. I don't want to do that, but…"

"But what, Miss Williams?"

"Well, that's why I was crying. Because sometimes I don't know what God is doing, and I get frustrated because I want Him to hurry up."

"Me too. I want Him to hurry up and make Mama happy so she'll stay home. And that way Tyrone and Big Boy…" Her eyes got as big as saucers, and she slapped her hand over her mouth. "I mean…I didn't mean…please don't tell on them, Miss Williams. Big Boy just got mad 'cause…excuse me, because he thought I was making fun of him because he can't read, and Tyrone was trying to get him to leave me alone. They didn't mean nothin'…I mean 'anything.' I just got scared. It was dark and Mama wasn't there and..." She tried to get up. "I better go...Mama will be mad if I'm not at home..."

"I really don't think it's wise for you to go now, Ari. It's dark and your mother still isn't home. We can talk about Big Boy and Tyrone tomorrow. But I can't let you go back home by yourself tonight." She patted her head and gently pushed her back down on the bed. "You need to get some sleep and let me worry about what to do. I'll take you back home in the morning, okay?"

"Okay." Ari yawned. "Miss Williams?"

"Yes, Ari?"

"I think God's gonna do it."

"Do what?"

"What you asked Him to do."

"From your lips to His ears."

"Huh?"

"Nothing. Now get some sleep."

"He answered my prayer. I think He's nice..." She drifted off to sleep.

"I just wish the world was as nice as He is." With that Jamilah tucked the covers under her chin and turned off the bedside lamp.

Rising from the bed, she tiptoed out of the bedroom. Tucking her feet under her on the couch, she drew a soft throw over her and up to her chin. She drifted into her own troubled sleep.

Before she answered the door she knew who was rapping loudly and impatiently. But she wasn't prepared for the sight of Ari's mother flanked by two policemen. Miss Jordan's eyes were flashing anger and indignation.

She pointed at Jamilah. "There she is, meddling wench! She kidnapped my baby!" Pressing past Jamilah, she dashed frantically into the room. "Where is she? Where is my baby? Ari? Ari? Where are you, baby?"

Ari wandered out of the bedroom looking bleary eyed. "Mama?"

Miss Jordan rushed to her, drew back, and then leaned forward to examine the black-and-blue mark on the side of Ari's face. "What did she do to you?" Her voice was shrill. She turned and glared at Jamilah. "What did you do to my baby girl?"

"I didn't do anything!" Jamilah fought her grogginess to make sense of what was happening. "She was attacked at your house…"

"That is not true! Nobody would do this…nobody!" Miss Jordan yelled.

"No! No, that's not…" Ari interjected.

"Be quiet, baby. Let me handle this. You don't need to be afraid of her…"

"I'm not…"

"I said be quiet! Mama's here now." She stood in front of Ari to shield her from Jamilah. "Officers, arrest this woman! This is the second time she's kidnapped my child!"

Jamilah stepped toward Miss Jordan. "That is not true and you know it!"

"What you gon' do? Attack me now? Right in front of the police!" Miss Jordan stepped back.

The police moved in to restrain Jamilah.

Ari started crying. "No, no!" she whispered.

Jamilah tried to explain, but no one was listening. The chaos was deafening between Ari's cries and her mother's hysterical accusations.

"You can explain at the station, ma'am. Right now you are under arrest for child abduction." He turned back to Miss Jordan. "Now move along, ma'am. We've got your statement. We'll contact you in the morning. Why don't you take your daughter home and put her to bed?"

From the backseat of the police car Jamilah watched Miss Jordan lead Ari away. She pondered Ari's last words before she fell asleep. *God is nice, huh? Right now I don't think He's being very nice at all.*

thirty-five

Corinne drove around the corner, apprehension rising in her throat. Something was very wrong. Her feeling of unease had escalated ever since her lunch the week before with the first ladies. Between the discovery of the photographs and her suspicions of what could possibly be plaguing Jada, she'd been consumed with what to do next. She'd already started developing a game plan for taking Jada and moving to her mother's until she was able to get on her feet financially. Her only dilemma was whether she should wait until Jada was finished at school, which was only weeks away, or move right away. She hadn't been able to pin Jada down to talk about it because she was in avoidance mode, which further exasperated her. So distracted was she by the rumbling in her spirit that she'd stopped drinking without thinking about it. Randall noticed before she did.

"What? No nightcap? Are we turning over a new leaf?"

"Maybe I am," she said without malice.

For the first time his words didn't agitate her. She was consumed with seeking God about how best to handle the situation with Jada. She hadn't had any confirmation of her suspicions, but she knew in her soul. She didn't know who it was, but she was going to find out. Fire rose in her. She was a mother tiger arising from sleep to find another animal trying to get to her den and kill her cub. She was not letting that happen. Her anger fueled her, giving her strength, and yet she didn't want to move without being sure of the best way to get to the bottom of the matter.

"Oh God, please forgive me. How could I have been so blind, so consumed with me that I allowed my household to disintegrate? Show me what to do, and I'll do it." The prospect of her daughter being in danger was the leverage she needed to oust her from her pity party and into action.

Pulling into the driveway she looked up at the house. Such a pretty place. It looked so inviting from the outside. She longed for it to be just as inviting on the inside. Randall was an incredible host, the consummate pastor and neighbor, inviting people over for dinner and holidays. Perhaps he too longed to feel warmth inside its walls. But that only seemed to happen when the house was filled with outsiders. She studied the facade, thinking how sad it was that the windows were dark as usual. When was the last time they'd eaten a meal together? What were they all avoiding? She leaned forward, peering into the darkness. *That's odd. Jada should be home by now. So should Randall, for that matter.* He'd canceled Friday night service and encouraged the congregation to enjoy the long holiday weekend as families. *When is he going to practice what he preaches?*

She wondered what his loving congregation would say about his secret life. They'd always been so pious toward her...so disapproving because she wanted nothing to do with ministry. And what about old pompous Pastor Masters and his wife, Ruth? Something wasn't right there, that's for sure. Poor Ruth. She seemed so mousy and subservient. Corinne always wanted to take her by the hand and get her to let that topknot down and put on some color. Her silver hair could be really attractive in a nice cut. And some nice colors would bring out her blue eyes and put some color on her cheeks. Instead she looked like she had just stepped off the prairie in frontier days. She was so subdued. A wallflower fading while Pastor Masters strutted around like a braggadocios peacock. What a couple. She wondered if they ever had sex. She couldn't imagine it. The thought made her giggle.

She opened the car door, grabbed her packages with one hand, exited, and kicked the door closed. Jostling her bag and packages, she put her key in the front door lock, only to have the door ease open on its own.

Maybe someone is home after all. But why didn't anybody turn on the lights? She set her purse on the table in the foyer and headed toward the kitchen to put away the groceries. Setting the bags on the counter, she realized something seemed wrong. She retraced her steps to the front foyer and stood at the bottom of the stairs listening.

Is that Jada's shower running? Why can I hear it? Jada always closes her door if she's in the bathroom. Slowly she climbed the stairs. "Jada?" There was no answer, and she didn't know why her heart was beating so hard. "Jada? Are you up here?" Still no answer. She picked up her pace. "Jada? Don't you hear me ca…" She stopped short. She had reached the top landing, and the door to Jada's room was open. Water had saturated the carpet and was beginning to snake out into the hallway. "Jada!" she demanded, not knowing if she should be angry at Jada's negligence or if something was wrong. Her shoes sank into the sodden carpet as she ran toward the bedroom door that was also open. She took a deep breath as panic gripped her. Tinges of red mingled with the water coming from the bathroom.

"Jadaaaaa!" she screamed, running toward the still form of her daughter lying in a pool of water, blood streaming from her wrist. The towel she wrapped around her arm had long given way. Jada's lips were blue, and her hair streamed around her, making her look like a strange gothic painting. Corinne fell to her knees. Grabbing Jada by her shoulders, she pulled her close. Jada's head fell back, her hair like a wet mop and her arms as lifeless as a rag doll's. Corinne shifted her to the floor and jumped to her feet. "Oh no, oh no! The devil is a liar. You are not going to take my daughter from me!" She rushed into the bedroom and grabbed the phone from its cradle on the nightstand. Dialing 911 she yelled at the recording, "I want a real person!" Relief flooded her when a real person answered. "Please, please! Somebody help me! My daughter, my daughter…she's bleeding! Oh God! Oh God!" Her eyes spotted the razor blade on the floor. "She's slashed her wrist."

"Do you know how long ago she did this?" The voice on the other phone sounded detached and way too calm for Corinne's taste.

"No, I don't know how long! Does it matter? She's lying on the floor dying! I need somebody here now!"

"Ma'am, I need you to calm down…"

"That's easy for you to say!" It was all Corinne could do not to throw the phone against the wall.

"I need you to calm down and give me your address…"

"It's 1619 Camden Drive. And I can't calm down!" She made her way back to the bathroom. Grabbing a towel she propped the cordless phone between her cheek and her shoulder while tying a tourniquet around Jada's wrist. She pulled the towel with all her might, focusing on stopping the bleeding. "Stop in the name of Jesus!" she demanded. Then her attention went back to the person on the line. "Get an ambulance here, and get them here fast!"

She slammed the phone down and used both hands to press Jada's cheeks, pinching them, looking for some sign of color. "Come on, girl. You can't leave me now. You've got too many songs to sing. Too many reasons to live. Momma's here. Are you listening to me, Jada? Don't you quit on me! Please don't leave me! Please don't leave me!" She jumped up and turned off the water, and then went back to Jada's side. She pulled the tourniquet even tighter. Satisfied that she'd stopped the flow of blood, she began sopping up the water around her, afraid to move Jada but not wanting her to be soaked even more.

She could hear sirens in the distance. She closed her eyes in gratefulness. "Oh God, please don't let it be too late! Please help me! Please help Jada!" She ran down the stairs, flinging the door open as the ambulance screeched to a stop in front of the house.

Completely oblivious to the stares of the paramedics when they saw her wet and bloody appearance and the gathering of nosy neighbors making their way toward her portion of the sidewalk, she took the stairs two at a time as she led the medics to Jada. She stood in the doorway, suddenly numb as she watched them hovering over her daughter, systematically doing their work. Lifting her onto a gurney, they proceeded toward the door. She followed behind them, trailing down the stairs like a frightened little girl.

One of the paramedics looked back. Gently taking her by the hand, she led Corinne to the back of the ambulance. "Would you like to ride with your daughter?" she asked.

Corinne nodded like an obedient child. "Is she going to be all right?" she whispered.

"Her pulse is extremely weak. We don't know how much blood she lost yet, but she's holding on. If you hadn't put that tourniquet on when you did, she might not have made it this far." She looked at her, as if seeing Corinne for the first time. "Hey, aren't you the minister's wife with the great big church? Then I don't have to tell you to have faith. Come on! Get in."

Corinne climbed into the back of the ambulance. The doors closed behind them, and she almost lost her seat as the van jolted forward. As they sped away she realized she hadn't closed the front door, and she didn't have her purse, her phone, or anything...and she didn't care.

Her dress clung to her, and her hair hung like bedraggled strings. And she didn't care. She didn't care that her neighbors had seen a fragment of her untidy life. Nothing mattered right now but Jada. From the pit of her stomach her words rose like a stream being released, gushing forth. She hovered over the still body of her daughter. Corinne prayed loudly, lapsing into groanings of her spirit to God. She didn't care if she looked like a woman who'd lost her mind. Looks wouldn't help in the midst of spiritual warfare. Looks had nothing to do with life and death.

thirty-six

Jamilah looked at the cell bars as she rehearsed the events that led her to this place. It was a blur from the moment Ari arrived at her door to the appearance of Miss Jordan at the door accusing her of kidnapping her child. Kidnapping! That woman was crazy. She'd glared and slung her unfounded allegations with malicious purpose.

If Jamilah hadn't been so shocked by what was happening, she might have strangled her while reminding the deranged woman of her sins as a horrible mother who was not worthy of having such a special daughter.

In the condo Jamilah tried to tell the officers it was Miss Jordan who was at fault. That she left Ari alone and in harm's way with Tyrone and Big Boy. But Ari's mother flatly denied doing so, saying she'd only run a quick errand and came back to find her daughter missing. Her contention was that Jamilah would weave any tale she needed to paint her as the villain, but it was the teacher who was guilty of wrongdoing.

Jamilah was speechless.

The more Miss Jordan went on, the louder Ari cried. Her mother stopped only long enough to soothe the child, reassuring her, "Mama is here now."

Stifling the urge to scream, Jamilah shook her head in disbelief as she listened to Miss Jordan's skillful dissertation. Obviously drugs had not muddled her ability to be scheming and deceitful.

Leaning back against the wall, Jamilah pondered her fate. She'd used her "one phone call," but no one was answering their phones. First she tried Dwayne, but even his cell phone was off. Her mother, who refused to have a cell phone, was still gone. As much as she hated to, she tried to call Tamara, whose cell phone was also off. The policeman was quickly losing patience. That left her at the mercy of Mr. Parker. She would never hear the last of it from him, she was sure. However, he'd agreed to come and bail her out, although he sounded none too pleased.

So here she sat.

Lord, how did I get in this mess? And how do I get out of it? No…how are You going to get me out of it? I'm so tired of trying to figure out how to make things happen. Did You allow this so I would come to the end of myself? It worked 'cause truly I'm in over my head, and I have no idea what to do or where to go from here. So, Lord, I officially give up.

Emotional exhaustion overtook her, and she fell into a fitful sleep.

She awoke with a start when an officer rolled open the door to her cell. "Williams, you have visitors."

"Visitors?" Jamilah wondered who they could be. Who else knew she was here besides Mr. Parker?

"This way," he said, guiding her down the hall and then into a small room.

She couldn't imagine who'd come. Sitting on the edge of a hard bench she waited. The door opened, and Mr. Parker entered with a man she'd never seen before. She felt very small and wilting beneath Mr. Parker's steely stare as he wordlessly studied her. She stood and prepared for the impending tirade.

Mr. Parker motioned to the gentleman. "Patrick Damon." He motioned to Jamilah. "Jamilah Williams." His eyes never left her face. "Mr. Damon is an attorney. I assume you will need one."

"I didn't do anything wrong!"

"That's what everybody in jail says."

"Mr. Parker! I am not 'everybody' in jail, and you know I'm not the kind of person who kidnaps kids. This is ridiculous!"

"I warned you something like this would happen. This is the last thing I need! A scandal with one of my teachers. What are you trying to do? Get my school closed down?"

"Mr. Parker, I *did not* kidnap Ari. She showed up at my apartment building and passed out in the lobby. Probably from running so hard. She had a huge bruise on the side of her face. All I could get out of her was that her mother hadn't been home, and two boys attacked her, but she got away and ran."

"That's a completely different story than Miss Jordan is telling. She says she was at home and only left briefly to do an errand. And you came and took Ari during her absence. She says there were no young men in her apartment. And Ari isn't saying anything. Miss Jordan's also saying you've taken Ari home without her permission before. So, Miss Williams, *you* have a problem."

To add insult to injury, he gave her an "I told you so" look.

"This is ridiculous. That is not true…"

"With the exception of your doorman, who could be viewed as a sympathetic witness, it's your word against hers," Mr. Parker added. "And since you've taken Ari home before without her mother's permission…and there are witnesses who say that's true…you are in major trouble."

Jamilah plopped down on the bench. "I don't believe this!"

"You'd better start."

"If I may interject," Mr. Damon said. "Hindsight is wonderful, but we need to come up with a solution. The first thing we need to do is get you out of here. I suggest you let me handle this. From what you're saying, Miss Jordan may be using you as a smokescreen to stay out of trouble herself. But we'll unravel that later."

It had to be a nightmare, she decided as she stood before the judge.

Rhetoric escaped her. Legalese swirled around as she wondered where Ari was now and what was happening to her. There was nothing she could do about that now. She had to concentrate on getting out of this fix.

"Your Honor, Miss Williams is not a flight risk. She's a respected and well-liked teacher. My client was nowhere near the home of the accuser. Ariana Jordan ran to Miss Williams' residence after two young men in her complex attacked her. Miss Williams called paramedics after the child passed out in her lobby and tried to contact her mother, who wasn't at home. So Miss Williams did what she thought best, allowing the child to remain in her care until her mother could be found. Unfortunately, her mother showed up and charged her falsely with kidnapping."

"Do you always get this involved with your students, Miss Williams?" The judge was looking at her.

Jamilah looked to Mr. Damon, who motioned for her to speak. "No, Your Honor, I don't. It's just that Ari's...Ariana's mother has failed to pick her up several times after school. I've escorted her home before to make sure she got there safely. On one occasion it was very late and Ariana's mother hadn't come home, so I took Ari home with me. I left a note and cab fare for Miss Jordan so she could come and get her daughter when she got home."

"That was generous of you. Did you report this neglect to DCFS?"

Jamilah looked at Mr. Parker, who didn't move. He didn't even look at her. She looked back to the judge.

"I didn't. Ari loves her mother...and I wasn't sure whether foster care was the best way to go, or where she would end up. I also thought I could help her."

"Miss Williams, Ari could end up where she almost ended up tonight if action isn't taken to remove her from an unsafe environment. Living at home might not be in her best interest at this time. This is about a little girl who needs a safe place."

Turning back to Mr. Damon, he hit his gavel against its pedestal.

"Due to the circumstances and since your client witnessed the neglect of Ariana Jordan, I will release her on her own recognizance while the matter is investigated. Miss Williams will immediately contact the Department of Children and Family Services and file a report."

He turned back to Jamilah. "Do you understand? You are to contact DCFS right away." Her stomach was sinking, and she looked down at the floor.

"Yes, Your Honor," Mr. Damon said. He grabbed her elbow and leaned in to whisper in her ear. "I suggest we get out of here before he changes his mind."

"But I can't do what…"

"Let's discuss this later."

"No really, I can't…"

"Is there a problem, Counselor?"

The judge was looking at her again.

"No, Your Honor." Mr. Damon looked at Jamilah, and his eyes made it clear now was not the time to discuss disobeying the judge's order.

Jamilah sighed and allowed herself to be led from the courtroom. The situation was getting more impossible by the minute. She was torn between the knowledge that she should yield to the authorities and the lack of peace she had every time she considered contacting DCFS. She'd always used her inner peace level as a monitor for what she should do, and now that she couldn't do that, she was confused. She just couldn't shake the feeling that she should not call DCFS. When in doubt, "don't" had always been a simple rule to follow…until now, when a judge was staring down at her. She wasn't sure if her unease was God's doing or her own selfish motives. If she reported Ari's mother to DCFS, Ari might disappear in the system. But Jamilah also knew she couldn't help her from jail. The law is the law. But did the leading of the Spirit override that? It was a catch-22. *God, feel free to show up anytime now!* she thought.

thirty-seven

Corinne roused herself from sleep feeling as if she were struggling beneath a million wet blankets. In the frantic aftermath of finding Jada near death and the anxiety of waiting for the doctors to get her stabilized, Corinne had been nearly comatose herself. When she found a phone to use, she realized she was so used to speed dialing Randall from her cell phone that she didn't know his cell number. And she didn't want to call her mother until she could balance the bad with something good, lest she upset her fragile health. She couldn't really think of anyone else to call. This left her time to stew over all that had occurred.

By the time the doctors came to deliver the news that Jada was resting and that she would probably pull through, Corinne was depleted, the last vestiges of her strength gone. She unfolded herself from the chair she was in and jumped to her feet. Her dress had dried and was sticking to her body. The diluted, dried blood created a tie-dyed image across the front, resulting in a crumpled effect that could pass as a deliberate fashion statement. She didn't care that she looked a mess. And it felt good not to care! She pulled the dress away from her body and made her way to Jada's bedside.

Jada was sleeping soundly, and color had returned to her face. Bags of liquid were replenishing all that had been lost, and a monitor beeped away steadily, noting her progress. In the midst of the equipment she looked so small, so innocent, so peaceful. Corinne's eyes filled with tears, causing her daughter's face to blur. Pacing back and forth, she prayed as she'd never prayed before. She pleaded for the life of her daughter and repented for not trusting God to take care of her. She confessed that part of the reason she hadn't asked for help before was because of her own pride in appearances. She admitted she'd been in denial. Though the truth had been clear all along, to accept it would have meant that something was wrong with her.

She prayed she hadn't learned too late that appearances had nothing to do with anything important. Appearances were simply that—a smokescreen that covered the truth of where everyone really lived, that covered what God already knew. How long had she been trying to dress up what only God could fix? Why had it taken her so long to come to the end of herself and call on Him? She squeezed Jada's hand. *Don't let it be too late, Lord. Please don't let it be too late!*

She let go of Jada's hand and paced again. *Where have appearances gotten me…or Jada, for that fact? I almost lost everything that was important over what? How shallow of me. Lord, forgive me, and help me have the courage to do the right thing for the sake of my child.*

If the truth, no matter how painful it might be, would make them free, it was time to face it head-on and deal with it. She sat down and waited for Jada to regain consciousness. The combination of what her daughter had been through and the harshness of the black hair that fell back from her face made her so pale she almost looked incandescent beneath the light that glowed softly above her bed. With her face scrubbed clean, devoid of the dark kohl circles she'd started surrounding her eyes with and the pale matte lipstick that took the life from her lips, she almost looked like herself again. Hints of the innocent, sweet, vivacious young woman she once knew lay sleeping more peacefully than she probably felt.

Obviously turmoil had raged beneath the surface for so long Jada couldn't take it anymore. Self-loathing washed over Corinne as the horror of what had taken place soaked in. How could she have been so selfish, so hopelessly consumed with herself that she missed all the warning signs? How could she have taken her daughter's pain as a personal affront to her...to the detriment of her only child? *Oh Jada, I am so sorry. Please, God, give me a chance to make it up to her.* There was nothing she could do but wait. Pray and wait. Wait and pray until exhaustion overwhelmed her, and she fell into a deep sleep of her own.

Jada moaned softly. Her eyes struggled to open.

Corinne woke and leaned forward carefully, not wanting to frighten her. Softly she smoothed Jada's temples, as if brushing hair from her face. "It's all right, honey. I'm here. Momma's here."

Jada's eyes fluttered again before opening. "Momma?"

"Yes, sweetheart?" Corinne forced a smile for Jada's sake, not wanting her to see how frightened she'd been. She wanted to be strong for her.

"Oh Momma, I'm sorry..." Jada's eyes filled with tears.

"Shhh...shhh...There's nothing to be sorry for."

"I'm sooo sorry..." Jada couldn't stop the tears.

"No, I'm sorry..."

"I couldn't do it anymore."

"Do what, honey?"

"He was hurting me...can't go back..."

"Who was hurting you? Can't go back where?" She tenderly stroked Jada's temples again. "It's all right. You can tell me. You don't have to go anywhere you don't want to. No one is going to hurt you anymore."

Jada's eyes closed, and her head rolled to the side.

"Jada?"

She didn't answer.

"Jada!" Corinne frantically pressed the call button for the nurse. She gently shook Jada, trying to rouse her. Almost instantly the door burst open. "She was talking to me and then she was gone..." she said to the backs of the doctor and nurse who hovered over Jada as they checked her vital signs.

They turned toward Corinne.

"It's all right. We gave her a strong sedative that might take a little more time to wear off. She's just sleeping."

"Oh! Thank you!" Relief washed over Corinne. She shot up a quick thank You to God too.

"She might go in and out for a bit before she's completely alert."

"Thank you. I'm sorry I panicked. I…"

"No problem. That's what we're here for. Call if you need anything else." With that they were gone, leaving Corinne to ponder what Jada said.

It felt like forever before Jada turned to look at her again. Corinne kissed her forehead gently. She traced soft patterns down Jada's arm, being careful to avoid the IV. She reached for her other arm to take her hand in hers. For the first time she noticed the marks on both her daughter's wrists. She pressed her lips together to stop herself from crying. A supernatural calm washed over her. No, she was not going to lose it…her mind or her daughter. Lifting Jada's hand to her lips, she turned it over, kissing the scars. Jada began crying softly.

"It's okay," Corinne soothed. "I'm here."

Jada continued to cry.

The floodgates opened inside of Corinne too. Softly mother and daughter wept in unison. Both saying nothing and everything in the midst of their tears. Corinne wanted to gather her daughter in her arms and hold her, but she was afraid to upset the equipment. She hovered over her until they were both spent. With no more tears left, it was time for words and new beginnings.

"Jada, I'm so sorry I haven't been here for you. But I'm here now. I love you so much! I…"

Jada's eyes filled with tears again. "But…"

"Let me help you. Tell me what happened. I *want* to help you. Who has been hurting you?" Corinne looked into Jada's eyes, but she turned away. Corinne took her chin in her hand and gently turned her face back toward her. "Please let me help you…"

Jada crumbled. "Pastor Masters…"

Corinne's hand flew to her mouth. "Oh no!"

"He…" And between jagged sobs the story of Pastor Masters' threats and abuse poured out of Jada as if a dam had finally given way. A torrent of pain gushed out.

Corinne struggled not to be swept away. Her mind went back to the pictures she'd found. Could it be possible that Pastor Masters sent them? What a filthy old man. How dare he defile her baby! Unadulterated fury spread through her veins. Her eyes flashed. He was not going to get away with this. Not on her watch. She took a deep breath. Almost too calmly she pressed her fingers to Jada's lips to stop her from descending into self-blame.

"Shhh. It's not your fault. Now get some sleep. Don't you worry… I'm going to take care of everything. Trust me."

"Momma?"

"Yes, baby?"

"I love you."

Corinne's eyes filled with tears. "I love you too. More than you'll ever know. And I never want to give you reason to doubt that again. I…" she stopped. Jada was sleeping again. Corinne's limbs felt leaden. She sank back in the chair, fully depleted. She would wait until Jada regained her strength, and then she would get to work. Now that the truth was out, it was time for everyone to be free…except Pastor Masters.

thirty-eight

Tamara held out her hand, accepting Kevin's help from the taxi. The driver set their bags on the curb in front of the airport with a finality that confirmed it was time to go back to the real world. Sad but true. The entire holiday with Kevin had been a dream come true. She'd never experienced a man so kind, so romantic, so thoughtful. He had been such a tender lover, even wiping away her tears of regret after that first time when she'd given in. He practically talked her out of the guilt she felt.

"Why would God create something so beautiful and not want you to enjoy it?" he breathed tenderly into her ear, kissing away her ability to reason.

She was of the disposition to agree. It seemed so unreasonable of God to allow her to go this far in life without enjoying the pleasures of intimacy. It was highway robbery! And for what? Bragging rights that she'd been celibate longer than most people she knew? At this point in her life she wasn't interested in setting records. She wanted to be loved, to be touched and caressed, to be considered and treated like a real woman. And that's exactly how she felt in Kevin's arms.

Then Kevin had kissed her and made his way to the washroom, leaving her to wrestle with the voices in her head.

"Offer your bodies as living sacrifices, holy and pleasing to God—this is your spiritual act of worship." Well, it just didn't seem that reasonable to her. She had given Him her life. Did He have to have her body too? *"Do you not know…you are not your own? For you were bought at a price; therefore glorify God in your body."* But it was her body. She was the one who had to struggle with her hormones and longings—not God. Why did He make her wait so long to be loved if He wanted her to stay holy? Why didn't He give her a husband a long time ago so she wouldn't end up in this position?

Jamilah would've had a lot to say about that, Tamara was sure. "Trust God's timing, blah, blah, blah…" She had trusted Him, and where had it gotten her? To the middle of her thirties without a man, that's where. Well, now she had one, and she wasn't going to let him go. God would forgive her like He did all the other folk who dipped and slipped. "Backsliding," Jamilah called it. Tamara liked to think of it as simply acknowledging her humanity and realizing she couldn't be as perfect as she would like to be. Staying celibate until marriage was an honorable thought, but it just wasn't realistic.

The weekend had been a haze of romance. Beautiful sunsets, walks along the beach, amazing love-making. She had to pinch herself to make sure she wasn't dreaming. Whenever the voices returned to speak spiritual reason to her, she shook them off and pressed deeper into Kevin's arms.

And now they were making their way through the airport and onto a plane. Returning home meant she would probably have to face the voices she'd run from all weekend. She wondered if Kevin was just as sad about going home as she was.

"Hey, I bet your apartment is going to feel pretty lonely without me in it now, huh?" she ribbed him, after settling into her seat and fastening her seat belt.

"Mmm, yeah." Kevin nodded to a colleague who passed in the aisle, yawned, kissed her on the cheek, and settled back in his chair. "Wow, I'm sleepy. I think I'm gonna grab a nap!"

She grinned and shook her head. He was such a high-energy person.

Small wonder he finally crashed. They had been going nonstop, but she was still too high from the weekend to be tired right now. She watched a couple of movies and read a book while he slept. All too soon they were landing in Chicago's O'Hare airport. As she stood, she suddenly felt something cold.

Kevin touched her arm. "Baby?"

When she looked back he looked concerned. He looked from her to the seat she had just risen from. It was drenched in blood. The heaviness she felt in her pelvis confirmed her thoughts. Her cycle had started early and with a vengeance. She struggled between fear and embarrassment. She'd been putting off going to the doctor about her cycle, which had grown increasingly heavier and heavier over the year. She didn't want to hear his doom and gloom predictions, especially since she wasn't able to address his suggestions about hurrying up and having a child before it was too late.

She sat back down, shivering from the coldness of the damp seat. Kevin summoned a flight attendant, who was very kind and understanding.

Wrapped in one of the airline blankets, she made her way to the bathroom to clean up as best she could for the ride home. For a moment she wondered if she was being punished by God, but then she decided that idea was silly. Still, her period had been heavy before, but this was the first time it had been like this. This was serious. The bleeding was out of control.

Kevin was still looking worried when she came out of the bathroom. "Are you going to be okay?"

"Yes, I'm fine," she asserted, struggling to maintain a semblance of calm. "I've been having a problem for a little while now, and I wasn't quite prepared. I wasn't due for another week." She wasn't about to reveal her panic to him.

"Well, at least you know it's here." He looked relieved.

"What does that mean?" She thought he seemed a little too happy about her period.

"Nothing. But I would get that checked out if I were you. My sister had that problem, and she had fibroids really bad. She had to have surgery. That's nothing to play with."

"Aren't you the clinical one?" She gave a nervous chuckle, trying to mask her fear.

"It's not funny, Tamara. Promise me you'll get checked out." His handsome face was sober as he searched her face.

"I will. Now stop worrying and let's get our bags. You've got a busy day tomorrow, remember?" With that she kissed him on his nose, pretending to be braver than she felt, and off they went.

As he tucked her into the car he'd hired to take her home, he leaned toward her again. "Promise me you'll make a doctor's appointment first thing tomorrow."

"I promise," she said.

"I'll call you later." He kissed her...a detached, hurried kiss...and then he was gone.

Suddenly Tamara felt cold. She shivered even though the early evening air was warm, even bordering on the balmy air she'd left on Grand Cayman. She didn't like how she was feeling, and deep down she knew it had to do with more than the turmoil her body was experiencing. But exactly what, only time would tell.

thirty-nine

Corinne glanced at her watch. It was three o'clock in the morning. Still no word from Randall. Perhaps this was a God thing. Jada's situation caused her to throw out her original plans. More immediate action was required. She still hadn't figured out what she was going to say to her husband. At this point she would deal with the chips falling where they may.

She'd left a message at his office and on their home phone letting him know where she and Jada were, but Randall seldom if ever checked for messages. She hoped he would when he began to wonder where everyone was. Or maybe a neighbor would let him know, depending on when he got home and if anyone in the cul de sac was around. Obviously neither had occurred, and she felt too weary to call the house again. Let him be the one who worried for a change. A sound at the door startled her. The silhouette of Randall filled the doorway. He made his way toward her.

"What happened?"

Corinne put her fingers to her mouth to shush him lest he wake Jada.

"Let's go outside and discuss this. I don't want to wake her," she whispered.

"I will not. I want to see my daughter." His voice was loud.

Jada stirred.

Corinne snorted in disgust, took his hand, and pulled him roughly from the room. She could feel the mother lion rising within her.

As soon as they got out the door and out of hearing range, she dropped his hand as if it had burned her and turned to him, a look of disgust on her face.

He took in her appearance, from her bedraggled hair to her sodden dress. His arm raised, indicating the front of her dress, and dropped. "What happened to you? What is going on here? I got home and no one was in the house."

"Where were you, Randall?" Corinne's tone was accusing.

"I got home around eleven. The front door was wide open but I figured you forgot to close it. I went into the study for something, sat down, and must have fallen asleep. I woke up about two thirty and started toward the kitchen for a snack. That's when I noticed your purse in the foyer, went upstairs, and saw the mess in the hallway, Jada's room, and the bathroom. I ran to our bedroom, and you weren't there. Then it occurred to me to check voicemail before I panicked. That's when I got the message that you were here. What happened, Corinne?"

Her shoulders sagged at the memory. "I got home and found Jada lying in a pool of blood in her bathroom!"

"What!"

"She slit her wrist." Even now the words seemed to come from outside herself.

"But why?" Randall demanded. "What reason could she possibly have for doing something so stupid?"

"That's a good question, Randall. What has happened to this family? To all that we had? To your love for your daughter? For me?" Corinne's voice was steady, her eyes clear as she stared a hole into Randall.

"Corinne, now is not the time to have this discussion."

"Oh but it is. Now is the perfect time. And believe me, I'm going somewhere with this…"

"You know what happened, Corinne. Your drinking disgusts me, and your 'poor me' attitude disgusts me even more."

Corinne shook her head slowly. "No, that is not it. I've finally figured it out…"

"Look, I don't have time for this. Our daughter is lying in there." He adamantly pointed a finger toward Jada's room. Color rose in his face.

"If you cared so much about our daughter you would have exercised more integrity in our marriage."

"What are you talking about?"

"I'm talking about your adulterous behavior…with men."

"What!" Randall was practically hissing, but she didn't allow it to deter her from what she wanted to say.

"I've been wondering to myself if it would hurt any less if it was with a woman. I've come to the conclusion it wouldn't. I wonder how your congregation will take the news that their illustrious pastor has been having affairs with men behind his wife's back? Perhaps they will finally like me."

She was surprised at how calm she sounded because a tsunami was raging in her soul now that she was finally getting out what she'd suppressed for so long.

Blood drained from his face, and he took a step toward her. "Are you crazy?"

"No, I'm not crazy. But I'm mad, Randall, very, very mad."

"If you dare breathe a word of this unfounded garbage…" He stepped toward her, his voice filled with rage.

"Are you denying the truth, Randall?"

"That is your truth, Corinne. Perhaps you're the one in denial about how undesirable you've been."

"That is low, even for you. This has nothing to do with why you won't sleep with me. This has to do with your character and how it has caused the demise of this family." Her voice also rose. She caught herself and ended with a hiss. She refused to let him ruffle her.

"And who do you think is going to believe your silly assumptions?

Where are you going with this artful story? To my loyal congregation?" He laughed in scorn. "That should go over big."

"I saw you, Randall," she said quietly.

"Saw what?" He looked at her in disgust.

"I saw you kissing that man in your study. You remember him, right? Tall, blond, good-looking? Perhaps he's moved on. I haven't seen him around since. And Randall, you don't need to just worry about me. You need to focus your damage control efforts on Pastor Masters too."

Randall looked as if he'd been rocked off his center. "What do you mean? What about Pastor Masters? I've got enough dirt on him to bury him if he even so much as thinks about saying anything against me."

"Obviously he's got enough on you too. It seems that Pastor Masters has known about your little secret for quite some time. He's been molesting Jada after worship rehearsal and threatening to expose you if she tells."

She stopped and watched his jaw go slack. Watched the weight of what she was saying sink in. "As you can see, I'm the least of your worries. I'm sure after Jada submits her report to the police he will squeal like a pig to cover his own tracks. That should be cute for your beloved congregation to watch. Both of their pastors quibbling over two shocking scandals. Talk about stealing the limelight from Jesus! That should really build up their faith."

"You have no proof, Corinne. And Masters is a liar. What you are talking about is just idle speculation. You sound like a woman scorned and grasping at straws."

"You wish! I have pictures, Randall." There! She'd said it.

"Pictures of what?" Randall practically spat at her.

Corinne felt powerful. "Pictures of you at a gay bar and locked in the embrace of another man. Pictures of you naked. Pictures of you..."

Randall held up his hand. "Why you little... Where did you get them? Did you hire someone to follow me?"

Corinne felt calm. She took a deep breath before delivering the death blow. "If I can put two and two together, I would say that your dear associate pastor had a plan B in case Jada stopped cooperating with him. Since she refused to go back to worship rehearsal, he decided to blackmail you."

Randall said nothing.

Corinne stepped closer, daring him to do something.

"Randall, don't play me so cheap. I am your wife. I loved you. We have a daughter. This isn't something that I relish, but it is reality, and it's time we deal with it."

Again she was amazed at how calm she was.

"This can't be about just you anymore, Randall. Think what you were subjecting your daughter to while you were off on your little trysts. I'll admit and absorb my part of the blame. I could have picked her up from church if I wasn't in the city 'feeling sorry for myself,' as you've put it. However you were right there…"

"Corinne…I…"

"There is nothing you can say. What does the Bible say about qualifications for a bishop or pastor? He should 'rule his own house well'? What happened to protecting us? Or did you think a fancy house was supposed to keep the wolves away?

"Why don't you practice what you preach, Randall? Your daughter almost died because of you. She would rather slit her wrists than expose her father…a father who hasn't been much of a father for quite some time now. And you put my health in danger. Did you even think about the fact that you were exposing me to the possibility of HIV and other diseases? As much as you 'despise,'" she made quote marks with her fingers, "my drinking, I chose to anesthetize my pain rather than confront or expose you."

She paused. Suddenly she felt very light. As if she'd been released of a huge burden.

"You know what? I'm done, Randall. I don't even have the strength to be angry at you anymore. I'm done. Stick a fork in me. I'm finished. I've come to realize that Jesus already died for your sin, so I don't have to. And I'm not going to let Jada do it either. I'm tired of dying by degrees because of you. It's time you own your filthy little secret and realize you have a problem. Yes, that's right! *You* have a problem, whether you want to admit it or not. My fault in this is I've been internalizing your problem. I've been owning it and blaming myself. But it's not about me at all. It's about whatever is broken in you."

She felt stronger than she had in a long time. "Don't you think it's time you displayed a little character and owned your own stuff? You can deny the truth to me all day, but you can't hide from God. And He will allow circumstances to force you to face and admit your secret. Remember the other prominent pastors who have fallen because of sexual sin? God will not be mocked, and you know it. What does the Bible say? 'Take note, you have sinned against the LORD; and be sure your sin will find you out.' Consider yourself outed, Mister. Pictures and all. I'm not covering for you any longer. I will not be your sacrificial lamb or enabler. And I certainly will not sacrifice my daughter for you."

She stepped closer to him.

"You've got two choices, Randall. You can continue to deny this and drag us through the muck and the mire or you can take the high road by admitting your problem and talking to your congregation before Masters or someone else does. My last official duty as your wife will be to help you do damage control on this for Jada's sake. After that I'm filing for divorce."

Randall put up his hand to stop her. "Not to justify anything that I've done because you're right, I hurt my family…

"You know, Randall, it's deeper than that. There's a difference between admission and confession. The bottom line is that you sinned against God. The fallout is you hurt your family. And I'm not sure you're really sorry about that yet. And God won't fix what you won't repent of and come clean about."

"That's true. But perhaps if you'd confronted me sooner things wouldn't have gotten this far. You are my wife, Corinne."

"I can't own your choices, Randall, and I refuse to. Only you can do that. I will give you this much though. Perhaps we were both broken in our own way, and neither of us was in any shape to help the other. That is so sad. The question is where do we go from here?"

"I don't know, but it will probably cost us everything we have."

"It already has, in my opinion."

"Let's continue this conversation later. Our first concern right now is to see Jada through this."

He headed toward her room but stopped and turned toward Corinne one more time. "I'm sorry for all the pain I've caused. I'm not happy this happened, but at the same time I'm relieved this all came out. Does that make any sense to you?" He hung his head, turned, and started toward Jada's room again.

Corinne followed. For the first time in a long time she pitied him. His logic wasn't so strange after all.

forty

Wednesday morning Tamara turned the key and stepped into the reception area of her office. She stopped short, looking into the disapproving eyes of Stella, who was seated at her desk early and ready for duty. She didn't look amused.

"I am so glad you could join us."

"Don't start, Stella. I'm not in the mood for your mouth this morning." Tamara marched toward her office, anger building on top of the exasperation already in place. Spinning around she made her way back to Stella's desk. "Just who is the boss here, anyway? Do I report to you or do you report to me? I don't appreciate you talking to me like that!"

Stella didn't flinch. "I guess that depends on who shows up in this office to field emergency calls that went unanswered all weekend, and who should let her assistant know she isn't coming to work so she can cancel and shift appointments before people start showing up. You were supposed to be back in the office yesterday, yes? So forgive me if I'm a little upset this morning. Especially since you must have turned off your cell and didn't return my calls or check messages. But since you are the boss, I have reorganized your calendar today and rescheduled yesterday's clients. And you have two urgent messages."

"What are the messages?" Tamara asked through gritted teeth, struggling not to go off on her disrepsectful assistant.

Stella picked up a message pad and said slowly and deliberately, "Let's see. Jamilah is in jail and needs you to bail her out. Corinne's daughter is in the hospital. Seems she slit her wrists, was being raped, and, well, I couldn't make out the rest of the message. It was really garbled because Corinne was crying too hard to make much sense." She glared at Tamara and handed her the pink pieces of paper.

Tamara snatched the paper from her hands. "Stella, stop being sarcastic. That's not funny!"

"Exactly my point. I didn't think it was very funny either."

Stella was looking very serious.

It dawned on Tamara as she looked at the first message that Stella hadn't made up or exaggerated a word of what she'd said. "Oh my!" she said as she dashed into her office and dialed Jamilah's cell phone. It went straight to voicemail. She left a message: "Jamilah! Where are you? I'm so sorry. I was out of the country this weekend, and I'm just now getting your message. Please call when you get this message. I...I don't know what to do!" She hung up the phone. She thought of calling Jamilah's mother, but decided not to upset her. She'd just have to wait.

She tried Corinne's home number next. The answering machine picked up. She took a deep breath. She couldn't sound frantic with a client. She was supposed to be a calming force. "Corinne, this is Tamara. I was out of the country this weekend when your call came in. Please give me a call at your earliest convenience. I'll keep you and Jada in my prayers."

The phone slid out of her hands. She caught it as it hit the desk and put it back in its cradle. She sank onto her chair. Placing both elbows on her desk, she put her head in her hands. She took deep breaths and tried to slow her thoughts. She felt like she was drowning, and she couldn't hold back the tears any longer. The floodgates opened, and all the pent-up frustration and pain gave way to sobs that echoed through her office. How could a time that felt so right end up so wrong?

First thing yesterday morning she'd called her doctor, who asked her to come in right away. As she sat in his office waiting on the cold, hard examining table with air shooting up her back she again wondered if God was pinning her to the wall because of her weekend.

Dr. Silvers, who had always been like family to her, was somber when he entered the room.

"Well, well, well. You can run but you can't hide huh, young lady?"

"I haven't been hiding…"

"Yes, you have. You know we should have taken care of this a long time ago. I don't need an ultrasound or an MRI to tell me what the problem is. Those fibroids have to come out. Unfortunately we'll probably have to do a full hysterectomy at this point."

Tamara felt the blood drain out of her face. "What? Wait a minute! Hold up! How did we get from a few little fibroids to this?"

"We got here because you wouldn't let me deal with those little fibroids when it was less drastic. I relented because you were holding out so you could have children. Have you gotten married or in a serious relationship since the last time I saw you?"

"No."

"Have you been sexually active?"

"Yes. Could that be the problem? Maybe it aggravated something?"

"Aggravated what?" He was looking at her as if she were a guilty child. "The only thing it could have aggravated is your conscience. I thought you were Miss Celibate Christian Girl?"

"What do you mean by that?" Tamara was indignant. "I came here for a medical opinion, not a sermon."

"Whoa, my friend!" Dr. Silvers put up his hands as if fending off an attack. "I didn't mean anything by it. You were the one who lambasted me when I suggested you hurry up and have a child. You informed me, quite self-righteously mind you, that you were a Christian and would not be having sex until you were married. How did I end up being the bad guy here?"

"I'm sorry. I overreacted." Tamara realized her guilt made her hypersensitive.

"Yes, you did." Dr. Silvers was looking at her like a stern father. "Now, let's get back to the real issue. I want to wait until the test results come back before making a final determination, but be prepared. I suggest you clear your calendar for a good month or six weeks. I'll call you tomorrow, okay?"

After she nodded, he turned and left.

Tamara wanted to plea bargain with God, though at the present moment she felt she had no right to ask Him for anything. She got dressed and left the doctor's office in a fog, moving through a haze of condemnation, angry stabs at the injustices of life, and resentment that some folks seemed to get away with everything and she never could. The scripture "as a man chastens his son, so the LORD your God chastens you" came to mind. Well, she wished God didn't love her so much.

Wandering home, Tamara plopped onto the couch in the living room, pulled a fluffy throw around her shoulders, and stared off into space. Her thoughts were a mush of nothing. She didn't know how long she sat there dozing on and off. Finally she awoke and the darkness pulled her back to the present. She left the couch to go to bed. In the back of her mind she noted that she hadn't heard from Kevin since he dropped her off the evening before. Exhaustion, physical and emotional, overtook her, wrapped her in its arms, and carried her away to a place where she felt no longing or pain.

When she awoke this morning, she'd felt drunk or drugged. She'd hated the thought of going to work but knew she must. And now she'd already dealt with Stella's mouth, discovered that Jamilah was in jail and Corinne's daughter had been raped and slit her wrists. On top of that was yesterday's news that her option to be a mother someday was probably gone forever. It was too much…way too much.

Stella was standing in the doorway looking at her. "Good thing I kept your morning open. Are you going to be all right?"

"Yes, it's just that…I had to go to the doctor yesterday…" She waved a hand as if it would finish the sentence for her.

The phone rang and Stella turned to answer it.

"Yes…yes, she is. One moment please." Turning back to Tamara she said, "Speaking of the doctor, that's him on line one." She turned back toward her desk as she closed the door, knowing Tamara would want privacy.

That's a first! Tamara thought before taking a shaky breath and answering the phone. "Hello, Tamara speaking." *Dear God, please have mercy on me.* She hoped He was still listening.

forty-one

Jamilah had never been so happy to see her classroom. She took a deep breath. Yes, even the bleach they used to clean the floors smelled good. On Tuesday Ari hadn't been in class, but she sat at her desk this morning, head down, avoiding Jamilah's eyes. Poor thing. She was in a very difficult place—torn between her mother and her teacher. Jamilah longed to hold her and let her know that none of what transpired was her fault. But she practiced restraint. She didn't want to jeopardize her already tenuous position at school or put Ari in greater emotional angst.

She could feel the air change when she entered the teachers' lounge later that morning. Obviously the news had gotten out about her little soiree in jail, probably thanks to Mr. Parker. He didn't say a word to her this morning, but the set of his jaw announced he was still highly annoyed by what he termed her unnecessary intervention in a situation she could never win. She almost agreed at this stage but hoped against hope that God would do something. She was standing on the scripture, "You will not need to fight this battle…stand still and see the salvation of the LORD." A child needed saving. She couldn't be Jesus to Ari, but she sure wouldn't mind being used by Him to bless her.

Mr. Parker met her in the hallway as she went to her classroom. "Miss Williams, have you called DCFS yet?"

"No, Mr. Parker, I have not." Jamilah steeled herself for his response.

"Why not?" His voice was tight with irritation.

"I don't have peace about it."

"You have greater peace about going to jail?"

"I don't think it will get that far. I don't think Ari's mother will stay sober long enough to follow through. She's just blowing smoke because once again she looked like an unfit mother. Even though she is, she doesn't want that to be public knowledge."

"All the more reason for you to proceed as you've been ordered to do."

"I can't. I have faith that…"

"Faith!" Mr. Parker snorted. "Faith has nothing to do with having sense, Miss Williams. Why would you put your career on the line for this little girl? Do you know how many other children are in the same situation? How many will be in your classroom year after year? Are you going to try to save them all? And are you really saving Ari by sending her back to the same hopeless situation day after day? I think you need to seriously rethink this."

The school bell rang.

"We'll continue this discussion later."

"I can't ignore what I feel in my spirit, Mr. Parker. I know you don't understand, but I can't and won't take matters into my own hands and call DCFS. I'm sorry."

"In that case, you have until the end of the day to reconsider and do the right thing. Do you understand me? I can't afford to have you bring anymore negative attention to this school. You either do what the judge has ordered you to or don't come back to work."

"So is this about me or the school at this point? I don't see how my decision to avoid having a child removed from her home and taken away from her mother has an impact on your school budget. I'm not saying I will never call the agency. I'm just saying I don't feel led to do it right now."

"All right then. Don't say I didn't try to help you." With that he headed down the hallway, anger evident in his stride.

She watched him as she prayed silently, *God, I'm not telling You what to do, but You have got to do something soon. I don't know what to do! I don't know what You have planned, but I'm trying to be still until this whole thing plays out. It's all on You!*

She thought of what her mother had said when she told her about going to jail. Surprisingly she hadn't seemed the least bit shaken when Jamilah relayed the events of her arrest. Her mom never missed a beat as she set their dinner on the table. She slowly sank down into her chair, more concerned with the condition of her knees than what Jamilah shared. Before giving thanks for the meal, she instructed Jamilah to stand fast. She was sure God was working everything out for the good.

"You know, sometimes things have to get ugly before you can appreciate the beauty of what God is able to do with your life. Jesus had to die before He could save you. You might have to die to your dream of saving Ari before anything can happen. Remember that just about the time you become convinced God isn't doing anything, that's exactly when He's working the hardest on your behalf."

"Are you sure, Mama? Because nothing has ever looked more impossible."

"That's because your focus is on the wrong thing. You're still trying to figure out how you can help God with this. Trust me. He does not need your help. And He loves Ari more than you do. The devil just wants to get you wound up in fleshly effort so you aren't in the right spot to receive your blessing. When you can't see what God is up to, you don't need to. Learn to stay out of His biz'ness and let Him do His work."

Jamilah was trying to do that. She just couldn't bear being the reason Ari was taken away from her mother. She knew Ari would see it as an act of betrayal, and Jamilah couldn't bear being the reason the girl ended up with strangers. Ari would never understand.

Interrupting her thoughts, the school bell rang. Jamilah entered the classroom and glanced at her students. She looked at her most forlorn student, wondering how to best break the ice.

"Good morning, class!" she announced.

"Good morning, Miss Williams!" they happily chorused back, not aware of the turmoil that swirled between Jamilah and Ari.

"Good morning, Ari. It's good to have you back!" She smiled her brightest smile.

Ari perked right up. "Thank you, Miss Williams. I'm glad to be back!" She looked relieved as her eyes searched Jamilah's face to make sure everything was fine between them. Satisfied that it was, her countenance relaxed.

With the air cleared, they were both free to continue their normal day. It felt good to settle back into the usual routine. The sameness that sometimes made her wonder if she wanted to remain in elementary teaching felt great today. The hours sped by. Jamilah glanced up to check the time and couldn't believe it was 2:55 already. Out of the corner of her eye she saw Mr. Parker outside her room talking with a woman and man. As the bell rang, he opened the door and entered the classroom. The two visitors came with him and watched as the children gathered their things and got ready to leave.

The principal came toward Jamilah looking rather grim. "Miss Williams, this is Mr. Stafford and Miss Wales from DCFS. Will you please ask Ari to wait for a moment?"

Ari looked up at the mention of her name. Jamilah felt rooted to the spot. She opened her mouth and closed it. She stared at Mr. Parker, who seemed irritated with her refusal to do what he asked. He turned to Ari.

"Ari, will you wait a moment, please?"

"Yes sir." Her eyes grew round as she sat back down in her chair. Looking to Jamilah she asked, "Am I in trouble?"

"No, Ari, you are not." Jamilah's voice was firm but barely audible. Her head was swimming.

When all the other kids were gone, Mr. Parker walked toward Ari with his two guests. The lady bent down, extending her hand to Ari and introducing herself. "Hello, young lady. How are you? My name is Miss Wales. Will you come with me?"

Ari looked at Jamilah for confirmation that she should go.

Jamilah was looking at the principal. "How could you do this?"

"You wouldn't, so I did."

"Miss Williams? My Mama told me not to go anywhere with strangers."

Again Jamilah looked from Mr. Parker to Ari and back to Mr. Parker, her look saying, "If you think I'm going to tell her to go with that woman you're crazy."

Mr. Parker leaned over and spoke reassuringly to Ari. "These are very nice people, Ari, who are here for your benefit. It's okay for you to go with them. They're going to take you to meet your mother. And then they've made arrangements for you to be in a safer place so no boys can hurt you."

Jamilah couldn't believe this was happening.

Ari began to cry. "But I'm safe here. I don't want to go anywhere else." She looked to Jamilah. "Miss Williams, tell them! I don't want to go with them. I'm scared!"

The lady gently tried to pull Ari from the chair. "There's no reason to be afraid. Your mother is waiting, and everything is going to be all right. You'll see."

"Why isn't she here now? I don't understand." Suddenly the light of understanding came on in her eyes. "Mama said if I misbehaved people would take me away from her. You're not taking me away from my mama, are you?" Her voice rose. She broke free and ran to Jamilah, throwing her arms around her waist. "Please don't let them take me! This is all my fault. I didn't mean to be bad. Please don't let them take me!"

"Ari, you are not bad. Don't blame yourself. This is not your fault." Jamilah cast an accusing look at Mr. Parker while trying to comfort her.

Mr. Parker didn't seem daunted or deterred from his mission. Firmly untangling Ari from around Jamilah's waist, he turned her toward him and knelt to her level. "Ari, no one is going to hurt you, and this is for your own good. Now these people have a very nice place for you to stay until your mother can get some help and get back on her feet. No one is going to take you away from your mother forever." He looked at Jamilah pointedly. "No one. Now everything is going to be okay. Be a good girl, and everything will be fine. I know you are very bright and good, so you know we would only do what's best for you. And if you care about your mother you want her to get help, don't you?"

Ari nodded. "She won't get sick anymore?"

Mr. Parker brightened. "That's right. Now run along. Your mother should be in the office waiting by now."

"All right." Ari looked back at Jamilah. "Will you come to visit me, Miss Williams?"

Mr. Parker interjected, "She won't be able to for a while, but everything will be okay. Isn't that right, Miss Williams?"

Jamilah nodded. She watched as Ari was led away by the two strangers. The door closed behind them.

The principal was still standing there, studying her face.

"I can't believe you did that. I hope you're satisfied."

"Indeed I am." He pulled himself up to his full height before heading toward the door. "I told you I have a school to run." He stopped, turned, and looked at her. "By the way, you're fired." He went to the door, opened it, and shut it behind him.

Jamilah wasn't surprised, just disappointed. Heading to her desk to pack her things, all she could muster was, "All right, Mama, I certainly hope this is as ugly as it gets. This is about as much ugly as I can handle."

forty-two

Lydia breathed a sigh of relief. She never thought she would get to the place where she considered Chicago home. But if home was where the heart is, this had to be it. Brandon was here, and a month away had been way too long, even though it had flown by work wise. She enjoyed seeing her old friends again and feeling the adrenaline rush of being in control of her environment. There was even the special thrill of completing a project on her own and making a name for herself. It gave her confidence to know she could get out there and make things happen. But she had missed her times of intimacy with Brandon. Those times of shutting the world out and reveling in their own romantic space…away from prying eyes and undesirable distractions.

While she was gone Brandon had been in the thick of filming. He sounded tired every time she talked to him. Last-minute changes had the entire cast and crew performing under tremendous stress. As Chicago forgot that it was spring heading toward summer, unexpected and erratic weather complicated the shooting schedule, stretching the work hours beyond the crew and cast's usual threshold for long days and nights. There were some days she didn't get to talk to Brandon at all. When he resurfaced, he sounded pitiful. Lydia felt so bad for him that she sent care packages, hoping they would cheer him up until she returned.

Now she was bouncing in anticipation of surprising him. After reaching her apartment and unpacking her luggage, she carefully applied herself to her toilette.

"I'm not trying to upset you or anything, but may I suggest you take the time to have a serious talk with Jesus? 'Cause I have a feeling you're going to really need Him soon." The words of caution Sylvia had spoken hovered in the back of Lydia's mind, but she pushed them away, hoping this time her friend was wrong. She deserved to be happy after all she'd been through. She'd agreed with her dear friend that, indeed, she had been ruled by her emotions and brokenness for a long time, but this was different. Brandon brought out a different side of her that she liked. She did not want to lose that part of herself.

She had had plenty of time while she was away to reflect on why her marriage to Richard had gone so wrong. She hated to admit it, but she did. A large part of the demise was her fault. She chuckled wryly. Tamara would have been happy to hear that. Wow! She'd come a long way. Perhaps it was the healing attributes of Brandon's attention that had freed her to really take a long, hard look at the contributing factors to her ability to repel the very thing she wanted. At any rate, she felt she'd finally owned her stuff and put it to rest. During her soul-searching she'd realized Richard was a lot like her dad.

"You've got daddy issues, girl," Sylvia said in her sage way. "You need to call him."

The moment Sylvia said it, Lydia knew it was true. She'd just never realized how much it affected her relationships with other men. Finally she did it. She called him even though she'd always felt her dad didn't love her, that he preferred her sister. She even thought he secretly wished she were a boy. When she expressed this to him, he was shocked.

"Do you know your sister felt the same way? She thought I loved you more than her and accused me of paying more attention to you!"

"What? That's crazy! You were so hard on me."

"I was hard on you because you were a strong-willed child. But I could see the promise in you. I didn't want you to take all that energy and creativity and charisma and ruin yourself, so I tried to keep a firm grip to teach you to channel all that in the right direction." He chuckled. "Lawd, have mercy, I can't win for losing. Your sister thought because I wasn't always on her case the way I was with you that I didn't care, and here you were thinking the same way."

Lydia felt the shackles breaking off. "So you did love me?"

"I did and I do! I love you very much, Lydia. Quiet as its kept, you were my favorite. I knew you were going to make me proud one day—and you have."

Tears flooded Lydia's eyes and for a moment she couldn't speak. "Daddy, do you know how long I've waited to hear those words?"

"Maybe I've gotten soft in my old age. But I wasn't raised to be running around hollerin' 'I love you' all the time. It wasn't the manly thing to do. If a man loved his family, he worked hard to provide for them. He disciplined his children so they didn't run crazy later on in life. I did the best I could, baby doll, so you could be your best. To me that was showing my love."

"Daddy?" Lydia sounded like a little girl.

"Yes?"

"I love you too. Will you forgive me for being so mean? I was just angry." Suddenly her negative actions against her dad seemed exaggerated and foolish.

"I know it, baby. Don't you know love loves in spite of all that ugly stuff? Just 'cause you wanted to poke out your lips and act haughty didn't stop me from loving you. Some things only age and time can fix. I knew one day we would have this conversation, so I just waited."

Lydia was grateful for his forgiveness. "Daddy?"

"Um hmm?"

"Can you feel me hugging you through the phone?"

"Can you feel me hugging you back?"

"Yes, I can!"

"Now run along. All this mushy stuff is making me embarrassed. Just don't take so long to call next time."

Lydia was so happy she thought her heart would burst. "I won't!" She laughed. "I love you, Daddy."

"Back at ya."

As Lydia hung up the phone she laughed again. She figured she'd quit while she was ahead. One confession of love was about all he could handle, but it was all she needed.

As she sprayed on the cologne she knew went straight to Brandon's head every time, she marveled at how much lighter in spirit she felt. She had hope for the future. Yes, her time away had been cathartic, giving her the space she needed to get to the bottom of her issues and start fresh. She felt free and clear. She wouldn't make the same mistakes with Brandon she'd made with Richard. She could understand Sylvia's concerns about Brandon; she knew they were the concern of any older woman dating a younger man. But so far the concern was unfounded, and what was love but one big risk anyway?

With that she swept out of her apartment and caught a cab to Brandon's hotel. She wanted everything to be in place by the time he got home that night. Armed with flowers and sundry spa items, she swooped out of the cab and into the lobby. The bellman looked surprised to see her. "Mrs. Caldwell! I mean…Miss…"

"It's all right, Jason. I'm happy to see you too." She swept past him and into the elevator. She pulled out her key. She loved hotels that still used real keys as opposed to those credit card things that were sure to stop working if you lingered for more than two days. She arrived at Brandon's floor, stepped out of the hallway, and walked to his door. She let herself in and stopped in the foyer. She took a deep breath. His cologne was in the air, and everything was just as she remembered. She'd called the set to see what time he would be finished and left a message for him to call her. He would be none the wiser that she'd returned early.

She set about placing her touches everywhere. She filled the room with candles and flowers and arranged them just so. The stereo was set to play a music mix she compiled while she was away. Dimming the lights, she stepped back and surveyed her handiwork. Now all that was missing was the champagne. She knew just the kind she wanted and where to get it. She glanced at her watch. If she ran out now, she would make it back in time to light the candles and greet him when he came home.

She headed out. Tripping off the elevator in a flurry, she was too excited to notice the paparazzi on her left as she stepped out and turned right. Suddenly she stopped short. Before her was Brandon, looking as fine as ever, helping a young woman out of a cab. She was very pretty and had a look of untouched innocence. It was clear she was totally smitten by him. Lydia was struck by the fact that she looked a lot like a much younger version of herself. Brandon bent and kissed her passionately before paying the fare and turning to guide her into the hotel lobby. He stopped in his tracks when he saw Lydia staring at him.

"Lydia, you're back!"

She stepped back as if he'd slapped her. "I thought you were working…"

"I was…I…" He was clearly at a loss for words. "Aw, man…" He rubbed his chin.

Lydia stood there saying nothing.

The young woman stepped forward, looking at Brandon with concern. "Do you know this person, baby?"

Lydia felt something in her brain snap. "Do you know this person?" The words sounded far away and slurred, like they were being spoken in slow motion. The scabs stripped away from her newly healed wounds and revealed the old scars on her soul. She unconsciously repeated what the woman said: "Do you know this person, baby?" Now she was up to full-speed as well as volume.

"I can't believe this! Who is this…this child?" Lydia started to wave her away, but then thought better of it. She stepped forward and focused her attention on her and smiled coldly. "Yes, he does know this person…very, very well! Who are you?" Her eyes flashed, and the young woman looked shocked.

"Lydia, stop it!"

She heard Brandon but she couldn't stop the torrent that spewed out of her mouth.

"Stop what? Stop loving you? Stop going ballistic because you've been playing me all along?"

"That's not true!"

"What do you know about truth?"

Click. Click. Click.

She didn't hear the cameras. "You're just an actor. A silly little boy living in a world of make believe where it's convenient to act like you're in love as long as it furthers your career." Tears streamed down her face. "I can't believe I fell for your drivel and let you use me. I hope you got what you wanted. All this time I've been killing myself to finish my work early to get back to you. To get back to what? To you cheating and carrying on?" She turned to the girl again. "Be careful, honey. He lies."

Click. Click. Click. The paparazzi were having a field day, and she was totally oblivious.

Brandon's companion lifted her head, linked her arm through his, and looked with disdain at Lydia.

"I'm sorry for your pain. I suppose it's understandable, but I find it totally unnecessary to create a scene." Turning to Brandon she said, "I think now would be a good time to let her know we've kissed, made up, and gotten engaged." She adjusted her ring to let the huge diamond catch the light as well as Lydia's attention. Turning back to Lydia she gave her a look of dismissal. "Excuse me. I'll leave you two to sort this out like adults." As she attempted to pass her, Lydia's arm snaked out and grabbed the girl's hair.

"Oh no, excuse me!" She was not going out like this—with some young thing who was still wet behind the ears trying to put her in her place. She yanked the girl's hair, satisfied that perhaps she was dismantling her haughty enemy's hair weave.

Brandon leaped forward, attempting to come between the two women who were now flailing on the sidewalk.

"Lydia, stop it!"

He ducked as his girlfriend's handbag sailed through the air.

Click. Click. Click. Click.

The frenzy of the cameras continued to be ignored.

Lydia was totally satisfied as she clung to a healthy chunk of hair.

"What is going on here?" Richard's voice broke through the din, causing Lydia to drop the hair she was holding. Richard and his companion were both looking at her as if she'd lost her mind.

And Lydia suddenly thought perhaps she had. All the work she'd done on herself was lost in frantic emotion over someone who wasn't worth it. Shame washed over her and the tears followed.

Richard gathered her in his arms. "Come on. Let's get you out of here." He gently led her into the lobby, leaving his companion standing on the sidewalk with the other spectators. Sitting her down in a corner away from prying eyes, he allowed her to finish crying, finally taking out his handkerchief and drying her eyes.

His eyes were full of compassion, yet it was clear he was at a loss for words. Finally he managed an awkward chuckle. "Humph. You never cried over me like that, and I actually loved you."

Lydia blew her nose, realizing she probably looked rather pitiful. She managed to squeak, "You did?"

Richard drew a deep breath. "Yup, I did."

"I loved you too, you know." She blew her nose again.

"Sure had a funny way of showing it."

"That's because I didn't know how." Then she shared the hurt and pain from her childhood up to the conversation she'd recently had with her father. She didn't know how much time passed, but she wished a camera was there to catch the expressions on Richard's face as a myriad of emotions crossed it.

His eyes were full of care as he smoothed her hair back from her face.

"So under all that hardcore woman was a little wounded girl. She's kinda cute. You should let her out more often. But tell her that grabbing people's hair weaves on the street is not very attractive." He smiled.

"I did do that, didn't I?" Lydia looked mortified. "I suppose the press was out in full force. They're going to have a field day with that one. Oh well."

Then she hooted and laughed until tears flowed down her face. It felt good to laugh, but she grabbed her chest and tried to compose herself. She was surprised to see Richard still looking at her, a slight smile playing across his lips. His eyes got her attention. They were filled with love and passion. She'd seen that look before…a long time ago. How many times she'd longed to see it again before her own eyes lost their light.

"Wow, there's the woman I met so many years ago."

His expression took her breath away. She looked down to collect herself and cleared her throat. Suddenly she felt awkward. "I'm sorry I took up your time. You probably need to get back to your friend."

"No need to apologize. I'm right where I want to be. So what happens next?"

"I—I don't know…"

"How does getting you home sound for starters?"

"That sounds good," she answered, rising. It was a good place to start.

forty-three

Tamara leaned back in her chair and breathed slowly. She prayed that Stella would not open her door any time soon. A cacophony of thoughts were brewing inside her head and flooding her heart. She couldn't believe she could be so close to happiness at last and have it blow up in her face. She had to admit that having children had not been on her list of things to do…well at least not close to the top. But she liked having the option. And now that was being taken away. There was something ironically unjust about it. Until now she hadn't used her body for anything other than basic bodily functions, and now she was told she was going to lose a part of herself. The part that, in her mind, defined her as a woman. It wasn't fair.

What had Dr. Silvers said the first time she'd seen him about this problem? Something about having a dysfunctional uterus. Fibroids out of control. Her abdominal cavity was distorted. It was a wonder she hadn't experienced more pain. She should have been more serious about having children earlier. "When a woman chose to have a child later in life, fibroids were the uterus' way of trying to make its own baby since you won't." That's the statement that got her. She wasn't sure she believed him anyway. She suspected he said that to challenge her faith and her choice to be celibate. God would never ask her to do something that would be a hazard to her health. She would give Him that much credit, even if she was still angry at Him.

Again she had to calm herself down and remember she hadn't been one of those women who were guilty of having a biological clock meltdown. She thought about Felicia, who had not been thinking about living holy when she got pregnant. She landed a beautiful baby and fabulous husband in one fell swoop. And here she was, having toed the biblical line for so long, and where had it gotten her? Nowhere. With nothing to show for all her hard effort and sacrifice. And now that she finally had a man she might want to have a child with, that choice was being ripped away.

Kevin. She wondered if he wanted to have children. They had never discussed it. They were too busy enjoying one another. She hadn't even pressed him about where they were going in their relationship because she wasn't sure herself. What if he said he wanted to get married? He wasn't saved. As rebellious as she had been of late, her history with God and her knowledge of right and wrong didn't allow her peace about taking that last step.

Rapidly zooming past conviction to deep condemnation after their holiday tryst, she found it hard to think clearly about where they stood or even where she wanted to go from here. She didn't relish the thought of feeling guilty every time she slept with him. And now that she had done it, how could she turn around and say no? And there was part of her that didn't want to. She enjoyed how she felt in his arms. But the other part of her tortured her and muted the joy she experienced with him.

Again she wondered if God was punishing her. Being villainous to prove that He was God and she was not. She could take her life into her hands and do whatever she pleased, but He would have the last say. He had the ability to shut her down if He wanted to. What had she been shaking her puny fist at God about for so long? A man. Well, she had the man she wanted. Now what? Suddenly her acquisition seemed minute in the scheme of things. Was she in love with Kevin? Yes. Did she want to lose him? No. Could she have him and God? She wasn't sure. And right now she didn't feel strong enough to let him go.

Suddenly she had an overwhelming need to talk to him. She needed him to hold her, comfort her, and tell her everything was going to be okay. It occurred to her that she hadn't heard from him all day. There had been a message on her home phone yesterday saying he was really under the gun and would call her today. That wasn't like him. He had been under pressure juggling different deals and clients before and always found time to call.

She thought about this puzzling change of behavior. All of her senses were tingling. She knew what she would tell a client in the same situation. When a man changes his pattern, something is going on. He either has unfinished business or he's decided to move on. But based on their last encounter, that didn't ring true. There had been no indication of him wanting to be anywhere except with her. He was far too generous, romantic, and sensitive to her every need to be in that frame of mind. Poor thing. He must really be under pressure, and a long weekend away probably hadn't helped. He was probably playing catch up.

She decided not to call him while he might be at work. If he was in the middle of something, that wouldn't be good. She knew how he was when he was in his zone, and she was feeling vulnerable from dealing with her own issues. She didn't want to put herself in the position to feel rejected if he was distracted and distant. *I'll just leave a message on his cell phone for him to call me when he comes up for air. I need him to be totally present when I tell him what I have to say.* The butterflies started in the pit of her stomach as she picked up the phone to dial Kevin's number. Her hands shook. What would he say when she told him about the surgery? Some men didn't handle news like this well. She would no longer be considered a good catch. It would take an understanding man to want a woman who wouldn't be able to have children when he was in his prime. It was an ego thing with most men. They wanted miniature versions of themselves. And now she wouldn't be able to deliver. She dialed. The phone rang, and rang,

and rang. Why didn't his voicemail kick in? Usually at work he had his phone turned off. Just as she was about to hang up a woman's voice answered.

"Hello?"

Tamara held the phone away from her ear and looked at it. Perhaps she dialed the wrong number.

The voice, sounding impatient, repeated, "Hello?"

"Uh…is this 312-555-0121?"

"Yes it is. May I help you?" Her voice was crisp.

"Is Kevin there?"

"Yes, he is. Who should I say is calling?"

She didn't answer the question. Something didn't feel right. "May I ask to whom I'm speaking?"

"Sure. You're speaking with Charlene." There was a hint of sarcasm in her voice.

Tamara frowned. Kevin's assistant was Donna. She heard her own voice repeating the name although she didn't realize she said it out loud. "Chaaarlene…"

"Yes, Charlene. His wife. Now, who may I say is calling?" She sounded irritated.

Tamara's mouth opened but no sound came out. She felt as if she was being sucked into a vacuum of devastation.

The voice on the other end was calling her back to the present. "Hello? Hello?"

"Uh, oh yes, I'm sorry."

"Hold on. Let me clear the other line and I'll get Kevin for you." She clicked over. Tamara considered hanging up, but her hand was super-glued to the phone…that's what it felt like anyway. Kevin… Charlene…wife. She kept trying to put the concept together but she couldn't. He was *her* man. At least that's what she had been led to believe.

She backtracked through their relationship, looking for red flags and warning signs. There had been no inconsistencies in his pattern. He called regularly—every morning, midday, and evening. But she had once seen a movie where a player was schooling another player. He told the young man that when he was juggling women to put them on a call schedule. A woman who heard from you regularly would be convinced she was the only one. It certainly had worked in her case.

Perhaps she should have been more suspicious when he was so willing to go home after dates, but she'd thought it out of courtesy for her stand about not being intimate. She hadn't worried about not having his home number because she had his cell, which she never used. True, he'd never invited her to his house. In retrospect she wondered how she had let that slide because her mother always told her you never know a person until you've been to his home. Environment told you things about a person he or she might not mention. But again, she thought nothing of it because of the way he squired her around town in very public places, introducing her to coworkers and friends. A moment of clarity came when she finally understood the flirtatious nature of his cohorts. If they considered her a well-kept mistress, they might assume she was open for better offers. Maybe that was the life of a high roller. She had gotten her fantasy man all right, but at a great price. She'd been bought, and no amount of money could get back what she'd lost emotionally and physically. Kevin's voice interrupted her thoughts.

"Hello?"

"Hello." She couldn't think of anything else to say.

"Yes?"

"Yes? What do you mean 'yes'?" Surely he didn't have the nerve not to recognize her voice!

"Ooh, Tamara. I didn't recognize your voice. Listen, I was in the middle of something. May I call you back?"

She was beginning to get angry, although she couldn't put her finger on who she was more angry at—him or her.

"No, that won't be necessary."

"Give me an hour."

She couldn't believe he was acting as if nothing was wrong. Perfectly normal. Pleasant even. That made her even madder.

"Honey, I am not giving you another minute!" She slammed the phone down, closed her eyes, and spun her chair in a circle. She would not be the pitiful other woman. No, she would not! She could at least walk away with dignity. What was that line? "Never let them see you sweat?" Well, she was not sweating...she was drowning...with no lifeline to help her surface from the depths of agony. Her entire world had crashed down around her ears in one day. And she had no idea which piece to pick up first or how to rebuild even a corner of her heart or world.

She gazed out at the cityscape. It served her right. She couldn't even argue with God about it. He was not obligated to protect her from getting hit by a car if she chose to stand in the middle of moving traffic. She would "take her licking and keep on ticking." The pressure in her lower abdomen called her attention back to what was immediately important. A phone rang in the distance. A buzzer sounded, and Stella's voice sounded over the intercom.

"Mr. Davis is on line one."

Tamara didn't answer. She couldn't move. She continued to stare out the window.

She heard the door open behind her...could feel Stella studying her.

Stella cleared her throat. "Hello? Mr. Davis is on line one." She waited a beat. "Obviously you're lost in thought. What should I tell him?"

"Tell him I'm out...permanently."

"Excuse me?"

Tamara swung around to face Stella. "You heard me. Tell him I'm out."

Stella put up her hand. "I got it...permanently." She turned back to her desk with a skip in her step. "Oh yes! God does answer prayer... never felt good about that man anyway. Hallelujah!"

"Thanks for sharing. Close my door, please."

She leaned back in her chair. Her mind was blank. Nothing there but pain. A pain that intellectually she knew would go away in time.

Right now it was all consuming. She wanted to scream, cry, and throw things all at the same time, but she remained frozen. She didn't feel justified in crying about her pain because she set herself up for it.

Trapped between reason and her emotions, she was suffocating. She felt like a fool. She walked into this with her eyes wide open, shaking her puny little fist at God. And look where it took her. She volleyed between being too ashamed to ask for forgiveness and needing Him more than ever. It was difficult to pray, to reach out to Him, even though in her heart she wanted to. She was torn between her anger, her pride, and her rampant sense of entitlement that still insisted that God owed her more than He was giving. She had no idea how to bridge the gap between her physical desires and her spiritual need. And so she sat suspended in her misery that was quickly deepening.

Suddenly Stella was standing in the door with a strange look on her face.

"Turn on the television!"

"What?"

"Turn on the TV!" Stella marched across the office and flicked on the television, frantically changing the channel just in time to reveal Corinne standing behind her husband at a press conference. She looked remarkably composed in light of what was being said. Tamara stood and made her way to Stella's side. The two women watched in disbelief. Stella wondered aloud what planet she'd been on to miss all this drama as she listened to Randall Collins.

The proverb "I was upset about having no shoes until I met a man who had no feet" came to Tamara's mind. Suddenly her problems seemed very small. Very small indeed.

forty-four

Corinne stood, head held high, behind her husband as he began his address. It was his second address since Sunday morning. He used the same speech for the media that he gave to his congregation.

"I am deeply saddened to resign my post as senior pastor of Trinity Assembly. Over the years I've felt privileged to serve such an outstanding group of people. However, in light of recent events and my own personal struggles for quite some time now, I feel the need to step down, seek God, and focus on spiritual and personal restoration. I am deeply saddened to know I've grieved the heart of God and have caused my family pain beyond measure. As a man of God I'm held to a high standard. I'm responsible for leading God's flock by example as well as word. There is no excuse for my actions. The bottom line is I have sinned..." His voice broke.

The hushed silence was almost deafening as everyone waited for his next words.

"I have sinned dreadfully. My daughter means everything to me. To think that I was in any way the cause for her pain is unbearable..." Again he stopped to compose himself.

Corinne laid a hand on his shoulder. She actually felt sorry for him. She had watched him go from defiant rage at being uncovered to absorbing the impact of the pain he'd caused his family. The jolt of seeing Jada in the hospital and learning of her trauma shattered the hardcore defenses he'd erected. In the end he had broken, weeping before his daughter and asking for her forgiveness.

"For too long my wife has paid the price for my weakness. For this I am truly sorry." He looked back at her, sorrow filling his eyes, along with tears that began to fall without reservation.

Cameras clicked but the supernatural silence prevailed as people waited for him to finish.

"I have sought the gracious Lord's forgiveness. Now I ask for yours." With that he turned, leaving an on-air reporter to fill in the blanks.

Since finding Jada on Friday evening, a whirlwind of events surrounded them. It seemed with each day another bomb dropped. After Jada filed her police report, the news had spread like wildfire through the congregation. By Tuesday four other girls from church stepped forward to file claims against Pastor Masters.

Corinne surprised herself by reaching out to comfort Ruth Masters. She was in deep distress. At first she responded with denial. There had to be some awful mistake. It couldn't be true. Her husband was one of the most godly men she knew. But as one girl after another added support to Jada's accusations, the truth had painfully set in, and Ruth retreated to her house, refusing to come out.

Corinne marched past the police barricades and the reporters to sit with her. She made hot tea and sat in silence as Ruth wept quietly. Not really knowing what to say, she silently offered her support. She too knew what it was like to suffer public shame. But she had lived with her husband's shameful secret for so long it was a relief to get it out in the open. Like a festering sore that needed air to heal, all the wraps had finally been pulled off. She had done most of her grieving ahead of time, so the pain wasn't as intense. Ruth, on the other hand, had been blindsided. Believing her husband walked on water all these years, the news had totally rocked her universe and scattered her little clutch of safe Christian friends. They had all dispersed as if she had a contagious disease, leaving her to sort through the rubble of her life on her own. She looked so vulnerable, so fragile that Corinne feared for her state of mind. She considered inviting her to stay at her house, but she didn't think the sight of Randall would help and she wasn't sure how Jada would feel. And there was too much turmoil at home anyway.

Ruth finally made a decision. She packed up her things and went to Indiana to stay with her sister until the storm blew over…or maybe longer.

Corinne only heard from one member of the First Lady klatch. Barbara had called to say she knew what it felt like to be in this place. She was praying for her, and if she needed anything to give her a call. Corinne felt she had a true friend in Barbara and told her she would take her up on her invitation once she got herself straightened out. None of the rest of the women called, and she knew she would be the hot topic at their next lunch.

Having found a good attorney, Corinne asked him to prepare the paperwork for a divorce. She asked him not to file them until after Randall stepped down from his position at church. Now that he had, she was free to proceed with her plans.

The church board stepped in and offered Randall a monthly stipend if he would agree to a restoration program, complete with counselors they selected. He agreed. And Corinne didn't know if it was guilt or generosity, but he signed the house over to her. She decided not to live in such a huge place with so many bad memories. A nice cozy apartment in the city would be just the place for Jada and her to continue healing. A change of scenery and environment would do them good. With the money she would get from the house, they would be able to get by until she figured out how to generate an income. Her mother had invited them to live with her, but she felt the need to spread her wings and discover the places in herself that had been long overlooked.

Strangely, she had more love for Randall now than she had in a long time. It was true. The truth does set you free. There was a new humility and tenderness when he addressed her, and when she watched him with Jada her heart went soft. It was apparent he had internalized her pain and been cut to the core. She prayed that he would be able to forgive himself, change his behavior, and move on. The bond grew between the two of them as they both focused on their daughter. She wished they had developed the friendship they were experiencing now a long time ago. Being realistic, she knew that sometimes a person has to experience great loss to know he really needs to change. She stuck to her guns about the divorce, resisting the temptation to remain.

Perhaps Randall would win the struggle with his sexuality, perhaps he wouldn't. She no longer could or would place herself in the position to not be loved by her husband. She wanted more. She refused to internalize his struggle and make it her own. If he was to rise to the occasion and become the man God created him to be, this was a war he had to fight and win without her. She would champion him from the sidelines, but she refused to place herself or Jada in the line of fire. Enough damage had already been done.

She gladly accepted the grace God was giving as she felt it wash over her, enabling her to forgive Randall. She'd been angry and upset far too long. She wanted to be gracious again for the sake of Jada and for herself. She wanted to be an example of love and grace to her daughter. She knew this was key to Jada's healing process. And she didn't want her daughter to repeat the mistakes she'd made because of unresolved daddy issues. So she refused to say an unkind word about Randall and purposed to pursue peace. She was surprised to find that this was much easier than holding a grudge. She could see the relief in Jada's eyes when they were all together, and she thanked God for giving them a respite in the eye of the storm.

She was surprised at the strength she'd found in the midst of these trials. Truly in her weakness God was strong. She was sick and tired of being sick and tired. It was a new day, and she was ready to flip the script on her life. Between the time Randall stepped down at church on Sunday and the press conference held Wednesday, the church had blown up into a cesspool of debate and accusations. No one in the family was unscathed. It was her fault. Her ice princess ways had caused her husband to fall. Jada enticed Pastor Masters. There were speculations about Randall as the news of the situation spread among the parishioners.

On and on it went. Someone even toilet-papered their house and the church lawn, leaving a note behind saying they were a blight to their community. Some resented the church board's stand to offer rehabilitation to Randall on their dollar, even though the board cited his years of illustrious service and the fact that he had single-handedly built the church into the institution it was today. They owed him that much, and besides, it had been said too often that Christians were the first ones to kill their wounded.

Which, of course, led to more rumors that Randall obviously had stuff on the board that made them afraid to oust him unceremoniously. Through all this, Randall did his best to shield his family. Corinne stood by him, causing him to remark, "Wow, you are something else! You have given new meaning to the phrase 'What doesn't break you makes you stronger'!"

She had to admit that must be true, though if someone had told her what this neck of the journey would entail she wouldn't have imagined she would still be standing. But indeed that had become her theme song. She was more than a survivor! She was determined for the sake of those she loved. And the rest of the people who didn't understand? Well, that was their problem. She had enough on her plate.

As she wheeled Jada out of the hospital and down the ramp toward the car Randall had waiting for them, she felt a strange mix of fear and excitement. For far too long she'd tried to create the picture-perfect life, when behind the scenes the truth was they were torn from the foundation up. Now the facades were gone. She had no idea what design God had in mind, and she was relieved to know it was totally out of her hands.

She was feeling adventurous, ready to embark into the unknown armed with her trust in God. She didn't know what tomorrow would hold, but for the first time in a long time she was determined not to be a victim. The prospect of victory was a foreign but delicious feeling.

forty-five

Tamara sat in her apartment with the lights out. Should she call Jamilah again? What could she say at this point? And she certainly didn't want to hear the words "I told you so." Yet she'd never felt so overwhelmingly lonely. She couldn't even squeak out a prayer. She'd tried but failed miserably several times. She was too angry, swinging back and forth between blaming herself and blaming God for the mess her life was in. Yes, she knew better, but if God had done something sooner she wouldn't have ended up where she did. Why hadn't He brought someone who was saved and wonderful into her life before she had to go looking for love in the wrong place? It wasn't fair! It just wasn't fair.

A knock at the door interrupted her thoughts. She went to the door, carefully peering through the peephole. It was Jamilah, looking very forlorn. Tamara slowly opened the door. Jamilah entered looking apologetic.

"I know I should have called but...the doorman wasn't downstairs... Hey, why is it so dark in here?" She plopped on the couch as Tamara turned on the lights. "Where have you been anyway? Boy, some people fall in love and don't have time for their friends anymore. That *is* why you have been 'incog-negro,' right?"

She waved Tamara's partial answer away. "Never mind. I'm not trying to dip into your business if you're not serving it up. Plus I have my own problems." She gave a deep sigh and leaned back, looking at Tamara now that she could see her. "Would you like to say 'I told you so' before or after I tell you all my troubles?"

"This wouldn't have to do with Ari, would it?"

"Ooh, you're good! Though I guess you wouldn't have to be prophetic to figure that out."

"I'm sure this is going to be juicy, especially the jail part. Would you like some tea before you begin your tale of woe and intrigue?" Tamara hadn't realized how much she missed Jamilah 'til now.

"That would be good. Hey, you got any food in this joint?" She put her hand up. "Never mind. I know better than to ask that question. Do you at least have some crackers?"

Once Tamara brewed tea and dug up a few things to satisfy Jamilah's munchies, she sat down and looked at her. "Okay, so give me the scoop. What did you do to land yourself in jail?"

"Well I was in jail because Ari's mother accused me of kidnapping."

"What! You didn't take that child home again, did you?"

"Nope!"

And with that Jamilah unfolded the whole story about how she'd purposed to "let go and let God." Ironically, that seemed to escalate the situation to impossible proportions. She told Tamara about Ari showing up on her doorstep, her mother having her arrested, and finally the details leading up to her getting fired and Ari being taken away to foster care. Suddenly she broke into tears.

"I don't know where she is, and I feel so terrible. She has to be feeling pretty betrayed right now. Dwayne is trying to track down her whereabouts through his friend that works at DCFS. I was going to see if I could foster her since I've completed filing all my paperwork, but now that I'm out of a job and being prosecuted by her mother I don't see that happening. It's such a big mess! I have no idea how it ended up being such a mess…" She threw her hands up in the air.

Tamara handed her a Kleenex, which she took and blew her nose loudly. "But enough about me. What about you? Where have you been? What have you been doing?" She looked at Tamara accusingly.

"When we're not around to hold each other accountable we end up in crazy situations. I'm not going to say 'I told you so' because I think we're even. Although you kind of set yourself up indirectly for what happened, it wasn't really your fault, which is more than I can say about my situation."

Tamara settled back into her chair and sighed. "You warned me, and I didn't listen." She looked at Jamilah, who simply looked back and didn't say anything.

"Remember the guy at the restaurant you warned me about?"

"How could I forget? I suspected that's why you weren't speaking to me."

"Yes…Do you forgive me?"

"Hey, girls will be girls. I figured you had to learn the hard way, and you'd be back eventually. Chile, you know it would take more than that to break our friendship after all we've been through together. So what happened? Do I need some fresh tea to hear this?"

"Probably." Tamara jumped up, relieved for a respite before delving into her story. As she poured fresh water she began her tale of how Kevin wooed and pursued her. The wonderful dinners and outings. All his best lines.

Jamilah listened with her eyebrows raised, her face an expressive canvas. "Girl, you had to be messed up behind all that. See, that's why I always say love is not discriminating, especially if a man is rapping and setting it out like that! Poor thing. You didn't stand a chance. It's a wonder you didn't fall with all that going on…"

"Oh…" With that she plunged into the trip to the Bahamas, the suitcase of clothes, the band on the balcony, her crumpled will power, the ride home, her doctor's diagnosis, and finally the phone call that capped off the romantic adventure. She was grateful Jamilah didn't interrupt when she got to the part about sleeping with Kevin, even though she looked disappointed.

When she was finished she could see the compassion in Jamilah's eyes. She spread her palms, signaling she'd come to the end of her tale of woe.

Jamilah leaned back on the couch and whistled.

"Wow, girl! You've been through it. I'm so sorry…"

"Not sorrier than me."

"How are you feeling really? Let's switch chairs for a minute 'cause I know how you stuff things. You do not need to keep this bottled up inside. It just wouldn't be good. Especially in your line of work."

"I've probably let several of my clients down at this point. As a matter of fact, I know I have. Especially one in particular. I just haven't been present because I've been so caught up in getting what I wanted and having an attitude about it. I missed important cues. But more than that, I'm having a real wrestling match with God right now. I feel like two people. One side of me knows I can't win if I choose to do things my own way. The other side is angry about that. Like if we really have free will, why can't I do as I please and get away with it? I feel like God owes me…"

"But you know He doesn't, right?" Jamilah interjected. "We've had this discussion before, Tamara. God doesn't owe you anything. Just because you've been a 'good little girl'" she made quote marks with her fingers, "doesn't mean He owes you a husband or anything else. Your obedience is what you owe Him. That should be your way of saying 'thank You' for what He's already done. Anything else He gives us in life is frosting on the cake."

"I know that intellectually, it's just that…"

"It's just that the flesh wants what it wants. I can get with that. If I were in that situation, you would have clocked that Kevin wasn't right and something was amiss five minutes out of the gate. But when we want what we want, we make things fit to our liking until the truth catches up with us. Unfortunately, by that time it's too late and pain is bound to follow. And God doesn't have to punish us too when all is said and done. The consequences of the choices we make do a good job of that all by themselves. The very thing that God was trying to save us from is what we end up experiencing. I think He feels bad for us, even though we made the choice. He can't save us from our bad choices because He gave us free will. But He does forgive us and restore us when we ask."

Jamilah stopped to ponder that thought for a minute, took a sip of her tea, and then continued. "I've learned this from my own situation. We can set ourselves up for pain or victory, depending on the posture we choose to take. We can get busy trying to make things happen on our own and eventually get our hands slapped, or we can wait patiently on Him and let Him work out His plan for us. And His plan is always far better than what we had in mind anyway. That's why He is God, and we are not."

"How can you be so sure of that, Jamilah? Especially with everything where it stands in your life right now? I don't believe you'll end up in jail, but what if you do? You felt you were doing the right thing. And how do you know when you should do something and when you shouldn't? I don't think we're always supposed to be passive..."

"It's not about being passive or being wimps. I think it's more about surrender. Either I believe God loves me, knows what's best for me, and wants it even more than I do...or I don't. And if I do believe that and He has a bird's eye view of my situation, I've got to believe that everything is as it should be until it's time for something different to happen."

"You lost me."

"Let's take your case. You want to be married, right? If God thought that was best for you right now, you would be married. Just because *you* want it now doesn't mean that now is the right time. And that might not have anything to do with you. It might be the person He has for you isn't ready. The man for you might be getting fine-tuned by God. But then again, you might be gettin' fine-tuned for him. God definitely has some attitude work to do on you, girl." Jamilah looked at her teasingly.

"In my case, I'm not sure what He's doing, but I know He's doing something." Jamilah's eyes filled with tears.

Tamara leaned forward and touched her knee. "Yes, He is. I can't say what He's going to do, but this much I do know. There's nothing left for either of us to do but wait on Him. I know I need to pray about my heart condition. I'm so angry!"

"That's because you feel entitled to what you want. Anger...and you know this, therapist friend...anger is unyielded rights. And you don't have the right to anything except salvation and the promises attached to that. If you truly said yes to God, you gave up your other rights in favor of having Him select what He knows is best for your life. I love Ari. I want Ari. But I can't decide I have the right to have her. All I can do is open my hands and tell God that if I'm best for Ari and Ari would be best for me, will He please put all the things in place to make it happen. I'm available for whatever He wants to do with my life because I've given my life to Him. My life is no longer mine."

"I guess I'm more selfish than I realized. I'm not quite there..."

"We all go in and out on any given day. That's the problem with a living sacrifice. It crawls off the altar now and then. What is it the apostle Paul said in 1 Corinthians? 'I die daily.' I think we die to ourselves and all the things we want by degrees. God uses life and its disappointments to pry our hands open inch by inch until we finally say, 'Okay, God, not my will but Yours.'"

Jamilah stopped for a minute, eyes closed. Then, as if suddenly snapping out of wherever she was in her thoughts, she said, "Well, enough of being deep. Can we go get something to eat? 'Cause you know you can starve a girl up in here!"

Tamara was relieved to move on. Jumping up from her chair she headed toward the hall closet to retrieve her coat. "I'm all for that. I'm feeling very Scarlett O'Hara about now. I'll worry about all this stuff tomorrow. I've had enough of trying to unravel it today. And now that you mention food, I realize I haven't eaten all day."

The phone interrupted her. She stopped, frowned, and continued toward the closet.

"Aren't you going to get that?" Jamilah asked.

"Nope. It's probably just Kevin again, and I definitely don't want to talk to him."

"Mmm, I don't think so. It says 'F. Sample' on your caller ID." Jamilah was studying the phone.

"Oh! That's Felicia!" Tamara grabbed the phone.

"Hey, Felicia, I am soooo sorry I missed you today…"

"I'm sorry. It's not Felicia, but she wanted me to call you."

Tamara didn't recognize the voice. "Who is this?"

"It's Carla. Something awful has happened…"

Tamara listened for a minute and then everything went silent. She felt the phone slipping from her hand, the floor giving way beneath her. "Noooo…" She heard Jamilah calling her name from far away…and then there was nothing.

forty-six

Ari gazed up at the oversized cross at the front of the church. It was huge. It seemed to hold up the entire building. She looked around behind her. The church was half filled with those who'd come for midweek service. She hadn't known people went to church on Wednesdays. She knew they went on Sundays, though she'd never been...and now here she sat. Her new foster mother, Mrs. Sanders, was smiling down at her. Ari smiled back. This woman was nice. And so was her husband, Pastor Sanders. They owned the church and adjoining elementary school. Two other foster children lived here too. They were around her age and named Brittany and Jonathan. They'd been with them for a year and seemed to really like being there.

The first night she went to the Sanders' house Ari had lain in bed crying after the lights were turned out. Brittany had climbed onto her bed and offered her a piece of candy.

"Don't cry..." she said as she gently wiped Ari's tears with a Kleenex. "I know you're scared, but you're going to like it here. Mama and Papa Sanders are really nice."

"I miss Mama and my teacher that's all..." After leaving the school with the lady and gentleman that had come to take her away last week, they had waited for Ari's mother at the office. She never showed up. Ari was sure she was angry at her, and it was all her fault that she couldn't go home again. Miss Wales had driven her to the Sanders' explaining that they were great foster parents and had been working with them for a long time, taking in children like herself until they could go back to their parents or be adopted by new parents. Ari couldn't understand why any parent would give their children away. Miss Wales explained that it wasn't because their parents didn't want them. Sometimes they were too ill or in no position to take care of their children, and they did what was best for their kids by letting someone take them who could care for them better.

Ari had looked at Miss Wales. "Like my mama? She gets sick a lot. But she is going to get well now, right?"

"I hope so..."

They had arrived at the Sanders,' and Mrs. Sanders was waiting for her. She was an attractive woman with a motherly air. She was a warm, paper-bag brown with slight gray streaks in her hair at her temple and was dressed in a nice knit skirt and top. Ari found it odd that she would be so dressed up at home. Her mama always wore jeans at home. Mrs. Sanders welcomed Ari warmly and gave her a tour of the house. It was a big place, but it was warm and inviting. Ari was in awe. She'd never seen a house so big. Even though she thought Miss Williams' apartment was beautiful, it wasn't big like this. Finally Mrs. Sanders showed Ari her room. She would be sharing it with a pretty girl named Brittany, who seemed very excited to have a temporary sister. After Miss Wales left, Pastor Sanders came home. He was brown and round, beginning to bald slightly on top, and wore little reader glasses that he was always adjusting. He had a big laugh that was contagious. He seemed truly glad to see her. He sat down in front of her, taking her hands in his.

"Welcome, Miss Ari, to your new home. I want you to know that God loves you and we do too. We want you to feel at home here. I know you must be worried about your mama, and I want you to know that we will be praying for her. We believe in prayer around here, and we know that God can and will work wonders. And if you need anything, you just feel free to ask. That is what we are here for." He smiled at her. "Any questions?"

"What about school?"

"School?" He looked confused for a moment. Then he brightened. "Oh! School! We'll get your information and grades from the school you were attending. Since school will be out in a week, you'll be fine missing the end. If you're still here at the end of the summer, you'll attend our school. It's a fine school that's owned by our church."

"Oh..." Ari was crestfallen.

"What's the matter?"

"It's just that my teacher, Miss Williams, I'll miss her." Ari brightened. "Can you pray for her too? I think I got her in trouble..."

"I doubt that, but sometimes when things happen in life that's God's way of trying to get our attention because He wants us to know Him."

"Oh she knows God. She told me to pray too."

"If she knows God then everything is going to be okay."

"I sure hope so..."

"You really like this Miss Williams, don't you?"

"I love her." Ari's eyes filled with tears. "I think she loves me too."

Pastor Sanders looked at her with a knowing look. "I'm going to pray special prayers for Miss Williams. Now, you know what I think? I think you need to have some dinner and get some sleep. You've had quite a day." With that he rose to his feet and gave her a pat on the head.

After dinner Mrs. Sanders had shown her to a bathroom that was attached to her bedroom and given her a pair of pajamas. They smelled just as pretty as they looked. Finally snuggled in bed, Mrs. Sanders had sat on the edge of the bed with a cup of hot chocolate.

She smiled. "When I was a little girl, hot chocolate always made me feel better if I was scared or sad."

Ari sipped the warm, sweet liquid. It felt good going down. "Thank you."

Brittany came to join them on the bed. When Ari was finished with her hot chocolate, Mrs. Sanders had them hold hands to pray. She looked at Ari, and then at Brittany. "Brittany, why don't you start. Ari, if you have anything to say to God, you can go after Brittany. The Bible says that when two or more people agree in prayer, God will grant their requests. So we will agree in prayer with you. Okay?"

Ari nodded and then squeezed her eyes shut tight as Brittany prayed.

"Dear God, thank You for bringing Ari to us. Don't let her be scared. Let her know everything is going to be all right and help her to like me. In Jesus' name. Amen."

"God, please help Mama not to be sick anymore. And please help Miss Williams not to be in any trouble. And please don't let Mama be mad at me. Amen."

Mrs. Sanders squeezed Ari's hand. "Dear Lord God, You are so kind and loving. And I know You know the plans You have for all of us and that You always work everything out for the good. I pray for Ari's mother, that You would relieve her suffering and make her whole. And that whatever the situation is with Miss Williams, You will work on her behalf. Please grant the desires of Ari's heart and reveal Your goodness to her. I pray that she will come to know how much You love her and that You will make Yourself real to her. I thank You for placing Ari, Brittany, and Jonathan in our lives for however long the season, and I promise to treat them like the gifts they are. May they come to know Your love through the love we show them. Fulfill Your plan for each of them. In Jesus' name. Amen."

"God has plans for us?" This was a new revelation to Ari.

"Indeed He does!" Mrs. Sanders leaned to hug her and then Brittany. She rose from the bed. "Now, you girls get some rest. I'll see you tomorrow. We're having pancakes in the morning." She smiled. "Good night!" With that she turned off the light and shut the door, leaving Ari to ponder her future.

What kind of plans does God have for me? Ari wondered. It seemed like every time she prayed, the opposite happened. But Mrs. Sanders said it was supposed to work out for the good, whatever that meant. All she knew was that even though these people seemed nice, she longed for what was familiar. She was worried about her mother, and she missed her teacher. No amount of pancakes was going to change that. And so she cried and tried to take Brittany's reassurances to heart.

Now, sitting in church and looking up at that great big cross, God suddenly seemed larger than life. Perhaps He really could fix everything, even though "everything" seemed messed up right now. A lady in the choir was singing, "I don't know what tomorrow holds, but I know who holds tomorrow." Ari liked that thought. If God was as big as that cross and held tomorrow, surely He could fix everything that had gone wrong. She hoped so anyway.

forty-seven

Jamilah turned to Tamara as she pulled the car in front of Felicia's apartment building. "You sure you don't want me to go up with you?"

"No, I'll be all right. I didn't mean to scare you. I've never fainted before. It was just too much all at the same time…you, Corinne, Kevin, my health situation, and now this. When does it end?"

"This is the cycle of life…mayhem…then peace…trial then respite. Makes us enjoy the quiet when we finally get it, I guess."

"You've become quite the philosopher, but I guess you're right. Well, I better get up there. I'll talk to you tomorrow."

"Okay. Please tell her I'll be praying for her."

"Will do." Tamara got out of the car and headed to the lobby. The doorman looked up.

"How may I help you?"

"I'm here to see Mrs. Sample."

"Yes, of course." He looked especially solemn. "Apartment 1117." He buzzed her through the doors.

Tracy opened the door when she got to the apartment. The sea of people parted when she entered the living room to reveal Felicia looking far too collected in the wake of the devastation. Simone was sitting on her lap crying, and Felicia was consoling her.

"Daddeee…I want Daddeeee."

Tears were filling Felicia's eyes. "I know…I know, baby. I want Daddy too, but he's not here. He's gone to be with Jesus." She looked at the others in the room, "She's used to him being home by now to play with her." She tried bouncing Simone on her lap.

"I want Daddeeee…"

"Don't worry. We'll see him again, honey."

Everybody in the room—Muriel, Brad, Adrian, Ron, Carla, Al, and Tracy—were watching her as tears streamed down their faces. Carla stood up and walked out of the room. Closing the washroom door behind her, everyone could hear her sobs through the door.

Felicia looked up.

"Hi, Tamara."

"What happened?" That is not what she meant to say first, but she had to know. Her mind was still reeling from the news that Kenny was dead. That had been the only thing she heard before blacking out. It seemed so surreal. It couldn't be true. He was so young, and they were so happy. Their lives were filled with so much promise.

"What happened?" she heard herself repeat. She couldn't get past that question.

Felicia handed an exhausted Simone over to Tracy, who clung to her.

"I don't really know. He came home early with another headache. I know I was supposed to meet you, but something told me to stay with him. So I put him to bed and gave him a massage, kissed him on his forehead, and told him I was going to fix him some soup. He smiled and said, 'That was good. I love you, babe,' and drifted off to sleep. I went into the kitchen to fix him the soup, and then I went back to wake him up to give it to him…" She stopped and swallowed. "He was gone. Just like that."

Tamara felt lightheaded and so cold. She hugged her coat tighter around herself, trying to find some heat.

Felicia continued. "I called an ambulance, and the paramedics declared him dead. I got hold of his doctor. He suspects it was an aneurism, but we won't know for sure until an autopsy is done. I don't know what else to say."

Tamara sat down on the chair that was offered to her. "How do you feel?" It seemed like a stupid question to ask, but she couldn't think of anything else.

"I don't know. It's very strange…almost as if I'm in a cocoon, a great big cotton ball. I know I'm in pain, but I don't quite feel it yet. I can't believe it. I just can't believe he's gone. I keep thinking I'm going to wake up and none of you are going to be here and he'll walk out of the bedroom wanting his soup. And then I'll sit and watch him eat it and we'll play with Simone. And I'll tell him right before we go to sleep that I'm pregnant."

Felicia didn't notice the sharp intake of breath as everyone reacted.

"…and he'll be over the moon, and we'll make love, and everything will be beautiful. At least that's what I'm hoping…" Her voice broke.

"You're pregnant?" Tamara thought, *Why can't you stop asking stupid questions?*

"Yes. I just found out this morning. He would've been so happy. We'd talked about having another baby right away because we didn't want Simone to be an only child. We both hated growing up alone. And now he's gone, and I'm alone again…"

"No, that is not true." Carla emerged from the washroom. "You're not alone. We're not Kenny, but you do have us…and God."

"That's right," Adrian quietly interjected. "He'll be your comfort in ways you could never imagine."

"I just don't understand it." Tracy was not to be consoled.

Felicia took Simone, who had managed to drift off to sleep.

"Tomorrow is not promised, Tracy. That's why it's good to have a relationship with God, so if you're the one leaving you know where you're going…and if you're the one left behind, you have Someone to cling to," Adrian gently said while squeezing Ron's hand.

"It's just not fair…"

"Life is not fair, Tracy, but God is." Muriel leaned forward. "There are some things we can't figure out. We have to accept them as part of a plan that is so much bigger than us that perhaps we won't understand how all the pieces fit until much later."

"It's kind of hard to care about a big master plan when your own personal world is being affected. When the pain you feel causes you to question your faith and God's goodness…and yet, in spite of it all, He comes through for us time and time again. And eventually, though you don't forget the experience, the sting of the pain is gone. But this takes time. Believe me, I know of what I speak." Carla blew her nose.

Tamara felt ashamed. She was still stuck back at the "question your faith and God's goodness" part. And yet she so wanted to get past that. To be able to accept that whatever God allowed to happen or didn't allow to happen was really good—no matter how bad it felt. This situation with Kenny wasn't sitting well with her either.

"How is this supposed to make Felicia feel better right now?"

"She might not feel better right now. Grief is normal and natural. But she does have a promise to live for. And in time that will help," Adrian responded, bringing balance back to Tamara's perspective.

"I've got more than a promise to live for!" Felicia stated. "I have the gifts I've already been given. Simone, a new life inside me, wonderful memories to treasure. I have…had…the love of an amazing man. I never have to wonder if true love is possible because I experienced it, no matter how brief. Isn't it something that the last thing he said to me was 'I love you, babe'? What if we'd had a fight and were mad at each other? I could have been out running around and missed the opportunity to be here for him. He could have died violently in some way that would have filled me with regret every time I thought of it. But he went quietly in his sleep, at peace with his Savior. And I was here to love on him. I was the last face he saw. A memory of love and peace was created before he went. And I don't have to worry about his salvation or if I'll see him again. I know I will. I've got that to cling to. Yes, I'm going to miss him. Do I want him back here right now? Of course! But do I feel robbed? No. I'm too rich from what he's left behind."

Everyone looked at Felicia in awe, so struck were they by the wisdom and maturity of her words. Brad finally broke the silence. "Wow, Felicia. I pray that each of us learns to nurture precious, sweet memories every day in the hearts of those we love. That's really all we get to leave behind."

"That's so true." Muriel squeezed Brad's hand that was resting on her shoulder. "Felicia, I'm so proud of you."

"Don't be proud of me yet. I'm talking a good game now, but I may have a meltdown at any minute." She laughed through her tears. Everyone chuckled with her, relieved to grab at a straw of levity.

In that moment Tamara thought Felicia was the most beautiful woman she'd ever met. As Tamara's heart broke, she swallowed the waves of pain that washed over her, willing herself not to break down in front of her dear friend.

Carla excused herself to go to the kitchen to fix tea for everyone. Felicia rallied everyone to help her plan the funeral. Tamara headed to the washroom.

She was acutely embarrassed by all the envy and jealousy she'd harbored toward Felicia. Her "perfect little world" wasn't so perfect anymore, and what a price she'd paid to experience that perfection. And now she was adding to Tamara's shame by responding to her shattered world with such grace. Leaning on the bathroom door as it closed, Tamara slid to the floor and buried her head in her lap. Exhaustion from fighting God swept over her. Her muffled cries drowned out her questions until she was beyond her anger and her pain, beyond the voices in the other room. Suddenly she felt as if someone gently put His arms around her. She sighed deeply. "God, please help me…" and she drifted off to sleep.

forty-eight

Tamara didn't know how long she slept on Felicia's bathroom floor. It was Ron who found her. Startled her rather, as the door prompted her back to the present when he tried to enter the washroom.

"Are you doing okay?" he asked, looking extremely concerned.

"Yes, I'm all right. I just got overwhelmed. I…"

"I understand. Well, we're getting ready to leave so Felicia can get some rest, although I think Tracy is going to stay with her. I'll see you at the funeral, I suppose."

"Most definitely."

"If you would like, Adrian and I can drop you off at home."

"I would appreciate it." She was relieved because she really didn't trust herself to get home without zoning out and wandering off.

The rest of the week went by in a blur until she entered the church for the funeral. Her eyes scanned the front pews. That had to be Felicia's mother. She looked like a movie star as she hovered like a mother hen over her daughter. There was Tracy. Yes, everyone else was already here. She decided she would wait until the service was over before she went up to pay her respects. She was afraid they would invite her to sit in front with them, and she wasn't sure she was strong enough to do that.

Adrian approached the podium and began to sing. When she got to "Whatever my lot, Thou hast taught me to say, it is well, 'It is well, with my soul…'" Tamara gave her high marks for having the nerve to sing. She didn't know how she did it without breaking down.

Adrian's voice filled the church as she transitioned to her own melodic thoughts, "I will not question when, or where, or how or why…for your faithfulness I never will deny…yes, weeping may endure for a night but joy comes in the morning as your plan comes to light…"

As the medley and words washed over Tamara's soul, they soothed away the residual pain and weariness she was feeling. She dabbed away the tears that were threatening to fall as Felicia's pastor came forward. He looked at Felicia.

Felicia smiled at him and nodded, as if giving him permission to begin.

"We are here today to celebrate the home going of Kenneth Jeffrey Sample. I want to start at the beginning of my knowing Felicia because her life and Kenny's are amazing testimonies. I first met Felicia at the altar here, albeit for a brief moment. She was pregnant, and as she was dedicating her life to Christ by saying the sinner's prayer, her water broke!"

The congregation laughed as they remembered that moment of delight and levity.

The pastor waited a minute before continuing. "Needless to say, there were two births that day. Her rebirth in the spirit and the natural birth of her and Kenny's daughter, Simone. Shortly thereafter I was introduced to Kenny, who grilled me about this thing called 'being saved.' He wanted to understand exactly what that meant. We spent some time investigating what it means to have a relationship with God that not only focuses on the end reward of eternal salvation and life in heaven but also on the immediate day-to-day intimate relationship and surrendering to experience life according to God's plan. He commented on the tremendous change he'd seen in the life of his wife, and he wanted to be all he could be so they could grow together. I was impressed by his love for her and her for him. They were a picture, I believe, of what God wanted a marriage to look like. So when I received the news of Kenny's passing, my first reaction was, 'How is Felicia going to take this?' I've been blessed and humbled by her response."

Tamara glanced toward Felicia, who looked surprised.

Her pastor continued. "I wrote down what she said because I wanted to make sure I got it right. 'Pastor, I can't sit and grieve my loss. Instead, I must consider what I have gained. To ponder what I "should have" versus what I have been blessed to experience would rob me of the joy God intended and make me an unnecessary prisoner of disappointment and frustration.' Isn't that amazing? And then she said, 'I've been given a testimony rich with the memory of God's goodness that I can constantly rehearse on those days when I feel down. I've been given more than what has been taken…and, actually, nothing has been taken—only moved to a place that will take me a while to get to.'" He looked out at everyone. "Let this wisdom help you and comfort you today in this time of grief."

And indeed it did as the import of what he was saying took root in Tamara's heart.

Still speaking, the pastor made his way down to the center of the aisle. "Her words remind me of Jonah, who found himself sulking in the belly of a fish. The Word of God tells us that on the third day Jonah prayed. I find it hard to believe it took him that long! In fact, I think he prayed from the moment he got in there…like we all do when we find ourselves in less-than-desirable conditions. Our prayer in those times is a simple one, 'Get me out of here, Lord! Help me escape my trial, my difficulty, my longings, my pain.' Funny how things never seem to change when we pray that prayer. It's not until we understand what Jonah realized on that third day that our prayer changes to one in line with God's will. Jonah said, 'Those who cling to worthless idols forfeit the grace that could be theirs.' Basically he was saying, 'If I keep insisting on life going according to my plan and my design, I will miss not only what God has already done for me but also the new thing He wants to do in my life and in the lives of those around me. If I insist on my way I will miss the greater way, the greater plan.'"

Arriving at the pew where Felicia sat, the pastor turned to her and rested his hand on her shoulder. He faced the rest of the congregation. "In my limited understanding of the plans of God, I don't understand why Kenny is no longer with us today. But if I stop and celebrate the time I got to spend with him, the possibilities are endless for my joy to increase, including doing something that would honor him. Kenny wouldn't want us to grieve today. He would want us to celebrate his new life in God's presence. I love the words of the song that says, 'If you could see me now, you'd know that everything is all right...'" An organ chimed in, punctuating the pastor's words. "'You would know that I've seen His face...I'm dancing in the light of His grace...'" He did a dance step back in rhythm with the rift of the organ. "Yes, if you could see me now..." He stopped.

"This may not be what you expected at a funeral, but Kenny and Felicia are not normal people. They are kingdom people. They don't ask God why; instead, they ask God what. 'What do You want us to get out of this situation, Lord?' 'What would glorify You, Father?' 'What greater thing do You want to work in us through this experience?' 'What would You have us share with others?'" The pastor paused. "Today I challenge you. What is standing between you and the joy God wants you to experience? Are you clinging to a picture of what your life is 'supposed' to look like? To a schedule of when things are supposed to occur? These are worthless idols that will rob you of the opportunity to experience the very present grace of God and the ability to see your blessings and rejoice in whatever state you find yourself in. Now is the time to come to God. Come and experience His grace. He stands with open arms, waiting for you."

The choir started singing faintly behind him, "Come...come... Jesus is bidding you come..."

Tamara could no longer see the front of the church because her vision was so blurred by tears. She couldn't move. She was rooted to the spot, though the greater part of her desired to leave her seat and move forward. She sat and watched Tracy go toward the front of the church. And then Felicia was at the altar, holding her as she wept and prayed with the pastor. She supposed the man joining them was Tracy's boyfriend. Was their love life starting at the altar?

The choir burst into a celebration as the men carried out Kenny's coffin, and his immediate family followed. Tamara stepped out as they passed her, and Felicia smiled while handing a sleeping Simone to her. Her weight felt good in Tamara's arms. The cords wrapped around Tamara's heart that were keeping her from total surrender were being gradually loosened. She gently squeezed Simone as she left the building, envying her peace and ability to sleep through the turmoil. Oh, to have the faith of a little child again! But, alas, she was no longer a child.

forty-nine

"Hello! Is anybody here?" Dwayne snapped his fingers in front of Jamilah's face. "Paging Jamilah Williams. Where are you, girl?"

Jamilah snapped back from staring into space to focus on Dwayne, who was studying her across the table at their favorite restaurant. "I'm sorry. I was just thinking about Ari and wondering where she is...how she is. I wonder if I'll ever see her again."

School had been out for two weeks now, not that it mattered since Jamilah was no longer employed. She'd been so drained she hadn't even begun to consider her options. Since that fateful day she'd been rising late, doing chores, and talking about taking advantage of the free time to organize her home and clean. Lethargy gripped her. "You're depressed," Tamara, who was preparing for her surgery in a week, told her. On the grounds that Tamara was in quite a state herself in the aftermath of her failed relationship and Kenny's death, Jamilah considered the source and didn't give much credence to the information.

She had gone on the Internet to do a job search, but her heart wasn't in it. She calculated she could live off her savings for six months. After that she would be in trouble. As for her court case, it quietly faded away. After the police investigated, they realized Jamilah wasn't a kidnapper. And, as Jamilah suspected, Ari's mother hadn't followed through. The last thing Jamilah heard from her attorney was that Ari's mother was missing. She'd never shown up to complete the paperwork for Ari's care and hadn't been heard from. Ari had been placed with a family, though Jamilah didn't know who or where. She prayed they were good people, and Ari was safe and happy. The child's whereabouts and welfare consumed her thoughts. And now here was Dwayne on a campaign to cheer her up.

"I'm about to start believing I'm boring because I can't seem to hold your attention," he pouted.

Jamilah giggled. "Being boring is the last thing you need to be concerned about. I'm just distracted. And to be perfectly honest, I'm just a little bit evil with you for abandoning me in my time of need."

"I would never abandon you! I wish I'd known! I would have planned to be there. You have to let me know these things in advance. Shoot, I would have enjoyed bailing you out of jail...holding you for ransom...taking advantage of the fact you needed me." He looked a little too happy for her taste.

"What? It would take me going to jail for you to think I needed you? What kind of nonsense is that?"

"You know how you get, Miss Independent. Swashbuckling your way through life. You can do everything for yourself, so step aside, you say. And so I do. I stand off the path, saying to myself, 'Just look at this girl wearing herself out. I guess at some point she'll stop and let somebody get a word in edgewise and help her behind.'"

"Dwayne, you need to stop it! I don't believe you. When have I said I don't need help? Men kill me with that whole 'independent women' speech."

"It's not what you say, though you've said plenty, probably without realizing it. And don't give me that 'men are killing me' mess. You women are killing us. It's your actions. Off you go on your own crusade without enlisting any help. You give me the list of what you're going to do and leave me to watch, wondering how long it's going to take for you to get to the end of yourself. Jamilah, you know people are not wired to function alone. Everybody needs help. But maybe women fear rejection more than we men do, so you just shoo away the very people ready to help you."

"Now, I've heard it all! Why don't you just step in and offer then?"

"What? And break up your groove? Mm mm. 'Hell hath no fury like a woman interrupted from her mission'!"

"You know you're silly, don't you?"

Dwayne feigned hurt. "Oh, now I'm silly. Well, I'll just keep my silly news to myself then." He took a bite of his food, looking totally absorbed in his dish.

Jamilah narrowed her eyes, impatient with Dwayne's baiting. "You know I'm about to reach across the table and hurt you, don't you?"

He threw up both hands and looked about for witnesses. "She's threatening me with bodily harm!" he said to a waiter passing by.

"Dwayne!"

"Oh all right!" He looked at her intently, studying her face. "I found Ari. I know where she is."

Jamilah shrieked, "Where is she?"

Dwayne shushed her. "Simmer down! You want to get us thrown out of here? I haven't finished my dinner yet, and I fully intend to." He turned his attention back to his plate, putting more food in his mouth and chewing with delight.

Jamilah hissed. "Where is she?"

"She's with a great pastor and his family on the south side. Good people. Great reputation. Good church. They run a Christian elementary academy too. She's in good hands. They take in children all the time and keep them until they are permanently placed." Again he was looking at her steadily.

"How did you find out?"

He was looking very pleased with himself. "I have my connections. I called my friend at DCFS and asked her to track Ari down."

"Can I see her?"

"It's up to the family. Charnette thinks it might be possible, but that it's best to give Ari some time to settle in to her new surroundings."

"Of course." Though Jamilah understood, she felt a bit deflated.

"You know, if they don't find Ari's mother soon she'll be a candidate for adoption." He was looking at her strangely again.

Jamilah's spurt of hope was quickly extinguished. "I guess I'm knocked out of the competition since I don't have a job."

"Yes, that's probably true. Boy, I bet a husband sure would come in handy about now."

"For who?"

"For you, silly girl. Being a foster parent was going to be tricky enough with you being single, but now single and broke…"

"I am not broke, Dwayne!"

"Chile, you ain't got no job. To the government that qualifies you as broke unless you have a stash somewhere I don't know about. Have you been secretly wealthy all along? You been holdin' out on me, girl?" Again he was searching her face. He hailed the waiter and asked for water. The waiter brought two new glasses of water and took away the glasses that had been on the table.

She dropped her eyes. "No, I'm not independently wealthy, as you well know. I guess you're right. They would consider me broke."

"I know I'm right. But as far as I can see, this is very fixable."

"It is? How?"

He looked straight at her and spoke slowly. "I figured it out this way. I'm a healthy, working man with a brand-new house in a good neighborhood. We could get married, and then we would be the perfect couple to adopt Ari."

Jamilah heard the words, but they sounded strange. They didn't quite connect and make sense.

Dwayne was leaning forward, handing her a water glass. "Why don't you take a sip of water. You look like you could use a drink."

She took the glass from him. "Thank you." She raised the glass to her lips, but suddenly stopped. "Something's in my glass!"

"Really?" Dwayne leaned forward, peering at the glass.

Jamilah lifted it to eye level to get a better look before she complained to the waiter. She gasped and almost dropped it. In the bottom of the glass was the most beautiful ring she'd ever seen.

Dwayne grabbed a fork to fish it out. "Should we call the waiter to take it away? Honestly, service is just so bad these days!" He was grinning.

"No! I mean…Oh wow!"

"So, now that you need me…Will you marry me, Jamilah?"

She narrowed her eyes and teased him. "Are you using that child to coerce me into marrying your butt?"

"Hey, a man's got to do what a man's got to do to get what he wants."

"You didn't have to use Ari to get me, Dwayne."

"You didn't make it easy, Jamilah, so I kinda think I did. Are you going to marry me or what?"

"Are you going to at least tell me you love me and do this right?"

"Oh yes…that…you already know! I love you! Now will you marry me?"

"Ooh, you are not starting this off right." Jamilah was shaking her head. She decided to milk it for all it was worth and enjoy watching Dwayne.

"Let me start over." He got up and stood by her chair. Lowering himself to one knee, he took her hand and looked up into her eyes. "Jamilah, I have always loved you. You are headstrong, difficult, and a piece of work…" He gave an audible, long, dramatic sigh. "But I love you." He shook his head as if he couldn't believe his own ears. "Seriously, Jamilah, you are the most beautiful, amazing, and wonderful woman I've ever met. I would love the opportunity to love you and serve you every day of my life. Now…will you marry me? Hurry up and answer me, woman, 'cause you know I got bad knees, and this floor is killing me."

Jamilah was laughing and crying at the same time. She grabbed his face with both her hands. "Yes, I will marry you, you old crazy man." She leaned forward and kissed him. It was a wonderful kiss that spoke a thousand promises.

Finally Dwayne drew back and kissed her on the tip of her nose before leaping to his feet. Throwing his arms into the air he exclaimed, "I'm healed! It's a miracle!" He looked at the people sitting at the next table and pointed to Jamilah. "She's going to marry me!"

Everyone around them applauded, and Jamilah put on her ring, holding her hand up for all to admire.

In the light the diamond cast prisms of rainbows onto the table-cloth. Jamilah took it as a reminder of God's covenant, a sign that this was the beginning of many blessings to come. From where she stood right now, the future suddenly looked very bright. Ari was in a good place, and so was she. The rest was up to God.

fifty

Tamara sat in the waiting room, completing the last of the paperwork before she was admitted. Jamilah had wanted to come with her, but Tamara felt this was something she needed to do alone...well, just her and Jesus. It had been a bittersweet moment for her when Jamilah told her about getting engaged to Dwayne. She could no longer argue that doing things God's way didn't work because that was exactly what Jamilah had done and she struck the mother lode. A good man who was fine, bright, financially stable, and loved the Lord to boot. It couldn't get any better than that. God had truly rewarded her friend for her faithfulness.

Jamilah had been patient, and even she was surprised when Dwayne finally "stepped up to the plate." Tamara envied the fact that Jamilah was marrying the only man she ever loved and that she'd saved herself for him. She could give Dwayne the precious gift of being her first and only lover. There would be no sexual baggage, no comparisons to detract from their relationship.

Tamara was happy for her friend but sad for herself. Her rebellion had gotten her pain, self-inflicted scars, and guilt. She thought of Felicia, whose situation had shown her that you can want what you want, but after you get it there is no guarantee on how long you'll enjoy it. Therefore, life could not be based on acquiring possessions or establishing human relationships. Those things were temporary at best.

As much as she'd battled in the past with God, Tamara now felt it was time to lay down her weapons and call a truce. She was tired of fighting with Him. Plus, the reality of the danger of the surgery itself and the potential complications of being administered anesthesia gave her pause. Now that she was staring the possibility of death in the face, the other issues she'd been fixated on seemed amazingly unimportant. What mattered most now was where was she in her relationship with God. And if she were honest, and why not be honest at this point, she was not close to God…and hadn't been for quite some time. All the obsessing she'd gone through seemed nothing more than a sad waste of time now. Well, she would have plenty of that to heal spiritually as well as physically while she recuperated over the next month to six weeks. She sighed and took a break from her paperwork. Her eyes scanned the room and landed on a familiar face. "Lydia?"

Lydia looked up from where she was sitting and filling out paperwork. Her face brightened. "Tamara! I didn't notice you. How are you? It's been a while. Boy, do I have a lot to tell you. I've been meaning to make an appointment, but so much has been going on." She got up and came to sit next to Tamara.

"You look great! I almost didn't recognize you with your pixie cut. Obviously life has changed a lot…along with your look. Are you still with the guy I saw you with at the restaurant?" Tamara asked.

Lydia blushed. "No. That turned into a hot mess. Where have you been! The whole scandal was all over the papers." She stopped and smiled shyly. "Richard and I got back together!" She looked like a little girl very pleased with herself.

"I've really been out of the loop. How did that come about?"

"You were right about so many things, and I was so angry that you were right that I refused to listen."

"I know a little about feeling like that." Tamara smiled slightly, thinking about her own stubbornness.

"I was so busy insisting on what I wanted that I didn't see what I wasn't giving. The more I tried to manipulate the situation to get what I wanted, the bigger a mess it became. It took two things to derail my self-destructive campaign."

Tamara looked at her in fascination. This wasn't the Lydia she knew. There was something softer about her...something beautiful. Lydia's words pulled her back to the present.

"First, I had this talk with my father. Tamara, it was amazing! I didn't realize how much I was acting out because of unresolved issues with him. I was punishing Richard for the way my father treated me. It was so unfair the things I put my husband through."

Tamara was truly floored. She couldn't believe her ears.

"But the straw that broke the camel's back was how Richard was there for me at the most embarrassing time in my life. I finally saw how much he loved me. I'd never really known or accepted it before. It was truly a humbling experience..." She went on to tell Tamara all the sordid details of her run-in with Brandon and his fiancée outside the Peninsula Hotel. She laughed at the expression on Tamara's face.

"Can you imagine? I'm shocked you didn't see the photo in the newspaper. It was quite the talk."

"I think I was away that weekend..."

"Ooh, with that fine man I saw you with at the restaurant? How's that going?"

"It *went.* I've moved on."

"I'm sorry."

"I'm not. Some things are best learned...even if it has to be later in life."

"Not a truer word has been spoken." Lydia hugged her clipboard. "I'd better finish filling this out. Hey, why are you here anyway?" She looked at Tamara's suitcase.

"I'm having surgery—a hysterectomy. You?"

"I'm doing a follow-up. I found a lump in my breast. After testing, the doctors said it's benign, but they want to do some radiation to be on the safe side. I tell you, that brought me to my knees. There's nothing like looking death in the face to put things in perspective. It was truly a wakeup call from God for me. All of a sudden a whole lot of troubles didn't seem so important."

"I know what you mean. Isn't it amazing how urgent issues seem… until you're faced with eternity. Then all of a sudden God becomes so huge, and you realize how distracted you've been and how little you really know about the person you're going to spend eternity with. It's a shame we spend so little time cultivating that relationship now because we're so busy trying to grab all we can, which isn't all that important or long lasting. It seems so ridiculously futile in hindsight."

"One of the things that has been most precious since Richard and I got back together is that we take the time to pray together and discuss God's Word. Our devotional time together is great! When we spend time with God, He fills us up with the love we need to love each other. And when we don't, we quickly fall into nitpicking. It's crazy. So we decided if our relationship was going to work, we were going to have to do everything God's way. When we're left to our own devices, it just doesn't work. We get in our own way, if you know what I mean."

"Indeed I do."

"I do feel sorry for the woman Richard was seeing. She really was a nice lady, even though I totally dissed her. Richard explained to her that he felt he needed to work on his marriage and honor the promise he'd made before God. She understood, although I'm sure that did little to ease the pain of losing such a good man."

"I'm sure."

"Lydia Caldwell?" a nurse called.

"Coming!" Lydia gathered her things in one hand, leaned forward, and hugged Tamara. Straightening up, she continued, "It really was great seeing you, and I'm glad we had a chance to catch up. I hope everything goes well with your surgery." She stopped and looked at Tamara. "I'll be praying for you. And thank you…"

"Thank you for what?"

"Thank you for putting up with me when I couldn't put up with myself. I was pretty hateful." She sighed. "We truly are a mess outside of God." Lydia smiled, turned, and was gone, leaving Tamara to ponder her last statement.

Just where did I think I was going anyway? How does a person take a vacation from the God of the universe and survive? She felt like the prodigal daughter, finally coming to her senses while sitting in a pig sty. Truly "sense" was not common, but if you had any, it makes good sense to stop volunteering for heartache and get your butt back home. And she intended to do exactly that.

fifty-one

Tamara was in the midst of a swimming pool, struggling to come to the surface. Taking deep breaths she finally felt herself rising.

"I think she's coming around," a man's voice commented.

She finally surfaced to realize she was lying in a bed with a warm blanket over her. An unfamiliar face peered down at her.

"How are you feeling?" he asked.

"Pretty mellow," Tamara responded. She felt like she was packed in a box of cotton balls.

"Any pain?"

The person, probably a nurse, Tamara decided, was adjusting the IV drips on the bags hanging around her. She examined the IV going into her arm. "Nope."

"Good! Your assistant and your mother are here. We'll observe you for a little while to make sure everything is all right, and then take you up to your room. Okay?"

"Sure." She drifted back to sleep.

When she awoke, her mother and Stella were seated next to her. They both rose.

"Welcome back to the real world!" Stella announced.

"How are you feeling?" her mother asked.

Tamara thought about that for a minute. "It's interesting. I feel... light...as if a burden has been lifted."

A beautiful bouquet caught her eye. "Wow! Who are those flowers from?"

"Lydia Caldwell, of all people. How did she even know you were here?" Stella wondered.

"I ran into her when I was checking in. Talk about a transformation! She's back with her husband."

"No! Really? Poor thing..."

"Actually, I think they're going to be fine. She's really come around and changed."

"Well, will miracles never cease."

"God is in the miracle-working business, Stella."

"Yes, He is. You also got some flowers from Felicia, and more from Jamilah and Dwayne."

"Stella tells me Jamilah and Dwayne are getting married." Her mother looked very pleased.

"Um hmm. Isn't that great after all these years?"

"We have to get this one married off next," Stella said, pointing to Tamara. "I scoped out a fine doctor working on this floor..." She had one eyebrow raised and a glint in her eye.

"Down, Stella! Leave that doctor alone. I'm fine where I am right now, and everybody does not have to get married, you know."

"You're not giving up, are you?"

"No, but I think I want to take the time to enjoy the garden I'm in for a minute. I don't think I've smelled all the roses where I am yet. I've been too busy envying everybody else's plot. It's time to fertilize my own bit of space."

"That's a new tune. What did they put in those bags? Mind-altering drugs?" Stella poked at one of the IV solutions.

There was a small tap at the door, and Jamilah stuck her head in the door. "Is it safe to enter?" She came in, Dwayne bringing up the rear. "Hello, Mrs. Watson," she said as she kissed Tamara's mother on both cheeks and hugged her.

"While they are engaged in PDA, how are you feeling?" Dwayne asked.

"I'm feeling fine, but I'm sure I'm not as good as you are. You finally got her!"

"Yup, I did." He was grinning like a Cheshire cat.

"And guess what else, Tamara?" Jamilah was practically bouncing in her shoes. "We saw Ari yesterday! She's staying with a pastor and his wife, who live not far from Dwayne's place...soon to be 'our' place." She smiled a shy smile as she touched Dwayne's arm.

"How did you find her?"

"Dwayne has a friend at DCFS who pulled some strings for us. It turns out Dwayne knows the pastor. Several of the kids that go to his church and the academy they operate are in his mentorship program. So Pastor Sanders agreed to let us see her. They already have two foster kids, so Dwayne and I are going to ask if we can become Ari's foster parents. If everything works out, we hope to adopt her."

"Will her mother object?"

Jamilah's countenance dropped. "She'd been missing for quite some time. They finally found her last week. I guess she died of an overdose."

"Oh no! How did Ari take it?"

"She was devastated. I think that's part of the reason we were able to get to see her. Pastor Sanders says she was inconsolable, but she kept talking about me and prayed and asked God to let me find her." Jamilah's eyes filled with tears. "Whoda thunk it, huh? After all that bellyaching, God really came through."

"I'd say! He came through big time." Stella was shaking her head in amazement.

There was another knock at the door. "Man, this place is Grand Central Station!" It was Felicia. "Hi, everybody!" She came in, followed by Carla, who tenderly kissed Tamara on the forehead and smoothed back her hair.

"How are you?" Felicia's eyes were filled with concern.

"I'm good."

"Really?"

"Yup. I just found out I'm going to be a mother."

"Huh?" Felicia was looking confused.

"Jamilah and Dwayne are adopting, so I'll get to be a mother—as in godmother!"

"Oh!" The light of understanding came on in Felicia's eyes. She smiled. "Hey, don't forget my two. You can add them to your surrogate mother list. I'm going to need all the help I can get."

Carla cleared her throat. "You can add my little one to the mix too. Wow! What's that scripture in Isaiah? 'Sing, barren woman, who has never had a baby. Fill the air with song, you who've never experienced childbirth! You're ending up with far more children than all those childbearing women.' That sounds about right." She smiled.

"Hey, that's true! Just call me Super Auntie as opposed to super nanny. I get to be Auntie Mame and return them when I'm done. That's a pretty cool arrangement. I'm going to like this. I get to be a mother and auntie without all the bills and work!"

"I might have to talk to Jesus about this. I don't know if that's fair!" Carla pouted with mock petulance.

"Oh, I think He knows what He's doing!" Tamara laughed and then winced in pain. "Ooh! Don't make me laugh."

Everyone laughed then.

"Hey! What do we have here? A party? Did you get permission from the front desk?"

The most gorgeous man Tamara had ever seen stuck his head in the door. He looked straight at her. "And how's the patient? Laughter is not allowed for the first 24 hours after surgery." He struggled to keep a straight face. As he entered the room Stella cast a conspiratorial look at Tamara's mother and then at Tamara.

Tamara ignored Stella.

"I'm fine, Doctor...?"

"Mathis. I'm one of the attending physicians on the floor, so I'll be checking on you. How are you feeling?" He regained his professional manner.

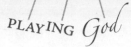

"I'm feeling fine." Out of the corner of her eye she saw Dwayne punch Jamilah. She pressed her lips together and focused on Dr. Mathis.

"Good. I'll be back in a little while to kick everyone out so you can get some rest." He smiled and turned to leave. Before closing the door behind him he turned and said, "I know that 'a cheerful heart is good medicine,' but keep it down in here." He flashed a brilliant smile at Tamara. "See you later!"

"That's the doctor I was talking about. Don't I have good taste?" Stella was looking after him with a very pleased look on her face.

"I'd be fine too if I had a doctor that looked like that," Tamara's mother said as she chuckled.

"He was yummy if I do say so myself." Jamilah chimed in.

"Hey, watch that! You're practically a married woman," Dwayne interjected.

"I can still look, can't I?" she shot back.

"No!" Dwayne answered, trying to look serious.

"Well, Carla, what do you think? Little Miss Matchmaker, is it a match?" Felicia too was smiling.

Carla rubbed her chin and did a Dr. Ruth impression. "I think the possibilities are endless. The combination of good looks, chemistry, admirable profession, and I believe he even threw in a Scripture. This could be the making of something really big."

"All right, all right. You people are out of control." In an attempt to switch the subject, Tamara looked at Stella. "Before I forget, did you get hold of Corinne?"

"Yes, I did. She's fine. And she will see you in a few of weeks when you get back to work. But let's get back to this doctor…"

Tamara feigned a groan. "There is no redirecting you. How about you guys stop playing God and leave the matchmaking to Him and His perfect timing, just in case He has someone else in mind. Isn't not doing that how we all get into trouble? I'm trying to get back on track here. Help a sistah out, okay?"

"Okay…but it sure is fun to speculate…"

They all laughed again.

Tamara's mother spoke up. "I do think he was right on one thing. We need to leave and let you get some rest." She put her hand on Tamara's and leaned over to give her a kiss. "Like we arranged, I'll be at your place. Call me if you need anything. Otherwise, I'll see you in the morning."

"I will. Thanks, Mom."

After exchanging a flurry of hugs and goodbyes, the quiet was like a kiss from God. Lying back and reflecting, she felt her life was very full. She hadn't lost anything at all. She'd made her peace with God, settled her issues, and gained some priceless understanding. A lot of women had given birth to children and still weren't "mothers." She had children in her life to give herself to. She had great friends and a profession that enabled her to help people and see lives changed for the better. Now that was true wealth that couldn't be taken away. From where she sat, Carla was right. The possibilities were endless.

Dr. Mathis stuck his head in the door. "It's awfully quiet in here. Everything all right?"

Tamara smiled. "Everything is perfect," she murmured as she drifted off to sleep.

fifty-two

The Chicago skyline was more beautiful than ever, or perhaps it was because she hadn't seen it in a while so she wasn't taking it for granted. It was good to be back at work. Six long weeks had passed, and she'd needed the rest. Tamara turned her chair around as Stella delivered a nice steaming cup of coffee to her desk.

"Here you go! Corinne and her daughter will be here in a few minutes."

"Great. I can't wait to meet Jada."

"Yes, poor thing. She's been through a lot."

"I'm curious to find out how she's doing."

"Well, you'll find out in a minute."

The phone rang. Stella reached down, picked it up, and answered, "Miss Watson's office. May I help you?" She paused. Smiled. Raised an eyebrow and looked at Tamara. "Who may I say is calling?" She could no longer suppress her smile as she hit the hold button. "A certain Dr. Mathis is on line one for you!"

Tamara smiled before shooing her out of her office. She waited a beat and then picked up the phone. "Hello?" His voice was nice on the other end of the line.

"And how's my favorite patient on her first day back to work?"

"Great and happy to be back."

"I'm glad to hear that. Listen, I won't keep you, but I was wondering if I'd be overstepping my boundaries if I invited you to dinner?"

"I think that would be nice. When did you have in mind?" Tamara sounded much calmer than she felt.

"Saturday evening perhaps?"

"Saturday would be good. What time?"

"Would you mind if we made it early? I'd like to catch the early service at church before I work my shift at the hospital on Sunday. Say around five?"

"That would be perfect."

"Good. I'll check back with you at the end of the week."

"All righty!" Tamara wondered if she sounded too chipper.

"Have a great day, and I'll talk with you soon."

"You too…have a good day, I mean."

"Yes, I got that piece." He chuckled. "In the meantime, keep all rowdy behavior to a minimum please. Bye." He hung up the phone.

Before Tamara could put the phone back in the cradle Stella was standing in the door.

"Well?"

"Well what?" She looked past Stella's shoulder. "Isn't that Corinne? Send them right in…" She smiled at Stella.

Stella stepped in the door, put her hand on her hip, pointed at Tamara, and whispered loudly, "You are an evil woman!" Turning back to Corinne and Jada she brightened. "Corinne!" Then shaking Jada's hand she said, "You must be Jada." She motioned toward Tamara. "Miss Watson is expecting you. Go right in." She closed the door behind them as they entered…but not before sticking out her tongue at Tamara.

Tamara smiled at her before turning her attention to the mother and daughter. They could have been sisters. Same blonde hair and crystal-blue eyes. Jada, for all that she had been through, was a picture of innocence. Clear eyed and pretty in a very clean, cover girl kind of way. Corinne had cut her hair in an angled wedge, very Posh Beckham-style, and it was chic and sophisticated. She looked more in control of her world now. They sat before her like matching bookends.

"Well, Jada, it's great to finally meet you. How have you been?"

Corinne leaned forward. "She's been doing quite well under the circumstances. I'm so proud of her." Corinne went on to explain that Jada had not backed down from the hard questions after pressing charges against Pastor Masters and had even reached out to encourage and sympathize with the other girls who had been victimized by him. "She's thinking about starting a support group with them."

Jada cleared her throat and leaned forward, smiling shyly. "I'd really like to have a youth group for other girls who have been violated by family members and strangers. Perhaps you could come and speak with them? And maybe advise us when we need it?"

"It would be my privilege, Jada." Tamara smiled at her, deeply impressed. "I know how traumatic this must have been...and still is...for you. I commend you on being open with your pain to help others. That's actually the quickest path to recovery."

Corinne was beaming. "She has been absolutely amazing. I always knew God had a special call on her life, but I didn't know the price she would have to pay for it."

Tamara looked at Jada, who was quietly smiling. "Someone once said 'Your mess becomes your ministry.' Kudos to you for turning your wounds into weapons."

"My dad always said you can't do anything about what happened to you in your past, but you have everything to do with how your future unfolds by the choices you make today."

"Very well said." Tamara was surprised by the strength of Jada's voice and conviction.

"Thank you."

Tamara looked at Corinne. "And how about you? Would you like to talk privately about where you are these days? "

"I'm comfortable sharing now. I'm being honest with Jada about where I've been and where I'm going. At this point, truth is our lifeline, and unfortunately, she's had to grow up fast." She squeezed her daughter's hand. "I think I'm in a good place. It would be easy to meander through the valley of regret and mourn over all the things that have happened, but I've done enough of that. Besides, it's not conducive to moving forward.

"The power of choice is amazing. Once I decided I wasn't going to be ruled by how I felt, I became free to do so much more than I ever thought I could!" She perked up in her chair and leaned forward. "You know what I've learned? Joy is a choice! Hah! Fancy that. For so long I thought happiness was based on what was happening or not happening in my life. Not true."

"Now that you've made this amazing discovery, what are you going to do with all this wonderful information?"

"I'm starting a new life. The divorce is still going through. Randall and I are communicating and responding to each other better now than when we were married, but we both need time and space to heal and be restored. Our marriage is over, but we have Jada in common, so we'll get along. We're selling the house and splitting what we have, which will give me a little wiggle room as I take the steps I need to be self-supporting. Jada and I are moving to the city, and I'm going to start a personal shopping business. I'll also take some night classes on business administration." She looked confident and excited.

As they continued their visit, Tamara marveled at how God was working everything out to His glory. How a girl who was robbed of her innocence could have her innocence restored and continue to trust God for her future. Through Christ, a shattered woman was daring to hope again and being renewed in strength and courage as she embraced a new beginning in the wake of personal devastation. Corinne had overcome bitterness, faced her demons, and come out victorious.

Gratefulness flooded Tamara. She realized that mountains were being moved and would continue to be moved by standing in faith and staying out of God's way. She felt free of worry as she too looked forward to trusting God for her future.

After Corinne and Jada left, Stella ushered in a new client. "This is Sandra Daley," she said, introducing the woman with her.

Tamara rose to shake her hand. "Hello! I'm pleased to meet you. May I call you Sandra?" Sitting back down, she studied her new client. Tamara recognized the look in her eyes. "So tell me, what brings you to my office?"

"Yes, you may call me Sandra." And then the floodgates opened, and tears streamed down the woman's face. "I think I'm having a faith crisis..."

Tamara grabbed a Kleenex box and extended it toward her. She leaned forward to listen intently as Sandra poured out her heart. Tamara had to concentrate on not smiling, lest her expression be misinterpreted. Life couldn't get any better than this. She was back, she truly loved helping people, and she felt that so much more was in store. Exactly what she didn't know...only God knew. And that was fine.

Many plans are in a [woman's] mind,
but it is the Lord's purpose for [her] that will stand.

PROVERBS 19:21

discussion questions

1. What cycles replay in your life? In your relationships? For the negative cycles, what can you do differently to change the end results?

2. How do you typically respond to rejection? In your last situation, what were your expectations? How did the other person fail you? When others can't fulfill your expectations, what can you do to not take it personally...to not look at it as a rejection of you?

3. What is betrayal to you? How do you respond when you feel betrayed? Which of your rights and which of the other person's rights were violated? How can you arrive at a peaceful compromise?

4. How do you deal with difficult issues in your relationships? How effective is your typical response? How can you change or adjust your approach to get better results?

5. When a disagreement arises, what is your goal in the relationship? How important is being right to you? Why is it important to "pick your battles"?

6. When and how can keeping a secret hurt you? The other person? When is it important to honor a secret? To break the silence? What does "covering someone's sin" mean?

7. How willing are you to be transparent and accountable? In what ways can isolation be dangerous? Why is
   it important to have someone you can get real with?

8. What does it mean to forgive someone? How does
   unforgiveness keep you in bondage? How does it affect
   your choices? What is your greatest struggle when it
   comes to forgiveness—giving and receiving?

9. What is the difference between setting boundaries
   and forgetting the offense? What boundaries should
   be set after forgiving to keep the relationship healthy?
   How can you communicate your relationship needs to
   someone else? What happens when you don't?

10. What disappointments have you repeatedly struggled
    with in the past? How has this affected your attitude
    toward yourself? Toward God? Toward others? What
    can you do to change your perspective? What do you
    need to let God handle?

11. What causes your faith to waver? How can placing
    your faith in the wrong thing set you up for disap-
    pointment? What is the difference between
    relinquishing your expectations and trusting God
    for the things you desire?

12. When God doesn't move according to your time
    schedule, how do you respond? What happens when
    you place conditions on God? How does placing con-
    ditions on God keep you from receiving His best for
    you?

13. What are you waiting on God for? What do you wrestle with while you wait? What have you learned about your character and faith during this struggle?

14. When trusting God's timing, how can you prepare for His answer? What do you think God wants to accomplish in you as you wait? How can you maintain your willingness to wait on God and trust Him?

15. What relationships from the past strongly impact your present relationships? In what way? If this is negative, how can you resolve your feelings and embrace a new attitude?

16. What situations continually cause you to have knee-jerk reactions? How can assumptions cause problems? How can you guard against jumping to conclusions or making assumptions in the future?

17. How can pride hinder transparency? What causes you to hide your pains and fears? How does the enemy of your soul use isolation to harm you? How can the truth of Christ set you free?

18. What does God mean when He says, "Guard your heart"? What is the difference between guarding your heart and being transparent? What are healthy guidelines for being transparent?

19. How do you handle unexpected loss? How can you cultivate a grateful spirit in spite of disappointments and trials? What do you need to believe about God in

the midst of your pain? What concrete steps can you
take toward healing and restoration?

20. What are the signs that it's time to let go or to hang
in there? What is the difference between striving and
actively waiting? What does resting in God look like?
What does giving up look like? What's the healthiest
attitude to maintain while waiting on God?

21. What happens when you "play God" in your life? In
the lives of others? In what situations have you done
this? What were the repercussions? What did you
learn from this experience?

To correspond with Michelle McKinney Hammond:

HeartWing Ministries
P.O. Box 11052
Chicago, IL 60611

E-mail her at heartwingmin@yahoo.com

or log on to her website at:

www.michellehammond.com
or www.thedivaprinciple.com

For information on booking her for a
speaking engagement:

1-866-391-0955

or log on to
www.michellehammond.com

Other Books by
Michelle McKinney Hammond

101 Ways to Get and Keep His Attention

The Diva Principle®

The Diva Principle®—A Sistergirl's Guide

Ending the Search for Mr. Right

Get Over it and On with it

How to Avoid the 10 Mistakes Single Women Make

How to Be Blessed and Highly Favored

If Men are Like Buses, Then How Do I Catch One?

In Search of the Proverbs 31 Man

The Last Ten Percent (a novel)

Lessons from a Girl's Best Friend

Playing God (a novel)

The Power of Being a Woman

Prayer Guide for the Brokenhearted

Release the Pain, Embrace the Joy

The Real Deal on Overcoming Heartache

The Sassy Girl's Checklist for Living, Loving, and Overcoming

A Sassy Girl's Guide to Loving God

Sassy, Single, and Satisfied

Secrets of an Irresistible Woman

Unspoken Rules of Love

What to Do Until Love Finds You

Why Do I Say "Yes" When I Need to Say "No"?